Fifty-seventh Street

By the same author:

THE NIGHT IS FOR MUSIC,
A Novel

Fifty-seventh Street

by *George Selcamm*

 W · W · NORTON & COMPANY · INC ·

NEW YORK

for
Pierre and *Genia Luboshutz*

Fifty-seventh Street

Although this novel is set in a milieu that will be familiar to many readers, it is entirely a work of fiction. The characters I have created and the events I describe are altogether imaginary.

G. S.

one

The artists' room was little more than a cubicle. Judith Conrad, seated at the dressing table, glanced at the brown leather sofa and the yellow wall beyond. For Carnegie Hall, she thought, this was on the shabby side. She turned back to the mirror, put on lipstick, and studied her reflection. Her jet-black hair, piled high on her head, revealed shapely little ears. The upswept coiffure gave her what she considered a Renoir look. The face in the mirror was still attractive. More important, it had character.

The dark-brown eyes that looked back at her gave no indication of the fear she felt. No matter how often she appeared in public she could not conquer the nervousness that gripped her beforehand. What if her heel caught as she came out on stage? Or she slipped on her way to the piano? What if, in the middle of the performance, she forgot? Against these terrifying possibilities her mind was powerless. They were akin to the fear of the dark she had had when she was little. Then there had been a simple remedy—she opened the door of her bedroom. Now a cure was not so easy to come by.

The sound of a Mozart symphony filtered in from the hall. Judith was unfamiliar with it, but knew that this was the final movement. There was a discreet knock at the door. Her agent, Birdie Harris, came clomping in. Birdie was plump and vivacious. The dirty-blond bun at the back of her head looked as if it had been stuck on at the last moment, as indeed it had. She served her artists devotedly, her duties ranging from publicity woman to nursemaid. "Darling," she exclaimed in the nasal twang she mistook for a tone of authority, "you look marvelous!" She kissed Judith lightly on the cheek while Judith kissed the air near Birdie's ear.

Judith rose and, sliding her hands down along her sides, surveyed herself in the mirror. "It's a Balenciaga," she said, pronouncing the designer's name as if she were saying "a Goya." He had sheathed her full figure in flame-colored satin; this was a gown for the stage. A little too unadorned for Judith's taste. Yet, as she watched the full skirt drape itself around her, its graceful folds shimmering in the light, she had to admit that he knew what he was doing. "I wanted black, but I'm glad I chose this."

"It's stunning. Absolutely!" Birdie stepped back for a better view. "How d'you feel?"

"Terrible." Judith's smile, with the full underlip curving a little to one side, gave her a sensual, almost gross look.

"You'll be fine once you get out there."

"Right now my insides are plopping out. Tell me, why do I inflict this torture on myself when I could stay home like most women and cook? Why?"

"Now she wants to stay home and cook," Birdie said to the ceiling. "What else would you be if you weren't a pianist? It's the one thing you've worked for since you were ten."

"What else? I'd be an average woman and lead a normal life." Fear exploded in her entrails. She made for the bathroom.

"It's all in the mind," Birdie announced.

A burst of applause in the hall signaled the end of the symphony. An usher stuck his head into the room. "Miss Conrad."

"It's time, dear," Birdie said gently. "Relax!"

Judith came out of the bathroom, smoothing down her dress. She hurried down the stairs that led to the side of the stage where the conductor, Paul Horvath was waiting for her. She had played with him the year before in Detroit and was flattered that he had re-engaged her. Although he greeted her with a smile of encouragement, there was something curiously remote about him. He was a formal man, with piercing blue eyes set deep in a bony face. Horvath was bald. The lofty forehead, fringed by iron-gray hair, gave him an intellectual air that Judith found extremely attractive. He took her hand, drew her in front of him, and followed her out on stage.

Automatically she put on her public personality—head high, shoulders back, exuding confidence. Her glance swept the two tiers of boxes; they were well filled. For her, a New Yorker, there was no hall like Carnegie. Where else would you find this combination of spaciousness and closeness to the audience? No matter where else she appeared—and there were several halls in the Midwest in which the piano sounded just as beautiful—to play in Carnegie meant coming home.

Judith made her way to the center of the stage. The applause that welcomed her was warm but of what she called the "show me" kind: this audience was friendly but waiting to be convinced. She bowed, sat down at the piano, and tucked her handkerchief into the far corner of the keyboard. Horvath had mounted the podium, which was between her and the orchestra, and stood waiting, baton poised in the air. She nodded to him to begin.

Out of the depths of the orchestra floated the opening triplets of Mozart's D-Minor Concerto, darkly mysterious. Judith turned the circular handles of the piano stool to raise it a little. Her hands were damp. She wiped them and returned the handkerchief to its perch. She looked straight before her, intensely conscious of the eyes focused upon her. The audience was a brooding presence in the shadowy reaches of the auditorium, an adversary whom something in her had to persuade, conquer, dazzle. Individually its members meant nothing to her. Why, then, was it so important for her to please them, to win their approval? It was a question to which she found no answer.

She glanced up at Horvath. His hands floated through the air, coaxing the sounds from the orchestra. The bony white face had a strange intensity. Judith became aware that her right knee was shaking. She tried to steady it with her hand, and with an effort of will fastened her mind on the music. The introduction was as spacious as the opening of a symphony, its sorrow tempered by a noble serenity. Presently oboe and flute engaged in a gentle dialogue that quieted her apprehension. Horvath turned to her and nodded. She raised her hands to the keys.

She shaped the opening phrase of the piano part, holding back a trifle in order to give each note its due. Horvath, catching the subtle inflection, deftly followed her. Judith, as she played, became aware of a multitude of unrelated details: a bald head at the end of the first row, the cool sound of the flutes, Horvath's decisive downbeat, the shift of the keyboard when she pressed down the soft pedal. Little by little she withdrew into the heart of the music, until it was almost as if she were playing for herself. Now she began to feel exhilarated; she was doing the thing she did best, and doing it with supreme ease. She was living in the most vital part of her, compared to which everything else she experienced must forever remain external, even trivial.

The Allegro ended. Judith took a breath and listened to the silence in the hall, punctuated here and there by a cough. She began the Romanza alone, with a tone that was limpid, caressing. The secret of this movement was neither to hurry nor to drag it; she felt she had hit upon just the right tempo. The muted violins answered the opening phrase, and she noticed that Horvath had understood it exactly as she had. Her fears had left her; she was at one with the music—nothing else mattered. This mood of assurance carried her through the difficulties of the final movement. Her hands bounced over the keys as the gay themes were tossed from piano to orchestra and back. She played with vivacity, Horvath giving her expert support, controlling the men with his crisp beat and subtly quickening the tempo when she hurried forward. The shadows of the minor key were dispelled for good as the rondo moved into a radiant D major. Judith attacked the scales of the final measures at a furious clip. It was over.

Loud applause filled the hall. She measured its intensity as she rose from the piano, and was pleased. Horvath stepped down from the podium, took her hand and raised it to his lips. She smiled at him and noticed the glint in his steel-blue eyes. Even now, while sharing this moment with her, he still had that remote air of his. She shook hands with the concertmaster and bowed to the audience, as did Horvath. She surveyed the crowded hall. The enemy out front had become a blur of friendly faces. Why had she been so afraid of them? If only she could taste the sweetness of this victory without having to go through the agony that preceded it! She returned for another bow alone, then brought Horvath out with her.

Birdie was waiting for her in the greenroom. "Darling, you were marvelous. Absolutely!" She kissed her.

"The third movement was too fast. I just couldn't hold back."

"Never satisfied. A perfectionist," Birdie confided to the ceiling, "that's what she is."

Judith laughed. "Is that bad?"

"Of course. Means you can never relax and enjoy your playing."

"Relax?" Judith made a face. "I'll tell you when I'll relax. When they plant me underground."

Boxes of flowers lay scattered around the room. She turned to the nearest one and read the card. Yellow roses from Bobby, her son. Next to it was a bouquet from Philip Lerner, the lawyer who had obtained her divorce and had subsequently advanced to a more intimate position. The greenroom was filling up. Judith moved to the back, where she received the long line of friends, colleagues, relations, and anyone else who wanted to congratulate her. In various versions they echoed Birdie's "You were marvelous." Even though Judith was not entirely convinced, she enjoyed their adulation sufficiently not to mind either the heat in the room or the hubbub. A young man with curly hair shyly asked for her autograph. She signed his program with a flourish.

Birdie hovered protectively about her, directing traffic. The dirty-blond bun bobbed to and fro; her voice shrilled through the din. "Walter, my dear!" She pulled Walter Stern forward, making it plain to the woman who was shaking Judith's hand that her time was up.

Walter, one of Judith's oldest friends, gave her a hug. "It was really first-rate."

Judith beamed. "Am I glad it's over."

"See you soon," he whispered in her ear and moved on. He was giving a party for her after the concert, to which many of their friends had not been asked. Judith had kept the invitations to a minimum. She was eager that Paul Horvath attend, and he was known to dislike huge gatherings.

She turned back to the line. "Olga, darling!" She embraced

an elderly Russian lady—a former singer—who had known her well in the early days of her career. "How nice of you to come."

"I loff your Mozart!" Olga guessed from Judith's excessive cordiality that something was up, and made a last-ditch bid for an invitation. "So much I haf to tell you, maybe ve can be togedder a leetle."

A dreamy look came over Judith. "Not tonight, dear. I'm simply exhausted. But real soon." She flashed a loving smile as Birdie firmly piloted Olga toward the door.

Max Rubin grasped Judith's hand. The famous impresario, well past seventy, was as spry as ever. He was a short stocky man with a bulbous head. "Good job!" he wheezed in a gutteral voice, blinking good-humoredly through his thick glasses. Some said he pretended to be nearsighted so that no one would suspect how much he saw.

Judith regarded managers as the natural enemies of the artist. They lived off the artist; they were parasites and exploiters all in one. It was their business to sell talent just as a salesman sold hats, shoes, brassieres. Consequently any relationship with a manager, she felt, ended by cheapening the artist. Her dislike of Max was aggravated by the fact that she needed him. She forced a smile. "I'm so glad you liked it."

"Of course, the last movement . . ." He raised his hand, fingers separated, and rolled it from side to side, very much the connoisseur. "Maybe a little too fast."

How the hell would you know? The words leaped to her lips, but she thrust them back. "It's a matter of taste," she answered pleasantly. For an instant she could not recall whether she had invited Max to the party; then she remembered that, at Birdie's insistence, she had. "You're coming to the Sterns, I hope."

"I should miss a party?" He grinned. "They live by the river, no?"

"Birdie will bring you." Judith turned from him and faced her son. "Bobby!" She threw her arms around him. "Did you like it?"

"Beautiful!" He grinned in the uncertain way he had when he felt that she was too busy to pay attention to him.

"The flowers are lovely. Thank you." Bobby was the one good thing to have come out of her first marriage. She adored him in spite of the fact that he reminded her of his father. He was tall and slender; his blond hair was a pleasant memento of the period in her youth when she was attracted to non-Jewish men. He was wearing his dinner jacket and looked, she thought, quite elegant. She straightened his bow tie and rearranged the hand-kerchief in his breast pocket.

Bob joined Philip by the door. Judith was pleased that her son and her lover got on so well. It made life simpler. She noticed that Philip did not come over to congratulate her. He was waiting for her to come to him. How petty! But she was too exhilarated to take his childishness seriously.

The line of well-wishers was coming to an end. She was tired of shaking hands, but continued the ritual of thanking her admirers until the last one had left. Birdie assembled the flowers and divided them between Bobby and Philip. Judith glanced about her. This little room with its bleak yellow walls contained everything that made her life meaningful. Her son. Her friends. Her public. And Philip, weighed down by two boxes of roses and a bouquet. She sighed. If only this moment could go on and on. If only it could always be like this.

2

Alice Stern fluffed up the cushions on the couch and turned on all the lights. She threw a practiced glance around the room. Everything was ready.

The living room reflected her horror of overstatement. Soft colors predominated—gray, pale yellow, blue. A street scene by Utrillo occupied the center of the main wall, its rectilinear houses bathed in the clean sunlight peculiar to that painter. Opposite hung a Rouault—a saintly, tortured face gazing out of purple shadows. Soon both would be hidden by a jabbering crowd.

Alice stepped out on the terrace. She was a slim, unobtrusive woman who stood out among the women of her circle by reason of her white hair, which emphasized the pink of her skin and gave her a surprisingly youthful look. The November night was mild. There was dampness in the air, and the vaguely acrid smell that enveloped the city at night. Eighteen stories below her the river gleamed, a dark luminous ribbon. An interminable

line of automobiles moved along the drive like golden-eyed
insects. Queensborough Bridge hummed, its gray lattice-like
structure floating above its black bastions at either end. On
the opposite shore, in Astoria, a red neon sign proclaimed the
virtues of Pepsi-Cola against the shrouded sky. Alice filled her
lungs. There was a sameness, she reflected, about her parties.
The food did not vary much, nor did the faces. When Walter
and she were younger they used to entertain his business asso-
ciates; in recent years he had surrounded himself with musicians. She could not see why he found them more glamorous
than the solid businessmen of the earlier period. They were
pretentious bores who talked incessantly about themselves: constantly kissing each other although they were quite ready to
cut each other's throats, and drinking your liquor as if they were
doing you a favor. How could anyone as sensible as Walter fail
to see through them? He had once dreamed of becoming a
violinist (how lucky for both of them that he had failed). Now
he enjoyed his role as a patron of music. When she questioned
some of his contributions he would remind her that they were
deductible.

Far below a tugboat passed. Alice watched its red light move
through the night. The thought of Walter brought an ache to
her heart. Long ago they had been in love; where had the joy,
the passion disappeared? Where, when you blew out a candle,
did the light go? Things had changed between them after Gene
was born. The child who should have brought them closer together had, strangely, driven a wedge between them. How could
a man be jealous of his own son? Walter had behaved as if the
more love she lavished on the boy, the less she had left for him.
As though love were like a cloth that, when pulled over one
end of the table, left the other bare. Surely love was indivisible:
what she had felt for her child could not be separated from
what she felt for her husband. Or could it? Alice leaned against
the glass partition that enclosed the terrace. What did it matter
now?

Was it possible that the fierce mother-feeling in her had sub-
tracted from the woman-feeling Walter had needed? In giving
herself to the boy had she unconsciously withdrawn from the
man? The event was too far in the past for her to be able to
judge. All she remembered was that, when she looked at Gene,
a happiness possessed her such as she had never known before,

compounded of all the pride and hope of which she was capable. And fear. Always the fear that this joy was too precious to last, that it would somehow be snatched from her. Alice pressed her hands against the partition. Even now she could not bear to recall the yellow slip of paper that had changed her life. It arrived on a rainy Saturday afternoon in 1944: *The Secretary of War regrets . . .* This was the moment she had dreaded since the day Gene was sent overseas, the moment she had always known must come. From then on, although she continued to go through the motions of living, the waiting was over. There was nothing more that could be taken from her.

A foghorn blew in a deep nasal voice; the tugboat threaded its way past the island in the middle of the river. Alice watched the red light move toward the bridge. What, then, had kept Walter and her together? Habit? Inertia? Fear of change? The same things that probably kept thousands of middle-aged couples chained to one another. Perhaps even the memory of their son. He had begun by separating them; now he had become a bond between them.

Alice went inside and rearranged the large white chrysanthemums on the piano. She stared at the brightly lit, stylish room that would remain empty for her no matter how many of Walter's cronies crowded it. The doorbell rang. She gave a start, fixed a hostess smile on her lips, and went to greet her guests.

"You like the new hall? I hear the acoustics are terrible."

"——gave me a standing ovation in Wichita. And in Duluth——"

"She had it lifted again, but it didn't take. You should see her face now."

"Khrushchev'll have to give in. If not——"

"——heard Callas in Paris, in *Norma*. She was awful!"

Alice looked around. Always the same conversation; she marveled that they never tired of it. These willful creatures who forgot to put their glasses on the coasters she had provided, who spilled ashes on the rug and food on the sofa—what possible connection did they have with her inner self? She felt as alien to them as if they belonged to another species. Reverting to a habit of childhood, she transformed them in her mind into the characters of an animal fable. Max Rubin, peering through his thick glasses and burrowing his way through a portion of salmon, would do well as a fuzzy old mole. Or a fox? Birdie, hovering about him in the hope of picking up bits of information that might prove useful to her clients, would make a bright-eyed squirrel. Judith, coiled on the sofa, head drawn back, was a cobra getting ready to strike. Bobby, standing uncertainly behind her, was obviously a young deer that had lost its way. Alice listened with a smile to the hissing and cackling of her private menagerie. The party was moving on its own momentum. She decided to make herself useful and crossed over to the dining-room table.

A cream-colored lace cloth set off two silver candlesticks with lighted candles and an assortment of cold cuts, cheeses, and a huge salmon. Musicians, Alice had learned, loved to eat. She placed herself behind the salad bowl. Walter came up and held out his plate; she scooped up slices of cucumber and tomato. He tasted the salad with an air of appraisal. "Honey, the dressing's just right."

Alice looked at him coldly. Whenever he used this affectionate tone with her she suspected that he was being unfaithful. His round good-natured face was flushed with excitement; his hair, gray at the temples, was damp. He enjoyed a crowded room, particularly when he was the host. He became expansive, told jokes, laughed boisterously at the punch line, and loved everyone. "It's a good party, don't you think?"

"Yes, dear." She glanced at his plate. "All that salmon? You know it's full of salt."

"This once won't harm. After all, we don't celebrate every night."

"That's the trouble. We do."

He threw her a do-we-have-to-go-through-that-again look. Max Rubin approached the table, Birdie in tow. "The lox is delicious," he said.

"That's not lox, Max," Birdie shrieked. "It's salmon. Nova Scotia salmon."

"Lox shmox . . ." He shrugged. "As long as it tastes good." He nodded. "I didn't have any dinner," he lied.

"You need someone to look after you," Alice said in a kindly tone, and then realized that she had committed a blunder. Max, at seventy-four, had just broken up his third marriage. His lips were pendulous; he was short of breath; he ate too much.

"There comes a time," he chortled, "when a man's old enough to look after himself."

Walter turned to Birdie. "Aren't you eating?" he asked with exaggerated politeness. They were having an affair. A few people in the room knew, a few suspected. The question was, did Alice know?

Birdie teetered over the sweets, torn between pineapple cheese cake and a chocolate cream puff. "My diet!" she wailed, and decided in favor of the cream puff.

"One won't make much difference," Alice said as Birdie bit into the soft crust. She disliked her and felt vaguely guilty because of it. She sensed that Birdie, beneath her curves and smiles and dimples, was tough. Her clothes were too frilly, her laugh too shrill, and the sharp points of her heels wrought havoc with the rug.

"Judith outdid herself tonight," Birdie said, for Max's benefit. "Absolutely!"

"Yeh. A good job," Max assented cautiously.

Walter felt that this was an opportune moment to introduce Max to his latest discovery—a young soprano from upstate whose studies he was financing. "She's loaded with talent. Take it from me."

Although perpetually on the lookout for talent, Max was wary of a layman's praise. "She really has it?"

"A gorgeous voice. Her name is Margo Scholtz. A young beauty from Poughkeepsie."

"Who's paying for her lessons?"

Walter grinned. "Not you, that's for sure." Of his varied philanthropies, he was proudest of his assistance to young musicians. "You'll have to hear her, Max. But first you must meet her." He put down his plate and, taking Max by the elbow, steered him into the other room. Birdie followed.

Judith's son approached the table. "How are you, Bob?" Alice said warmly. "I didn't get a chance to speak to you at the concert." She filled his plate.

"That's enough, thanks."

"Your mother played beautifully tonight." She gave him an encouraging smile. He was shy and easily flustered, which surprised Alice in view if his good looks.

"Yes, I thought it went very well." Bob drew his plate away but remained where he was, waiting to be dismissed.

"She looked lovely too." Alice tried to make contact with him, but the distance between them was too great. Bob was about the same age as Gene had been when he was drafted. The irony of it struck her: she would have been only too happy to devote her life to her son, but he had been snatched from her, while Judith filled her life with so much nonsense that she barely had time for hers.

The young man still faced her, uncertain as to how to take his leave. "Would you like some beer with your supper?" Alice asked. "Or wine?" She motioned toward the bar in the foyer. Bob moved on.

Margo Scholtz appeared. "What a lovely party!" She helped herself to cold cuts and stopped before the salad bowl. Alice put a scoop of cucumbers and tomatoes on her plate. She liked everything about Margo, her dark prettiness, her small oval face with its diminutive features, her childlike excitement at finding herself in the big city. She would have liked to say to her, "Go back to Poughkeepsie, my child, and become Margie Schultzberger again. Forget about fame and career before you become like the creatures in this room. Marry a nice young man, have three kids, and spend your years happily baking apple pie." She knew Margo would not listen. Besides, had she managed her own life so well that she could give advice to others? "I'm glad you're enjoying it, dear." She noticed that Judith's son was sitting alone and added, pointing, "Why don't you join Bob Conrad?"

Philip approached the table and held out two plates. "Very little for Judith. She doesn't feel like eating. I think she should."

Alice put a small helping on Judith's plate and a larger one on his. She felt sorry for Philip, as she would for any victim of Judith's. He was a likable chap and a competent lawyer. What did he see in Judith? Alice smiled. She would never know.

Philip returned to Judith. Her legs were drawn up under her. She had taken off her shoes, and her wide skirt fell in shimmering folds over the side of the sofa. Her voice rose querulously as she confronted Max. "What're you trying to tell me? That we have to give the public what it wants?"

"I'm telling you that music is a business. The hall, the advertising, the programs . . . it all costs money, no? Somebody has to pay for it." His pudgy hand came down decisively on the arm of his chair. "That's all I'm saying."

"I disagree!" As always, when she argued, Judith was vehement. "Music is *not* a business, it's an art. The artist must try to educate the public."

"People go to be entertained, not educated. And if they make up their minds to stay away from a concert, you can't stop them."

Judith did not join in the laughter that greeted this remark. "In Europe art was supported by kings and princes. They were the artist's public."

"Yeah. But they had their heads cut off. Nowadays the public has to pay for it."

"We have patrons in this country too. Boards of directors, foundations, private individuals."

"Sure. Opera they support, symphony they support. But a piano or violin recital—no! They buy a few tickets and think they're doing you a favor yet." He shook his head obstinately. "I'm telling you the whole thing is a question of dollars and cents. And when Max Rubin tells you, you can believe."

Judith flushed with anger. She suddenly saw in Max the whole race of hucksters who grew fat off the artist's talent. "Dollars and cents?" she burst out, eyes flashing. "It's people like you who pull the artist down, and the audience with him!"

Philip, still holding the two plates, leaned over the back of the sofa. "Sh . . . take it easy, dear."

She turned upon him, breathing fire. "Don't you shush me!"

He smiled weakly. "Max only meant——"

"I know perfectly well what he meant. And I don't like it." She had no patience with Philip's fear of antagonizing people. He called it tact, she regarded it as cowardice. The lawyer's occupational disease.

"Judith, we're here to enjoy ourselves," he expostulated, "not to bang our heads against a wall."

"Then go ahead and enjoy yourself. I don't mind banging my head against a wall. Usually it's the wall that gives!"

Silenced, Philip handed Judith her plate. Max settled back in his chair. He disliked women with minds of their own, especially if they contradicted him. "You know what she wants?" he wheezed. "She wants the government should support artists. Socialism we should have yet." His pasty face took on an injured look.

"Socialism, my eye!" Judith countered. "Every government

ın Europe has a ministry of fine arts. That's what we'll have here one of these days."

"Oy, will you have a headache!" Max retorted triumphantly.

Walter thought it was time to intervene. "Break it up, children. We're not going to solve the world's problems tonight." He brought Max a scotch on the rocks.

Paul Horvath arrived. He had exchanged his white tie and tails for a turtle-neck sweater and slacks. His entrance changed the atmosphere. In Walter's circle the performing artist was much sought after, but a famous conductor stood several notches higher. Horvath was then at the height of his career. He was admired for his prodigious memory—he conducted the most complicated modern scores by heart—as well as for a fanatical dedication to his ideals that permitted no concessions to the public.

Alice hurried over to him. "Maestro, how nice of you to come."

He kissed her hand. "I'm delighted you asked me." His voice was deep, calm, pleasant. A Hungarian by birth, he had studied in London and spoke English with a faint central-European accent.

Walter greeted Horvath warmly and introduced the conductor to his guests, leading him around the room as though displaying a trophy.

"Maestro," Birdie fluttered, "it was a marvelous performance. Absolutely!" Horvath was one of her clients. As a rule she was on a first-name basis with the artists she represented, but Horvath was too European for such familiarity.

He sank onto the sofa beside Judith and rubbed his hands along his thighs. "It's good to relax." A smile softened the severity of his features. "You did very well tonight."

"So did you." She fixed her gaze upon him in the boldly inquiring way she had. She found his ascetic face uncommonly interesting. The high cheekbones made a dramatic contrast with his sunken cheeks. Once again, as when he kissed her hand on the stage, she was aware of the enigmatic look in his steel-blue eyes.

"We were having quite a discussion," Walter called from the bar. He brought Horvath a vodka and tonic and summarized the argument.

Horvath listened intently, trying to relate the discussion to his own convictions about the nature of music. His had been a solid European education based on Latin, Greek, and classical philosophy, expanded by a passion for reading unusual in a musician. "In the great periods of art," he said at length, "such as the time of Pericles or the Renaissance———" He spoke slowly, weighing his words, seeming almost to see them. Indeed, his ability to visualize, whether a page of music or a string of telephone numbers, was the basis of his infallible memory. At rehearsals the men in the orchestra never failed to be astonished when, without a score before him, he would stop them and say, "Gentlemen, would you begin again, please, three measures before letter *L.*"

He explained his view that the artist was part of his society and could not hope to rise above its shortcomings. In ancient Athens, as in Italy during the sixteenth century, political and social forces worked together to create a climate favorable in the highest degree to art. "But in our society everything depends on big business. So the forces working against the artist are stronger than those working for him. I am convinced that———"

Walter listened with the delight of a producer watching a successful first night. This was the kind of evening he liked to have in his home: good food, plenty of liquor, attractive well-dressed women, and interesting conversation (from which he excluded three topics—business, politics, and religion). "Makes sense," he whispered to Alice, putting his arm around her.

"He certainly does." The conductor was the one man in the group whom she found interesting. In a flash of intuition she realized that Horvath and she—so far apart in background, outlook, experience—had one thing in common: both of them were solitaries. Outsiders.

The party broke up a little after one. Walter and Alice accompanied their guests to the door. There was an epidemic of kissing and the synthetic warmth that came with it. Alice was delighted to see them go.

Walter was in an expansive mood. "This was one time I enjoyed my own party." He always said this. "I think they had a good time."

"I'm sure they did." Alice went around the room emptying ashtrays into a metal container.

"For a while Judith got hot under the collar. She has a temper, that girl." His face was flushed; he felt wide-awake. "I think I'll get a breath of air," he announced with elaborate casualness, "and pick up the *Times*." What he had in mind was a nightcap with Birdie. In the old days, walking the dog had served as an excuse for his nocturnal perambulations. Now there was no dog.

Alice emptied the last ash tray. Did he have to explain where he was going when he knew very well that she didn't believe him? "Good," she said wearily, and turned to the maid. "Let's clean up the mess."

"You wouldn't call it a mess," Walter said testily, putting on his coat, "if you liked my friends."

"Are you asking or telling me?"

He shrugged and left.

3

Walter walked briskly down the deserted street. Under the glare of the neon lights Second Avenue wore a tired look. The man at the newsstand huddled in his booth. Walter bought a *Times*, turned in at Fifty-second Street, and entered a brownstone house near the corner. He pressed Birdie's bell twice.

As he came up the stairs she waited at the door, wearing a pink housecoat that made her look taller and brought out her curves. Too vain to wear glasses, Birdie for years had wandered in a fog from which she was rescued by contact lenses. She drew Walter inside the apartment and slipped into his arms.

Birdie's living room was warm and cozy. Wherever you turned there were lamps, knicknacks, cushions. One corner bulged with a bright-red hassock. As much as Walter appreciated the quiet elegance of his own apartment, he felt more relaxed here. He kissed Birdie and ran his hands slowly down her back.

"I'm getting fat," she said coyly.

"And it's all mine." He grinned.

"You were supposed to contradict that statement."

"Why should I? Too many women are skinny nowadays. Ugh! I like something to hold on to."

She threw back her head and laughed. It was a bawdy laugh

that never failed to excite him. Then, mussing his hair, she disengaged herself from his arms.

"What are you drinking?" He sat down on the couch.

"Vodka."

"I'd love one."

She sat down at his feet and gazed up at him. "You know you're not supposed to have any. Would you like a glass of milk?" In the intimacy of her home she became less assertive, her voice was gentler.

He made a face. "At home I'm bullied by Alice. Here it's you."

"How else? Weak men attract strong women. That's your fate."

"It's been a pleasant one. Better than I've deserved."

"Stop feeling guilty. Sure you've been lucky, but it couldn't have happened to a nicer guy." Birdie had a theory that flattery got you everywhere. "I'll bring you the milk," she said, and pulled herself off the floor.

"Not yet," he pleaded, and caught her in his arms. He drew her down on the couch and stretched out, resting his head in her lap. "Did you enjoy the party?"

"You know I love parties." She pronounced her *t*'s with exaggerated distinctness, which gave her speech a slightly affected sound. "The chitchat, the gossip. Plus the fact that I was asked." She was silent a moment. "Although I must say your wife wasn't exactly cordial."

"My friends bore her. You know that. Besides, you two are so different—what could she find to say to you?"

"I can think of a lot of things I'd like to say to her." She ran her forefinger over the rim of his ear. "But I guess I'll never get the chance."

"Something to be thankful for."

"You must realize," she said with sudden intensity, "I'm at a terrible disadvantage with Alice. How do you suppose it feels to be entertained by a woman with whose husband I'm—how shall I put it?—involved? It's like a grade-B movie."

"Are we on that again?"

"Not at all. Let's just dismiss the situation. Pretend it doesn't exist."

Walter hated to waste time on problems for which no solution was possible. Birdie's grievance belonged to that category.

"What would you have me do?" he asked wearily. "Divorce Alice?"

"If you could have done that, you would have long ago. Fact is, you're still in love with her."

"Would I be here if I were?"

"Sure. You could love her and still need a fling." Bending over him, she held his chin as though to force him to face the issue. "Trouble is, I'm the fling."

He freed his chin by moving her hand down to his chest. "You're being unfair."

"No, I'm not. Deep down you consider me good enough to be your mistress but not your wife. That's what hurts."

Walter assumed a pained look to hide the fact that she was right. He was grateful to Birdie for all that she had given him. Nevertheless, his image of what his wife should be like had been shaped by Alice's cool elegance. Never in a thousand years could he picture Birdie receiving his friends or presiding at his table.

He put his hand guiltily against her cheek. "Look, sweetie, I never tried to fool you about where we stood. You were over twenty-one, you knew what you were doing. You must admit I was honest with you."

She smiled. "As honest as any man is when he's hot for a dame. He does all sorts of nice things for her, to make her forget that he can't give her the one thing she wants—a wedding ring And she keeps telling him she understands. They're both kidding each other. But by that time she's in love with him, so what can she do?" Birdie sighed. "It would have been a lot easier for me if you had been faithful to your wife."

"I was mad about her in the beginning," he said defensively.

"What went wrong?"

"I needed a hot-blooded woman, and she was always so-so about that." He moved his hand tentatively in the air.

"You think it was her fault, she probably thinks it was yours."

Walter looked back over the years with as much fairness as he could muster. "It's never one person's fault. What goes wrong is the combination. She didn't share my enthusiasm for making love, so she pushed me away a little. I felt she didn't want me, so I pushed her away a little. As the years passed each of us pushed in turn—out of hurt pride, spite, revenge, God knows what. In any case, I had to look elsewhere. And once you look, you find." Raising his hand, he chucked her under the chin. "Fortunately."

She pouted. "How many others were there before you got to me?"

"They were fly-by-nights. If you hadn't come along I'd have ended up as one of those dirty old men who pinch girls' behinds."

Birdie stared before her. She hated to nag. Besides, what good would it do? As if he had read her thoughts, Walter sat up and took her in his arms. "You've been wonderful for me, sweetie. Don't think I don't appreciate it." He tried to draw her down on the couch.

Birdie's myopic gray eyes looked at him lovingly, but she felt she ought to make a show of resistance. "Is *that* what you came for?" she asked.

"Would you prefer it if I came to discuss books?"

"Oh, no!" she cried, and snuggled down beside him.

He pulled her to him.

Alice lay under the bed lamp, propped up by two pillows, a copy of the *New Yorker* in her lap. She enjoyed every aspect of the magazine—its cartoons, its stories, and the lush advertisements that made luxury so attractive. She turned the pages idly, picking an item here and there that engaged her wandering thoughts.

The bedroom was uncluttered. A television set faced the twin beds; the white rug gave the room an antiseptic look. On the dresser stood a picture of Gene in his Air Force uniform. Near it was a small vase with a few sprays of marigolds. She changed the flowers according to the season but kept them simple—daisies, lilacs, tulips, pompons. She had left Gene's room as it was on the day he went away. His suits hung in cellophane wrappers in the closet; his shorts, shirts, and socks were neatly stacked on the shelves. Walter said she was being morbid. Only when she emptied the closet, he maintained, would she finally accept the fact that Gene was gone. Alice refused to be intimidated by a man's way of thinking. The things in the closet were all that remained to her of her son, her last link with his physical presence, and she could not bring herself to give them up.

The years after the war had been the hardest. At first it needed only the sight of a young man walking beside his parents to fill her with bitterness. So many had come back, why could he not have been among them? She regarded mothers more fortunate than herself with a fierce envy that filled her with guilt. She had no right, she told herself, to act as if she were the only one who had lost a son. Millions all over the world were bereaved too; yet the thought of that shadowy multitude did not alleviate her despair. Walter suggested that they adopt a war orphan, but the prospect agitated her. How could she ever again invest her love and hope in a child when some unforeseen catastrophe might snatch him from her?

People kept telling her that time would heal the blow. It did, on the surface. Bit by bit she resumed the outer pattern of her existence. She visited friends, read an occasional novel, went to the theater; she bought clothes, laughed at jokes, accepted invitations. Yet this vaunted healing of time was a fake. Beneath the resumption of life was a void, a stillness that cut her off from the world. She hid it from her friends and sometimes succeeded in hiding it from herself, but it was there even as Gene's clothes were behind the closet door, and she knew that it would never leave her.

Alice turned the page of the magazine and studied the hairdo of a model wearing a sapphire necklace. $5500.00. With earrings to match, $6800.00. It was well past two. Where was Walter? She had no desire to wait up for him, but knew she would not be able to sleep until he came home. If she put out the light, part of her would be listening for the sound of his footsteps in the hall. She could see the innocent look on his face when he returned. He would give her a cock-and-bull story that would humiliate her all the more in that he considered her naïve enough to believe it. She knew all his tricks, and put up with them as a tired mother did with the deceptions of a naughty boy. In the early years of their marriage she had felt betrayed by his philandering; he never understood that his unfaithfulness struck a mortal blow at her pride as a woman. Somehow she always found out about his escapades. Was his inability to hide them from her a form of revenge? Time and again she decided to leave him. He would come to her full of repentance and implore her to reconsider. They seemed to be engaged in a kind of dance in which each step of the one mtached that of the other: he must repeatedly hurt her and she must repeatedly forgive. He had a crazy theory that just because a man was occasionally unfaithful to his wife it did not mean he didn't love her. At times he even managed to convince her of this. In the early years she remained with him for Gene's sake; it would not be right, she told herself, to deprive the boy of his father. When Gene was grown she stayed out of inertia. After Gene's death she stayed because she was too crushed to go anywhere. In this darkest period of her life Walter was infinitely kind and patient; she needed him desperately. And now? Now she put up with him because it was too late to do anything else. They were approaching the end of their journey; did it matter whom he jumped into bed with? If he still had to prove himself a man, that was his problem, not hers.

She heard the key in the lock and tried to look absorbed in what she was reading. He came into the bedroom. "Still up?"

"I was catching up on book reviews."

"My head ached, so I took a walk."

"Feel better?"

"Much." He took off his jacket, arranged it carefully on a hanger, and hung it in the closet. "That was a fine evening, hon," he said.

"I think your friends enjoyed it."

"Don't you mean *our* friends?"

The hour was too late for argument. "Of course, dear," she said smoothly.

He shook his head. "You just don't like them. Once you make up your mind not to like someone, it's finished."

"Look, Walter——" Her voice rose ever so little. "They're your friends, because you picked them, not I. But when they come here I do everything possible to make them feel at home, and I think they enjoy coming." She stopped as though the subject were closed, but could not resist adding, "Although they'd probably go anywhere as long as they got a free meal."

He flushed. "That's not a nice thing to say." He undid his tie and began to unbutton his shirt. "You're saying it to hurt me."

"If the truth hurts, it's not my fault."

At once the room was filled with the residue of a thousand clashes between them. "Honestly, I don't know what you have against them," he brought out petulantly. "Would you prefer it if I brought home some idiots who spent the evening discussing real estate?"

She regretted having given him an opportunity to feel aggrieved; this was a role he thoroughly enjoyed. "I don't have anything against them, except that I see them as they are. They're mean and petty and completely out for themselves."

"Who isn't?"

She ignored the interruption ."They're name droppers. Celebrity hunters. Worst of all—bores!"

"You say this because you're a snob."

"On the contrary, it's you who are the snob."

"Look——" Walter made an effort to sound reasonable. "We had Judith Conrad tonight. We had Paul Horvath—one of the finest conductors in the country. Max Rubin's been a top figure in the musical world for forty years. Doesn't it mean anything to you to have people like that in your house?"

"Frankly, no." She stared at him coldly. "I don't need them around to make me feel important."

"You resent them," he struck back, "because they make you feel like a nobody. You'd rather be surrounded by nobodies. Then you could be the queen bee."

"A psychologist yet," she sneered.

"What's the use?" he muttered, throwing up his hands in disgust. "Where are my pyjamas?"

"On your bed."

By *your bed* Walter understood not the twin bed on which the coverlet was turned down invitingly, but the couch in the little study off the hallway. He had slept there for almost twelve years, following a scene in which she had ordered him to leave their bedroom and he had sworn never to return to it. He no longer remembered what had precipitated the crisis, but he had kept his vow. Turning on his heel without a good night, he stalked out and shut the door behind him.

Alice put out the light. She felt a momentary glow at having had the last word; but it quickly subsided, leaving in its place an all-too-familiar emptiness. She wanted to call him back and tell him she was sorry for what she had said. Her pride prevented her. Instead she turned on her side and stared before her. A soft glow filtered into the room from the lights on the bridge; the half darkness pressed down upon her. Her heart was heavy, and the taste of tears stung her lips. How strange it was that the need to hurt—and be hurt—could be as powerful a bond between two people as love.

4

Judith lolled in an armchair, her feet on the low table in front of her. The exhilaration induced by the concert had worn off, giving way to depression. By some mysterious arithmetic her depressions equaled in intensity the exhilaration that preceded them. This accounted for what she called her roller-coaster existence: going up was more pleasant than coming down.

Philip sat on the low piano bench, watching her. Her dark brooding eyes were fixed on the middle distance; she appeared to have forgotten him. "What's wrong?" he asked, resenting the exclusion.

"What's wrong?" she said irritably. "Everything." During the concert she had been persuaded that she was in top form. Now, swinging to the other extreme, she was dissatisfied with everything she had done. She glanced at her watch. "The papers'll be out soon."

"Why are you so anxious? You did your best, no? What difference does it make what some newspaper critic writes? He's only putting down his opinion, he's not God."

"He has more power than God, because a million people are going to read his review tomorrow morning. They can't think for themselves. He makes up their minds for them."

"Seems t'me that if I were an artist I wouldn't even read the reviews."

"Don't worry, you'll never have that problem." This sounded more cutting than she had intended. "Every artist dreads a bad notice. There it is in cold print for the whole world to see. You feel as if you've been stripped naked in public. And you've no one to complain to—the critic has the last word and knows it." How could he not understand what was so obvious to her? At first she had found him refreshingly different from the musicians she knew. He had conducted her divorce suit with skill and obtained a much better settlement than she had expected. Now he was beginning to irritate her. "Trouble with you, Phil, it that you have both feet on the ground."

"What's that supposed to mean?"

"It means that you're the kind of man who moves strictly within the limits of his personality."

"And where am I supposed to move?"

"On the mountaintop. From where you can see the whole world!" She flung out her arms in a grand embrace.

"You should've been an actress." He looked at her appraisingly. "The trouble with me, you're trying to say, is that I'm satisfied with my life. As a matter of fact I am. When a man's seen the kind of things I saw in the war, he's happy just to be alive. Want to know something? Most of the people around here don't know how lucky they are."

This kind of talk bored her. "Phil, why don't you run down and pick up a paper."

"The *Tribune*'ll be out by now," he replied. "Not the *Times.*"

"Why d'you argue with me when you see I'm upset?" she flared up, unloosing upon him the full impact of her eyes.

Without answering he threw on his coat and went out.

Judith decided to make herself comfortable. A huge couch stood against the wall, covered with faded green velvet—a relic of her parents' day. On it were strewn several back copies of the *Times,* the second volume of Beethoven's sonatas, and a pink scarf. She transferred the sonata volume and the scarf to the piano bench, threw the newspapers on the floor, and lay down. She kicked off her shoes, slid one arm under the back of her head, and stared up at the ceiling. The clock ticked. Now and again the honking of a taxi horn strayed into the room.

In the beginning everything had been easy. Her father had been endlessly proud of the little girl who took to the piano, and never tired of showing her off to his friends. He was a successful doctor, handsome and fun-loving. Judith adored him. At an early age her music-making became an inseparable part of her need to win his admiration; already her daydreams centered about the famous pianist she was going to be. Her parents had no doubts about the brilliant career that awaited her, and allowed her to entertain none. Besides, her playing was an easy means of gaining the attention of her world—that German-Jewish, solidly middle-class world which brought to this country so profound a belief in the superiority of its tradition. Bach, Mozart and Beethoven, Schubert, Schumann and Brahms, Goethe,

Schiller and Heine—these were the names her elders taught her to revere even before she knew why they were worthy of reverence. When she found herself, at seventeen, in Berlin, where her parents had passed their youth, she felt almost as if she had come home. She studied with Edwin Fischer and Backhaus, and became passionately devoted to the German idea of music as a moral force, a poetic experience of transcendental significance. This well-nigh mystical concept she found embodied in the German classics to such a degree that she was rarely impelled to play anything else.

Her stay in Germany was cut short by the triumph of Nazism, an event that was hardly noticed in the hermetic world she inhabited. If the early excesses of the Nazis made little impact upon her, it was because she had never identified herself with Jews. Her parents thought of themselves as Germans and looked with majestic disdain upon the Russian-Polish Jews New York was full of. Throughout the twenties and thirties they maintained that there would have been no anti-Semitism in Germany were it not for the east-European Jews. They paid lip service to their religion by attending services (reformed) on the high holy days. With the years even this perfunctory rite was abandoned. Where men were concerned, Judith favored non-Jews. Her parents were delighted when she married a blue-eyed Episcopalian who looked like the perfect foil for her duskier charms. Eustis Conrad III. He wore brownish tweeds, smoked a pipe, had a tiny cleft in his chin, and worked for an excellent Wall Street firm. What had she seen in him? Looking back across the years, Judith could not even remotely imagine.

It was only at the war's end, when the world learned the full measure of what the Nazis had accomplished, that she became aware of herself as a Jew. She faced the realization that in the gas chambers no distinction was drawn between the westernized German Jews and their less cultivated Russian-Polish brethren. Among the victims were her grandparents, who had resisted every inducement to leave what they regarded as their homeland, and an assortment of aunts, uncles, and cousins whom she remembered from her student days in Berlin. Her identification with them awoke a complex of emotions of which she had never been conscious before. She was Jewish, it came to her, not because of a religious faith she had never shared, but simply, inescapably, because if she had lived in Germany she would have perished with the others. She was a Jew because Hitler had said so. Against that judgment there was no appeal.

The question that tormented her was, How could the nation that produced Bach and Beethoven, Goethe and Schiller also have created Auschwitz and Buchenwald? How could the com-patriots of Mozart and Schubert have perfected such ingenious techniques for transforming people into soap and lampshades? Everything that her parents had taught her about the land of their birth, everything that had made her regard Germany as the citadel of art and culture, turned out to be untrue. How could they have been so tragically mistaken?

Her husband was a mild young man who, for all his good manners, bored her. She parted from him without sorrow. Her second husband was Jewish and made her extremely unhappy. Ralph Rothstein embodied all the traits that her parents con-sidered obejectionable in the Russian Jew: he was aggressive, arrogant, selfish, crude, and loud. His only virtue, it seemed, was a gift for making money. If, from her first marriage, she emerged with a beautiful baby boy, from her second she came away with a healthy alimony that would cease only when she married again. She had no intention of making life that easy for Ralph. Besides, she was finished with marriage.

From her earliest years she had lived under the spell of a promise: the world would lie at her feet if she worked hard and devoted herself to her music. This condition presented no prob-lem, for she loved the piano and spent hours at it. All the same, she discovered that the promise was not easily translated into reality. It was not enough to possess talent; you needed also the talent to sell your talent. This involved meeting the people who could be useful to you, manipulating them to your advantage, finding—or creating—the right opportunities, competing with a host of other pianists for the attention of the public, dickering with managers, and trying to control a variety of factors among which luck was not the least important. What had begun as a simple goal that seemed well within her grasp turned out to be a delicate operation whose complexities had challenged her ingenuity for the better part of two decades. She found them be-wildering, tantalizing, and infinitely absorbing.

Philip returned with the papers. Judith snatched the *Times* and opened to the music page. She plunged into the review; it belonged to what she called the "give and take" school of criticism; what the critic gave with one hand he took back with the other. He praised her tone, but suggested that she had over-pedaled. Her phrasing was sensitive, but in the fast movement her beat had been unsteady. In the end, however, he came through with a quotable statement. She read it to Philip with relish: "To anyone who has watched her growth over the years, it is clear that Miss Conrad is developing into one of the important women pianists of her generation."

The reviewer of the *Tribune,* on the other hand, found fault with everything she had done. According to him she had barely scratched the surface of the concerto. Judith, enraged, flung the paper on the floor. "The idiot! Can't do a damn thing himself, but it's so easy to tell others!" Critics, she insisted, were frustrated pianists, singers, composers who couldn't make the grade, so they took out their frustration on those who did.

Philip tried to calm her. "Why upset yourself? It's his job to criticize—that's what he's paid for. Anyway, you got a fine notice in the *Times.* More people will see that one."

This failed to mollify Judith. It was the bad reviews that impressed themselves on her mind, never the good ones. "Ridiculous!" she cried. "According to the man in the *Times* I turned in a fine performance, and in the *Tribune* you read exactly the opposite. Each of these clowns is convinced he's telling the truth. How can you take them seriously?"

"Then why do you?"

Judith's underlip curved in that sensual smile of hers. "My trouble is, I want the whole world to love me and refuse to face the fact that it's not possible. I couldn't get this through my head when I was a little girl, and I still can't." She tore out both reviews for her scrapbook. With a final glance at the smaller column she dismissed its author with, "I could wring his neck!"

"You're too intense," Philip said.

"You mean, I'm too alive?" She smiled.

Now that the ordeal was over she was ready for pleasure. No matter how abruptly she went from one mood to the next, she expected Philip to follow her. In their love-making it was generally she who took the initiative and he who submitted. She pulled him to her and overwhelmed him with her caresses, giv-

ing herself completely to the surge of passion. And at the height
of it, somehow, it was he who lay on his back while she came
out on top.

Philip raised himself on his elbow and followed the even rise
and fall of her breathing; she was asleep. She fascinated him,
she puzzled him, just a little she repelled him. He had never
known anyone like her, and he wasn't sure he enjoyed the experience.

She lay on her side, head slightly back, one arm coiled around
the pillow, looking very feminine. Even in her sleep she lied.
Beneath those softly rounded contours was an iron will driven
by boundless ambition and pride. Her need to conquer, to imprint her image on the world, extended into every facet of her
personality. Even love, for her, was a form of conquest. She liked
to say that she could love only a strong man, but this was self-
delusion. Actually, it occurred to him, only a weakling would
submit to her domination. In the early months of their friendship he had been fascinated by the vagaries of the artistic temperament; now he found them trying. She seemed unable to
keep her mind on anything that was not directly related to herself. During the negotiation of her divorce she had followed his
work with the greatest concern, but took no further interest in
it once he had obtained what she wanted. He could not put his
finger on what was wrong between them. He knew only that
when he was with her, in some curious way he ceased to exist.
That was just about it. Her way of enjoying a man was to wipe
him out.

Was the trouble, perhaps, that there was so little gentleness in
her? Basically she was unable to share. What she thought of as
love was really desire—a volcanic upsurge that held her in its
grip until her needs were satisfied. She reminded him of those
female insects who, once they have enjoyed their mate, devour
him. She would devour him too if he let her. But he wasn't going to.

He let out a sigh. Here he was, lying beside her, already thinking of their affair as something in the past. Soon they would
be to each other no more than a memory. He had enjoyed much
in their relationship, yet he relinquished it without regret. He
was not the kind of man who took on more than he could handle.
Anyone who took her on was courting defeat.

Philip bent over her, a smile on his lips. She was something, this girl. She really was . . .

5

The basement was a long narrow room enveloped in cigarette smoke. Bob and Margo sat in a booth, between them a little square table covered with a red-checkered cloth. He watched the three musicians on the dais as he followed the shifting patterns of sound. The bass player slapped his instrument with the flat of his hand, the guitarist shaped pinglike tones that were amplified electrically to a throbbing intensity, while the clarinetist embarked on a rapturous improvisation. Bob's left hand beat a tattoo on the tablecloth. His head jerked back now and again in a kind of counterrhythm, almost as if his response to the beat were being dragged out of him by force.

Margo smiled. "You love this music, don't you."

He beamed at her without interrupting the motion of his hand or head. "It turns me on." The clarinet wailed its way up the scale. "Beautiful!" he cried out, his eyes alight.

She liked his enthusiasm. He was almost too good-looking, she thought—his thin face was highly expressive, his blond hair took on a golden sheen under the light. He was quite different now that he was away from his mother's friends. His timidity had dropped from him; he was spontaneous, outgoing.

The music came to an end. Bob slumped against the back of the booth. Margo sipped her drink. "Did you enjoy the party?" she asked.

"I never enjoy those people. They're a putdown." On his lips the phrase sounded like an affectation, contrasting as it did with his generally conventional speech.

"I find them fascinating."

"That's because you didn't grow up with them. I've had to be with that crowd since I was a kid. What a drag!"

"Why?"

"They don't like you for what you are. You have to be somebody, you have to set the world on its ear. Take you. Ordinarily you'd be thinking about marrying some Joe and settling down.

Instead you're all hopped up about a career. That's all you think about, your whole life is one long hassle to make it." He grimaced.

She looked at him in wonder. "What's wrong with that? If you have some talent, why shouldn't you try to develop it?"

"Because something happens to you while you're trying. You get caught in the rat race, you become tough and bitter until nothing is left of the person you were."

The music began again. Bob resumed his tapping. "Don't you have any ambitions?" she asked.

"Sure. I want to be myself. I want to be free inside. That means throwing off all the hang-ups the world forces on us from the day we're born." He had soft green eyes with tiny black pupils—cat's eyes. She thought them beautiful. "When you're a kid," he said, "your parents make you feel they love you because you're clever or good-looking or talented. Then you spend the rest of your life trying to win their love—or the world's love —through your cleverness or beauty or talent. That's all wrong. They should love you because you're you, because you're theirs. Without conditions attached."

"There are always conditions," she said. "That's what makes you toe the mark."

"It's all wrong! In our society everyone competes. There are other societies—in the Orient, for example—where life isn't based on competition. Believe me, they're happier."

The idea that one could simply *be* was new to Margo. "If you don't have a goal in life," she expostulated, "how are you going to make something of yourself?"

"That's the way my mother thinks," he said quietly. "It's for the birds. The goal should not be to prove yourself to the world. The goal should be inside you."

It astonished her that she responded so readily to his moods, to the play of light and shade on his face, the inflection of his voice. His ideas, however alien to her way of thinking, reached her in an easy, intimate way. She smiled up at him. "How strange! I'm talking to you as if we were old friends."

"Not strange at all. People build walls between each other. They don't have to."

He made it sound, simple, almost inevitable; yet Margo felt that everything connected with this evening—the smoke-filled basement, the wild music, the look on his face—was rare and never to be forgotten.

Just before they left he disappeared into the men's room. He stood in front of the urinal, studying the obscene drawing penciled on the wall. The door opened. A thin young man in a red blazer took his place at the adjoining urinal and glanced at the door. As he did so he passed two diminutive cloth bags to Bob, who slipped him a ten-dollar bill. The exchange took a moment; the young man vanished. Bob dropped the little bags into the inside pocket of his jacket, flushed the urinal, and rejoined Margo.

MacDougal Street was crowded; the air was cool and moist. She filled her lungs. "This is like a holiday," she said. "I've been working so hard."

"How come?"

"We're giving *Madame Butterfly* at school. I have the main part. It's a big opportunity for me."

"Scared?"

"Sure. But once you're on stage you have too much to think about." Her face was radiant. "It's wonderful!"

"Look at what you have to go through before you get the chance."

"That's part of it. You hope and dream and work your head off. Finally, if you're lucky, something comes your way."

They reached Washington Square. The street lamps threw a wan light on empty benches. Trees stood bare in the November night, their branches outstretched.

He looked down into her face. "That means, you spend half your life living in the future."

"What's wrong with that?"

"All I know is I'm alive today. What's now is real—and it's great! Tomorrow may never come."

"Most of the time it does." She tried to see the world as he did, and it was suddenly radiant with color and light. The houses on the north side of Washington Square, their gracious stoops set back from the curb, looked fresh, transformed. A waning moon floated over the arch and enveloped her in its gentle glow. He slipped his fingers through hers; they walked hand in hand. "I think your mother's a fascinating woman," she said.

"She's all right. Trouble with her is, she's *on* too much of the time."

"On?"

"Puts on an act. Even for herself. Then she can't tell which part of her is real and which is make-believe."

His matter-of-factness took her aback. "Don't you love her?"

"I suppose I do. Just because you love someone is no reason not to see them as they are."

"I think you're wrong. When you love someone you see him as he ought to be, or as you'd like him to be. When you see people as they are it means you no longer love them."

He laughed. "Then I don't, I guess. We're supposed to love our mothers, but sometimes it's more complicated than you'd imagine."

Could he love me? The thought left her startled. She realized that she was holding his hand too tightly and loosened her grip. "Your mother's an artist," she said evenly. "She has to project her personality. In order to do that you have to dramatize what you feel."

"It's one thing to dramatize as part of your job, it's another when you do it in your spare time too. Believe me, this can be a bore." He was no longer gentle. It occurred to Margo that he loved Judith either too little or too much.

He hailed a cab. Neither of them spoke after they got in. Margo sank back in her seat and reflected on her reaction to him. He brought with him a way of looking at things, a quality of awareness that filled her with excitement. At the same time there was something unreal about the experience. She had the sensation of being both in it and outside looking on, and knew only that she wanted to prolong it indefinitely. The problem was what to do when they reached her door. The lights along Fifth Avenue sped past her; she watched them through half-shut eyes. Should she invite him up? She brusquely dismissed the thought, yet it kept returning.

They alighted in front of a brownstone on East Twenty-second Street. A neon sign on the corner went on and off, flooding the street with waves of pink light. He followed her to her door. "I'm glad you decided to ask me up," he said.

She turned around sharply. "What makes you think I did?"

He grinned. "I could feel the vibrations in the cab."

Her embarrassment vanished, "As a matter of fact I shouldn't."

"Why not?"

"I hardly know you."

"Not true. I've told you a lot about myself. Much more than I usually tell someone I just met."

His earnestness conquered. She held out her hands in a gesture of yielding, and led the way up the stairs to the third floor.

Her studio apartment contained a small upright piano and a record player. The bed was disguised as a couch, the kitchenette was a little alcove. She motioned him to the armchair by the window. "Coffee?"

"Don't bother. Let's just talk."

She settled herself on the couch. "You still haven't told me what you want to be."

"Yes, I did. I said I wanted to be myself."

"That's hardly a career."

"Oh, you mean how I intend to make a living?" He threw back his head and laughed. "Shall I tell you the truth? I haven't the faintest idea. When I finished college I went to graduate school. Columbia. Mainly because I couldn't think of anything else to do. I was going to take my M.A. in English lit. But it's such a stuffy place that I dropped out. Did that upset my mother!" The thought seemed to give him pleasure.

Margo looked puzzled. "But what do you do? I mean, when you get up in the morning. Surely you have some kind of goal."

"Oh, that. As a matter of fact I'm trying to write. The question is, have I anything to say? I like to put words on paper. Once they're down, though, I'm not sure they're worth much." He leaned forward, scrutinizing her. "You must understand that my way of looking at life is different from yours. You've set yourself a goal and you chug toward it every hour of the day. That's your thing, and it's fine for you. With me living is the most important thing. Writing is a by-product. If I get anywhere with it, fine. If not——" He shrugged.

Margo watched him intently. Clearly he stood outside—or was it above—the way of life that she had been taught to accept as the only valid one. Yet so great was her desire to agree with him that she was willing to concede the limitations of her outlook. If he needed a year or two to find himself, who was she to object? "Of course," she said, thoughtful, "you have to live first. Otherwise what'll you write about?"

He smiled. "Then let's say I'm gathering material."

A silence fell. Bob suddenly rose and came beside the couch. Kneeling in front of Margo, he raised one hand and passed his fingertips across her cheek and around the oval of her chin, gently, unhurriedly, as if it had been long understood between them that this was what he must do. "Would you like me to go now?" he asked, and cupped her chin in his hand.

Margo hesitated. "Part of me wants you to stay, and the other part tells me to send you away."

"Which part is stronger?"

"The one that wants you to stay."

"Beautiful." Bending forward, he rested his cheek against hers. Then he put his arms around her and kissed her.

His lips felt soft and warm on hers. The tip of his tongue pressed against her mouth, seeking to enter. For a moment she made a show of resisting, then parted her lips to receive it. There was neither surprise in her nor fear, only delight that the evening had followed its preordained course. He drew back, slipped one arm behind her back and the other under her knees as if he were going to lift her, and laid her flat on the couch. Lying down beside her, he cupped one hand on her breast, then let it trail to her thigh. Again his lips were on hers; she felt his body stiffen against her. Suddenly he left off, raised himself on his elbow, and looked at her intently. "Tell me one thing. The truth."

"What?"

"Am I the first?"

She weighed the question. "No," she finally said. "There was a boy back home."

"Good. I wouldn't want to be the first."

"Why?"

"Too much of a responsibility."

"You mean, if I'd said you were, you'd have gone away?"

"Yes."

"Then I'm glad I told the truth."

"Did you love him?"

"I thought I did. We were both too young."

"I see," He rose and flicked off the light. She watched him drop his jacket, tie, and shirt on the armchair. The neon sign on the corner swept the room with its rhythmic alternation of light and darkness. Now he was in his undershirt and briefs. It was dark for a moment. When the sign changed he stood naked before her, slender, golden-haired, enveloped in light. And it seemed to Margo that he was the most beautiful thing in the world.

He returned to the sofa. It was very still in the room. Gently he undressed her, removing first her shoes and stockings, then the rest of her clothes, which he dropped on the floor. She heard the quiet rhythm of his breathing. His hands made love to her, his lips were at her breast. For an instant she had again the sensation of being both inside the experience and apart from it, looking on. He drew her hand down over his body. She felt the rise and fall of his belly and let her hand rest where he left it, ashamed to proceed further, almost fearful. As if he had read her thought, he guided her fingers still lower until they touched the fuzz of soft hair at the base of his stomach and came to rest on his swollen sex. Suddenly she was no longer ashamed or frightened or reluctant. She was a woman exploring the body of her lover, wanting to know every part of him, to receive him, hold him, feel him inside her. Again responding to her thought, he raised himself above her. She felt her body yield, welcoming him, sucking him in, and becoming one with him. Thought and feeling, past and present melted into an encompassing oneness. Her hands rode hard over his body. She felt the little hollows in the sides of his buttocks as he pushed into her, and responded in a rhythm that carried her beyond herself—the life-giving rhythm that was stronger than will, stronger than thought, for it reached back to the beginning of time. No longer was she outside the experience looking on. She was in the blazing center of it, indissolubly at one with it, clutching him to her, digging his fingers into his back, wanting to squeeze all of him into her, lunging forward in total response to him until the primeval force swept her to the final surge of desire and release.

Her cheek rested against his chest; she was aware of the pounding of his heart. She lay still, savoring their intimacy. He sighed and gently withdrew. Lying on his back, he stared at the ceiling while the pulsating light from the sign on the corner ebbed and flowed over them. Then he turned on his side and passed his fingertips over her face. "You have a little nose," he whispered, "a little mouth, and the tinest ears. You're lovely."

She smiled. "I'm glad you like." It came to her that he had never once mentioned love. The realization saddened her, since she knew with utter finality that he was the one she wanted. She had loved him before she knew him, and she always would.

He went to the bathroom; she heard the toilet flush. Then he returned. "You better wash up," he said, and she knew what he was thinking of. She rose from the couch, slipped into a robe, and went into the bathroom. When she returned he was smoking a cigarette. She lay down beside him and ran her fingers through his hair.

He blew rings of smoke through pursed lips. "Tell me about yourself."

She put her head on the pillow, next to his. "Not much to tell. I was born in Poughkeepsie and sang in the church choir. Everybody said I was going to be a singer, and I believed them. Three years ago I came to New York to study. At Juilliard. One night I sang in a concert at the school. Your mother's friend Walter Stern was there. He liked my voice and decided to help. He and his wife have been wonderful. That's about it, I guess."

"Isn't there any more?"

"No. I've been so caught up in my studies I haven't had time to think of anything else. That's why tonight has been so—wonderful."

"Did you know," he said, "that the simplest organisms in nature, like amoebas, don't have sex. Neither do they die. Only the creatures who know the pleasure of sex have to face death."

She put her hand against his cheek. "Why d'you think about death when I feel so full of life."

"Because it isn't a separate thing, it's part of life. Who knows, maybe another kind of life."

"I never think of dying," she said. "It never enters my head that I will."

"The amoeba can't create life, yet he's immortal. Not that it means anything to him. But we, who are able to create life, die. Buddhists believe that when a man dies his soul passes into the body of a child born at that moment. The individual is a link in the chain, and the chain never ends."

All this sounded extremely profound to Margo and quite beyond her depth. She sighed happily and hoped he would continue.

He did. "When I discovered sex—I guess I was about twelve—I used to think about it every night when I went to sleep. It was such pleasure, I was sure I was going to die from it." He smiled.

His linking of sex with death was too foreign to her way of thinking to strike her as anything but a poetic fancy. "I'm glad you didn't," she said, and kissed him.

He looked into her eyes. "It's incredible to me that you're so

sure about your future. Don't you sometimes wonder whether
or not you'll make it?"

She thought a moment. "I don't have the time. My feeling is
that if I learn to sing as well as I can, everything else'll take
care of itself."

"You're lucky. If I were that sure, I'd have it made. Sometimes
I go to the library and stare at all those books on the shelves.
Can it be that some day I'll write one? It just don't seem pos-
sible." He put his arm around her and drew her close.

A melody ran through her head. She hummed it.

"What is it?" he asked.

"I was rehearsing it today. From the first act of *Butterfly*. The
love duet." She sang the phrase softly, spinning out its bitter-
sweetness in a long lyric line. *"Dicon ch'oltre mare se cade in
man dell'uom ogni farfalla, d'uno spillo è trafitta ed in tavola
infitta!"*

"Meaning—?"

"Pinkerton has just told Butterfly she's well named. She an-
swers, 'They say that over the sea'—she means in his country—
'if a butterfly falls into a man's hand he sticks it with a pin and
sets it on a table.'" Suddenly Margo realized that she had just
asked him not to hurt her; her face went hot. At that moment,
fortunately, the neon sign was dark.

"What does he answer to that?"

"Let's see . . ." She pretended that she was trying to remember. *"Un po' di vero c'è* . . . 'There's a bit of truth in that,' he
says. 'You know why? Because then the butterfly can't fly away.'
Lo t'ho ghermita . . . 'I've caught you, I hold you trembling,
you are mine!'"

"I don't go much to the opera," he said quietly, and she was
grateful to him for having given the conversation another turn.
"But if you sing, I'll come."

"Promise?"

"Promise." Without a word of warning he seized her. He ran
his lips over her breasts, caressing her nipples with the tip of
his tongue, exploring her body as only a lover of women could,
inhaling its fragrance, revealing its capacity for pleasure in ways
she had never imagined. He had endless zest for the physical
side of love-making. She yielded to him eagerly, completely.

When it was over he rose and began to put on his clothes. She watched him, taken aback. "You can stay over if you like," she said.

He knelt beside the couch and took her hands in his. "After I've been this close to someone, I just have to be by myself awhile. To restore the balance, like."

"A woman is different. I thought it would be nice to fall asleep with your arms around me."

"I wouldn't sleep, I'd be too aware of you. And I'd only keep you up."

"Then you'd better go. I've a lesson tomorrow and a rehearsal." She was silent a moment. "What'll you do when you're married?"

"Separate bedrooms, I guess." He grinned. "Anyway, that hassle's a long way off."

She accompanied him to the door. A delicious drowsiness enveloped her. "What time is it?"

"Don't look. Clocks only tell you what time other people think it is. In this room we make our own time. I've been here for weeks, months, years. Ever since you were born." He took her face between his hands and kissed her forehead, her eyelids, and the tip of her nose.

"Will I——will I see you again?" she asked, and was sorry to have asked it.

"Strange, you're so sure of your work yet so unsure of me."

"That's because——" She groped for an answer. "—I know my work better than I know you."

"I'll call you tomorrow." He opened the door and gave her a final kiss. Half way down the stairs he stopped and looked back. "Don't worry," he said with a smile, "I don't stick pins in butterflies."

She went inside and, pulling the robe around her, stood by the window. A vast hush hung over the city. A truck rumbled past on Second Avenue; the sign on the corner had ceased its gyrations. The stars looked wan and remote, except one in the eastern sky that trembled with a great light. She was sure it was Venus, and her heart overflowed with happiness.

6

Bob stopped before a brownstone on East Sixty-second Street. The house had been bought by Judith's father before the war; it was now worth four times what he had paid for it. Originally there was a flight of stone steps in front that led to the parlor floor. Judith had had the front modernized; you entered on the street level through a door painted an elegant black with a thin red border.

Bob let himself in and made his way down the corridor on the ground floor. His room was at the back of the house. He closed the door behind him with a sense of relief, shutting out the world of will and activity in which, even when he most enjoyed it, he felt himself a stranger. The bed, unmade, occupied one corner, flanked by a desk with a typewriter on it, a television set, and a record player. Book shelves and record albums took up what little space was left. He knew the location of every book and record. Only one feature failed to meet his approval. The window, which faced the back yard, was protected by three iron bars that Judith had had put in several years before. Times had changed, she maintained, since the days when her parents had lived there. Bob considered the bars an eyesore even though, in response to his protests, they had been painted white.

He threw off his clothes and looked at himself in the full-length mirror on the closet door. Clothes were part of the armor people wore to protect themselves against the world: artificial trappings, false and constricting. It followed that a man was truly himself only when he was naked. Bending over the record albums, Bob pulled out the one he wanted—Ravi Shankar's *Sounds of India*—and put it on the phonograph. The music floated into the room, filling the air with delicate patterns of sound repeated with hypnotic insistence. This melody was far removed from the activist music of the West; it was peaceful and soothing—music for meditation.

Bob lay down and shut his eyes. The evening had left a glow. It was so difficult for him to make contact with others that when he did he was filled with a sense of achievement. The mind, he reflected, expressed its thoughts through words that were more or less misleading, but the body communicated its desires directly, unmistakably. Sex, consequently, was the most immediate way of achieving oneness with another person. Margo's gentleness had encouraged him to take the initiative. He had come off, he felt, with flying colors.

Despite the glow, he was not unaware of possible complications. Two people jumped into bed and had fun together, but they had a hard time keeping it that way. Inevitably one of them began to make demands on the other, the fun became tangled up with all sorts of headaches. If a man's first duty was to develop himself as fully as possible, anything that tied him down could become a threat. As he listened to the gentle tinkling of the sitar, Bob became aware of a basic contradiction in his nature. On the one hand he wanted to be loved, on the other he wanted to remain free. Torn between the two, he was unable to move decisively toward either. He remembered reading that when the Crusaders finally caught sight of the Holy Sepulcher they approached it by taking three steps forward and two back. Was this, he wondered, how he approached life?

The ceiling was veiled in shadows. Words and images floated through his mind—he saw the beginning of a short story. An old man is cared for by his daughter. She is torn between her love for him and her resentment at being tied down; he, similarly, is torn between his dependence on her and his fear of losing her. Bob pictured father and daughter, he heard their voices and saw the dingy room in which they lived; but when he tried to set the characters in motion they faded from his view. He was continually beginning stories in his mind that he was unable to continue. When he tried to capture them on paper they eluded him or turned out to be pale copies of films he had seen, books he had read. In his favorite daydream he imagined himself a famous writer like Norman Mailer or Tennessee Williams, sought after and welcomed everywhere. All who had doubted him were finally persuaded of his gifts, especially his mother. Now that he had convinced them, he was finally able to believe in himself.

The record came to an end. Leaning over, Bob brought the needle back to the beginning. The melody unfolded in delicate curves, like the traceries he had seen in pictures of Indian temples. Somebody once said that architecture was frozen music.

Who? He lay very still. Ambition, desire for fame and success, hunger for love or sex or power—these were the chains that bound a man to the world, hiding from him knowledge of his true self. In order to free himself from these delusions he had to throw off the Ego, to withdraw into the innermost part of him where there was only pure being. Bob tried to empty his mind of thought. He could almost hear the pulsation of his blood, a gentle flow attuned to the rhythm of the universe. He aspired to the rapt contemplation achieved by the mystics of the East, a state of will-lessness incomprehensible to our machine-made civilization. He wished he had grown up in India or Tibet, in a simple patriarchal society whose code of behavior was handed down from one generation to the next, where he would have felt protected and been capable of making a place for himself. He might even have joined one of the monastic orders that relinquished the world and its distractions. Instead he had been set down by fate in this Babylon-on-the-Hudson, in a chaotic, insanely competitive scene where he did not belong and never would. He wondered what he might have been in a previous incarnation. It seemed to him that only a thin wall separated him from the mystery. If he could but find the door . . .

Bob listened to the rise and fall of his breathing. There were moments when his body overflowed with energy and became a thing of wonder to him. He passed his hand over his stomach and placed it on his penis, recapturing in his mind the pleasure it had brought him at Margo's. He fingered it lovingly until it grew hard, and held it aloft, away from his body; he was proud of its size. At school, in the shower room, he used to measure himself against other boys and feel sorry for those who had been shortchanged. At times he enjoyed playing with himself almost as much as the real thing. For one, it was less of an effort. Besides, he had never quite decided which was more exciting—the lascivious scenes conjured up by his imagination or what reality had to offer. Tonight, though, he was glad he had made the scene with Margo. Giving pleasure to someone else added to the enjoyment. It was the sharing that mattered, even to one like himself who was by nature not a sharer.

The sages of the Orient achieved such control over the body that they could walk on broken glass or flaming logs without pain; they could suck in water through the anus and transcend

the force of gravity. They induced a state of mystic contemplation in themselves through sheer strength of will. Some day he,
too, would be able to do this. In the meantime he had to rely
on external means. He brought out one of the little cloth bags
he had hidden in the inside pocket of his jacket and emptied its
contents in the palm of his hand—two tiny white cubes impreg-
nated with the magical substance that freed the mind from
bondage to reality (or from the illusion that most people regarded as reality). A wild excitement gripped him as he put one
in his mouth. He tried to calm himself, to prepare for the moment of rapture. Soon time and space would dissolve, even as
the cube of sugar dissolved on the tip of his tongue. He would
be transported to another dimension of consciousness, to a state
of inner illumination which those who had never experienced
could not even remotely image.

The record came to an end and automatically stopped. The
clock ticked softly. Its beat grew louder and louder until it
merged with the beat of his heart, with the beat of the bass
drum in the basement on MacDougal Street, with the beat of
the universe. Time stopped. The room filled with a flood of
light that was not only light but joy, brilliant, vibrating light
that streamed from shooting stars and planets, so intense he
could taste it, touch it, feel it. Light flooded the world, dissolving the wall of fear and aloneness that had shut him in. He
floated on its infinite current, weightless, unconquerable, enveloped by clouds and colors more vivid than any he had ever
seen—pink, red, orange, blue. They formed changing patterns,
shifting images, visions compared to which reality seemed a piti-
ful sham. His consciousness grew larger, deeper, until it took in
all time and space. He looked into himself and glimpsed his
soul, his essence in all its truth, the veils and the lies stripped
away. His body came alive. He felt the power stored in his
muscles, in the ceaseless expansion and contraction of his vis-
cera; he was at one with the universe, with the infinite mystery
that kept the stars and planets on their course. All that had been
hidden in his soul floated up into the light. Events that had
taken place at different periods of his life swam together in a
miraculous simultaneity. It seemed to him that the experience
he was going through was unique—never before had anyone
known such ecstasy. Therefore he, too, was unique! The realiza-

tion set him apart from other men, lifted him high above them. And from this vantage point they all looked so puny.

His body was dissolving. Arms and legs trailed off into space. Only his heart remained, pumping a river of blood that flowed over mountaintops and pulsed in time with the rhythm of life. His senses were so gloriously alive that he could almost see his pores. He had shaken off the bonds that chained ordinary men. He was a cloud, a fountain, a star, free at last to see the truth, the naked truth. And it was more beautiful than anything he had ever imagined . . .

7

Patty's Corner was discreetly east of Second Avenue. You went down several steps and found yourself in a narrow crowded bar. Patty, a fat Lesbian with a raucous baritone voice, had a theory that people would go anywhere if it was dark enough. Bluish lights veiled the room in chiaroscuro while Patty, accompanying herself on a tinny piano, sang ditties calculated to titillate her clientele. Her rendition of "Hands in Each Other," against a background of rippling arpeggios, never failed to bring down the house.

Paul Horvath sat toward the back of the bar. In the semidarkness the conductor's bony face had the pallor of a death mask. He wore the same turtle-neck sweater and slacks in which he had attended Walter's party; he was drinking a gin and tonic. He could barely discern, in the mirror behind the bar, the features of the young man beside him who was nursing a beer. Paul enjoyed the atmosphere of anonymous eroticism that prevailed at Patty's. It was a pleasure to be in a place where no one could possibly recognize him.

He finished his drink and ordered another, trying to muster up the courage to address his neighbor. It was extraordinarily difficult for him to strike up a conversation with a stranger, especially if the stranger happened to be an attractive young man. Here, the darkness was a help. He thrust a cigarette between his lips and went through the motions of looking for his lighter. Then he turned, his throat tightening as he said, "Do you have a match?" It seemed to him that his voice boomed through the bar.

The young man appeared to have been expecting the overture. "Here y'are." With a friendly smile he produced a book of matches.

Paul jerked the pack of cigarettes in the young man's direction. "Care for one?"

"Thanks."

Paul struck a match. In the flickering glow he saw a boyish face with straight black eyebrows that almost met over the ridge of a perky nose. The young man puffed at the flame; Paul shifted the match to his own cigarette. Now that he had taken the first step, he relaxed.

The young man let out rings of smoke. "Where ya from?" he inquired.

"Where d'you suppose?"

"You sound like an Englishman."

"I am," Paul said smoothly.

"My name's Don."

"Paul."

"Pleased to meetcha." Don held out his hand and smiled, revealing a row of very white teeth.

Patty was back at the piano. After some introductory arpeggios she went into a number entitled "Fanny, Where Are You?" Her admirers guffawed; the bar was enveloped in a heart-warming salaciousness. "She's a gas," said Don, laughing.

Paul laughed too, mainly out of a desire to share Don's delight. The young man reached the end of his beer. "Have another?" Paul said.

"Don't mind if I do."

Paul ordered another round of drinks. "What do you do?" he asked Don, although he had a fairly clear idea.

"You mean, for a living?"

Paul nodded.

"I'm in between jobs. I came to New York to be an actor, but it's tough to break in."

Paul nodded sympathetically. "Where did you grow up?"

"Minnesota. Ever been there?"

Paul had conducted several concerts in St. Paul. "No," he said. "How do you like New York?"

"It's too big. Too noisy. And lonesome."

"Where do you live?"

"On the West Side."

"I do, too," Paul said casually, although the young man had not asked.

Their conversation followed a set pattern, as in a game in which the individual moves may vary but the outcome is assured. Ultimately Paul paid for their drinks, Don preceded him out of the bar and waited for him at the corner of Second Avenue, they found a taxi on Fifty-seventh Street and headed west. It occurred to Paul that the young man beside him interested him considerably more than had the guests at Walter and Alice's; he felt guilty about this. Leaning against the back of the cab he moved his hand slowly over the leather seat until it touched Don's; their fingers interlaced. The cab stopped for a red light; another cab pulled up alongside it. Paul withdrew his hand.

They alighted at Sixth Avenue and walked toward his hotel. "I'll go in first," he said. "Come up in a few minutes. Number 618." As he passed through the lobby he nodded affably to the night clerk. He had persuaded himself that, as long as he was not seen coming in with a young man, neither the night clerk nor the elevator man would suspect his proclivities. They did nothing to disturb this fiction.

Once inside his suite he turned on the light, removed his coat, and sat down in the armchair that faced the door. The room was square, its walls covered with old-fashioned oak paneling. A grand piano filled one corner. Chairs and sofa had the nondescript look of hotel furniture, except for a chest—a magnificient example of Spanish Gothic—on which stood two ornate silver candlesticks with thick white candles. Between them, on the wall, hung a large crucifix and a colored print of Mantegna's *Saint Sebastian*. Paul lit a cigarette and inhaled deeply. He drew two ten-dollar bills from his wallet and slipped them into his pocket. In the hall the elevator clanged open; he gave a start. A moment later there was a quiet knock on the door, and he admitted the young man.

Don looked around. His glance fell on the chest. "Nice place," he said.

Paul's eyes met Don's; he smiled. "You're charming," he whispered emotionally. In a few moments Don would be lying in his arms; the prospect filled him with excitement. He felt protected by his anonymity. The young man knew nothing about him, they met on a single level that excluded all others, that enabled him to surrender to the pleasure of the moment without interference from any conflicting feeling. Even the knowledge that he was paying for Don's compliance did not interfere with his enjoyment. On the contrary, it guaranteed that his emotions would remain uninvolved, his potency unimpaired. As strangers they met and as strangers they would part. Only in this way could he protect himself from the tyranny of love, and the anguish of losing the loved one that in his mind was inseparable from love.

He led Don into the bedroom. A wave of desire surged through him, and with it, tenderness. He put his arms around the youth, kissed him, and drew him toward the bed.

Paul sat sipping a Scotch and soda. He wore his favorite dressing gown—a battered robe with a maroon satin collar. The robe hung open at the neck, showing his barrel chest covered with a thick mat of dark hair streaked with gray, over which hung— suspended from a thin chain—a golden cross. His white bony face hardened into a grim expression. Now that Don had left, the glow of well-being that followed the orgasm had begun to dissipate. Once again the happiness he sought had eluded his grasp. He felt cut off from the world of normal men and women who found solace in each other and in the children they created. The price of freedom was an icy loneliness that at times plunged him into despair. Helpless, he clutched the cross over his heart.

His religious feeling went far beyond adherence to dogma. The guilt engendered in him by his sexual deviation found solace in a vision, almost childlike, of a merciful Father in heaven who understood and forgave. Precisely where and how God wrought his wonders was not altogether clear to him; surely the Creator was all around us, within each one of us. This mystical view of life dominated Paul's thinking to such an extent that in his youth he had seriously considered becoming a monk. Only the impulse that drove him to music—and the intensity of his sexual desires—prevented him from dedicating himself to the religious life. But the desire for spirituality never weakened its hold upon him, nourishing his joys and comforting his sorrows.

He had little patience with the theory that homosexuality was basically a maladjustment of the personality traceable to a childhood situation. The concepts of the psychologists were as alien to his thinking as was their jargon; he was convinced that he had been born the way he was. What was natural for other men was unnatural for him; what was natural for him they regarded as unnatural. He deplored their narrowness of view. If the Creator had meant him to consort with women He would not have endowed him with so powerful a hankering for young men. In following the deepest impulses of his nature, consequently, he transgressed not the laws of God but those of man.

At the same time he could not remain oblivious of the fact that the Church regarded his foible as a mortal sin. Inevitably he was led from dogma to mysticism. He became a God-seeker rather than a churchgoer, and strove for passionate communion with the suffering Son whose agony redeemed the sins of men. This search required the intermediacy of neither priest nor ritual: he addressed God directly and knew that he was heard.

Especially he addressed Him through the miraculous language of music. In the pure medium of tone, which soared high above the earthbound, Paul found ideal expression for the volcanic emotions that seared his soul. The constrasting moods of a Beethoven symphony, from the Promethean conflict of the first movement to the serenity of the second, from the joy of the third to the triumphal affirmation of the last, became the symbol of his own travail. Was not Beethoven's motto *per aspera ad astra*—"through hardships to the stars"? At times Paul achieved a healing oneness with God, when it seemed to him certain that the spiritual part of his nature must ultimately triumph over the carnal. True, these moments were rare, but they were never to be forgotten. His gratitude for this sign of divine mercy strengthened his dedication to his art and gave it a profoundly spiritual quality. As a matter of fact, his life was almost monastic in its discipline. Music making was for him an act of redemption, just as sex was the evil from which he had to be redeemed.

Head bowed, eyes riveted to the floor, Paul plunged into the nethermost circle of his private hell. Presently he dropped to his knees, the robe slipping from one shoulder. He pressed his palms together, the golden cross between them, body bent forward in an attitude of supplication. Despair tore at his soul. From the depths of him rose the words of the psalmist, which repetition had branded upon his memory: *Have mercy upon me, O Lord, according to Thy loving-kindness. According unto the multitude of Thy tender mercies blot out my transgressions.* The muscles of his jaw twitched, a look of terror tightened the bony face as the walls of his prison closed in upon him, shutting him off from all who were in a state of grace. *Against Thee, only Thee, have I sinned, and done this evil in Thy sight. Purge me with hyssop and I shall be clean; wash me, and I shall be whiter than snow.* The image of snow brought back a scene from his childhood in Hungary: he sat bundled up on his shiny new sled while his father pulled him across the freshly fallen snow; he felt sad that his father's footprints had to mar the pure white surface. The memory brought a surge of longing for the lost innocence of childhood. Tears welled up in his eyes and rolled slowly down his cheeks.

The silence was heavy, tense. He seemed to be waiting for a sign from heaven. It came. He remembered that God was compassionate and understood his sorrow. Was He not, forever and ever, the all-forgiving Father? A miraculous calm enveloped Paul. He pulled himself to his feet, tied the belt of his robe, and sat down at his desk. Before him lay the score of Mahler's First Symphony, which he was going to conduct the following night. He opened to the first movement. The architecture of the movement, with its mysterious introduction, rose before him in all its spaciousness so that he saw at a glance, as a simultaneity, what existed only as a succession in time. He followed the opening melody as it was sung by the strings, hearing it in his mind at the tempo he intended to take it, a little faster than in the recording by Bruno Walter but not as fast as Szell. Looking up from the score, he could picture the printed page. The little black dots formed patterns before his eyes, and the patterns sang,

The telephone rang. Paul glanced at the small clock on the piano. Almost three. At this hour it could be only his indefatigable press agent. He picked up the receiver and heard Birdie's genteel "Maestro!"

"Aren't you in bed yet?" he asked. Although she telephoned him every night, he always managed to sound surprised when she did.

"As a matter of fact I am."

At first Paul had resented this intrusion on his privacy. Then he realized that she might be calling out of loyalty, to tuck him in, as it were, and was touched. In time he even began to look forward to the nightly ritual.

"I just thought," Birdie said, "I'd check to see if everything's ready for tomorrow."

"I know the music, if that's what you mean," he answered in his deep resonant voice. "I cannot guarantee that the orchestra will be there, or that the public will come. But my part is ready."

"That's all I wanted to know. Why don't you go to bed and get some rest?"

"That's exactly what I was about to do." He hung up and sat wondering. What did she know about his private life? Did she guess the truth? Was this her way of satisfying herself that nothing untoward had happened to him? On the other hand, since she herself sent out stories to the press about his habit of meditating and studying through the small hours of the morning, might it not be that these nocturnal conversations were no more than they pretended to be—a pleasant way of saying good night? He would never know, nor did he want to.

He lay down and turned out the light. He remembered that he had asked Don to phone him later in the week and hoped the young man would keep his word. A smile curved his lips. He fell asleep.

8

Max Rubin opened his eyes. He was having trouble with his prostate and had to urinate several times during the night. He sat up, lowered his legs over the side of the bed and felt for his slippers.

The bedroom was large, with tall windows that extended to the floor and opened on a small balcony. Fifty years ago the hotel had been one of the most elegant in town and a favorite dwelling of musicians; its thick walls allowed them to practice until all hours of the night. Now the building, along with the neighborhood, had deteriorated. The elaborately carved pilasters, crystal chandeliers, and faded red carpets bore witness to vanished splendor. Max had occupied the same suite for thirty-eight years and saw no reason to move. Where would you find such high ceilings and roomy closets? The new houses were like rabbit warrens; they had tissue paper for walls—if a man burped in the next apartment or made love to his wife, you heard. No, thank you. He was going to stay put until they carried him out.

He shuffled into the bathroom, his bulbous head inclined slightly to one side, and leaned over the toilet bowl so as not to wet his pyjamas. The stream no longer leaped out in a curve; it dribbled. The doctor said that if they could postpone an operation for a few more years the problem would solve itself. The old man smiled. A few more years were all he needed.

He was not afraid of death. He had had a full life but he was not yet ready to leave it. When his time came he hoped he would go with a minimum of fuss. People were fools to speak of the meaning of death. Only life had meaning; death was simply the absence of meaning. Max flushed the bowl and went into the oval-shaped living room. He looked about him with approval; they didn't build rooms like this any more. An elaborate mantelpiece of white stone fringed a fake fireplace. On it was a bronze nymph who reclined on a rock, an ornate clock in her belly, flanked on either side by two bronze urns that rested on luxurious bases of black marble. Max had acquired these objects d'art, along with the crystal chandelier that dominated the room, in the early twenties. He had regarded them then as the ultimate in elegance, and in the forty years since had found no reason to change his mind.

It was pointless to go back to bed. He slept intermittently nowadays and was astonished at how little sleep a person needed. He sat down in his enormous green-leather armchair; it raised his legs as it swung backward and brought his head down so that it was level with the rest of him. Max had a theory that the body relaxed completely only in a horizontal position, when the heart was not obliged to pump blood against the force of gravity, and spent as much time as possible on his back. He took a cigar from the box on the table, bit off the tip and lit it. Sounds and voices floated through the windows from afar. Even Broadway was muted at four-thirty in the morning.

The wall opposite the fireplace was covered with signed photographs; Kreisler, Rachmaninov, Josef Hofmann, Godowsky, Marian Anderson, Mischa Elman. He had known the great ones and had served them well. Step by step he had guided those who put their careers in his hands, until their names were as well known in Wichita and Dubuque as in Boston and New York. He had quarreled with some of them, broken with others; several had grievously disappointed him. But he could truthfully say that those who had stuck with Max Rubin had never regretted it. Puffing at his cigar, he shook his head and looked to one side as if appealing to the judgment of an invisible bystander. Was it an accident that Max Rubin was the biggest name in the business?

The reasons for his success were not hard to find. First, he was able to make up his mind. Most people didn't know if they were coming or going—when they said yes they meant a little bit no. With Max Rubin, yes was yes and no was no. And if any decision of his turned out to be a mistake he wasted no time in useless regrets. Second, he had been honest—or as honest as a man could be in this shitty business. He had been ruthless when it was necessary, maybe he had stepped over a few bodies on his way, but he was able to look any man in the eye, he had done nothing he had to be ashamed of. Third, he never allowed his feelings to interfere with his judgment. Whether or not he liked a particular artist as a person made no difference. Once Max Rubin took someone under his management, he did his best. Fourth, he was not afraid to take chances. He was a gambler by nature and the stakes were high. True, he had gone under several times in the course of his career, but he had always bounced back.

Max had been one of the first to realize that the concert industry was big business. He had bought out the competitors he could not crush, and had merged with those he could not buy out. He had organized groups of cities into circuits, so that his artists could proceed from one engagement to the next with a minimum waste of time and money. He had organized popular-priced series in which one big-name performer helped sell four or five others of lesser magnitude. And when the vogue of soloists was somewhat on the wane he had concentrated on group attractions, importing exotic novelties from the four corners of the earth. Always he had been one step ahead of the public, not so much to give it what it wanted as to make it want what he gave. Not for nothing had Max Rubin become a legend in his own time; behind all his manipulations was a vision. In his native Russia music had been for the upper classes; the muzhiks knew nothing of Beethoven or Tchaikovsky. It had been his dream to create a broad popular base for serious music, so that Beethoven and Tchaikovsky might nourish the lives of all. Through a combination of talent, perseverance, and luck he had been able to achieve this goal. And because he had been the right man at the right time in the right place, his efforts had been crowned with spectacular success.

His critics, such as Judith, accused him of pandering to public taste. In doing so, Max felt, they vulgarized his life's work. On the contrary, he had the greatest confidence in the taste of the masses. Given a choice between good and bad, in the long run they always preferred the good. For this reason he had exerted himself to bring them the best that money could buy. Thus it came about that a penniless immigrant from Odessa, who after fifty years in this country still spoke its language with a heavy accent, had helped mold the musical taste of a nation and had contributed, not unworthily he thought, to the cultural explosion of our time.

Max half shut his eyes as he inhaled the aroma of the cigar. Nature, he reflected was wise in her dealings with old age. She took away your pleasures one at a time, dulled your senses little by little—first your eyesight, then your hearing—so that when your time came you were ready to go. Sex had been the first to drop out; then his need of sleep; alcohol, cigars, and chopped liver remained. Having lived his life in majestic disregard of doctors' orders, Max was not disposed to make concessions now. However, he balanced his indulgences with a passionate addiction to yogurt, which aided digestion, he had heard, and lengthened life; and made up for his daily infractions of diet by consuming two containers a day.

Remembering his dispute with Judith, Max pursed his pendulous lips in displeasure. Women like her were too smart for their own good. Didn't she realize that pianists were a dime a dozen? Didn't she understand that a pianist was helpless unless he had a manager who stood squarely behind him? It was the manager who built the artist's career. Indeed, except for the few top names, the manager created the artist (and the demand for him) in the same way that the director on Broadway created the actor. So wasn't it foolish of her to give herself airs? Max stared moodily at the photographs on the wall. She wasn't anywhere near big enough to defy him. The place she had made for herself—more accurately, that he had made for her—could go to half a dozen others. And would, by God, if she didn't behave herself.

At seventy-four he was free of women and glad of it. The worries they brought more than balanced the pleasures they gave. At last he was no longer a slave to his balls. When he thought of love it was his first wife he remembered. His whole life would have been different if she had not died. Her successors —there were two—had been poor substitutes. A man's love, Max believed, was a coat that he hung now on one peg, now on another—it might fit one better than the other, but it was always the same coat. Finally the hanger wore out and there was no use trying to hang it up any more.

His son had disappointed him. Jerry was on his own, in California. A schlemiel. They saw each other once a year, during the summer; that was enough. Max removed the cigar from his mouth, stared hard at it, and thrust it back between his lips. He was alone and liked it. What a relief it was to come home at night to an empty apartment. Not to have to listen to chatter. For the first time in his life he was able to think. He had never had time enough to read; now he was making up for it. History, biography, books about the war, anything but novels, most of which he regarded as silly. Why should he be interested in a story made up by someone who probably knew less about life than he did? Novels were a waste of time unless they were by Tolstoy or Dostoievsky. Theirs he read over and over again. As far as he was concerned, these two masters constituted the entire domain of fiction.

Puffing on his cigar, Max shuffled over to the window. The sky was paling in the east; the stars looked wan. They were millions, billions of miles away, yet man was impudent enough to suppose that the creator of this infinite machine had nothing better to do than to take an interest in his affairs. How could grownups be so naïve as to imagine that the universe revolved around them, or that there was someone up above who kept tabs on them? Did they think they solved the mystery of the creation by calling it God? Considering the state of the world, he always said, it would be the greatest insult to God to suppose that He existed. No, Max Rubin had not looked for God in heaven; he had sought Him in man. Man was the godlike creature who created art, science, history; who learned and reasoned and changed the world. Max scanned the sky. In his own small way he had served the divine in man; he could say with truth that he had led a useful life. Now he was ready to call it a day, whenever his heart decided it had had enough. He was quite clear about the manner of his departure. He would be found in bed one morning by the chambermaid. Some people would be sorry, others glad. There would be a column in the *Times;* he would be cremated—he had made provision for this in his will—and there would be a short memorial service at which five of his artists would play the first movement of Schubert's C-major Quintet. No speeches.

The pallor from the east flowed gently over the sleeping city. High over the canyon of Broadway the star that Margo had mistaken for Venus sang a hymn of praise to the new day. Max padded into the kitchen, foraged about in the refrigerator, and brought out a container of yogurt. He stirred the layer of strawberry preserve at the bottom. It was delicious.

two

The office was quiet at the end of the day. Through the Venetian blinds came slanting shafts of light in which a thousand dust motes danced. Philip sat at his desk, head resting on his hands, and followed the luminous specks in their endless gyrations; his eyes returned to the sheet of paper before him. "Dear Judith . . ." How to go on? How was he to tell her that he did not wish to see her again? Whichever way he phrased the thought it sounded hurtful, and he had no desire to hurt her. Or did he?

He sat staring, wondering if he had ever really loved her. It was as futile to accuse her of being self-centered or overbearing as it would be to charge him with weakness of spirit or the inability to stand up to her. Probably with the right man she would be different, as he would be with the right woman. He tried to imagine the kind of man who would be right for her. He could not.

As for the woman who would be right for him, he did not have to wonder. Her name was Andrée; he had met her during the war. For Philip everything connected with the war was wreathed in an unreal glow. This was the time of his youth, the epic period of his life when he had proved himself capable of deeds he now only remotely associated with himself. The dedicated OSS lieutenant who had been parachuted into France to work with the Maquis seemed a total stranger to the Philip he now was. The actions in which he had participated were larger than life, as if they had taken place in one of those war films in technicolor that were shown on an extra-large screen. Life had been heroic then, lived at a pitch of intensity to which he could never rise again. The bonds between himself, Andrée, and Jacques were such as could exist only among people who lived daily in the shadow of death. It was futile to try to explain to Judith—although he had tried—what Andrée and her husband had meant to him, or he to them. Life had a purpose then and a goal. How often they dreamed together of what awaited them when the war was over. What awaited them was simple— she remained in France to nurse Jacques back to health, and Philip returned to America. But he carried away with him an indelible vision of what a woman could be like at her finest. Against that measure all others had been found wanting.

Philip lifted the paperweight on his desk and set it down again. A splash of orange light caught the wall on which hung his diploma from New York University. At what point, he wondered, had the young lieutenant of the OSS become the prosaic lawyer he now was? His hair was thinning, he had put on weight; he lived a comfortable, trivial existence and longed for his youth. He ate in French restaurants, went to French films, enjoyed French wines; he paid his alimony on time, and sometimes dreamed of Andrée. He who at twenty-five had been concerned with matters of life and death now passed his days with clients who were concerned with dollars and cents. He who had helped to mine bridges and blow up trains now sat behind a large desk, his weapon a telephone. There was a time of peace and a time of war, just as there was a land of the living and a land of the dead. The one had no connection with the other.

And now he was saying good-bye to a woman he could not bear. She and her friends thought they belonged to an elite that stood miles above the average man. He had news for them. Many an average man had gone through experiences they would not even remotely approach if they lived a thousand years.

"Dear Judith . . ." Philip took a deep breath and wrote his
letter. Then he wrote another, to Andrée.

Judith read with mounting anger. When she finished she
crumpled the letter in her hand and hurled it into the wastebasket. Her rage, she knew, had nothing to do with love, since
she had been wondering for some time how she could get rid of
Philip. But that he should be the one to break off the affair
was infuriating.

It served her right for having taken up with him in the first
place. He was thoroughly ordinary, like a thousand other lawyers in town. He had a good head on his shoulders and a kind
heart, and was adequate in bed—but no more; and he should
have been grateful that she had even bothered to look at him.
Instead he had the nerve to call it quits. How about that!

Her dressing gown hung open. She drew the sides together
and tied the belt, then picked up the crumpled sheet, smoothed
it out, and reread it. Her eyelids burned. Was she going to shed
tears over someone she didn't really want? People thought they
were suffering because of love when it was only their pride that
was hurt. The faded green expanse of sofa was littered with
newspapers. Judith swept them to the floor and sat down. To be
perfectly honest, she was not made for love. She had neither the
time nor the inclination for it. The world was full of weaklings
who clung to each other because they were afraid to stand on
their own feet. What most of them thought of as love was no
more than the body warmth produced by occasional friction.
The strong, on the other hand, were self-sufficient; that was the
secret of their strength. She took a final look at the crumpled
letter. Very deliberately she tore it to bits which she threw into
the wastebasket, then brushed her hands as if washing them of
the mess.

She sat very still, staring at the stacks of music against the
wall. Why was she attracted to men unworthy of her? Why, for
a change, did she not take up with someone strong and distinguished whom she could respect? The image of Paul Horvath
came to her mind; she remembered the sense of mastery he
gave her the night he conducted for her. Men like him went
their solitary way through the world, untouched by the multitude's need for togetherness. He was probably as incapable of

giving love as she was. Yet if she failed with someone of that caliber she would at least carry away the satisfaction of having met her equal. To fail with a nobody like Phil was humiliating . . .

She remembered that for the past year he had taken care of her affairs; he could hardly drop them now. Whether they were lovers or not, he had to remain her lawyer. Surely he would understand that. She looked at the clock; it was almost half-past eleven. He would be getting ready for bed; he had a thing about getting eight hours of sleep. She decided to call him, lifted the receiver, and put it back. This was the worst thing she could do! He would think that she was pleading with him to stay. She decided to write him a letter and began to compose one in her mind, but did not get beyond the first sentence. A letter left too many questions unanswered; only by talking things over did you get somewhere. She argued the wisdom of the telephone call at some length, examining all the pros and cons yet knowing all the time that she would end by phoning him. At five to twelve she gave in.

"Phil?" She made her voice sound casual.

"Hi."

"I just read your letter."

He said nothing.

"There's very little to argue about," she continued blandly. "Two people stay together because they feel they've something to offer each other. When one of them no longer feels that way, the other has to accept it. It's as simple as that."

"We agree then." He sounded relieved but wary.

"All the same," she said affably, "I don't think this has anything to do with your being my lawyer. You can resign from one job," she chortled, "but that doesn't mean you have to give up the other."

There was a silence. Then, "Judith," he said quietly, "we're not children and we shouldn't kid each other. A break between us means exactly that. As I said in my letter, I feel it would be better for both of us if we went our separate ways."

"But Phil, be reasonable." Her voice rose a little. "You know I'm not the kind of woman who would try to hold on to a man. As far as I'm concerned you're a free agent. But you can't stop being my lawyer just like that. It would leave me in a terrible mess."

"Julith——" He spoke slowly, as though reasoning with an obstinate child, "I can't remain your lawyer because that would mean I'd have to go on seeing you. And all the things that have been wrong between us would continue to be wrong. I don't intend to drop your affairs tomorrow. I'll wind up what has to be done and hand it over to anyone you choose. People change their lawyers every day in the week, so let's not get carried away."

Her voice hardened. "And what exactly has been so wrong between us, may I ask?"

Again a silence. Then he said, "It would take too long to explain. You probably know just as well as I do. I'm not myself with you. I feel as if my balls were cut off. I've been through a lot in my life. What I want now is peace and quiet."

"Peace and quiet?" she shouted into the mouthpiece. "That's what a cow wants."

"So I'm a cow," he said pleasantly. "Or an ox, to be exact."

"Look, Phil, it doesn't matter to me one way or the other. But I think you owe it to me——" What precisely did he owe her? "When two people have been together for a year and a half they owe it to each other not to part like silly children."

"That's why I don't want to go on seeing you. We owe it to each other not to hurt one another. The only way to do that is to say good-bye."

It unnerved her that he was standing up to her. For the first time. "I did everything in the world for you," she cried bitterly, "and this is how you thank me."

"That's right! You stood over a hot open stove and gave me the best years of your life."

"I don't ask for gratitude, that's the worst thing a person can ask for. But I do expect a certain amount of appreciation."

"You're not going to get it," he said with finality. "Anything a woman gives a man or vice versa has to be measured in terms of the price. In this case the price was too high."

"Too high?" she cried, sarcastic.

"You wiped the floor with me and I took it. But I don't intend to any more. You're a domineering woman, Judith, and I'm an easy-going man. That's why we're no good for each other."

"But——"

"There is no 'but,' " he broke in. "And now, if you'll excuse me, I'll hang up, I've a rough day tomorrow. Let me know who your lawyer is and I'll send him the papers. Good night."

The receiver clicked, the dial tone buzzed in her ear. She slammed down the telephone, swept by an impotent fury that was directed at herself no less than at him. Why had she demeaned herself? Too agitated to sit still, she rose from the couch and began to pace up and down, arms across her chest, hands clasping her elbows. A pain throbbed against her temples, she swallowed hard, yet she saw the irony of the situation. Now that she respected him because he had stood his ground, now that she really wanted him, she had lost him! It had always been like this. The men she had had she didn't want, the men she had wanted she couldn't have. Her lips trembled, tears rolled down her cheeks. How ridiculous to be crying over a man she did not even care about!

Too wrought up to fall asleep, she decided to take a pill. She went into the bathroom, opened the cabinet and drew out a small bottle. To her surprise it was almost empty. She swallowed two green-and-black capsules in half a glass of water, and studied her reflection in the glass. Her skin was her least attractive feature; she worried over its rough texture—what the girl in the beauty parlor described as enlarged pores. The old remedy was still the best—she dabbed cold cream on her fingertips and with a gentle circular motion rubbed it into her cheeks. Now she mustn't cry any more. Tears and cold cream did not mix.

Her outburst had left her spent; she lay down and floated off into a pleasant drowsiness. Just before falling asleep she remembered the enigmatic look in Paul Horvath's eyes. Finally she knew. It was the look of loneliness.

2

The promise of spring was in the air. Margo was in love. Moods and feelings whirled through her that left her in turn exhilarated, bewildered, fearful, ecstatic. When she lay in Bob's arms she felt so completely at one with him she could almost read his thoughts; but after he left her she fell prey to uneasiness. What had he meant by this word, that phrase? When they were together she dreaded the moment of his departure; when they were apart something in her perpetually waited, longing for his return. If he was late, as he invariably was, she was convinced that he would not come at all; and when he finally did appear she was convinced that he would not stay long enough. The center of her life had always been within herself; now the control had passed to another. It frightened her to think that he could grant or withhold happiness as he saw fit, yet she would not have had it otherwise. This was the paradox she did not understand: only now, when she no longer was complete within herself, did she experience life more completely than she had ever thought possible.

Her singing had been the focal point of her existence. If her studies had confined her, they had also protected her. Suddenly, as in the fairy tales of her childhood, she had been awakened from her long sleep by a kiss. Her Prince Charming, with his golden hair and green eyes, was more beautiful than any she had envisioned. For the first time in her life she felt herself flowing out to somebody in an overwhelming need to give, to share. Millions of people must have discovered love in the same way, yet what she now felt seemed to her miraculously unique.

Love, unfortunately was the one thing he hardly ever mentioned. She found him extraordinarily reticent about his feelings. It was as if he felt that by revealing them he would put himself in her power. Therefore, by all sorts of stratagems, she must make him assure her that he loved her, for the sheer pleasure of hearing it. "You little goose," he would say, "would I be here if I didn't?" Or, in a tone of resignation, "Funny thing, no matter what subject we start with, politics or music or anything, it always ends up with 'Do you love me?'" To which she would shrug and ask happily, "What else matters?"

Precisely because he was not able to put his feelings into words, the act of love took on special importance for her; it was then that the man in him spoke directly, compellingly to the woman in her. In their passionate embraces his reticence melted, his defenses fell. When she felt him inside her or heard the racing of his heart against her ear she knew that he needed her. Thus sex came to play a role in her love apart from the pleasure it gave, reassuring her, bringing her as close to him as she would ever come.

He was a moody lover. He might lie peacefully beside her while they listened to records or chatted aimlessly. Suddenly he would clutch her to him, gripped with desire. She liked to leave the light on so that she might enjoy the sight of his body, but he preferred the dark; she was grateful for the neon sign on the corner that filled the room with pulsating waves of light. The violence of his orgasm was frightening. He trembled and cried out as if he were being rent apart. She once caught a glimpse of his face. The expression on it was as close to pain as to pleasure; his teeth were clenched, the muscles in his jaw twitched. Gasping, he buried his head in the pillow. Presently he looked at her gently; the demon had vanished. "Y'know, I'm beginning to understand what makes a man push for dear life when he's in heat. He's trying to get back to where he came from."

The life of the senses was pre-eminent for him. To smell, taste, touch her body had a meaning for him as important as the act itself. "Wouldn't it be terrible," he once said to her, "not to be able to see."

"Or hear."

He thought a moment. "No. If I were deaf I could at least think words in my head. But to know that the world is full of color and not to be able to see it—to live in darkness—that's the worst! If I were a soldier I don't think I'd fear dying so much as losing my sight."

"What an awful thing to think about!" She cradled him in her arms, intensely aware of his fragility. Could it be that she, so slight compared to him, was the stronger?

He was extremely visual. The world existed for him in terms of colors, shapes, movement. Walking down a street with him was an experience for Margo. She became aware as never before of the color of the sky, the quality of light, the shapes of clouds and houses; she saw the city with fresh eyes. On their way back from a walk in Central Park they would pass the new skyscrapers on Sixth Avenue. He would point out one building—for example, the Hilton—as as monstrosity, another, such as Saarinen's for CBS, with its magnificient buttresses, as a masterpiece, and would explain the reasons for his judgment. Margo, clinging to his arm, was convinced he should have been a painter or architect.

She sometimes worried that her love was drawing her away

from music. But she was also aware that it gave her an understanding she had lacked. For the first time in her life she knew what she was singing about. She had mastered the notes of Butterfly's part. Now she mastered their meaning. What was Puccini's opera about, if not the life of the heart? In the final weeks of the year her teachers were amazed by her deepened understanding of the role. Margo noted with amusement that they attributed this to their efforts.

The performance took place on a Tuesday in May. It was her first big opportunity and she was eager to make the most of it. She awoke that morning in a state of anxiety. As the hours wore on her apprehension subsided; this, she was convinced, was her lucky day. She ran through her part from beginning to end, then went to the hairdresser. In the late afternoon she rested, ate lightly, and set out for the Juilliard. It was the first week of daylight-saving time. A lavender haze enveloped Riverside Drive. The dome of Grant's Tomb rose in classical simplicity against the azure sky. Across the Hudson, high above the Palisades, floated an array of salmon-colored clouds. Margo walked with a lilt, swinging her bag. Buildings, boats, people were bathed in a golden light.

She had a moment of panic before the curtain went up. What if the first note stuck in her throat? The orchestra struck up the busy little overture. Presently, surrounded by geishas under their brightly colored parasols, she climbed the hill to Pinkerton's cottage. Her first notes floated jubilantly over the harbor of Nagasaki. Was she not the happiest girl in Japan? Pinkerton came forward to greet her. She bowed low and responded to his greeting with touching simplicity.

Walter and Alice sat toward the front of the hall. He was as nervous as if he himself were making his debut, but when he heard Margo's first notes he stopped worrying. She moved about the stage with a natural grace that he found enchanting. As he followed the soaring line of the duet at the end of the first act he felt proud of his protégée, and more than a little virtuous because his interest in her was strictly platonic. Some men collected stamps, others books, coins, chessmen; how much more rewarding a hobby it was to help a girl like Margo, to watch her grow and set out on what he was convinced would be a great career. After one of her high notes he turned triumphantly to Max

Rubin, who sat on his left. "What did I tell you?" He had had a hard time persuading Max to come; the impresario had pleaded a headache, a cold, a previous engagement, and capitulated only when Walter said he would send his car.

Max pushed out his lips. "Not bad," he conceded, "not bad at all." Coming from him, this was praise indeed.

Alice was moved. She had never become friendly with Margo, perhaps as a reaction against Walter's preoccupation with the girl. For a time she had wondered whether his affection for her was as innocent as he made it out to be, but she soon realized that it was; Margo probably took the place of the daughter he should have had. In any case, as she listened now she saw her in a new light. The girl sounded lovely and made an appealing little figure on stage. Walter had insisted that they give a party for her after the performance. She had refused at first but was glad she had changed her mind.

Judith shifted restlessly in her seat. She had come because Walter insisted. She disliked opera, which she ranked far below symphonic, chamber, and piano music (Mozart's operas excepted); and she loathed Puccini. The love duet in the first act made her think of Philip. She put him out of her mind, focused her attention on the stage, and was delighted to find that Walter's faith in Margo was justified. She would have had to tell him the truth, no matter how unpleasant; now she could honestly say to him that Margo was gifted. In a curious way she found herself envying the girl. Envying what? Margo's talent, youth, charm, figure? Not any one of these but perhaps a little of all. Mostly she envied Margo the excitement of the first time, the hope and expectancy that went into an evening such as this. The atmosphere of the school brought back memories of her own student days. All these bright-eyed youngsters playing in the orchestra, singing in the chorus, milling around in the halls —gifted, unbalanced children filled with all sorts of illusions about themselves, who twenty years later would be nonentities holding down a teaching job in Podunk or tootling away in a provincial orchestra. Would she want to be young again? And make the same mistakes? No, thank you.

Bob sat beside his mother, intent on the stage. He tried to reconcile the image of the girl who lay naked in his arms with the polished singer before him. The girl who dug her fingernails into his back and cried with passion was one Margo, the doll-like geisha on stage was another. Now that he saw this side of her he felt that he had never really known her. How could it be that she who was so unobtrusive when they were together, so submissive to him, could dominate the stage with her presence? As the act wore on he, too, like Judith, felt jealous of her, but for another reason. From now on she would be different. In spite of all her protestations she could never belong to him alone. Even as she whispered words of love in his ear she would be passing out of his reach, leaving him behind. Was he sad at this or relieved? He followed the luminous curve of her voice above the orchestra, and wondered.

It was not until the second act that Max committed himself. A burst of applause greeted her rendition of "Un bel dì." The old man turned to Walter. "It's a strange thing in this business. One girl sings the notes in a fine voice but leaves you cold, you don't give a damn about her. This girl tears your heart out."

Walter beamed, "In Hollywood they call it star quality."

"Star shmar . . ." Max's pudgy hand cleaved the air. "It's very simple. Most singers can't act, and if they act they can't sing. Your girl does both." He thought a moment. "In a year or so she'll be ready. Bring her to me."

Walter drew a long breath. At last Margo was on her way.

In her second-act encounter with Yamadori and the consul she revealed herself as an actress of diverse moods; those scenes crackled with temperament. The stage director had had a novel idea. Since Butterfly throughout this act maintains that she is Pinkerton's wife and that hers is an American home, he made her discard her Japanese costume for something resembling an American dress. In the third act, when she realizes that Pinkerton has betrayed her and decides to kill herself, she returns to her kimono, to die as a Japanese. Margo's final scene moved Walter deeply. She made the little geisha a noble figure, infusing her last moments with a pathos that brought tears to his eyes. The hall rang with bravos when she came out for her bow; he could not have wished for a warmer reception.

Later, backstage, she was surrounded by her family and friends. Walter hugged her, Max patted her benignly on the shoulder, Alice kissed her, Juith congratulated her. Margo's eyes wandered around the room, seeking Bob. He stood by the wall and waited until the crowd had thinned. Finally he came over. "You were great," he murmured, but so quietly that none of his enthusiasm came through.

"You really liked it?" She looked up at him, eager for his praise. "I was afraid you mightn't."

He roused himself from his reticence. "You were beautiful. Beautiful!"

She wanted to throw her arms around him, but smiled at him instead. Others came up to congratulate her. Bob moved off.

When she arrived at Walter and Alice's, the guests were assembled. She was flattered that Judith and Max had come. Walter had invited her teachers as well, and a number of her fellow students. She greeted Bob casually; as though by prearrangement, they said very little to each other. Walter brought out champagne for a toast. Margo emptied her glass with the others. "You're not supposed to do that," Walter said gaily. "We're drinking to you."

She laughed. "I didn't know. It's the first time anyone ever toasted me."

"But not the last. We must do it over." He refilled the glasses and raised his. "To Margo, and many more evenings like this!"

The party broke up early since she was tired. Bob left with his mother; Walter sent Margo home in his car. Flushed with her triumph, she was unable to fall asleep. Bob's face hovered in the darkness before her. With a stab of sorrow in her heart she knew—he did not welcome her success. Deep down he wanted her to fail. She pressed her cheek against the pillow and sighed. It was the one sacrifice she could not make for him.

3

A gray light streamed through the windows of Birdie's apartment. The slanting rain seemed quietly determined to continue all afternoon. Walter poured himself a drink and settled in an armchair. The vodka tasted all the better because he was not supposed to drink it. His blood pressure made it necessary for him to avoid salt, tobacco, alcohol, and several other items, each of which immediately took on the deliciousness of forbidden fruit. Luckily sex was not on the list.

He did not mind waiting for Birdie. The quiet was pleasant. The cluttered living room reflected her personality: a little disorganized, a little pretentious, but warm and cozy. He could do without the reproductions of Picasso and Monet on the walls; he never could persuade her that the humblest original was preferable to the finest print. And he certainly could do without the red hassock in the corner.

This was the kind of day when a man was disposed to count his blessings. First and foremost, that he was still here to enjoy them. Second, business was booming. The city was in a fever of building. Apartment houses mushroomed in the unlikeliest places. How could anyone pay the rents they were asking? It was beyond him, but this was not his problem—his job was to build. Through a combination of fortuitous circumstances, his company was in a position to reap the greatest possible benefit from the boom.

Life had been generous to him. He was in no sense an exceptional man. On the contrary, he considered himself only slightly above average. He had had the luck to marry the daughter of a big real-estate operator (he never forgot that he owed his career to Alice). In addition, he had guessed shrewdly now and again. He began to buy plots on Second Avenue before the elevated train was torn down; it took no additional wisdom to repeat the procedure on Third. He bought IBM stock before most people did. He realized that New York would need a spate of new buildings after the war. In each case he had been in a position to translate his hunch into action. For this society had rewarded him handsomely.

There had been a time when he was less favorably disposed toward a system based on free enterprise. In his senior year at City College he entered into a violent flirtation with Marxism: he tried to read *Das Kapital*, pored through Engels, devoured Lenin. The Hoovervilles and apple sellers of the thirties constituted irrefutable proof, as far as he was concerned, that capitalism was on its way out; he marched in May Day parades, bought *The Daily Worker*, and regarded the Soviet Union as the workers' paradise. If in later years he looked back on these youthful indiscretions with nostalgia, it was because this was the only period of his life when he was genuinely interested in anything outside himself.

The love affair with the proletariat was as brief as it was intense; once he married Alice he found himself on the other side of the class struggle. A decade after his youthful shenanigans he swung to the other extreme. The notion that a society could exist without capitalists struck at the very root of his security. He now had to be assured that free enterprise would not only last his lifetime but would endure forever. He turned against the Soviet Union and looked upon every upheaval there as a sure sign that communism would not work. From this position he found his way to a vague liberalism that suited his easy-going nature. He foresaw a rapprochement between the two systems: ours would grow increasingly socialistic while the Soviet Union would grow ever more capitalistic. In any case the Cold War made no sense once both sides possessed the atom bomb. His desire for an understanding between them was based on his reading of history. As a result of the First World War capitalism had lost Russia; as a result of the Second, China and eastern Europe. Clearly the system would not survive another blood letting.

The great regret of his life was that he had not taken part in the war. Those who had, he felt, knew things forever closed to him. By the time the draft reached him he was overage. He made several attempts to have himself reclassified, but Alice managed to persuade him that the country's industrial machine had to be kept going and that he could serve best by staying at his job, especially since he was participating in a sense through his son. He never forgave himself for having listened to her. What held him back, more than her remonstrances, was his reluctance to put himself in a situation where he would be measured against younger men. The war had been the great experience of his generation, that forced every man who was in it to face up to what he really was. Walter wondered how well he would have met the test. He would never know.

Those years had been extremely painful for him; the more his affairs prospered, the guiltier he felt. He could not understand why he should be safe and comfortable, making piles of money into the bargain, while other men were risking their lives on the battlefield. He would scan the lists of casualties in the newspapers with an inexplicable feeling that he somehow was responsible for their misfortune. The war underlined for him in the cruelest way that inequality in men's luck which operated just as inexorably in peacetime. He never questioned the turn of fortune's wheel that caused one man to become rich while another remained poor. Why, then, was he unable to accept the rulings of an inscrutable destiny that permitted one man to survive while the fellow next to him was blown to bits? In time he came to suspect that his guilt was a universal feeling which left no one untouched. Those who came out unscathed felt guilty toward those who were wounded, those who came back felt guilty toward those who did not. Similarly, in the frame of civilian life, those on top of the heap felt guilty (or should) toward those on the bottom, and tried to expiate through religious observances or the various charitable contributions that could be written off at tax time. For years he was incapable of passing a beggar on the street without depositing a coin in his box. In time he persuaded himself that the man probably owned a house in Flatbush, and gave no more.

His own sacrifice had been the heaviest anyone could make— his son. It was morbid to suppose that Gene's death was the price he had paid for his own safety; the notion was irrational. Yet there occurred to him repeatedly, during his time of grief, the parable of Abraham about to sacrifice Isaac on the altar of the Lord. Throughout the building of his empire he had been spurred on by the image of Gene as his successor. He needed an heir to give him a sense of creating something that would endure beyond his lifetime. Gene's death left no one to continue his work. Alice was so crushed that his first duty was to minister to her; he never let her know how hard he had been hit. He reproached himself for not having been a better friend to Gene and, when the torment became too great, found refuge in the memory of a camaraderie that never was. On several occasions he had taken the boy rowing on the lake in Central Park. These were transformed in his mind into a series of outings that extended over the years. A random visit to the Museum of Natural History, an excursion to Bear Mountain were seized upon as evidence of the closeness between them. When he said to someone, "My son was a lieutenant in the Air Force," grief mingled with pride; nor could he regard Gene's death as a purposeless accident. It had meaning in terms of his son's stake in the war both as an American and as a Jew, a meaning pinpointed by the fact that Gene was shot down during the celebrated raid on

Dresden. Phrases such as "He made the supreme sacrifice" or "He gave his life for his country" might sound like clichés to others. To Walter the words meant precisely what they said.

His wound healed better than Alice's. This, he decided, was not because he loved his son less but because he was a man and not given to morbidity. He understood why she kept Gene's room as it had been and placed little bunches of flowers near the picture in her bedroom; but he did not approve of such gestures. He honored Gene's memory in a more constructive way, by instituting a series of scholarships for young musicians. He expanded the scope of these gifts through the years and provided in his will for a foundation that would continue the program after he was gone. This aid to young people made his life's work seem less purposeless. And it somehow brought him a little closer to his son.

Birdie alighted from the bus and clattered through the rain on her spindly heels. They threw her body off balance, so that she met life at a precarious angle. She had no umbrella, it was impossible to get a taxi, her hair came straggling over her forehead, her stockings were wet. The open-toe shoe, she decided, was the greatest curse imposed on woman since childbirth. She hobbled to her doorway, stopped to draw breath, and made her way up the stairs.

Walter grinned at her when she came in. "Where've you been, sweetie? You're a sight."

"I'm done in. Completely!" She dropped on the couch. "Here I've been out battling the world, and when I come home what do I hear? That I'm a sight."

"Not even a kiss?"

"Even the way I look?" She smiled, mollified.

He took her in his arms. "You better change before you catch cold."

She went into the bedroom, threw off her clothes, put on a pink housecoat—the one he liked—and fresh make-up.

"That's better," he said when she returned, and handed her a drink. "Why were you battling the world?"

"Max. That sonofabitch." The dirty-blond bun at the back of her head bobbed decisively. "He cut Judith's concerts down to almost half of last year's. Out of spite."

"What d'you expect when she treats him like dirt?"

"Is she supposed to kiss his ass because he gets her a date? That's not her style. She's going to speak her mind no matter what."

"Then she must pay for the pleasure."

"Guess what he had the nerve to tell me. 'It's not easy to sell women pianists.' 'What about Guiomar Novaes,' I said, 'and Gina Bachauer?' 'They're exceptions,' says he. 'Besides, they're not American.' Know what he did? He dropped Judith from his main series in the Midwest. A dirty trick. I just don't have the heart to tell her."

"Sweetie, say what you will, she's an aggressive woman and you know it. Sooner or later she gets aggressive with the wrong people. After all, Max doesn't need her, she needs him. She only makes things difficult for herself when she attacks him as she did at the party."

"I get it. Power is what you must never quarrel with. That's what makes it power," she said, astonished at her own profundity.

Walter thought a moment. "It's a strange thing with people like Judith. If you're in a position to do them a favor, they have to show you they're not fawning on you, so they go to the other extreme and kick your teeth in." His eye fell on the Picasso. "I meant to tell you, sweetie, why don't you get rid of those prints?"

"Why?"

"Because what's on your walls should be original—something that's only in your room and nowhere else. A print can be duplicated in the thousands."

She was about to say, *Buy me an original and see if I turn it down.* Instead, "That's plain snobbism, Walter. I'd rather have a Picasso print any day than a piece of junk by a nobody."

He shrugged. "Have it your way. The rain certainly put you in a mood."

She ignored his comment. "I ran into Paul Horvath near Carnegie Hall. He said," she mimicked Paul's British accent, " 'I guess I'll see you at the Wardwells Thursday night.' What are you supposed to answer when someone tells you that?—'I wasn't invited'?"

"So that's what's eating you."

"I wouldn't mind if they didn't ask me because I offended

them or something. But I hate to be——" she looked for the right word, "ignored."

"Look, sweetie, you go to a hundred parties during the winter. What's one more or less, especially when you see the same faces and hear the same gossip at all of them."

"You're going, aren't you?" she said sullenly. "So don't give me that hooey."

Walter knew, as did she, that a phone call from him would bring the coveted invitation. But it was not a phone call he was prepared to make. "You're just afraid," he said, "that for once something interesting might happen."

"In my profession," she brought out querulously, "it helps to be seen at the right parties whether they're interesting or dull." Actually she never found them dull. Like Walter, she enjoyed the pervasive excitement of a crowded room, the body warmth, the spurious friendliness, and the sense of superiority that came from having been invited when so many others had not.

"Such a fuss over a party!" he exclaimed impatiently. "Now, really——"

Suddenly her face collapsed. "Oh, Walter," she cried, "don't you see how wrong the whole thing is! How difficult it is for me. Don't you suppose I'd enjoy going with you, as your——" She stopped short. Her lips trembled, tears blurred her contact lenses.

He put his arm around her. "Now, now . . ." He brought her head down on his shoulder and said gently. "You're being childish to make such an issue of it."

"I know," she sniffled, but . . ." She nuzzled her forehead against his jacket. "People make such a mistake when they think I'm tough. If they only knew what a softie I am."

Miraculously, he had come prepared. With his free hand he drew from his pocket a little box covered with black velvet. "I got this for your birthday, but there's no law that says you can't have it four days in advance."

She glanced down and noticed that the box said Tiffany. Walter opened it. Within lay a delicate spray of little diamonds and sapphires.

"Darling!" she exclaimed, "what a lovely surprise!" She saw through her tears that the brooch must have cost two thousand. At least.

Walter beamed. "I thought you'd like it."

She wiped her eyes and blew her nose. "You're a dear to re-

member! Let me see how it looks." She lifted the pin out of the
box and, turning to the mirror, held it up against her chest.

Standing behind her, he put his hands palms flat on her hips
and slid them up till they rested on her breasts.

"Walter!" Birdie gently disengaged herself, returned the pin
to the box which she deposited on the sideboard, and gazed up
at him tenderly. Life was a mess whichever way you looked at it.
You couldn't get what you wanted, so you had to take what you
could get. People called it making an adjustment. They were
right. Absolutely!

4

Judith crouched over the keyboard, a look of intense concen-
tration on her face. The secret of good practicing, she always
said, was to make every minute count. She listened carefully to
her playing, matching each motion of her fingers with the sound
it produced.

The large Steinway filled the far side of what her parents
used to call the parlor; she referred to it as the music room.
This was a spacious room, with the tall French doors and par-
quet floor of a bygone era. Books, papers, stacks of music, and
record albums were scattered everywhere, along with the gloves
and stockings that Judith had forgotten to put away. She had
grown up under a mother who made a fetish of neatness.
Twenty years after the good woman's death Judith was still
disobeying her. She was always on the verge of putting the room
in order so that she could give a party, but never got around to
it. She was enough of a celebrity, she felt, for people to want to
entertain her without expecting to be invited in return.

She was working on the opening of Brahms's Piano Concerto
in B-flat. She heard in her mind the serene horn melody that
launches the work, and played the answering triplets. Always,
in working out a passage, she analyzed the music in terms of the
specific problems it presented. The first problem here was to
take advantage of the rich sound of the bass register without
overshadowing the right-hand part. The second, to move
smoothly from triplets to eighth notes and back, with an occasional shift to the three-against-two rhythm of which Brahms

was so fond. And third, to build very gradually the crescendo that prepared for the entrance of the orchestra. She divided the opening passage into little sections, practicing each hand alone over and over until she was completely satisfied, before trying both hands together.

Judith was fascinated by the technical aspects of her art. A pianist had to be in full control of his muscles, like an athlete. Only then was he free to express what he had to say. The spiritual content of music, consequently, had a purely physical basis, depending upon the perfect co-ordination of arms, wrists, fingers, joints. However, it was precisely here, she felt, that so many pianists of her generation made their mistake. They ended by worshipping technique for its own sake, playing everything as fast as possible without the slightest concern for the meaning of the music. What could be drearier?

In earlier years she had devoted a good part of her practicing to technical exercises. Now she preferred to derive those from whatever piece she was studying. She played the first two pages of the concerto in different rhythms, varying accent and touch, shifting the weight of attack from shoulder to forearm to wrist. And always she listened to the sounds that billowed through the high-ceilinged room. She loved everything about her piano—its ebony case, its slightly worn pedals, the keys that responded so sensitively to her fingers, the dark resonance of the bass, the gentle sound of the treble, the brilliance of its upper register. At times it seemed to her that the instrument was a part of herself. At such moments she could scarcely regard this marvelous box of wires and hammers as an inanimate object. Somewhere within its dark entrails there must be a soul.

Now that she had the details under control she was ready to play through the entire section. This involved what seemed to her the most important problem of all—to weld the details into a unity, so that the ear would grasp the architecture of the whole. This, Judith felt, was something she was particularly good at—she had a sense of the big line. She tried to get fullness of tone without pounding, power without strain. It was a great mistake, she maintained, for a woman to try to play the piano like a man. How much wiser for her to take advantage of her femininity.

Judith lost all track of time when she worked. To guard against this, she set the alarm clock for noon. She was startled by its ring and turned off the alarm with a sigh of regret. How quickly the morning had passed. It seemed to her that the hours she spent at the piano were the happiest she knew. There was no sacrifice she would not make, no pleasure she would not forgo in order to achieve this blessed solitude. Alone with the music she became truly herself, rising above the pettiness of daily existence. In this room she was free, she was alive, she was at her best.

At the head of the stairs stood a long narrow mirror, the old-fashioned kind that reached to the ceiling and had legs carved in the shape of griffins. Judith glanced at herself before going out. She was wearing her new spring suit, a green and black tweed for which she was a trifle plump; she had to lose at least five pounds. She made her way down the stairs and knocked on Bob's door. "I thought I'd stop in for a minute," she announced in an elaborately cheerful tone; she did not want him to think she was snooping. Somebody once told her about two people who lived in the same house and communicated only by letter. This, she often thought, would be the ideal solution for Bobby and herself.

Bob, in slacks and a pullover, sat by the window reading. He remembered, the instant she came in, that he had forgotten to make his bed.

"What are you reading?" She sat down in the swivel chair in front of the typewriter.

"Sartre. *The Words.*"

She would have felt at ease had he said Dickens, Thackeray, or Balzac. But the writers he read had come up in the last few years, when she no longer had time for reading: Genet, Becket. Ionesco, Camus, Sartre. They were the architects of a new intellectual world in which she had no part, and the way he said "Sartre" showed that he was aware of this. "How's my boy doing?" she brought out uncertainly, and knew at once that she should not have said it.

"Fine."

She leaned over the typewriter and began to read the sheet in the carriage.

"Don't," he cried, "it's not ready. It's a story I just began."

She stopped reading. "You're always beginning stories. I'd be happier if you finished them."

He jumped up, pulled the sheet out of the carriage and flung it face down on the desk. "Look, mom, it's a beautiful day, you're wearing your new suit, I'm in a good mood—why d'you want to come in here and spoil it?"

She held out her hands innocently. "I don't want to spoil anything. I just thought I'd come in and take a look at you. If you weren't so sensitive——"

He returned to his chair. "I'm not being sensitive. I just don't like to show a piece of work before I'm satisfied with it. You'd be the same, I'm sure.

"That I would," she answered placatingly.

There was a silence. She smiled. "I remember when you were a little boy, you would toddle along at my side asking all sorts of questions. It was so easy for us to talk to each other then. Now . . ." She threw up her hands.

"It figures," he said. "I belong to one generation, you belong to another. Why should it be easy for us to talk when my way of looking at life is completely different from yours."

"Does it have to be? Don't you suppose if you said something sensible for a change I'd see it was sensible?"

It was his turn to smile. "Nothing I say would make sense to you, mother. I'm in a different bag than you."

"But certain things make sense no matter what your bag is." It made her feel very advanced to use his phrase. "I'd like to see you stand on your own feet. I'd like to feel that you know where you're going."

"The world's in danger of blowing itself up, and you want me to know where I'm going?"

"My darling, the world has always had its problems. You're just using that as an excuse for not solving your own."

Bob thought a moment. When he was unsure of himself he curled his left hand into a fist and tapped one end of it lightly against his chin. "Would you be happier if I spent every day from nine to five in some idiotic job that didn't interest me in the least? Just so I could pay the rent?"

"Paying the rent is not the most disgraceful thing a man can do," she retorted. Now she was on the defensive; she hated to be accused of being money-minded.

"Look, mom, if you couldn't afford it I'd go out and get a job tomorrow, and you know it. But you don't need the money, and if you didn't have me on your hands you'd spend it on something else. Why shouldn't I take advantage of the opportunity and try to get where I want to? Why should I join the money grubbers and make myself miserable? For all I know I may be dead tomorrow."

"Stop being romantic. You won't be."

"Since you are able to help me out, why shouldn't I write?"

"If I thought you were on the right track," she said, perplexed. "Believe me, it's not the money. I'm not asking you to become a businessman—you obviously aren't cut out to be one. I'm an artist myself, I understand the artistic temperament. But it seems to me you're drifting."

"I live in a time when the world is drifting."

She ignored his remark. "Lots of young men follow a simple path. They want to be lawyers, doctors, engineers, what have you. All they need to do is pass their exams, and that's it. But someone who wants to write, or paint, or compose, or act . . . it's all so vague."

"What if they had tried to stop you when you said you wanted to be a pianist?"

"I never said it, I just fell into it. Besides, I was a girl, we were well off, there was no problem."

"But no one stopped you, and you made it."

"I'm not so sure I did. Anyway, we're not discussing me. It's you I'm worried about. I want to be proud of you, I want you to get somewhere, and you don't seem to care."

"I can't live just so that you'll be proud of me. That's your hang-up, not mine," he said coldly. "When I was a kid you were always showing me off, showing me off."

"Now you're paying me back. Is that it?"

"Perhaps I don't want to be shown off any more. Maybe it's more important for me to be me."

"And who is that, may I ask? A beatnik?"

"Come off it, mom."

"Why can't you go back to college and finish your M.A.? Then you could teach, and write on the side. That would be practical, and I'd feel you were headed somewhere."

"Because I hate graduate school. It's stuffy—it bears no relation to anything real. Besides, I don't want to teach. That's not my thing."

"Then what d'you propose to do? Sit here stewing in your juice, turning out a story now and then that gathers rejection slips?"

He flushed. "Some great writers started out by gathering rejection slips."

"Yes. But gathering rejection slips doesn't necessarily make you a great writer."

"D'you enjoy taking away my confidence? Then go ahead." He lifted his hands and dropped them in a hopeless gesture. "I don't know why it is, but we always seem to go around in circles."

"Not at all. I know perfectly well what I'm saying, and I know what you're saying."

"No, you don't. I'm saying that you measure everything by success." He spat out the word, contemptuous. "You live in a world where everybody's busy getting ahead. You can't even imagine a world where people just want to be—not get anywhere—just be! I remember when I was growing up, I'd be walking with my friends who were taller and I'd feel your eyes on me, measuring me against them. I'd straighten up and try to look as tall as I could. It was no good, always being measured, always trying to live up to what was expected of me."

"Ah, now we're on solid ground." Her voice took on a sarcastic note. "I'm to blame for everything that's wrong with you."

He ignored the interruption. "Sometimes, just as I'm falling asleep, I remember something that happened when I was around six. You took me somewhere, a department store I suppose, and told me to wait until you came back. Then you disappeared into the crowd at the counter. All of a sudden I guessed the awful truth—you had brought me there to leave me, you were never coming back . . ."

"And what did you do?"

"I let out a yell, that's what I did."

She leaned forward. "You forget the end of the story. When you yelled I came running, didn't I?" She leaned back in the swivel chair. "The trouble with all you young people is that you read too much psychology. Too much Freud. People got along fine for centuries without him, now they have a label for everything that ails them."

"All the same," he said quietly, "you didn't love me enough."

"That's what *you* thought." She slapped the top of the desk, suddenly angry. "Listen, young man, the trouble was I loved yon too much. I smothered you in love, with the result that now you can't stand on your own feet. What I ought to do, for your own good, it turn you out of this house and cut off your allowance and force you to look after yourself." She saw the hurt look in his eyes and stopped. Why, she wondered, was she unable to maintain an even keel with him? Either she was too loving and spoiled him, or she was too severe and humiliated him. "I'm sorry," she said. "I shouldn't have said that. But I will say—and I say it not in anger—that I can't let you go on like this indefinitely. I have a duty to you—to see that you make something of yourself."

"You mean, to see to it that you get something back on your investment."

She controlled her temper. "The issue, as I see it, is simple. If you supported yourself you'd have every right to lead your life as you saw fit. On the other hand, as long as you live in this house and I'm paying the bills, I have a right to approve or disapprove of what you do." She was standing now and looking down at him, which gave her the advantage. "Sooner or later I'll have to put my foot down and say, 'Young man, either obey me or get out.' You won't like it when I do. You'll think it's because I don't love you enough, and you'll be wrong. But I can't help that. When you were little and I refused to let you have your way, you would lie down in the street and beat your head against the pavement. A kind of blackmail. I gave in to you then, but I can't now."

He did not answer. She glanced at her watch. "I have to go. I'm sorry if I disturbed you," she added, suddenly polite and distant as she went to the door. They gazed at each other across an unbridgeable gulf. She sighed. "I hate to leave you looking so glum, but what can I do? I don't know my own child any more. I suppose no parent does. I don't know who your friends are, where you keep yourself, what you're thinking. In a way you're right—we live in two different worlds, and they're far apart. It's not my fault or yours, it's the way things are." How strange it was. She had brought him into the world, a pink, helpless little thing that she bathed and fed and diapered, and now he was someone apart from her. A stranger. Worse—an enemy! The thought unnerved her. Impulsively she crossed over to the window, bent down and kissed him. "Oh, Bobby, why can't it be like it used to be?" She ran her hand over his hair, and walked away. At the door she turned and said sadly, "But what I told you still holds. I'm sorry." She went out.

Bob stared before him, his face rigid. He tried to go back to his reading but was too agitated to follow the subtle web of

Sartre's thought. His eyes fell on the three vertical bars outside his window. A helpless anger seized him, akin to the anger of his childhood when he threw himself down and beat his head on the ground. If he could only go away and never see her again! But she was right: he was not yet ready to stand on his own feet. This was what hurt, even more than the things she had said.

A dull pain pressed against his temples like a leaden weight. It grew and grew until it was greater than he could bear. He stood up, rummaged in the top drawer of his desk and brought out a yellow envelope that contained the green-and-black pills he had stolen from his mother's medicine chest. He took four and swallowed them hastily. Almost immediately he felt a little better.

5

Alice walked briskly up Fifth Avenue. Her silver-gray hair tossed in the May breeze, framing her pink skin; she breathed deeply, with pleasure. She was returning from her class in painting at the New School. Sunlight splashed over the sidewalk, contrasting sharply with the oblong shadows cast by tall buildings on the opposite side of the street. The world was filled with purples, greens, and yellows that she had never noticed before.

Twice a week she rose at seven in order to be on time for the class, which began at nine; she put on a smock and threw herself into the work. This was something she had wanted to do for years. Now that she had taken the step, she enjoyed the sessions immensely. She hung her first two pictures in the dining room. When visitors looked at them she would murmur, "I'm afraid they're not very good." Whereupon Walter would say, "Stop apologizing! At this rate you'll be selling like mad in a year!" He was delighted that she was doing something on her own. It was, he insisted, the best thing in the world for her.

She stopped now and again to look into a shop window. At Twenty-second Street she remembered that Margo lived not far away. The girl had not been feeling well; Alice decided to drop in on her. She wondered what she could bring her, and noticed a book store farther up the street. She went in, browsed awhile, and found an autobiography of Mary Garden that would be of interest, she imagined, to a young singer.

As she left the shop a familiar face swam out of the crowd. "Bob Conrad! What are you doing here?"

Bob was on his way to Margo. "I was just going to pick up a couple of books," he said, pointing to the shop.

"Strange, I almost never run into people I know. You'd think it would happen often in a city like this, but it never does."

"Has something to do with the theory of chance, Mrs. Stern. If you have a hundred people in a village, they're bound to meet every couple of days. If you have eight million——" He was a trifle stiff with her, as he always was with his mother's friends.

"*Mrs. Stern* sounds awfully stuffy. Why not Alice?"

"All right . . . Alice," he said, trying to make it sound natural.

It came to her that she had never paid much attention to him when he was at her house. "Know what? I'll take you to lunch."

Bob did not know how to refuse so friendly an invitation; he was too afraid of being rebuffed himself. "That's very kind of you," he murmured, "I'd enjoy it very much."

They reached Schrafft's, which at that hour was filled with women eating fruit salads with cottage cheese. Alice ordered one. "Have something more substantial—" she said, "—you're a growing boy."

"I have news for you. I haven't been a growing boy for a long time." He ordered a veal cutlet. The situation was not as forbidding as he had thought it would be. She was older than his mother, but she didn't come on as his mother did. She was gentler. And he liked her white hair.

Alice leaned over the salad. "I know so little about your generation."

He put down his fork and considered her remark. "I could tell you about myself for days and days, and when I finished you probably still wouldn't get the picture. Then again I could tell you about myself in five minutes." Unable to manage *Alice* with ease, he avoided her name altogether.

"Make it fifteen."

"I shan't need fifteen," he said. "I got out of college and began my M.A. in English lit. But it bored the hell out of me, so

I dropped out. I guess I'm not cut out to be a scholar. Now I'm trying to write. And live. That's about it."

She realized that, for all his casual manner, he was shy with her, which made her shy in turn. "What are you writing?" she asked.

"Short stories. I've also begun a novel, but I haven't made much headway with it. I get bogged down by technical problems."

"Take your time. It's not as if you had a wife and children. As long as you're alone, you're free to try one thing or another until you find what suits you best."

"I wish my mother took that view. She's in an awful hurry for me to get somewhere. It's her hang-up, but it becomes mine as well."

"She loves you."

"There are different kinds of love. Selfish love, destructive love, possessive love." He tapped his chin in that tentative way he had, with the end of his fist. " 'Children begin by loving their parents and end by judging them.' Oscar Wilde said that."

"He might have added that if they grow up, the chances are they'll go back to loving them."

Bob smiled. "So I didn't grow up." He thought a moment. "Tell me, Mrs.—uh—Alice, if you had a son what kind of person would you like him to be?"

"I did have a son."

"I'm sorry . . . I remember, my mother told me."

"I think Gene would have been a scientist. He was good at physics and that sort of thing. What kind of person I'd have wanted him to be? Any kind he wanted." She noticed that he had finished the cutlet. "Have some dessert."

"Apple pie."

"Why not ice cream with it?"

"Thank you."

Halfway through dessert he looked at her gravely. "I didn't mean to be severe, but it's always a hassle between parents and children. They keep trying to get close to each other, not realizing that it's impossible. Come to think of it, what have they in common? They have to lie, if only to spare each other's feelings. For instance, I began by telling you a little about myself. Believe me, if I really did you'd be shocked out of your mind. What I tell you is the part that can be told, like a campaign biography.

It's what parents present to their children, and vice versa. Each tells what he thinks the other would like to hear. How can a real relationship be built on this basis?"

"You're looking for absolute truth. That's because you're young. Any relationship between two people involves a certain amount of what you call lying. It's not really that. We can't ever reveal ourselves completely to another person. Something has to be held back."

He jabbed his fist against his chin. "The Greeks had a myth that if you saw Zeus naked you dropped dead."

"Then they understood that the complete truth is dangerous." Her cheeks dimpled when she smiled. "Let's say two people meet, and each carries away an impression of the other. It doesn't have to be the complete truth, just close enough to the truth to bring them closer together."

"What impression will you carry away of me?"

"That you're young and sensitive. Shy. Maybe talented. And ——" She stopped a moment before she added, "maybe a little mixed up."

He smiled.

"And what picture," she asked archly, "will you carry away of me?"

"That you're very honest. I like your hair. It's natural. My mother and her friends haven't a gray hair on their heads. It's all hoked up."

"Again you're judging harshly. I may have let my hair go natural for the same reason that they didn't. To make an effect." She was coquettish now. "White hair happens to suit my complexion. It's as simple as that. Besides, it has a blue rinse." She thought a moment and added, "Maybe at a certain point I wanted to look older. Maybe I didn't want to compete any more. You see, I'm being honest with you. At any rate, honest enough."

She told him how she had passed the morning. "It's wonderful," she said, rubbing her thumbs across the other fingers, "to do something with your hands. And to have no other goal than the fun of doing it."

"Only the amateur," he observed sententiously, "can allow himself that pleasure. The artist has a responsibility. To his talent. To his work." As if the idea had just occurred to him, "Maybe the real way to enjoy art is to be an amateur."

She leaned forward confidingly. "When you reach a certain

age there's the danger that you'll get to feel life has passed you by. A hobby can be a marvelous cure for that. But why am I telling you this?" She glanced at her watch. "I was going to drop in on Margo Scholtz—she lives nearby. But the time passed so quickly, I'll leave it for tomorrow. D'you remember her? You met her at my house."

"Yes," he said vaguely. "I remember."

"A very talented girl—Walter has great hopes for her. She hasn't been feeling well. Working too hard, I guess." Alice motioned to the waitress for the check.

They finished their coffee and left. He hailed a taxi for her.

"Can I drop you anywhere?" she asked.

"No, I'm going downtown."

"Good-bye, Bob." She wanted to add, "Let's do it again some-time," but was too shy. Instead, "It wasn't too bad, lunching with an old lady."

"Now I'll be honest with you," he said gravely. "I enjoyed it very much."

"You didn't expect to?"

"Frankly, no. It was a pleasant surprise."

She entered the cab. Bringing her face to the open window she said, "It might also surprise you, if you had told me more about yourself, how little you'd have shocked me." She waved as the cab drove off.

"Thanks for lunch," he called, waving back.

When she came home Walter was in the living room. "Where've you been?" he asked, in a tone meant to indicate that he had been waiting impatiently for her.

She told him about the encounter. "He's a likable young man. I imagine it's not easy to have Judith for a mother."

Walter would have concurred if Birdie had made the state-ment. With Alice, however, he felt he had to defend his friends. "If you think it's easy to have Bob for a son, you have another guess coming."

Alice poured herself a glass of sherry. "I thought I'd find it a little difficult to be with him. On the contrary, it was very pleasant. We sat chatting like old friends."

"All the same, I don't blame Judith for worrying about the lad. He seems to be completely without ambition."

"Does everybody have to be an eager beaver? Give him time. He'll find himself."

"You weren't so permissive when I was starting out." *Permissive* was a recent addition to Walter's vocabulary. He loved using it.

"You had a wife and child. Remember? Bob is free. Let him spread his wings a little. Besides, I'm forty years older."

"That makes a difference?" he said in mock astonishment.

The wine spread a glow through her. "I had a wonderful day. The painting went well. I took a walk on Fifth Avenue—it felt great to be in the sunshine."

He glanced at her. She looked surprisingly pretty. "I haven't seen you so . . . alive," he murmured, putting his arm around her, "in a long time."

The light waned in Margo's room. They sat in the half darkness. "I didn't have to defend myself," Bob brought out quietly, "or explain. She accepted me just as I was. I guess that's why I enjoyed it." He looked up at the wash of orange in the sky. "She had a son killed in the war, so she must be over sixty. We hit it off fine. Funny thing, when I was a kid everybody over thirty was old."

Margo held his hand. "I'm glad you got to know her a little. They've been awfully nice to me. She was a bit distant at first, but she's become friendlier lately."

"She was going to look in on you, but it got late."

"Did you let on about us?"

"Of course not. What's all this about your not feeling well?"

Margo laughed guiltily. "They asked me over several times when I had a date with you. I didn't feel like telling them the truth, so I made excuses. Once it was a sore throat, the next time a virus."

He smiled. "Wait till they find you out." Color faded from the sky, causing the roofs to be silhouetted against the twilight. Directly north, lights glimmered in the windows of the Pan Am Building. "Looks like a gigantic beehive," he said. "No, a rabbit warren."

His thoughts reverted to the luncheon. "Strange. We were two civilized people spending a pleasant hour together. And all the time I kept thinking, Why can't I have this kind of conversation with my mother? No accusations. No problems. Why was I able to be myself with this woman whom I hardly know, yet I get all churned up with my mother?"

"You've explained it yourself. You can be free and easy with a stranger. With parents it's not that simple, they're too close to us." She slipped her fingers through his. "Oh, Bobby, it's good to sit here like this."

"Yes."

"In a way I'm afraid."

"Why?"

"I always thought that if I studied hard everything would turn out fine. All that isn't enough any more. I've found out that there are other things just as important, and it frightens me."

"Why should being in love frighten you?"

"Because it's not as simple as I thought. You can practice your scales and study your lessons and sit at the head of the class, and things may still go wrong."

"They don't have to."

Her eyes shone with a somber light. "I'm no longer sure of anything." Her fingers tightened in his, and her little oval face was intense. "Tell me. Have you ever been in love with all your heart and soul? Have you ever loved anyone the way I love you?"

He tried to imagine the quality of her love as a deaf man might try to imagine music or a blind man light. A pale darkness enveloped the room. He stroked her hair. If only they could remain like this. Always. He pulled her to him, and a sadness filled his heart.

6

The train droned its way through Long Island. To Paul all the stations looked alike. That morning he had regretted having accepted Judith's invitation; he hated week-end visits. Now that dazzling sunlight poured out of a cloudless sky he was glad he had come.

When he alighted, he took a deep breath. The air had the tang of the sea. He looked for Judith. A tall young man in white shorts and sandals stepped out of the station. Paul wished he knew someone like that. To his amazement the young man approached. "Hello. I'm Bob Conrad. Don't you remember me?"

Paul took the outstretched hand. "Of course. You're Judith's son."

They climbed into a jeep. "She bounces a bit," Bob said, adopting the casual manner that best hid his shyness, "but there's nothing better on a sandy road." They drove off, Bob's hair tossing in the breeze.

Paul filled his lungs. "I have not been near the ocean in a long time. It smells good."

"It's a bit cold for swimming, but the bay is warm. Did you bring your trunks?"

"Of course."

"We'll take a dip if you like."

The cottage was one of a row of six on a sandy strip facing the sea. Judith was waiting for them on the porch. Heavily rouged, with her jet-black hair piled high on her head, she looked out of place in a beach house in spite of her bright red cotton dress. "You finally got here!" she cried, her joviality a trifle forced because it was she who had taken the initiative. "I was sure you'd be lost."

"I followed your instructions. They worked like a charm." He came up the stairs, put down his bag, bent slightly, and kissed her hand.

She led the way into a sitting room bright with chintzes. Sunshine streamed in through a large picture window that looked over the ocean. "We're very simple here," she said. "I hope you won't mind."

He smiled. "No, I do not mind."

"Bobby, show the maestro to his room."

Bob preceded the visitor up a steep staircase. Three bedrooms, their doors open, clustered around a square landing under a skylight. "This one's yours," he said and, pointing to the fourth door, added, "the john is here."

They entered the room. Bob went to the window and threw it open. "Look!" Paul joined him. Before them stretched the Atlantic, a sheet of blue shot with gold. Little breakers curled along the beach. "You have to grow up near the ocean to love it. Did you?"

"No." As Paul leaned on the window sill his hand brushed the young man's. He drew it away. "I grew up in the mountains. That is where I feel at home. But this is beautiful too."

"The sea has its moods. One day it's gray and gentle, the next it's boiling mad. Today it's basking in the sun. I never get tired of watching it."

Paul changed into gray slacks and a polo shirt; they went downstairs. Bob mixed martinis while Paul joined Judith on the porch.

"I never thought we'd get you out here," she said.

"I am delighted you asked me." His lean, ascetic face looked worn. "I do not realize how tired I am at the end of the season."

Judith found his low-pitched voice most pleasant. It accentuated the impression of inner strength that had drawn her to him from the start. His was a calm imposed by an effort of will, beneath which she sensed unslackening inner tension. She liked, too, his rather formal manner of speech. "It's nice to see you in sports clothes instead of tails," she said.

"Both are uniforms." He smiled. "Clothes do not make the man, they only cover him."

"I don't agree with you," she retorted with the decisiveness that most men found excessive. "You put someone into a policeman's uniform or a soldier's, and something happens to him."

"The change is not so much in him as in those around him, no? They react differently to him, with the result that he too is different."

Bob brought their martinis. From the beach came the soothing murmur of the waves. "In the city," Judith said, "any noise keeps me awake. Here the ocean puts me to sleep."

Paul raised his glass. *"Prosit."* He drank. "I am chained to Manhattan all year. I forget how beautiful the world is outside."

"That dreadful island," Judith said. "Filthy, noisy, crowded, and the air is poison. Yet we stay there year after year, grubbing away like ants."

Bob sat on the railing. "You know you couldn't live anywhere else, mom," he said. "You'd be bored."

She turned to Paul. "He's right. We're probably cutting years off our lives by staying there, yet by now I need the poison. Take it away—and I'd collapse."

When they finished their drinks Bob said to his mother, "Maybe the maestro would like a swim?"

"Promise me you'll stick to the bay." She turned to Paul. "Don't let him tempt you into the ocean. Your toes'll fall off."

They changed into their swimming trunks in the wooden shed

behind the cottage. The gloom was soothing after the brilliance outside; a muted light streamed in through dust-encrusted windows. Bob threw off his clothes. He had already acquired a tan but was white across the middle. Paul looked away as the young man drew on his swimming trunks. He removed his shirt, revealing the cross that hung on his hairy chest.

"Better take that off," Bob said. "You might lose it in the water."

Paul arranged his slacks and polo shirt on the bench and, lifting the gold chain over his head, deposited his cross on them. Bob looked on. "I don't have any kind of religion," he said. "I don't like the Jewish god—he's too vindictive. And I don't like the Christian god—he's too meek and gentle. Besides, no one takes him seriously."

"Religion means a great deal to me," Paul said quietly. "That is why I never discuss it."

"I'm sorry," the young man said and led the way to the beach.

They walked along the water's edge where the sand was hard. Neither spoke. Like many men who spend much time alone, Paul liked to talk when he was with others. To his surprise, he did not mind the silence that settled between Bob and himself. The salty air, the feel of the sand under his feet, the endless expanse of sea and sky induced a mood of sensuous pleasure that made conversation unnecessary.

It was Bob who broke the silence. "Do you enjoy conducting?"

"Yes and no. I see the world as Will and Idea, as Schopenhauer called it. When you conduct you build a structure; more accurately, you reveal the Idea that is hidden in the notes. The shape of the whole is clear in your mind, even though you reveal it one detail at a time. Like a man who tells a story—he knows the outcome but his audience does not. As you build the structure you create, you experience what the composer felt when he wrote it. What you are doing is close to revelation. Which is why the artist is more than an entertainer. He is a prophet!" Paul stopped and looked at Bob. "This, my friend, is the 'yes' part. The 'no' part has to do with controlling the situation—in other words, with power. The orchestra is the instrument you play on just as the pianist or violinist plays on his—an instrument consisting of a hundred men. Actually a hundred spoiled children. You must impose your will, your vision, your revelation upon them. They resist you. Why? Because the multitude always resists the leader. Each one of them is thinking as he fiddles or blows, 'Why am I sitting down here following him when I should be up there giving orders?' To describe their childish tricks I would have to write a book." He shook his head. "Day by day you fight their mediocrity, their laziness, their refusal to rise above themselves. And the more you try to raise them the more they hate you."

He fell silent, his thin lips pressed together. "But they are only half your problem. The other half is called the board of directors. Some of them are there because they love music, although they know nothing about it. Some are there because they want social position or a place in the musical world. Some are fools, others are knaves, but all of them have money—that is why they are on the board. And all of them have wives. You must go to their dull dinner parties and listen to their silly views. You must be pleasant to them. Why? Because the orchestra runs a deficit and they are the ones who pay it. Since they pay, they feel they have a right to interfere. They want to know what artists you engage, what programs you plan. They love Beethoven and Brahms, therefore you must play Beethoven and Brahms season after season. And they have protégés whom they expect you to hire. In a word, they give you gray hair and shorten your life."

"Sounds pretty grim."

"It would be but for the music. The moment finally comes when you stand on the podium, you raise your hand, and all that went before is forgotten. You stand face to face with the vision—the world as Will and Idea. This is the moment that justifies all. This is why you put up with the nonsense, why you come back again and again. At that moment you are happy that you did not give up and turn to raising chickens or selling bath-robes."

"You mean, there are times when you want to leave it all?"

"Often." He raised his hands in a gesture of helplessness. "But the music will not let me."

The sun was still hot. They reached the bay. "My mother's afraid I'll catch cold in the ocean. It don't warm up till August."

Paul glanced at the youth. "English is not my language, but should you not say *It doesn't?*"

"Why? *It don't* sounds perfectly good to me."

"But there are laws of language, no?"

Bob smiled. "Laws are made to be broken. Surely you know

that. Everybody breaks some law or other. It's just a matter of picking the ones you want to break."

"To me," said Paul gravely, "*it don't* sounds like an affectation."

Bob's eyes lit up at being understood so well. "That's exactly what it is. Or was, at first. Now it comes natural."

They waded into the water up to their knees. "If it disturbs your mother so, why do you not swim here instead of in the ocean?"

"Fish. I'm afraid a fish'll touch me."

Paul laughed. "But the fish is afraid of you."

"That's right. Each of us is scared of the other." The breeze tossed his hair over his forehead; he pushed it back.

"But there are just as many fish in the ocean."

Bob shrugged. "You're assuming that the mind is rational. I have news for you. It isn't."

They dived into the water. Paul swam vigorously away from shore while Bob hung behind. Then, with swift powerful strokes he overtook the older man, outdistancing him by several lengths, and waited for him to catch up.

"Ah, you like to compete," Paul said.

"Only in certain things."

Paul submerged and opened his eyes. He could see Bob's body through the water, weightless and graceful as if he were executing a slow dance. Paul pushed down till he touched bottom and returned slowly to the surface. Bob floated past, an arm's length away, grinning at him. Paul smiled back and was horrified to think that he had almost turned down Judith's invitation.

It was after six when they returned to the shed. They took turns at the shower; Bob produced two huge towels and proceeded to rub himself down. Paul remembered the passage in one of the ancient Greeks—was it Plutarch?—describing how, the wind having lifted the mantle of Alcibiades, Socrates became inflamed at sight of the youth's body. As before, he averted his eyes; but every now and again, as if against his will, they stole a glance at the naked young man beside him.

When they came out of the shed the sky was pale green and saffron. A hush hung over the earth. Paul had not felt so contented in a long time.

The slabs of the breakwater were still warm from the sun. Judith looked up. The sky was festooned with stars, tier upon tier of golden dots strung across the velvet blackness. In the soft glow of the summer night Paul's face lost its severity. They sat where two slabs formed a natural bench. From below came a gentle gurgle as the tide rose through the breakwater. Three sailboats were anchored off the beach, their lights shimmering over the waves.

She leaned back against the flat stone. She was discussing a subject that never failed to upset her—modern music. "I've been a musician all my life," she said decisively, "and I think I know something about it. How do you suppose I feel when I sit in a hall and hear sounds that make absolutely no sense to me? Shall I tell you? It's as if I came to that cottage," she pointed, "which I've owned for years, and was told that it no longer belonged to me." She thought awhile. "That's just about it. These new composers are taking something away from me that I thought was mine, and I don't like it."

"But every generation has to create something new, something in its own image. Was not Beethoven different from Haydn, Chopin from Beethoven?" He turned sideways, so that he could see her. "And at every change the conservatives protested."

Judith turned too; her face was close to his. "Maybe it's a question of degree. Music today is so far out that it's left most of us behind."

The crickets hummed sibilantly against the night. Paul looked up at the stars. "Somebody asked Beethoven if the *Razumovsky Quartets* were really music. He answered 'Not for you—for a later age.'"

"That's too easy. Don't tell me that the great composers weren't understood in their own time. Beethoven certainly was, so were Haydn and Mozart and Bach and Handel. Even if a composer didn't catch on at once, a decade or two later he was accepted. Yet here it's almost a century since Schoenberg was born and I still can't make head or tail of his later works. Webern makes no sense to me, yet all the young composers are following him. When I hear a concert of the new music I go into a depression. I'm convinced the world is coming to an end."

"Maybe it is. Certainly the world that we knew." He was enjoying this conversation; she was bright, assertive, with a mind of her own. He regarded these traits as masculine and liked women who displayed them. It was the cuddly type he could not abide. Unfortunately, even the assertive ones ended by demand-

ing from him what he could not give, so that much as he admired Judith he was wary of her.

"For thousands of years," she continued, "composers tried to
make beautiful sounds. But today's music is so ugly. I sit and
wonder, What do the new composers hear? What do their admirers hear? It's very discouraging." She noticed that he glanced
at his watch. "You must be tired after that swim," she said.
"Shall we go?"

He helped her up; she held on to him as they crossed the
breakwater. The feel of her hand was not unpleasant, even
though it brought dangerously close the mysterious world of
womanhood he had never had the courage to explore. She released his hand when they came to the beach. "I think," he said
in the low baritone she found so musical, "that we are on the
threshold of a new kind of music, different from any the world
has ever heard before. Maybe instrumental music has come to
its final stage and electronic music will take over. How I wish
I could hear the things that composers will be writing a hundred years from now."

"You conduct a lot of new music. Do you understand it?"

"Some I do, some I do not. But I strongly feel that it deserves
a hearing. Is it not madness to feed the public the same dozen
symphonies of Beethoven, Brahms, and Tchaikovsky year after
year? We live in twentieth-century houses, we wear twentieth-
century clothes, and think twentieth-century thoughts. Why then
should we not listen to twentieth-century music?"

"But do you like the new composers? Honestly?"

"That is not the point. I may be too old for some of them,
but they could still be on the right track. If I do not understand
them now, perhaps a later age will."

"No!" She waved her forefinger vigorously. "Just because we
don't understand a piece doesn't make it another *Razumovsky
Quartet*. Don't give me that."

He was thoughtful. "Composers today face a new problem.
For the first time in history music is supposed to be for everybody. What with radio and television, recordings and concerts,
music has become a democratic art. But who do you suppose
listened to Haydn's symphonies? The guests of Prince Esterházy
—in other words, the elite of society. Not the workers and peas-
ants, I assure you."

"You don't approve of democracy?"

"Not really. Music is for the chosen few. We degrade art when we try to give it to the masses. Let them listen to Rodgers and Hammerstein, or Shostakovitch. I believe very strongly in an elite. Otherwise you pull everything down to the level of the herd."

She threw him a quizzical glance. "Don't let anyone hear you," she said. "Such views are not popular in this country."

"I never discuss political questions, because nothing comes of such discussions. We convince only those who already believe. I will say, however, that I consider the French Revolution one of the catastrophes of history. Most of the evils that plague us today began with that dreadful event."

"I didn't know you were for Marie Antoinette," she said, amused. Then, "You're an unusual man, maestro, the kind that stands out from the mass. Maybe that's why you think in terms of an elite. All the same, it's a dangerous doctrine. I hate to remind you, but the last time they tried it out was only twenty years ago. Millions of people died."

His lips tightened; he made no reply. The moon had risen and the breakers soothed the silence with their murmur. "I'm glad I got to know you a little better," Judith said. "I always thought you were rather remote, except when we made music."

"Have you changed your mind?"

"No. I still think you're not easy to know." Her lips curved in a smile that was both childlike and sensual.

"Is anybody? We live inside ourselves. How can anyone really know another person?"

They reached the cottage. "Would you like a nightcap, Paul?" It was the first time she had called him Paul. They were both aware of it.

"Not especially."

"Then I think I'll go to bed."

They tiptoed up the stairs. The door of Bob's room was open; he lay curled up in a sheet, head back on the pillow, his bare chest pale in the moonlight. "He still falls asleep with his door open," Judith whispered. "It's a habit from his childhood. He was afraid of the dark." Her face softened. "Bobby's a good boy. We have our spats now and then, but he's a real person." She held out her hand. "Good night, Paul."

"It has been a lovely day."

"I'm glad you enjoyed it."

"Good night, Judith."

Paul shut the door behind him. He put on his pyjamas and lay down. The moonlight streamed into the room, throwing its luminous pallor over the wall behind the bed; the waves never ceased their murmuring. Paul thought of the handsome youth on the other side of the wall. What would happen if he were to tiptoe into Bob's room and awake him with a kiss? What would happen indeed! A smile softened his face. He fell asleep.

Judith, seated in front of the mirror, reviewed the events of the day. She was delighted that she had invited Paul. What a pleasure it was to be with someone who belonged to her world. A glance, a word, and he understood. He was extremely intuitive, she thought, and when he spoke about music he was first-rate. True, there was something elusive about him. But that, if anything, made him more attractive.

With little circular pats she rubbed cold cream on her face. Her skin looked less ragged now that she was taking care of it. She wiped off the excess cream and went to bed feeling immensely pleased with herself.

The next morning, after another swim and an early lunch, Bob drove Paul to his train. The jeep came to a halt outside the station. Bob jumped down and lowered Paul's suitcase to the ground.

Paul got out. "I thoroughly enjoyed my visit," he said.

"Didn't you expect to?"

"Frankly, no. I hate the bother of leaving town. I had no idea that it would be so pleasant.

"Now that you found the way I hope you'll come again, maestro."

"Why not call me Paul?"

"I hope you'll come again, Paul."

"Your mother asked me for the Fourth of July. If it is at all possible I will."

The train rolled in and came to a halt. They shook hands.

"Good-bye, Bob. Next time I will recognize you."

"Ciao."

As the train pulled out, Paul put his head out of the window and waved. Bob waved back. In some strange way, without having to put it into words, he knew. He had the older man in his power.

7

Max Rubin lay in his green leather chair, reading. He was on the last page of the last volume of Churchill's history of the Second World War, and felt profoundly satisfied at having concluded so formidable a task. Throughout he had underlined words he did not understand or was not sure of in order to look them up in the dictionary; he wrote their definitions in a notebook that he kept especially for this purpose. Two words were underlined on the last page—*reconstituted* and *unswerving*.

For two hours he had been borne along on the majestic current of the Englishman's prose. He removed his glasses and shut his eyes, pressing thumb and forefinger against his eyelids. One pattern throughout history, he reflected, was constant—men killed each other. The reasons and the methods changed, as did the slogans that justified the killing. All else remained the same. How utopian, then, was any plan for creating a better world as long as man remained the destructive animal that he was.

Max was fascinated by the subtle relationship that bound the leader to his time. Which shaped the other? People used to believe that the destiny of nations was determined by kings and generals, queens and mistresses. Yet it was clear to Max that the time created the leader as surely as the leader put his imprint on the time. The leader gave expression to the powerful forces dormant in the masses whom he led, just as the wave upon the surface gave shape and movement to the submerged mass of the sea. It was precisely this ability that made him a leader. For instance, the 1930s were a time of hesitation and appeasement in England, a nonheroic age; therefore it produced nonheroes like Stanley Baldwin and Neville Chamberlain. But the 1940s demanded a hero. Consequently a Churchill appeared, to give expression to the nation's will to survive.

Max rested the book on the wide arm of the chair and lay back, eyes shut. The half century of his career, he reflected, had extended over two world wars and a depression between them. Throughout those turbulent decades he had been troubled by a question that was not easy to answer: Of what importance was art in a world racked by poverty, strife, and a staggering array of problems? True, his work as an impresario had given him a pleasant way of earning a living, but like all men who take themselves seriously Max needed greater justification for his life. It was history, ultimately, that gave him this. Who cared why Sparta fought Athens or vice versa? But the sculptures of the Parthenon still shed their luster. Who remembered why Napoleon entered Vienna or which emperor fled when he did? The *Eroica* and *Fidelio* lived on. Could anyone have foretold that kings, dukes, and popes would be known to us only because their lives had been touched by a Mozart, a Bach, a Michelangelo? The political events of our time seemed more important than what the artist did only because we stood so close to them. Fifty years from now they would appear in a different light. What Hitler or Stalin did on a particular occasion or how their generals executed a certain campaign would have less relevance for each succeeding generation, while the works of art produced during those years would have more and more.

Max pushed the chair into an upright position, shut the book, and replaced it on the shelf beside the four other volumes of the set. Then he pulled out the hard-covered notebook in which he charted the activities of the artists and groups under his management. He rarely consulted the elaborate files in his office that were drawn up by his staff; all he needed was this notebook. In its pages he could see at a glance each performer's engagements for the coming season. Between one entry and the next he left several blank pages in which he jotted down everything that occurred to him concerning that artist: plans, evaluations, promotional ideas. The notebook, in effect, was a master plan— the map of his empire. He could not leaf through it without a feeling of pride, for on its pages were inscribed names admired throughout the world. To him they were pawns on a gigantic chessboard, to be shifted about as he saw fit. Each of them knew only the part that concerned him but he, sitting back in his green leather chair, saw the whole. He could truthfully say that Max Rubin used his power for their advantage rather than his own.

He came upon the page on which, after hearing her *Madame Butterfly,* he had written in his sprawling script the name of

Margo Scholtz. His plans for her were still nebulous; he was in no hurry. For the coming season he would find her a few minor engagements—a concert here, a local opera group there; then a year or two in Germany, at one of the smaller opera houses, where she would acquire the necessary polish. He did not believe in rushing a young artist; the way to build a career was to move slowly, to build on solid ground. Nothing in the world was as exciting as to discover a new talent and guide it step by step to the spot where it deserved to be. This gave him the sense of achievement he needed, the feeling of creating something out of nothing that transformed him into a small copy of the God he did not believe in.

A scowl settled on his face as he came to the page devoted to Judith Conrad. He noted with satisfaction the decrease in the number of her concerts, even though it meant a lower fee for himself. She had to be taken down a peg—no question of that. A stone soaring through the air might think it was going somewhere, unmindful of the hand that threw it. Just so an artist might take it into his head that he was moving under his own steam, forgetting that Max Rubin stood in the wings directing his movements. Judith, he always said, was too smart for her own good. Didn't she realize that he could make or break a dozen like her if he felt like it? He had only to let it get around that she was difficult, and no other manager would touch her. Max pushed out his pendulous lips; his breath came with a rasp. Actually he would not be maligning her, she *was* difficult. And that was the one thing no artist could afford to be—unless he was at the top of the heap, which she certainly wasn't!

He recalled for the twentieth time her suggestion that he had made his success by pandering to the public's taste; he resented it deeply. The great impresario, he felt, played the same role in the entertainment world as the great leader did in the political world—he brought to the surface the shapeless forces hidden in the masses. It was ridiculous to say that he gave them what they wanted, since most of the time they didn't know what they wanted. Actually he shaped their taste, directed their impulses. By sensing their needs he gave them an image of what they would like to see and hear, and in the end made them want what he gave them. Thus he played his part in the shaping of art just as the political leader did in the shaping of history.

Letting the notebook rest in his lap, Max sat listening to the silence. He loved the small hours of the night when the city was quiet; it was the only time a man could think. The nymph on the mantelpiece was enveloped in shadow; her belly showed a quarter to two. Max went into the kitchen, foraged in the refrigerator, and brought out a container of yogurt. Coffee flavor. He savored each spoonful, reflective. At seventy-four a man no longer worked for money, fame, success; these were the trimmings. At seventy-four a man was free at last to work for the only thing that mattered—the work itself.

He returned to the chair, sat down, pushed it into a horizontal position, and pressed a switch. The green leather began to purr and vibrate, giving him a gentle massage. The old man felt the little tremors against his back and smiled with pleasure. Why shouldn't Max Rubin relax like anyone else?

8

The train emerged from the tunnel into the light of day. The change struck Paul like a shift from minor to major. As on his previous visit to Judith, the sun poured golden light out of a clear blue sky, putting him in a holiday mood. The tracks of the railroad yard sped past him in shifting patterns. Presently the flat landscape of Long Island took shape outside his window. He noticed all sorts of details that had escaped his attention on the first trip. Then he leaned back, shut his eyes, and pictured the young man in white shorts and sandals awaiting him at the end of the journey.

He had mixed feelings about falling in love. On the one hand he dreaded an emotional involvement, on the other there was an emptiness in his heart that cried out to be filled. His concept of love had been shaped by the one romantic attachment of his life. He was twenty-two and had just returned to his native Budapest, after three years of study in England, when he met Baron Kurt von Vischer, an attaché at the German embassy. Kurt was ten years older than he. To the young musician he epitomized the man of the world. The baroness was rich, fat, and considerably older than her handsome husband. She made almost no demands upon him. Kurt introduced his protégé into the brilliant social circles of the capital. Their becoming lovers seemed to Paul as inevitable as it was beautiful. For the first time he knew what it meant to share every thought and feeling with someone who understood him completely. Kurt, a scion of the East Prussian aristocracy, began by regarding Hitler as an upstart. However, as the thirties wore on and each of the Fuehrer's bloodless victories brought closer the emergence of a greater Germany, he was won over—and won over Paul as well.

Given Paul's talent, he would have made an international career in any event. What Kurt did for him was to open the right doors and accelerate the pace of his advance. Paul was twenty-five when he conducted his first *Rosenkavalier* at the Budapest Opera; within two years he had appeared in Prague and Vienna. The following summer he accompanied Kurt on a visit to the latter's ancestral estate. They stopped in Munich and Nuremberg. The journey was a powerful experience for Paul; he saw about him a nation reawakened, preparing for its rendezvous with destiny. The open-air rallies that he witnessed were like great pagan rituals accompanied by a display of military might no pagan ever dreamed of. Behind the oratory he discerned an idea that spoke to him in the most immediate way, a philosophy based on power, on youthful vigor and hope. He had always known in his heart that the earth belonged to the strong, the brave, the few. In the flaming swastikas, massed banners, and frenzied salutes he saw a magnificent affirmation of this truth.

Offered a conductorship in Switzerland, he was on the point of refusing, since it would have meant separation from his friend, but Kurt felt that this was too great an opportunity to turn down. Besides, war was imminent and Paul would be safe in a neutral country. After it was over—Kurt was convinced that the Nazi victory would be swift and decisive—they would be reunited. Paul yielded. Their last night together was sad. They lay in each other's arms in Kurt's room while the baroness lay snoring in hers. Kurt held him tightly, protectively, and Paul's heart overflowed with love. He wept when they parted. They never met again.

His years in Switzerland gave him invaluable experience in his craft. They were also the agonizing years when the easy victory promised by the first Nazi bulletins receded, month after month, year after year, until even the most ardent believer fell prey to doubt. Paul was stunned by Hitler's defeat. Who would have dreamed that the decadent democracies, weakened by the rule of the many—in effect, the rule of the mediocre—would triumph over a philosophy based on the rule of an elite? Ironically, the Allied victory helped his career. When musical life resumed on the continent there was a sudden shortage of conductors, since several of the best ones—Karajan, Boehm, Furtwängler, Krauss, Knappersbusch—were waiting to be de-Nazified. At that moment there was room at the top for a gifted young man who was not compromised politically. Although Paul had believed in Hitler as fervently as some of his more famous colleagues, his years in Switzerland had kept him untainted as far as officials were concerned. His star rose rapidly, first in Germany, then in England. In 1950 he was invited to the United States. After several fruitful years in the Midwest he came to New York.

The baron did not survive the war. Summoned back to Germany in 1944, he was implicated in the plot against Hitler and summarily shot. Paul enshrined Kurt in his memory as the most perfect human being he had ever known. His sense of loss was too great for him to try to fill the void left by his friend. As the years passed he separated sex and love. The profound experience that he had shared with Kurt remained untarnished by his casual encounters with the young men he picked up in bars. In one respect he took over Kurt's role: although he grew older, they were always in their early twenties, as though he recaptured in them the youthful charm Kurt had found in him.

The ideology of the Third Reich, based as it was on the promise of total victory, could not continue to hold him once victory had turned into defeat. Paul had never resolved the conflict between Nazism and Christian ethos. He gradually drifted back to the religious mysticism that lay at the core of his personality. Imperceptibly he turned from the Superman of Nietzsche to the Man of Sorrow, from Wagner to Bach. As the Third Reich receded into history his youthful involvement with Nazism sank into the lower regions of his unconscious, like a geological layer covered over by the accretions of subsequent eras. Occasionally the remembrance of the earlier period filtered into his awareness, where it became part of the general atmosphere of guilt that enveloped the landscape of his soul—a guilt from which he found surcease only through repentance and prayer, bolstered by innumerable readings of the Psalms, the Gospels, and his favorite author, St. Augustine.

The train came to a halt. Paul seized his bag and made his way to the platform. Then he caught sight of Bob waving to him. The sun shone, the air was salty, and his heart sang as he realized how much he had missed the youth.

When they came out on the beach an hour later the sky clouded over briefly, making a gently diffused light. "You're much darker than you were," Paul said.

"I've been out in the sun." When Bob smiled his teeth stood out whitely against his deep tan.

They walked along the water's edge. "I looked forward to our meeting again," Paul said, hoping the young man would attach a deeper significance to this remark.

"So did I," Bob answered pleasantly.

"Have you been in the city?"

"Once."

"Why didn't you ring me up?"

"Didn't occur to me you might want me to."

The sun came out, casting two long shadows sharply before them. "What have you been doing since the last time I saw you?" Paul asked.

"Nothing."

"How can one do nothing?"

"It's not easy," Bob said gravely. "Takes a lot of effort to attain a state of pure being."

Paul thought a moment. "I never learned how. Either I study scores or play the piano or read or see people or think about my next concert. I am simply not able to do nothing."

"Try one day to sit still and empty your mind of all thought. You'll find that you can't. Words and ideas will keep popping into your head, soon you'll be thinking of the same old things. If your mind could stay empty, that is, keep itself from being distracted by thoughts, you might be able to hear the beat of life. The beat of your own being."

"And you have been doing this? Sounds fascinating."

"That's what people say at cocktail parties when someone tells them he's been training seals or hunting for buried treasure."

Paul looked at him, taken aback. "What I like about you is that you are not quite polite. But then, you are not insulting either."

"I didn't mean to be either."

"What I really like is that you say the unexpected."

"You mean I don't say what you expect. But that's a statement about yourself rather than about me."

Paul was won over by the young man's directness. "You remind me," he said, "of someone wandering naked in a room where everyone else is in tails."

"Maybe I'm the one who's properly dressed."

"That is quite possible." Paul smiled. It seemed to him a miraculous thing that the two of them, so different in age, background, and point of view, should understand each other so readily. "But surely you do not intend to spend your life emptying your mind so that you can hear the basic beat."

"Everybody asks me what I intend to do. I don't really yet know."

"Your mother tells me you want to write."

"I'd like to, but I'm not sure I've anything to say."

"You strike me as talented."

"What makes you say that?"

"A feeling I have about you. But—if I may speak frankly—talent is not enough. A lot of people have it, but nothing comes of them. It is what you do with the talent that counts—the discipline, the persistence, the hard work."

"What you're saying is, I'm going to have a tough time making it."

"Yes. You should have something to fall back on in case you do not reach your goal."

"When the time comes I will. Meanwhile I just want to find out where I'm at." He looked very young as he said it.

Their shadows lengthened over the sand; they reached the bay. The sun, still high in the western sky, cut a golden swath through the water. "I was three years old when my mother was divorced," Bob said quietly. "She didn't marry again until seven years later. You know something?" He turned to Paul. "It would have been easier for me to grow up if my father had been around."

They swam.

Water gurgled through the rocks of the breakwater. The crickets made insistent music while Judith told Paul about herself. "I remember the first time I played in public, I was around nine and wore a starched white dress. I was excited and frightened, exactly as when I have to play now. My parents were very proud of me, and I was convinced the whole world loved me and always would. I was mistaken."

He smiled. "If you had to do it over again . . . ?" Plum-colored clouds drifted lazily across the night sky; fireflies darted about in crazy patterns.

"I'd want to be someone ordinary."

He thought her reply a shade arrogant—only an extraordinary person had a right to say this. "Why?"

"You've a better chance to be happy. Or at least satisfied."

"You are not?"

"No. I never seem to get the things I want, and I don't seem to want the things I get."

"But that feeling is not limited to artists. There must be thousands of people who are familiar with it." He leaned back against the stone slab, which was still warm from the sun.

"The trouble is, I feel it about my work too. No matter how well I do, I'm not satisfied. How can I be when I know what I failed to achieve?"

"Perhaps you are too honest with yourself."

"Could be. One should shade the truth, pretty it up. I don't." She threw back her head, looked up at the stars, and sighed. "I should like to have had either a big talent—so big that I'd never have any doubts about it—or none at all. As it is, I'm somewhere," she moved her hand from side to side, "in between."

She smoothed back a strand of hair that had come loose in the breeze. As she did, she leaned slightly to one side so that her body touched his. Paul stifled an impulse to move away. At that moment, with painful vividness, he pictured her voluptuous body naked in his arms. The image filled him with panic, and with a revulsion akin to what he had felt as a boy when he realized for the first time that his mother must have done *that*. "Doubts one must always have," he said smoothly. "I mean, enough to spur us on to do our best, but not enough to crush us."

"You are a great artist," she said. "For you it must be easy."

"It is never easy." At what point had he taken the wrong turn? Was it because he had loved his mother too much and must safeguard her purity by excluding all women from his embrace? Such fanciful speculation led nowhere; he had been born the way he was and must learn to accept his infirmity as men accepted any malformation of body or soul. In any case, his position on this accursed breakwater was becoming precarious. How could he tell her that she had him at her mercy only because he was falling in love with her son? "Easy it cannot be, because art demands that you sacrifice every other interest. Have you ever heard musicians talk about anything else but their work?"

"It's easier for a man to put his work above his personal affairs. I've been torn all my life between trying to be an artist and trying to be a woman." She turned to him, suddenly coquettish. "It will amuse you to know, Paul, that my first impression of you was of a man with almost no personal life."

"Really?" He was beginning to sweat; the rock was too warm. He squirmed sidewise so as to face her, managing thereby to put a few inches between them.

"That night you conducted for me I noticed the look in your eyes. I couldn't put a name to it. Later it came to me that you must be a very lonely man."

She's discussing my eyes! I'm going to strangle this woman. He smiled affably. "It's always interesting to hear what impression one makes on others."

"Was I right?" she inquired archly.

In God's name, how do I get her off this rock? "Loneliness is —how shall I put it?—part of the human condition. We are born alone and we die alone. People spend their time trying to escape the inevitable. They cling to each other, marry, and breed, all in order to escape their aloneness. The artist, by his very nature, is doomed to solitude. That is his destiny, and nowhere is he more alone than in the midst of the crowd."

"Must he be alone?" Her large eyes were upon him, brilliant and voracious. She moved forward so that her breasts almost touched him, and the sweetness of her perfume hit him like a bludgeon. "Plenty of artists have families and friends. Stravinsky, for example, or Picasso."

"For each of these you have a Beethoven, a Schubert, a Tchaikovsky who went through life alone. Do you know what Heine said? 'Out of my great sorrows I make my little songs.' "

She gave him a loving smile. "You remember everything you read. It's extraordinary."

His antennae warned him that she was almost ready to strike.

How to ward her off without hurting her feelings, particularly since she was one of the few women whose company he enjoyed? He chose the least noble way. Clutching his head with his hand, he let out a gasp of pain.

"What's the matter?" she cried.

"Nothing. I get these attacks now and then. Especially when I am overtired. Have you an aspirin?"

"At home. Maybe you were out in the sun too long." She half rose. "I'll give you two aspirins and a cold compress."

He helped her to her feet. Her solicitude touched him; now that he was out of danger, his hostility passed. He rewarded her with a second performance, this time contorting his face in a spasm of pain.

The attacks grew less severe once they reached the beach; Judith mothered him through the short walk to the cottage. The moon had risen, round and white, pouring its silvery radiance over the sea. When they reached the house Judith hurried to the medicine chest and brought out a bottle of aspirins. Paul, carrying the comedy to the end, obediently swallowed two tablets in a glass of water, whereupon she made him lie down on the chintz-covered sofa with a cold compress on his forehead.

It was past eleven when she led the way up the narrow stairs. They stopped on the landing. As on his first visit, the door of Bob's room was open. Bob lay on his back, sheet coiled around him, a patch of moonlight across his bed. Judith gazed at him, then turned to Paul. "Get a good night's sleep and you'll be as good as new."

He felt guilty for the deception. "So sorry I put you to all this trouble."

She patted his hand. "Don't be silly. We're friends, aren't we? Good night, Paul."

"You are very kind. Good night."

He closed the door behind him, undid his sandals, and took off his clothes. The window was open; the smell of the sea pervaded the room. He looked out and filled his lungs. In the distance, the breakers streaked the night with their white crests. A wild thought careened through his brain: What if he tiptoed into Bob's room? Only for a moment. He dismissed the idea as madness. But who would know? If Bob awoke or Judith opened her door he could explain that the lad had cried out in his sleep and he had gone in to see if anything was wrong. The longer he dwelt upon the prospect, the more alluring it became. He felt tense, alert in every nerve; he knew he would be unable to sleep until he had executed his plan. It was very quiet in the house. He finally tiptoed across the room and, stopping before the door, stood still, listening. At length he turned the knob slowly, noiselessly. Bob's room adjoined his. One step, and he was over the threshold. Two more, and he stood in front of the bed.

His heart was pounding, his throat was dry. He knelt in front of the bed and gazed at the beautiful youth lying before him. The patch of moonlight had moved toward the wall; half of Bob's body was in shadow. There came back to him the passage about Alcibiades. A vast longing filled his heart, powered by a desire that overrode reason. Slowly, almost reverently he lifted the sheet from Bob's body and feasted his eyes on the one kind of loveliness that was able to move him. Then his fingertips moved ever so lightly over the young man's wrist and forearm, up to the elbow and beyond.

Bob opened his eyes, and Paul realized that he had been awake. He looked at Paul without surprise, as though he had been expecting him. A smile curved his lips; he seemed to be weighing the choices before him. Suddenly he pointed to the door with a circular motion of his hand. Paul understood. He rose and crossed over, quietly shut the door, returned to the bed, and lay down beside Bob. Raising himself on one elbow, he passed his lips lightly over Bob's cheek until they came to rest on his mouth.

Judith awoke. The sky was still dark except for a pale streak in the East. She had to go to the john but did not stir. If she were choosing a cottage now each bedroom would have its own bathroom. It was too inconvenient, when there were guests in the house, to have to go into the hall. What if she ran into Paul as he came out on a similar errand? This was hardly likely, she knew. Still . . .

Her thoughts reverted to their evening together. There was much about it that puzzled her. He obviously enoyed her company, yet she sensed his withdrawal as soon as she came too close—it ringed him about like a protective wall. But if he didn't want her, why had he come a second time? She had seen through his play-acting, of course; the timing was too perfect for his pains to have been real. Yet, just possibly, he might have had a headache from too much sun. Maybe she wasn't young enough for him. No, he didn't seem like a cradle-snatcher. Impotent? He seemed virile enough. Preferred men? No, there was nothing effeminate about him. Maybe he needed a short, fat girl of fifteen with a mole on her right cheek, wearing high leather boots and brandishing a whip. That was it! She sighed. Whatever it was, he had his reasons—and she had to respect them. She should have known beforehand—it looked too good to be true.

She slipped into a housecoat and went out on the landing. A sliver of yellow light showed under the door of Bob's room; Paul's was empty. She heard them talking softly, and was pleased to know that Bob was coming in contact with a first-rate mind. She sighed, remembering the years when she had sat up half the night talking to people who interested her. Those wild, wonderful conversations. If her hair weren't in such a state she would have gone in and joined them. It was considerate of them, she thought, to shut the door so as not to disturb her. A wisp of dawn filtered in through the skylight, enveloped in shadow. She made her way to the bathroom. Then she went back to sleep.

The next morning there was a heavy mist that reduced the sun to a sullen smudge in the sky. Judith was the first to come down. She puttered about in the kitchen; soon the odor of fresh coffee filled the cottage. While waiting for the others she sat down at the piano and played a Schubert Impromptu, the songful one in A♭. Music, she decided, was much easier to understand than people, their minds, their motives, their thoughts. Bob came down at ten, Paul shortly after. When they finished breakfast Judith suggested to Paul that they play duets. The piano was an old-fashioned square grand she had picked up at an auction, that had retained its tone in spite of the sea air. They sat down before its yellowed keys while Bob curled up in the window seat with a book.

They played the great F-Minor Fantasy of Schubert. Judith took the treble part. The poignant melody was romantic as only Schubert could be, and she played it romantically. Paul carried the bass part. His rhythm was stricter than hers. He avoided the subtle nuances—a hurrying forward here, a holding back there —that came naturally to her. She found herself following his beat and could not but admire the classical purity of style that characterized his music making.

"It's amazing," she said when they finished the first movement, "the way you read at sight."

"A conductor has to read scores all the time. What is so amazing about it?"

"I do it so badly. If I haven't gone over the music beforehand, I'm lost."

"This is because you never read at sight. The trick is for the eyes to move ahead of the hands. By the time you finish playing one measure, your eyes should have taken in the next."

She sighed. "I'll never learn—it's too late. If I want to play a piece, I simply have to practice it. Not that I mind!"

He leafed through the second movement. "What a pity that we hear this music so rarely. And only in the concert hall, where it does not belong. These duets are house music. They should be played as we are doing it, for the pleasure of the players, or for one or two friends." When they finished the piece they talked at length about Schubert, and she played him the first movement of the posthumous Sonata in B-flat.

Later he stood with Judith on the porch while Bob brought the jeep in front of the cottage; he was taking an early train. "Now that we're old friends," she said, holding out her hand, "you must come again." She knew he wouldn't, and she was not sure that she wanted him to.

"Just ask me!" he replied with false fervor. He kissed her hand, clambered up beside Bob, and the jeep drove off.

A silence fell between them. Bob had no desire to refer to what had occurred the night before, yet it seemed trivial to make small talk. Presently Paul raised his hand toward the wheel and brought it down on Bob's. "It has been wonderful," he said.

Bob did not reply. Then breaking into a smile, "Would she be sore," he said, "if she ever found out." There was a shade of triumph in his voice.

"She will not," said Paul hastily, "so there is no problem."

The road curved away from the sea. Paul wanted to say something tender, but he sensed that the young man was in no mood for intimate avowal. "Your mother is a charming woman," he said.

"When she wants to be. She can also be a bitch."

The jeep approached the station. Paul removed his hand from Bob's. "Do you know anything at all about love?" he asked softly.

"Very little. There's a girl in love with me at the moment, she says I love only myself. She's wrong. I can't bear myself."

"You are a beautiful person."

"Perhaps to you. Not to myself."

"Perhaps I see you as you really are."

"No. You see me as I could be—if I were someone else."

Paul was seized by the longing he had felt the night before, mingled with infinite compassion for the fragility of youth. "I think I am going to love you very much," he said gently.

Bob did not answer. He brought the jeep to a halt outside the station. A whistle blew.

"Will you be in the city this week?" Paul asked.

"Thursday." He was coming in to say good-bye to Margo, who was going home for the summer.

"You will not forget to call me? At the hotel."

"Sure thing."

"Can we have dinner together?"

"No. I'll come after."

The train arrived and ground to a halt. They walked toward it. "Thank you for everything," Paul said quickly. "You will never know how much it meant to me."

Bob jabbed his fist lightly against Paul's arm, twice. "Have a good trip."

"Till Thursday, then."

"Ciao." Bob returned to the jeep, thoughtful. How strange, that Paul and Margo—so different in every respect—had the same quality of urgency in their voices when they took leave of him. An urgency he did not, could not share.

9

The waiting room had an impersonal air; the dark wooden benches were empty. Margo and Bob sat in a corner, her valise on the bench beside them. She held his arm, her body against his. "I ought to be ashamed," she said, "to cling to you like this for the whole world to see. But I'm shameless."

She wore a yellow cotton dress whose brightness accentuated

her dark complexion. "I used to look forward," she said, "to spending the summer with my parents. Now all I can think of is how I hate to leave you."

"I'll be here when you get back."

"I know it, but only with my mind—my heart keeps telling me you'll go away and I'll never see you again."

"Listen to your mind. That's what it's for."

"Will you think of me everyday?"

"I promise."

"Will you write me?"

He made a grimace. "You know I'm no good at letters. Takes me two days to find an envelope and stamp, two more to remember to mail it. Why don't you phone me when you feel like it?"

"My parents'll get the bill and ask questions. I'd rather not tell them about you . . . yet."

"Call collect. I'll be coming home from the beach around six."

She made a face. "I hate long-distance conversations. I'll shout into the phone, 'How are you? Having a good time? D'you miss me?' And all the time I'll be thinking about the money it's costing you."

"Why don't you write me first, then I'll answer on the phone. This'll combine both methods, to the satisfaction of all concerned."

Two sailors in white uniforms sat down on the bench opposite them. They were young and sunburnt, and sat without speaking. A dumpy woman with a torn valise plumped down not far from them "All these strangers," Bob said. "I wonder who they are, where they're from, where they're bound for, what they're thinking about. I'd like to hold out my hand to touch them. But they pass me by."

"All you can hope to know are a few friends whose lives touch yours. From them you can guess what the others are like."

"Millions of people in the world, each one with his story. All those stories I'll never know."

A voice over the loudspeaker announced that the train to Poughkeepsie was ready. Bob lifted the valise from the bench; she took her bag and Mary Garden's autobiography. They made their way into the main hall of the station. Margo, her hand in his, looked up at the vast expanse. "It's so big, it used to make me feel insignificant."

"Now it don't?"

"No. Because you're here."

They descended to the lower level and walked to the center of the platform. Bob put down the valise and faced Margo. She gazed up at him. "How do I look?"

"Like a small-town girl in a yellow dress going home to visit her parents. The *Daily News* would describe you as a petite brunette."

"What's wrong with that?"

He grinned. "Nothing."

Passengers were boarding the train. Margo went in, followed by Bob. He lifted the valise onto the rack overhead, bent down, and kissed her.

"I'll call you Sunday," she said, her eyes large and intense.

"Ciao."

"Sunday night. Be there."

Bob went off and walked along the train until he came to her window. She pressed her face against the pane and said something; he jabbed both forefingers against his ears to signify that he could not hear. A whistle shrilled. She blew a kiss and flattened her hands against the glass. He put his hands on the pane directly against hers. The train pulled out; he walked beside it for a few paces and was left behind.

He mounted the cream-colored ramp that led to Forty-second Street. The night was humid. A stillness hung over the city; the streets had a "nothing doing" look. It was too early to go back to Long Island. He wondered whether he should see a movie, suddenly remembered that he had promised to call Paul, and made for the nearest phone booth.

The deep baritone leaped out of the receiver. "Ah, you did not forget. I am delighted. Where are you?"

"Near Grand Central."

"Come along."

Bob took a bus to Fifty-seventh Street and walked crosstown to Paul's hotel.

"How nice that you came," Paul said at the door and led him within.

Bob glanced around the square-shaped sitting room. "I like the oak paneling. Has that 1910 look." His eyes came to rest on the Spanish chest beneath the crucifix. "Beautiful."

"I picked it up in Barcelona when I conducted there."

Bob studied the elaborate carvings. "You know a person better," he said, "when you see him in his pad."

"You would, if this were my home, but it is only a place to stay in."

"Where's home?"

Paul shrugged his shoulders. "Wherever I am conducting. Which means, it is always temporary."

Bob looked up at the *St. Sebastian.* "Who's it by?"

"Mantegna."

The young man fastened his gaze on the column to which the martyr was bound. "His eyes are on heaven, which is where you'd expect them to be with all those arrows in him."

"Would pain diminish his ecstasy?" Paul asked sternly. "He rises above the physical. That is why he is a saint."

You really believe that nonsense? Bob suppressed the remark. He decided to change the subject. "You're so orderly," he said, pointing to the pencils stacked neatly on Paul's desk. "I'm like my mother, I leave everything lying around loose."

"I have to know where things are, otherwise it would be impossible." He smiled. "Even if I were not, the chambermaid would bully me into neatness."

Bob sat down. The air conditioner filled the room with a low, steady hum. "What will you drink?" Paul asked.

"Scotch. On the rocks."

"What have you been doing?"

"Swimming, mostly. And you?"

"Recording." Paul brought him his drink and poured one for himself. He lifted a record from the desk. "Came out today. Mahler's First."

"Congratulations." As in the case of Margo, Bob had mixed feelings about Paul's achievement; it brought home to him that he himself had accomplished nothing as yet. He examined the record. Paul's picture was on the jacket, the ascetic face with its thin lips, sunken eyes and bald dome staring dramatically out of a dark background. "Where's Mahler?" he asked with a smile. "After all, he only wrote the piece."

"That is precisely what I told them. But they sell the conductor, not the composer. You cannot argue with Madison Avenue. Would you like to hear it?"

"Of course. But why don't I phone home first. My mother expects me back on the nine-twenty. I better tell her I got hung up."

"Exactly what does *hung up* mean?"

"Anything you want it to mean."

"The telephone is in the bedroom." He indicated a closed door.

Bob went into the adjoining room and spent five minutes expostulating with Judith. Upon his return he let out a sigh of exhaustion. "She hates it when I change plans. She'd like everything to run on schedule, like in one of those eighteenth-century pieces she plays, where every detail is in its appointed place. She don't understand that life isn't like art."

Paul drew the disc from its cover and set it on the turntable. The mysterious open fifths of the introduction floated into the room. "What a way to begin a symphony! And a first symphony at that." He drew a footstool in front of Bob's chair and sat down. "Mahler wanted it to sound *wie ein Naturlaut*—like a sound of Nature." The main theme of the Allegro sang out. "It has the quality of folk song," Paul said softly. "So simple. So inevitable. I can hardly believe he was a Jew, it sounds so Austrian."

Bob glanced at him in surprise. "What a strange remark." Then, "I'm half Jewish. Did you know that?"

"No. You do not look it."

"What's a Jew supposed to look like?"

Paul shrugged. "In any case, you do not."

"My mother don't believe in mixed marriages any more. Because of the children. She says they're neither Jew nor *goy*. They don't know where they belong."

"Is that how you feel?"

A faint smile curved Bob's lips. "I wouldn't belong no matter what I was. I'm not the kind."

Paul took the young man's hand in his, interlacing their fingers. They listened in silence to the rest of the movement and the eerie march that followed. When Paul rose to turn the record he said, "Not bad, considering the conditions under which we work." He sounded detached, as though evaluating someone else's performance. "We record after the concert, from midnight until God knows when, in a single session. The men are so tense they actually play better."

"And you?"

Paul smiled. "I am always tense with Mahler. Tension is the essence of his music." He placed the needle. "The Scherzo is pure Austrian folk song. Mahler got it from Schubert, with a bit of Bruckner thrown in." He returned to the footstool and again took Bob's hand.

It was the fourth movement that made the deepest impression on the young man. Powerful masses of sound were hurled against each other in an apocalyptic vision. This was the demonic kind of music for which Paul had a special affinity. From the inferno emerged a broadly flowing melody charged with Mahler's passionate lyricism; then the storm raged again. At the very end the symphony returned to the "Nature" sound of the beginning.

Paul stopped the machine. Bob said nothing. Finally, "Did you like it?" Paul asked.

The youth hid his emotion. "Very much," he said in a judicious tone, as if measuring out the proper amount of approval. "You sure put a lot of juice into the last movement."

"I find it easy to understand Mahler. His music came out of tremendous inner turmoil. You have to breathe with it. When I finish conducting one of his works I can hardly breathe at all."

Bob listened intently. "A movement such as the fourth," Paul was saying, "depends on the greatest possible contrast between the dramatic and lyric elements. Do you understand, little one?"

Bob laughed. "Little one? I'm taller than you."

Paul remembered. Kurt used to call him *mein kleiner,* and he would laugh in reply just as Bob had done and say, "I'm taller than you." Spurred on by the bright look in Bob's eyes, he continued his explanation. To mold a young man's mind even as Kurt had molded his, to leave an imprint on a young man's soul even as Kurt had left an imprint on his . . . this was supremely worth doing. He leaned forward, looking up into Bob's eager face. This would be happiness!

three

 Philip Lerner sat at his desk. The late-afternoon sun threw its amber glow over the furniture, which was in the blandly impersonal style that used to be known as Swedish modern. His secretary had gone; the office was quiet. This was the hour when he was able to think most clearly. The letter before him needed thinking about. It was from Andrée, and brought the news that Jacques was dead.

The sorrow he felt was sharpened by a wedge of guilt. He had never permitted himself to think *If only Jacques died.* Now it no longer mattered what he thought or kept himself from thinking. A chapter had ended for Andrée and him—a new one was about to begin. Philip studied her neat, feminine handwriting. The two of them were free at last, to give each other what happiness they could in the time that was left to them. They were at an age when two people did not adjust easily to a new situation, yet he faced their future without apprehension. She was the only real thing in his life—everything else had been play-acting.

He recalled an August day when the three of them had been

sent into Toulon. The port was swarming with Germans. He was supposed to be a deaf mute, so that his accent would not give him away. The three of them practiced sign language all the way into the city. Anyone looking at them would have thought they were on a holiday excursion—except that their laughter was a shade too gay. Philip remembered Jacques's self-possession and quick thinking, the qualities that had brought the three of them safely through the war. Jacques's generation was beginning to die out. When its last survivors were gone the war would cease to be part of the living past—it would become an event to be read about or seen in films or mentioned by people as something they had heard about from their fathers. Jacques's death cut another of the ties that bound Philip to the most significant period of his life.

He rested his elbows on the desk and stared before him. The noise of traffic floated up from the street. Jacques had been a good man: this was the only way Philip could sum up what his friend had meant to him. He had been a hero without heroics. He had risen above personal interests in order to dedicate himself completely to what mattered most to him—which happened to be what mattered most to his time. That, Philip decided, was as close as he could come to the definition of a good man.

Yet might not a Nazi have served his cause with equal self-sacrifice and conviction? Would he, then, have been a good man too? Yes—if his cause had won. Philip was startled by this conclusion. Could it be that a cause was just not because of its inherent morality but only because it was victorious? Suppose the Nazi factories had produced more tanks and planes than we did, or had found their way to the atom bomb first? Then the shoe would have been on the other foot: Hitler, Mussolini, and Tojo would have been revered as heroes of the century, while Truman, Churchill, and Stalin would have been hanged as war criminals. In effect, what gave the Allies their victory was not the justice of their cause but their military strength.

Or was there a logic in history, a secret purpose that moved the world forward, that could not permit Hitler to win because his sense of reality was false? If the Nazis had won, the clock would have been turned back a thousand years; the logic of history could not allow this to happen. Yet where was the logic in the victories of Genghis Khan or Tamerlane or, to take an example closer home, of General Franco? They won in spite of the logic of history, because they were either stronger or luckier than their opponents. Could it be that there was no absolute standard of justice and goodness, that these were merely relative concepts to be interpreted according to which side you were on?

It began to grow dark in the room; the street noises abated. Philip roused himself, turned on the light, and lifted the telephone. His voice trembled as he said, "I'd like to send a telegram."

The plane shot along the runway with a great roar and began to slow down. Philip stood on the observation deck wedged among the crowd. The plane halted, stairways were rolled into place, passengers disembarked. Joy burst into his heart as he recognized her.

She made her way across the field and into the building. The people around him surged from the outside deck to the waiting room. He followed. He stood pressed agianst the glass partition, oblivious of the din. Then she appeared, a slim, hatless figure in black. She looked up, searching; caught sight of him, smiled, waved. He watched her as she steered a little steel cart to the baggage racks and shepherded her valises through customs. Finally the glass door opened, she stood before him.

"Andrée!"

"Pheeleep!"

He held her in his arms; they kissed. Behind her, the porter wheeled the baggage. She wept a little and he stroked her hair. The dream had come true.

2

Summer ended; Margo returned to New York. The visit with her family had been restful. She loved the rolling hills alongside the Hudson, the tree-lined streets of her childhood; she enjoyed the hours spent with her parents and sister. While she was with them her life in New York seemed unreal. Even her love for Bob became a gentler, saner thing. Now, however, the country town with its comfortable frame houses and broad lawns receded into the realm of the unreal as the city sucked her back into its turbulent rhythm. There was no mistaking which was the dream and which the reality.

She threw herself into her work; her days were taken up with solfège, new roles, acting, diction. She was moving into the French repertory—Micaela in *Carmen*, Marguerite in *Faust*—and found herself responding to French lyricism even as she had to Italian. They were as different as the two languages that nourished them. Bizet she put on a par with Puccini; Gounod moved her less. She was increasingly aware of the conflict between her life—by which she meant her love for Bob—and her work. There was only one way in which this opposition could be resolved: to be so sure of him that her love and her work would strengthen each other instead of pulling her in opposite directions. But how was she to achieve this security? It seemed to her at times that love was a kind of illness, like smallpox or measles, against which a person ought to be able to be vaccinated. How much smoother life would be if she were able to go to the doctor and receive a shot against emotional upset.

One day early in October Walter telephoned her. "Max is offering you a contract," he informed her jubilantly. "Not much for this year, but it's a start. I can't tell you how pleased I am."

Margo knew that this was a momentous step forward in her career, and felt a surge of excitement that afternoon when Walter brought her to Max's office near Carnegie Hall. The room was carpeted from wall to wall; Max sat behind an impressive desk. He rose and took her hand. "How are you?" His accent made it sound like *havayoo*. "Real glad to see you." He motioned her to a chair.

She was fascinated by the collection of signed photographs on the wall. Her eyes came to rest on a picture of Geraldine Farrar. "Did you know her?"

"I didn't handle her. I was young then and small potatoes. But she was always nice to me." The old man sighed. "She was the greatest. Greater even than Mary Garden. Her voice was like silk. And she knew when her time was up. She stopped while she was still on top. The way an artist should."

Margo's glance traveled along the wall. Alma Gluck, Lucrezia Bori, Bidú Sayão, Zinka Milanov. "It's thrilling," she said, "to think that some of them might have been in this room, might have even sat on this chair." For the first time she felt the full impact of the opportunity that was opening before her.

The old man smiled. "My artists didn't come to me, I went to them. When you and I do business in your hotel instead of here—that's how you'll know you're a star."

"Is that the only way I'll know?"

"There'll be plenty of other ways." He thought a moment. "Today little girls sing opera. They sing the notes. That's enough to make you a prima donna? No, my dear!" The bulbous head shook emphatically. "Those women," his pudgy forefinger indicated the wall, "weren't just singers, they were personalities. They had class. That's why the public was crazy about them. Don't let anybody tell you you can fool the public." The pudgy forefinger swooped down on the desk. "In the long run people know!"

Margo signed the paper he put before her, and he showed her the blank page in his notebook where he had written her name. "It's empty now. Someday it'll be full. I don't want you should think it's easy. In this business you have to take the good with the bad. But if you have the stuff," he orated grandly, "take it from Max Rubin, there's more good than bad."

When they left the office Walter insisted that she come home with him. "This is a special day in your life—we have to celebrate. You'll stay for dinner."

"I'm afraid I can't, Mr. Stern. I—I have to be home."

"Then come for a drink. Alice'll be delighted at the news."

In the car Margo said, "There's something I'd like to tell you. How much I appreciate all you've done for me."

"I know. You don't have to say it."

"Also——" She hesitated, embarrassed. "Now that I'll be earning something, I'd like to start paying you back what I owe you."

He put his hand on her shoulder. "Child, you don't owe me a thing. It's been fun watching you grow. When I see you where you belong . . . that's how you'll pay me back."

"Still, it's not right that I should always take from you. If I do earn some money, why can't I try to pay back?"

"There'll be time enough when you're rolling in dough. Then you'll need tax deductions, and I'll be one of them." The prospect delighted him. He dropped his hands in his lap, fingers interlaced, and sat beaming.

They found Alice in the living room. She congratulated Margo and kissed her. Walter said to his wife, "Honey, why don't you persuade her to stay for dinner?"

"Would you like to?"

"I'd love it," Margo said, reddening, "but I have to be home. A friend is coming over."

"Don't insist, Walter. She has a date. We'll make it some other time."

Walter scowled. "There you go, putting ideas into her head. She shouldn't be having dates now. Her mind should be on more important things."

Alice smiled. "That's not for us to decide." She looked at Margo. "Actually, I agree with Walter. For the time being you should stay free, so you can concentrate on your work."

"It's not what you think," said Margo hastily. "It's a girl friend . . . a girl I grew up with. I promised to cook dinner."

"No problem. We'll make it some night next week," Alice said kindly.

Walter told his chauffeur to bring Margo home. After she had left, "I'm afraid we embarrassed her," Alice said. "You mustn't get carried away. After all, she has a right to her own life."

"Has she?" He pursed his lips, annoyed. "Too much is at stake for her. She's got to understand that."

"Walter, she's a young girl! Maybe she's in love."

"She said it was a girl friend."

"Could be. Could also be we put her on the spot, so she lied."

"She shouldn't!" he said righteously.

"Why? You never lie?"

"That's not the point. She owes me the truth."

"If she lied, it was because we forced her to. We shouldn't make her feel she's at our beck and call."

He opened his newspaper—a sign that he had lost the argument. "All right," he grumbled. "I meant well."

She brought him a glass of milk.

The black Cadillac came to a halt. Margo jumped out impatiently; Bob was at the door. She thanked the chauffeur and waited till he had driven off before she hurried to her lover. "Bobby, I've wonderful news!"

"I been waiting half an hour," he said sulkily.

"Sorry, darling. They wouldn't let me go. Guess what happened." She told him as they went up the stairs.

Once inside her apartment she threw her arms around him. "Isn't it thrilling?"

"You should be very happy. And proud."

"I am. Are you?"

"Of course. How else would I feel about your getting such a break?"

The thought slipped through her mind that she would feel even happier if she could be sure he loved her, but she was silent.

"What are you thinking about?" he asked.

"If I told you, you'd be angry."

"Try it and see."

She did.

He stroked her hair. "You're wrong, I'm not angry. Only puzzled. Just because people talk about love it don't mean they know about it. Love," he announced loftily, "is a mystery. You can't see it, taste it, touch it, smell it. What more can I tell you?"

"That you love me and—" She hesitated, then plunged ahead, "—and want to marry me."

"Margo!" His face assumed an expression of mock pain. "That's not my bit and you know it. Just hearing the word makes me nervous."

She kissed him again and again, thrusting the tip of her tongue between his lips, then threw herself on the sofa and gave him a detailed account of her day. She had a childlike certainty that he would want to hear about all the things she had done and the people she had met. "I sang the Jewel Song from *Faust* at my lesson. Have you ever seen the opera?"

"No. It's a French corruption of Goethe's play," he added severely.

"Nobody ever reads Goethe's play, so who cares what the French did to it? It makes a fine opera, which is all that matters. Marguerite is innocent and sweet; I understand her. And I understand why she'd want to have a child by Faust."

"Why?"

"Because it's natural, if you love a man, to want to bear his child. It means that you and he have created something."

A look of alarm crossed his face. "Margo, you're taking those pills I gave you."

"Of course, silly. Why wouldn't I?"

He looked relieved. "Because you might get opera mixed up with real life. They're different, you know."

"Are they? Operas are about love and hate and jealousy. What's unreal about that?"

He brought his fist against his chin, thinking. "The emotions in a work of art," he pontificated, "resemble those of real life, or people wouldn't recognize a novel or play as true. All the same, the resemblance is not as close as people think. Fact is, art has its own reality. That's what makes it art." To impress her he added, "Although Aristotle did say that drama should purge our emotions through pity and terror."

"You're so smart!" She sighed in admiration.

He stayed late. When he had gone Margo lay on the sofa, daydreaming. As far back as she could remember her fantasies had revolved around a packed opera house that cheered her performance. Now another image made its way into her consciousness: she saw herself nursing a baby with golden hair and green eyes. Strangely, this vision gave her as much pleasure as the other; then she pictured herself in front of a house on a quiet, tree-lined street, with two youngsters playing on the lawn. She had been so firmly set on her career that she had never imagined herself as a wife and mother, yet the other image must have lain hidden at the back of her mind, waiting to be released. It saddened her to have to choose between the two. Why couldn't she have both?

She realized that Bob would never grow up unless she forced him to face responsibility. What if she were to make him a father? Then she would hold him to her as women had held their men since the beginning of time. After all, the pill in which he put such faith was not one hundred percent dependable. Suppose she became pregnant. He could never prove she had done it on purpose. More important, he would face an experience that could not but mature him. He had been a child long enough. Suppose she helped him become a man!

The neon sign across the street pumped intermittent waves of light into the room. As she fell asleep a smile spread over her face, wise and joyous. Just suppose . . .

3

Birdie finally confronted Judith with the bad news about the coming season. Judith responded with a headache and a severe depression. "I'd understand it if it were my fault. But audiences love what I do. I sold out in Duluth last year. In Wichita they gave me a standing ovation. And that bastard cuts down on my concerts."

"Darling, you should go out of your way to be nice to Max. Instead, you never miss an opportunity to antagonize him. If you don't mind my saying so, you don't have much talent for public relations."

"What d'you expect me to do? Crawl on my hands and knees for a few concerts?"

Birdie passed her hand over her hair, as though to make sure that the bun at the back was there. "You got to tell people what they want to hear," she announced, "otherwise . . ." She shrugged.

"I can't help it if I'm honest."

"I'm not saying you should kiss his ass, but you don't have to kick him in the teeth."

"I'm not a hypocrite," Judith announced proudly. "I told him what I think. He should be man enough to respect me for doing so."

Although Birdie had objected to Walter's analysis, she now passed it off as her own. "You're a funny girl, my dear. You're afraid Max'll think you need him, so you go to the other extreme to show him that you don't. You're not being realistic. He's the one who gets you the dates."

"If it's not Max, it'll be someone else."

"With someone else you'll have the same problem, and he won't be half as good."

Judith's lower lip pushed forward obstinately. "He's going to hear plenty from me. And he won't like it either."

"Why d'you make things difficult for yourself?" Birdie raised her hands in a helpless gesture. "It's as if you enjoyed killing your chances. I'll never understand."

By the time she confronted Max, Judith had worked herself

up to the proper pitch. It added to her zest that she was wearing her green and black suit. Max rose as she entered. "Look who's here." His Russian-Jewish gutturals imparted a warmth to his greeting that he did not feel. "So how are you?" He motioned her to the chair beside his desk.

She sat down, crossed her legs, and came to the point. "How d'you expect me to be when my concerts are cut in half?"

He extended his hands philosophically. "It's the ups and downs of the business. You know, the fat years and the lean."

"The fat years and the lean were sent by God," she said, eyeing him coldly. "The ups and downs are made by you."

"God I'm not. Miracles I can't make."

"I'm not asking for miracles. All I expect is that your salesmen should do their job."

"My salesmen work very hard. Take it from Max Rubin, they try their best for you. If they can't sell an artist, nobody can."

"Your salesmen sold me fine," she countered. "They sold me down the river."

A crafty light shone in the old man's eyes. "Why they would do that?" he asked gently. "The more concerts you play, the more they make."

"Yeh. But they make out just as well by pushing someone else on your list. They do what you tell them."

"Since when you are a mind reader?"

She ignored the remark. "It's disgusting, what you do. This year you push one favorite, next year another. We're pawns in your hands and you push us around any way you like. Churchill was right," said Judith, confusing him with Lord Acton, "power corrupts, and absolute power corrupts absolutely."

Ever since he had finished the five volumes, Max considered himself an authority on Churchill. He did not recognize the quotation, which made him angry. "Listen," he said sternly. "I been running my business for fifty years. I don't need you to tell me how."

"I'm not telling you how to run your business," she cried, her voice rising. "I'm only saying that what you do takes away from the dignity of the artist."

"You don't like it here maybe? No one is forcing you to stay."

"And where am I to go? You have the field sewed up—you and a few others who are no better than you. We're at your mercy."

"In all the years I been in business I never heard complaints. Maybe you'll be happier some place else. Believe me, from the profit I make from you, I don't have to listen to insults."

"It's not I who insult you, Max. It's you who insult the artist and his art. You like to think you're bringing culture to the masses. Let me tell you the truth—you prostitute art!"

"Phooey! Such language I got to hear?"

"You'll hear the truth whether you like it or not!" Her eyes grew hard. "For fifty years you've vulgarized everything you've touched. That's the secret of your success. Vulgarity, and nothing else!" she shouted, and stood up to give herself the advantage of looking down at him.

"You come here to make me trouble?" Max inclined his bulbous head to one side. "Trouble I don't need. For six years I did my best for you, but you don't appreciate. You know what? Max Rubin needs you like a hole in the head!" The pudgy hand cleaved the air in an imperious gesture. "Don't do me any favors. Next year you can go some place else!"

Judith swept out of his office aglow with the joy of having told him off. Max watched her depart with a determined look on his face. He took out his hard-covered notebook and opened it to Judith's page. His pendulous lips tightened in a satisfied smile as he ripped out the page, crumpled it, and threw it into the wastebasket under his desk.

Judith's elation returned as she described the scene to Birdie, who grew paler with each detail. "My God, you didn't say that!" Birdie gasped.

"Why not? It's time someone stood up to him."

"It had to be you?"

"Yes! I'm not going to let anyone ride over me."

"But you made an enemy out of him."

"So what? The little he did for me anyone can do."

"You don't know Max. He'll spread the word that you're difficult, as he calls it. Once that gets around——"

"Don't panic, Birdie. I'm not going through life on my knees."

Birdie kept her peace. How could she explain anything to someone who not only slammed the door in her face but was overjoyed at having done so? That afternoon, as she finished telling Walter what had happened, Birdie was thoughtful. "Y'know what?" She had the look of having stumbled upon a profound truth. "She's her own worst enemy."

"The world is full of such people. They have a will to fail."
This phrase was another recent acquisition, and Walter was
proud of it.

"It's as though she enjoyed punishing herself," Birdie said,
puzzled. "Crazy!"

"Couldn't you explain this to her?"

Birdie looked at him in surprise. "Of course not. You can't
tell people what they don't want to hear." Then, pensively,
"Sometimes I think Max put his finger on it. She's too smart
for her own good."

Judith sat in her hotel room looking out the window. It was
raining; the pavements glistened under the street lamps. The
drapes were adorned with a flowered pattern that matched the
furniture covers. She hated them, as she hated everything about
Cleveland. Mae West was right—every city in the United States
outside New York was Bridgeport, Connecticut.

Her head ached, she was depressed. A letter from Birdie had
informed her that Philip had married his Frenchwoman. Judith
had not thought of him in months, yet the news of his marriage
upset her. Was it because he had found happiness while she
had not? Or because another woman had taken her place? In
any case, the more she thought of him and his French bride the
more she felt sorry for herself, alone in this hideous room on a
rainy night in Cleveland.

In addition, her concert in Cincinnati the night before had
not been well attended. As a seasoned performer Judith knew
that not every concert could be a gala event. Any one of a number of factors might cut down the size of an audience: bad
weather, a competing event, an exciting television program,
insufficient publicity, even a political crisis that turned people's
thoughts elsewhere. For whatever reason, she had not fared as
well as on her previous tour of the Midwest. Also, while solo
recitals were fine in their way, what counted were engagements
with orchestras, and of these she had only one. Nor had she
been at her best in Cincinnati—only two encores. She was stuck
in Cleveland for another day, then Detroit. Max had not spaced
her dates well. For her money he could drop dead.

The euphoria that followed her quarrel with him had faded.
Although she hated to admit it, she knew she had made a mistake. She should not have tangled with him; her tongue had
run away with her. She'd have to find another manager, which

was not easy. There were too many pianists around; if only half of them could be exported to Australia. She wondered if the breach was irreparable. He would make her eat crow if she tried to win him back. Her lower lip pushed out—she was not going to humiliate herself. Birdie would have to find a way to patch things up.

Judith turned away from the window and plumped down on the day bed. To what extent, she wondered, did one determine the events of one's life? Suppose there had not been a piano in the house when she was growing up? Suppose her parents had not imposed their dreams and ambitions upon her? At that point she could have been bent in any direction; or was her future course already set? *Mark my words, she's going to play in Carnegie Hall some day . . . she's going to be somebody!* Well, she had played in Carnegie Hall, she had become somebody, and much good it had done her. Here she was, dragging her suitcase from one hotel room to the next with two evening gowns, two nightgowns, and an extra jar of cold cream. Still chasing the childhood dream. What for? When she ran across people who had known her in her youth, they seemed to be impressed. "I've heard so much about you," they would say, or, "It must be *exciting* to be famous." Judith's lips curved in a mocking smile. They should see her now.

Yet even if she abandoned the dream, where could she turn? What would she do if she were not traipsing across the country from one concert to the next? Could she at this point settle down as a happily married matron in suburbia—assuming that she found a husband to settle down with? How much freedom of choice did she have? This was the life she had chosen—more accurately, that had chosen her—and she was stuck with it for better or worse. She looked at herself grimly in the mirror. At the moment, it seemed, for worse.

Whom did she know in Cleveland? The lady at the head of the concert committee. The local manager. She could not face an evening with either, and decided not to phone them till the following morning. Somebody would be giving a party for her after the concert; they would serve peanut-butter sandwiches and she would have to be pleasant on the chance that she might be invited back. Not next year—"Our public likes variety," they always said—but the year after. It irritated her to think that she had to please these provincials. How far all this was from the dream that had gilded her youth. Judith found her reflections too melancholy and decided to take a walk.

The rain had stopped, a dampness hung in the air. She peered listlessly at the dummies in the department-store windows. Somewhere a clock finished striking ten; another began. The street was deserted—they pulled in the sidewalks at night. She found herself outside a bar. In the window a neon sign wrote *Budweiser* in orange letters; the room looked inviting. She had never been in a bar alone. What did it feel like? She smiled as she realized that she was finally going to find out.

She went in, glanced around with assurance, sat down and ordered a Scotch on the rocks. It was important to her, for some reason she could not fathom, to give the bartender the impression that she was accustomed to this sort of thing. She opened her bag, brought out a pack of cigarettes, placed one between her lips, and began to look for her lighter when a voice at her left said, "Here y'are." She turned. Her neighbor was a blondish man in his forties. He flicked his lighter and brought the flame to the tip of her cigarette; she drew and thanked him.

"Awful night," he said. He had a little cleft in his chin that reminded her of her first husband.

"It certainly is."

A sign hung over the mirror facing Judith. "In God we trust," it announced in square black letters. "All others pay cash." The stranger said, "Where ya from."

"Albany. And you?"

"Fort Worth."

She assumed that he, too, was lying. "I've been there," she said.

He sipped his beer. "You here on business or pleasure?"

"Y'might call it business. And you?"

"Both." He gave her what he obviously considered a mischievous look.

"Take care one doesn't get in the way of the other." She decided he was a traveling salesman, although what he sold she could not imagine. Most likely a pillar of the community, with a son in high school and a daughter not yet, or the other way around. Yet here he was on the prowl, and wanting her to know it.

"I wouldn't let that happen. What kind of business you in?"

"I'm only passing through, really."

"Where ya headed for?"

"Reno." It was apparent to Judith that his questions sprang not so much from curiosity as out of a desire to prolong the conversation.

"Awful lonesome, isn't it," he said, "when you're in a strange town."

"Quite. Are you married?"

"Yes."

She liked him for having admitted it.

"Are you?" he asked.

Judith moved her hand from side to side. "Sort of."

He did not press her. She had finished her drink; he asked if he could buy her another.

"If you like. What would your wife say if she saw you flirting with another woman?"

"I'm not flirting. I'm only trying to be friendly."

"What would she say if she saw you trying to be friendly with another woman?"

He grinned. "She ain't gonna see me. So that's one bridge we don't have to cross."

This, Judith told herself, was far from stimulating conversation, but since it was the first time in her life that she had been picked up in a bar the encounter held the charm of novelty. In her present mood she was glad he had spoken to her. It struck her that whereas in a normal social situation two people tried to find out as much as they could about each other, in this instance the information that each sought—and gave—was kept to a minimum. He was not interested in her as Judith Conrad, with all the complexities of personality that made her what she was; for him she was simply someone to go to bed with. To her astonishment, this anonymous relationship, in which each partner caught a fleeting glimpse of the other through a peephole, as it were, could have a certain attraction if the circumstances were right. Tonight they seemed to be.

"What's your name?" he asked.

"Irene. And yours?"

"Dan. Hi." He extended his hand and clasped hers. Then, half disengaging his, he let his forefinger lightly tickle her palm.

Her lower lip curved in that sensual smile of hers. "Fresh, aren't you."

"If this weren't a public place," he replied, "I'd put my arms around you and give you the squeeze of your life."

She laughed. "And what would your wife say?"

He winked. "I told you not to worry about her."

Judith raised her glass. What would her son say? Or Birdie? Or Walter and Alice? They'd say nothing because they would never know. But she would know, and she would be thoroughly ashamed of herself. To go to bed with a stranger—— It was appalling even to consider the possibility, yet she was not appalled in the least. Judith studied his reflection in the mirror behind the bar. The neon sign in the window cast its orange glow on his regular features. He had a clear skin and was on the lean side. Fortunately, since plump men did not attract her. His pocket handkerchief matched his tie in the same way that the drapes at the hotel matched the furniture covers. She tried to picture him with his clothes off and was astonished at how easily she could.

He put down his drink. "Shall we go?"

She heard herself say, "When I finish my drink," and realized for the first time that she was going through with the adventure.

His hotel was around the corner. They walked without speaking; he held her hand like a lover. But this was madness, she told herself; there was still time to change her mind. Why should she? She was not married or in love. Whom was she betraying—except herself? She had known sex only with a husband or lover, as part of a relationship. But it could also be enjoyed as a thing in itself, a purely physical experience that relieved body tension just as emptying the bladder or bowels did, only more fun. During the war years there must have been thousands of men and women, uprooted and lonely, who had this kind of fling. What harm was there in it? On the contrary, he had already done her some good. Her headache was gone and she felt at least five years younger. Most important of all, she had shaken off her depression. True, this was not the sort of thing she would ever permit herself in New York. But this was Cleveland.

They reached his hotel. "It's okay," he reassured her. "As far as they're concerned you're my wife."

"I see."

"Besides, they mind their own business. They'd go nuts if they didn't."

They entered the lobby. He picked up his key at the desk and led the way to the elevator. She could feel the desk clerk's eyes on her back and walked very erect, bracing herself for another inquiring glance when they reached the elevator; but it was an automatic one. He led the way to his room. Once inside, he threw off his coat and gave her a quizzical look. "Make yourself comfortable," he said, and took her in his arms. He made a ritual of kissing. First his lips lightly brushed hers, barely touching, as though he wanted to tantalize her; then he swooped down and sucked them into his mouth. She found herself lying on the bed, his hand ascending expertly between her thighs. "You'll wrinkle my dress," she said.

"Take it off." He watched her undress with intense interest, while his hand stroked the crotch of his trousers. For an instant Judith thought he was going to masturbate; then she realized that this was a gesture of arousal, and that his cockiness covered a not unengaging timidity. However, when she lay in his arms he recovered his assurance. His ardor communicated itself to her, and she was glad she had come.

When their passion had abated, "Gee, you're terrific!" he said, as one artist to another.

"You're not bad yourself."

"Let's go again. I came too fast," he brought out almost ruefully. "This time I'll make it last longer." He did.

It occurred to Judith that sex on this basis was simpler than the kind she was used to. When she slept with someone she cared about she was concerned that he share her feelings, and this concern could become so intense as to interfere with pleasure. But where her feelings were uninvolved she could concentrate on her own enjoyment without worrying about his.

"Why don't you stay all night?" he whispered when it was over.

"I wish I could, but I have to leave early in the morning." She turned on the light, dressed, and put on fresh make-up. She glanced at him curiously. They had shared the most intimate human experience, yet they remained strangers.

He had slipped into a terry-cloth robe and followed her to the door. He tried to put his arms around her but she was no longer in the mood. "I really must go now," she said, stopping his hands.

He accepted the rebuff good-humoredly. "It was a pleasure to meetcha." He held out his hand.

To this there was only one answer. "Likewise, I'm sure."

Again his forefinger tickled her palm. She freed her hand. "Little man must go to bed."

"You think you'll find the elevator?"

"Of course."

"If you ever get to Fort Worth, look me up."

"I sure will," she said with fervor. "Good night."

"Take care."

She took the elevator down. The lobby was empty. She passed the desk clerk with unseeing eyes. It had grown colder, the sidewalks were dry. Judith buttoned her coat. As she approached her hotel her high spirits vanished; her depression returned, sharper than before. It was terrible to think that she had submitted to such degradation. And even worse, that she had enjoyed it.

4

Paul sat reading, waiting for the doorbell to ring. He grew tense whenever Bob was late, even though he knew in advance that the young man was likely to be. At last Bob arrived, unconcerned.

"Where the devil were you?" Paul snapped.

"I got hung up."

"You know I do not like to be kept waiting."

"Cool it, Paul, it's not as if you were standing on a street corner. You've got your books here, scores, records. What's the difference if I turn up a bit late?"

"It is the principle." Paul knew that it was silly to attach such importance to a trifle, yet he was helpless against the wave of anguish unloosed in him by the young man's seeming indifference to his needs.

"Punctuality isn't a principle, Paul. It happens to be part of the German tradition in which you grew up. Like German thoroughness or German efficiency. Much happiness they brought into the world."

Instantly Paul's petulance disappeared; he threw the youth an affectionate glance. "When we are together I keep comparing what I was at your age with what you are now. I must admit, you come out ahead."

"It was another time, another generation."

"You make it sound like a century ago."

"It was a world war ago."

"Granted I am old enough to be your father. Does that mean I speak another language?"

"If you want to know, yes. On certain subjects we've absolutely nothing to say to each other."

"Then why say it?" It was precisely when Bob put a distance between them that Paul felt most keenly his need of him. He took the young man in his arms and kissed him.

Bob freed himself. "Please, Paul. You know this isn't my thing." He wiped his lips with the back of his hand.

"Very flattering," the older man brought out acidly.

"You make problems. If you want someone who'll enjoy kissing you, you should find yourself a queer. Town's full of them."

"Not interested."

"Or one of the hustlers you told me you used to go with."

"I no longer want that." Paul's face was taut with emotion. "You do not understand, Bobby. I love you."

"But I like to kiss girls. Is that such a crime?"

"You did not object that first night." Always, in the battle of wills between them, Paul harked back to the one occasion when Bob gave himself without hesitation.

"Maybe I was curious. Maybe I was flattered." He grinned. "Maybe I enjoyed taking you away from my mother."

"You scoundrel!"

"She made it pretty clear she was after you, so I rescued you. Be grateful."

"You should love your mother. That's what we were taught in my day."

"I do. All the same, maybe I enjoyed being one up on her for a change."

"Was that the only reason?"

"You know it wasn't. I admire you very much, Paul, and I'd like to have you for a friend. But you want me for a lover, and that, to be perfectly honest with you, is not my bag." As a matter of fact he was not being perfectly honest. He enjoyed his power over the older man and knew that the more unattainable he made himself, the greater this was.

He dropped into the armchair by the window. Paul drew up a footstool and sat down in front of him. "I was glancing through Plato while I waited for you." He picked up his worn copy of the *Dialogues*. "Let me read you a passage from the

Symposium." He read slowly the philosopher's celebrated defense of homosexual love: " 'Each of us when separated, having one side only, like a flat fish, is but part of a man, and he is always looking for his other half. Men who are a section of that double nature which was once called bisexual are lovers of women, but they who are a section of the male follow the male, and while they are young, being slices of the original man, they hang about men and embrace them, and they are themselves the best of boys and youths because they have the most manly nature. And they embrace that which is like them.' " Paul looked up. "The wonderful thing about Plato is that he understood the nature of love, not as desire for pleasure but as a longing for the ideal." He returned to the book. " 'When one of them meets with his other half, the actual half of himself, the pair are lost in an amazement of love and friendship and intimacy, and one will not be out of the other's sight, as I may say, even for a moment. For the intense yearning which each has towards the other does not appear to be the desire of lovers' intercourse but of something else which the souls of both desire and cannot tell, of which they have only a dark and doubtful intuition.' " He glanced at Bob, who had been listening intently.

There was a silence. Then Bob said, "It worked fine for them. They were pagans, their society accepted it, their poets and generals and philosophers were like that, and they had a great thing going. But our society don't accept it and never will. In our world if you're that way, you're queer, and that's all there is to it."

"What has the world to do with it?" Paul cried. "In this room there is only you and me. We build our own world, we make our own laws. We—we alone decide!"

Bob was touched by his intensity. "Granted, in this room we make our own laws. Even then it can't work."

"Why?"

"Because the love of a man for a woman has everything going for it. This kind has everything against it."

"That is nothing but prejudice."

"No, Paul. I'm not speaking from a moral point of view—what you call prejudice—because I haven't any. I mean the nature of the love itself. It's not stable, it can't last. What attracts you to me is the fact that I don't give in." Now, for once, he was trying to be honest. "If I did you'd get tired of me in a week, as you did with all the others in your life."

"Is this what you fear?"

"It's inevitable. Sooner or later we'll break up, for one reason or another. And you'll go on looking for the same damn thing over and over again. Looking for the one thing you'll never find."

Paul left the footstool and knelt before him. "You will never know how much I need you. It can work if you will only give it a chance." Taking Bob's face between his hands, he drew it down and kissed him. This time the young man did not resist.

Paul gazed at him, lost in thought. "You are wrong to say I am attracted to you because you do not yield. I am attracted to you because you are beautiful. I do not mean only your body, I mean all of you. Inside."

Bob smiled. "I'm not beautiful inside. Take my word. You don't see me as I am. You have some image in your mind that resembles me a bit, you've attached my name to it, and think it's me. That's how it is in love. Someday you'll discover your mistake and blame me for it."

"Since you seem to know so much about it, tell me: have you ever loved anyone? I mean completely, madly, the way I love you?"

Bob smiled, remembering that Margo had asked the same question. "How about some music?" he said.

By "music" he meant Mahler's First, which Paul had played for him repeatedly and which had become "their" piece. He had grown sufficiently familiar with it to be able to hum some of its themes, and could even anticipate their appearance. With its abrupt alternations of mood the symphony had come to represent for him the special atmosphere that pervaded his evenings with Paul. He knew that he would never again be able to hear it without picturing this square room, with its dark paneling, from which the hostile world was excluded, within whose four walls he did not have to prove himself but had only to sit back in order to be surrounded by adulation.

When the piece was over he glanced at his watch. "It's after ten!" He jumped up. "I got to go."

Paul looked woebegone. "You are not staying?"

"No. I've a date. With a girl," he added, as if that legitimized his leaving.

"I was hoping you would stay over," Paul murmured help-lessly.

"I'm sorry, Paul. I can't."

There was a silence. Finally Paul said, "It is not fair, what you do. We made a date for last Sunday. You postponed that, and postponed it again until tonight. When you finally do get here, it turns out you have another engagement." He spoke quietly but very distinctly. "I accept the fact that you do not feel for me what I feel for you. All the same, you should show me more consideration."

Bob let out a sigh. "We've been through this a dozen times. Why? We've had a great evening together, and now I have to leave. What more d'you want?"

"You know very well what I want."

Bob's face tightened. "Do we have to make the scene every time I come? Seems to me you should be interested in me as a person, not just as someone you drag into bed. Don't you see how it cheapens our friendship if you treat me like a sexpot?" He felt himself on solid ground now and became self-righteous. "I'm not not of those boys you used to run around with. "I'm——" He stopped. What precisely was he? "I'm a person. I'm a human being."

"You are the one I want." Paul's deep baritone sounded mournful. "Since you came into my life I no longer want sex that is only sex. Is that so difficult for you to understand?" His gray-blue eyes had lost their steely look; they were sad and beseeching.

Bob relented. "But I do have this date," he said. "What d'you want me to do?"

"Break it. Or postpone it. You do it to me, surely you can do it to your other friends."

"I'll see." Bob went to the telephone and dialed Margo's number. He sensed that Paul suspected him of lying, and welcomed the opportunity to prove that there really was a girl in his life.

"Hi, babe," he said into the mouthpiece. "I got hung up. Could we make it tomorrow night instead?" Margo, it turned out, had had a grueling day and was quite amenable to the change. She tried to prolong the conversation but Bob cut her off. "I'm with people now. Seeya tomorrow. Dinner? Sure. I'll be there at six thirty." He put down the receiver and grinned. "No problem."

Paul relaxed. He went over to Bob, put his hands on the young man's shoulders, and gazed into his eyes. "Thank you," he said gently.

Now that he had rebuffed Paul, Bob was all acceptance. In the darkness he submitted to the older man's caresses even as he had in the little room by the sea, so ardently that one would hardly have suspected he genuinely preferred women. He savored the delight of being made love to, of having someone older, wiser, stronger worship his body, and experienced a pleasure at the climax that almost equaled the intensity of his orgasm with Margo. Then he curled up in the blanket and slept.

Paul, leaning on his elbow, watched him. A great tenderness filled his heart. He would remember this night as he remembered the night by the sea, because all barriers between them had been swept away. For once they had achieved that union of two bodies, minds, and souls of which Plato spoke. Tonight each of them had found his other half. It was moments like these that a man lived for.

5

November twilight flowed into the little kitchen. Margo cut a grapefruit in half, put the bottle of wine in the refrigerator, and chopped up a green pepper and onion. Since this was to be a special night, she was eager that the dinner be exactly right. She had never enjoyed cooking and had spent as little time in the kitchen as possible. Now, to her surprise, she found great pleasure in preparing a meal for Bob. She put two yellow place mats on the small oblong table and brought out two linen napkins. Between the two settings she placed a little vase filled with pink carnations. She listened for his footsteps on the stairs. As usual, he was late.

Sitting quietly, she felt a boundless joy at the thought of the child inside her, a tiny bundle of cells growing, taking shape, becoming eyes and skin and hair, finally to emerge as a living thing perfect in feature and limb. How miraculous was the act of creation, yet so simple that everyone was capable of it, and thereby became like God. She was so absorbed in her thoughts that she did not hear him come up the stairs

He kissed her and sniffed the air. "Mm . . . smells good. I'm starved." He had picked up a record by Ella Fitzgerald in a shop on Third Avenue and was impatient to hear it. While Margo put the finishing touches to their dinner, the dark velvety voice filled the little studio with its lovesick plaint:

> *My mamma don' tol' me when I was in pigtails,*
> *My mamma don' tol' me, "Hon,*
> *A man's gonna sweet talk an' give you the big eye,*
> *But when that sweet talk is done,*
> *A man is a two-face, a worrisome thing*
> *Who'll leave you to sing the blues in the night."*

Trumpets and saxophones moaned in the background; the drums beat a lazily persistent rhythm. When Margo brought in the veal he was sitting with his eyes half shut, head thrown back, his left hand beating a tattoo on the tablecloth as on their first night together in the basement on MacDougal Street. He stopped the record; Ella was too important to be dinner music.

Margo sat down and served. He tasted the meat. "Sensational!" For a few moments he ate in silence, savoring the food; then he looked at her inquisitively. "So—?"

This was an invitation for her to tell him about her day. As she described each event she saw it through his eyes, and it forthwith took on a quality that had been missing before. For dessert there were stewed peaches and cookies. When they finished their coffee Margo washed the dishes while he returned to the record. The drums filled the air with their capricious rhythms, the throaty voice resumed its complaint:

> *"The evening breeze'll start the trees to cryin'*
> *And the moon will hide its light*
> *When you get the blues in the night.*
> *Take my word, the mockingbird'll sing the saddest kind of song.*
> *He knows things are wrong,*
> *And he's right!"*

Bob listened, transported. "She's great!" he called into the kitchen. "She's beautiful."

Margo did not resent his not offering to help with the dishes. If they were married she wouldn't want him in the kitchen. Instead of drying the plates, she placed them upright on a plastic rack and let the water drip.

> *"I been to some big towns, heard me some big talk,*
>   *But there's one thing I know,*
> *That a man is a two-face, a worrisome thing*
>   *Who'll leave you to sing the blues in the night . . ."*

The voice trailed off into its private anguish. Margo removed her apron and joined him in the other room. He sat facing the record player. The long-awaited moment was at hand. She took a deep breath. "Bobby, I have something to tell you." Her heart skipped a beat but her voice remained steady as she heard it say, "I'm going to have a baby."

He wheeled around. "What?" Without thinking he lifted the needle and clicked the turntable to a halt.

"I said I'm going to have a baby."

He jumped up. "You mean—you mean you're pregnant?"

"Yes."

"It can't be!" A look of bewilderment crossed his face. "I gave you those pills to take. What went wrong?"

"Nothing went wrong. I just——" She held out her hands in an entreating gesture.

He tapped his fist against his chin in that tentative way of his. Suddenly he fixed his eyes on hers, and there was an anger in them she had never seen before. "I know," he cried, "you did it on purpose! It was on your mind all the time." His forefinger shot out at her in accusation. "You did it to trap me!"

"No, I did it because I love you." The words came out before she could stop them, and she realized to her horror that she had confessed to what had unaccountably taken on the dimensions of a crime.

"You did it to trap me!" His face went gray, and the wrath in his cat's eyes was streaked with fear. "I told you I won't be pinned down. Not now and not for a long time. I got to stay free, don't you understand? You're not going to have that baby! You can't!"

Her heart sank at the hatred in his face. She wanted to cry out, "Bobby, don't look at me like that!" Instead she stepped back and faced him. "You've no right to tell me that," she said quietly. Her voice trembled, then steadied itself. "I was hoping you'd want to be a father. I thought it might make you grow up and want to be a husband too. But you don't have to do any-thing you don't want to. You owe me nothing, and I've no claim on you." There was a firmness about her now that was as un-yielding as his fury. "I won't take you to court, so you've noth-ing to worry about. But you have no right to tell me I can't have my baby. Nobody's going to take my baby away from me —not you or anybody else."

Bob paced up and down, jabbing his left fist against the palm of his right hand. "I should have known," he muttered. "I should have known you would try something like this. God damn it! You betrayed me, damn you! You tricked me into this."

"Don't, Bobby. Please!" She began to sob. "You've no right to talk to me this way."

"You pull a trick like this," he exploded, "and I've no right? You must be nuts!"

The tears rolled down her face, yet even in her anguish the thought raced through her mind that he was thinking only of himself, "I'm telling you again," she said, "I won't try to hold you. You're free to go. This minute, if you like."

She stared helplessly as before her gaze the golden-haired angel turned into a demon, with his face contorted, eyes glitter-ing, the pupils off center like the eyes of a doll laid on its side. It was as if the tenderness she had come to expect of him had never existed; in its place was a loathing that terrified her. "You tricked me, God damn you!" he raged. "You fuckin' cunt! Cunt!" Suddenly he turned and began to bang his fists against the wall with all his might.

She ran to him. "Don't, Bobby, you'll hurt yourself."

He pushed her away and with a final "God damn you!" rushed out, slamming the door behind him.

Margo collapsed on the couch. Her blurred gaze moved slowly toward the phonograph and came to rest on the record. His parting gift. Her shoulders shook; a convulsive sob broke from her lips.

He trudged aimlessly across Manhattan Bridge. His feet hurt. He stopped to rest, crossing his arms on top of the railing. It felt cold. To his left the sun hung above an endless huddle of Brooklyn roof tops. Southward, the cables of the old bridge crisscrossed in lacy patterns against the light. In the harbor be-yond, the bronze goddess held aloft her torch. The railing vibrated with the hum of a passing train; the air had an early-morning freshness that tickled his nostrils—what he thought of as "the smell of arithmetic examples." This was the hour when he used to start out for school after a breakfast of scrambled eggs and cocoa, his books and ruler under his arm. The streets of his childhood were quiet and sunny. Everything was so simple then. Why couldn't it have remained so? He sighed and, resting his head on the railing, watched the dirty green current below him swirl sluggishly northward. If he had his way life would be one perpetual childhood. It was growing up that caused all the trouble.

There came back to him the bitter taste of Margo's betrayal. He should have guessed her intention. As a matter of fact he had. The night she spoke of Faust and Marguerite he knew at once what was on her mind. Did she really believe he would want to be a father when he wasn't even able to take care of himself? How could she be so stupid? He thought of all the bright young men who had started out with high hopes, only to be saddled with a wife and children before they knew what had happened to them. Trapped for life. He was not going to end like them. He would not let himself be caught.

Why had he clung to her so long? He should have cut out sooner. Just because a fellow enjoyed balling a chick was no reason for him to sign his life away. He picked himself off the railing and continued toward the New York side of the bridge. Far across the bay an ocean liner glided toward the end of its voyage, its white decks veiled in a lavender haze. Directly below him a tugboat moved downstream, trailing a plume of gray smoke. Automobiles crawled along the East River Drive like ants. She looked soft and frail, but within that little body was a will of iron. Once she had made up her mind to have the baby, he'd never be able to talk her out of it. He didn't want to talk to her again, or even see her; the very thought revived his rage. Yet he was tired of hating her—it made his head ache. The trouble with hate was that it destroyed the hater along with the one he hated. But if he didn't talk to her, who would? Who would drive some sense into her head? If his mother were back from her tour . . . No, he could never tell her what had happened. With her strange ideas about life she'd probably insist that he marry Margo at once.

He reached the end of the bridge and walked down the broad

flight of stairs that led into the plaza. When he came to Canal Street he turned to look back at the semicircular row of columns; it was supposed to be a copy of St. Peter's in Rome. The city was getting ready for another day. People were on their way to work, youngsters were carrying schoolbooks under their arms as he had done long ago. Crowds made him uncomfortable— they oppressed him with a sense of his unimportance—yet he loved the city.

He passed a hot-dog stand, realized that he was hungry, and bought a frankfurter. The meat was tasty; he washed it down with orangeade. Beyond was a little square with a playground surrounded by a steel-wire fence. Three benches were drawn up in front of it, freshly painted and empty. He sat down on the first and leaned back against the fence. The sunlight warmed his face; he dozed off. A truck stopped directly before him with a screeching of brakes; he awoke with a start. Who'd put some sense into Margo's head? The answer came, clear and simple. Alice.

He saw a phone booth across the street, went over and looked up her number. He was about to insert the coin but changed his mind. If Walter answered it would be awkward to explain why he was calling so early in the morning. He remembered her telling him, the day they had lunch together, about her class in painting at the New School: three mornings a week at nine. Today was Wednesday. Or was it Tuesday? No, Wednesday. He had left his wrist watch home and asked a passer-by for the time. Twenty after eight. He started out for Twelfth Street, striding purposefully. The prospect of being able to confide in someone heartened him; he no longer felt tired.

He passed a succession of flophouses on the Bowery, their hallways dingy in the bright sunlight. A drunkard lay in a stupor between two ash cans. People walked past, glanced at him, and went on; no one cared whether he was alive or dead. That was New York for you. Cooper Union looked quaintly old-fashioned against the new buildings that were going up around it. He cut across to Washington Square; the park looked bright and fresh even though the leaves were beginning to turn. He remembered the walk with Margo that first night. What fun they had had! If he could have foreseen what lay ahead, how quickly he'd have turned back.

He reached the New School and stood near the curb opposite

the glass door, watching people go in. Presently he caught sight of Alice coming down the street. She was hatless; her white hair framed her face. She was walking briskly, swinging her bag as if she enjoyed it.

She stopped in surprise when she saw him. "Bob! What are you doing here?"

"Waiting for you."

"Oh?" She gave him a searching look.

"I'd like to talk to you. That is, if you have time."

"Of course I have."

"I mean," he tapped his chin with his fist, "I could see you after class if it's more convenient."

"The class can wait."

They walked to Sixth Avenue. "Shall we go back to Schrafft's?" she asked.

"It's too far. This'll do." He pointed to a coffee shop on the corner; there was an empty booth near the window. They went in.

"You've been up all night."

"Yes."

"Then you'd better have breakfast. What would you like?"

"Scrambled eggs and cocoa. I saw the kids on their way to school and remembered, that's what I used to have in the morning."

She glanced at the menu. "They don't have cocoa. Will hot chocolate do?"

He nodded. She gave the order, adding a cup of coffee for herself.

"You see, it's like this . . ." He stopped, wondering how to begin. Then the words came tumbling out as he told her about Margo and himself.

Her face was sad when he finished. "Poor girl," she murmured.

"You don't understand. I can't marry her. I can't!"

"Why?"

"For any number of reasons. Mainly because I don't want to. I don't love her."

"Why did you hang on so long?"

"She was sweet and giving—it's pleasant to be loved. Someone feeds you, waits on you hand and foot, thinks about you all the time. It's very flattering. The catch is, nobody gives you anything for nothing. What they want in return is you—all of you, past, present, future—and there's no trick they won't use to gain their end. Love is the greatest con game in the world."

She smiled, although her face remained sad. "That's one way of looking at it. Maybe five years from now you will have found another."

"She didn't have to get pregnant," he said morosely. "We could have gone on and on if only she hadn't. She did it on purpose. To get me where she wanted me. Is that love?"

"Yes, that's love."

"You see it from her point of view."

"I'm a woman. How else would you expect me to see it?"

"But I need your help. You've got to talk to her. You've got to explain to her that it won't work. If I married her, I'd hate her, and I'd hate the child too. There's too much I have to learn. I mustn't be chained yet. To anyone. I need time; I need my freedom. I'd never forgive her for taking it away from me, and I'd never forgive myself for letting her."

"In the old days she'd go home and tell her father. He'd come after you with a shotgun and lead you to the altar."

"And we'd live in hate forever after. Fat lot of good that would do. By the way, you won't tell your husband. It'll upset him, and it might hurt her career."

"This is the first time you've thought of her end of it."

"You think I'm selfish. Go on, say it."

"Don't ask me to sit in judgment on you. You have to judge yourself."

He pondered that. "This is the best I can do now," he brought out softly. "I've got to accept myself as I am."

"If people did that, how would they ever get better?"

"Maybe they don't. Maybe they only think they do. Anyway, that's their problem. Mine is to see to it that Margo gets some sense into her head." He was thoughtful. "It was a beautiful thing we had."

"You speak of it in the past tense."

"Because it's over. There's no use playing games."

"But you're letting love slip away from you."

"Is that so terrible?"

"Yes."

"I can't love now. Maybe someday I'll be able to." His face came forward, tense. "Will you help me? Will you talk to her?" There was fear in his voice that she might not.

"Can't you?"

"No. I don't want to see her any more. It's no use." He studied Alice's face, serene in its sorrow as if she had long ago resigned herself to whatever troubled her.

"I do want to help you, Bob, believe me. But I don't know her very well. How can I suddenly barge into her life? Yet I'm involved in all this because of Walter. He's terribly concerned about her—she's like a daughter to him." Alice thought a moment and sighed. "Yes, I'll talk to her."

Bob looked relieved. "You'll know what to say?"

"I'll know." She called for the check and paid. When they came out she said, "Go home and get some sleep."

"I will." He took her hand. "I feel a lot better now. Thanks to you." He kissed her on the cheek and walked swiftly away.

Alice looked after him. Without being aware of it she raised her hand to the spot where his lips had touched her face; her eyes filled. He reached the opposite side of Sixth Avenue, turned around and waved.

When he got home he dropped onto his bed without taking off his clothes. But he was overtired and could not sleep. His nerves were taut; he had the sensation of something crawling up his back. How could he be exhausted and alert at the same time? The anxiety that held him in its grip was all the more frightening in that he did not know what he was anxious about. When he could bear the tension no longer he got up, opened the top drawer of the dresser, drew out the yellow envelope, and took from it four of the green and black pills. He swallowed them one after the other and lay down again.

The sharp edges gradually blurred; the clamp of fear around his forehead loosened its grip and dissolved in a pink-gray haze. He hated no one, neither Margo nor himself, and he blamed no one. Out of the blur swam two lips, soft and inviting. He thrust his forefinger between them; abruptly they turned in a half circle to a vertical position like a screw being tightened. He tried to withdraw his finger; the lips opened, disclosing two rows of teeth. He could not free his finger, the harder he pulled the tighter their grip. With a tremendous effort he yanked his hand away, leaving his finger between the teeth. To his amazement he felt no pain; his arms and legs detached themselves from his body and floated off into the distance like balloons, then his head and legs and trunk, all floating lazily into the pink-gray void. He looked down from a great distance and saw that the earth resembled a big red apple, opened up as if a knife had sliced it down the middle, and at its core was a worm, a long, thin, pink worm with an ugly head that turned this way and that. He looked away so as not to have to see it. But he knew— he knew it was there.

6

Alice leaned forward in her chair. "It was the shock, Margo, that upset him." From where she sat she could see that the kitchenette was bright with sunlight. For some reason this made her task more difficult. "You've got to realize he's not able to face up to it."

"But he's responsible, isn't he? It's his baby the same as mine." The hurt look on her dark, thin face accentuated its childlike quality.

"Of course. But he feels that it's your fault because you made yourself pregnant. Is that true?"

Her mouth tightened as though she would keep it from answering. Then, softly, "Yes. I love him and I thought——" She stopped. "It doesn't matter what I thought. I was mistaken. But he needn't worry, I'm not holding him to anything."

"Then what do you intend to do?"

"I'll have my baby, and I won't ask him or anyone else for anything."

"My dear child, I don't think you've thought it through. Having the baby is only the first step. Then what?"

"Then I'll do my best for it." She spoke decisively, as if trying to convince herself. "Who knows? Maybe when he sees it he'll change his mind."

"You're thinking only of yourself and him. What about the child? How will you support it?"

"I'll work."

"And what about your career?"

Margo stared before her, the furrows deepening between her brows. "Maybe that's not so important any more. Maybe there are other things in life."

"Margo, please listen to me. You've worked too hard, you've come too far to give up now."

Margo looked up. "Tell me, what would you do in my place?"

"That's an unfair question. We're so different, you and I, how can I advise you? If you were an ordinary girl I might say 'Go ahead and have your baby.' It's possible these days for an unwed mother to make her way. But you're not an ordinary girl. You stand at the beginning of a great career. You have an obligation to your talent, and you mustn't let anything interfere with it."

The white face turned sullen. "What are you trying to tell me?"

"As far as I can see you have three choices. You can have the baby and bring it up as best you can. But that might mean sacrificing your career. Or you could give it away for adoption. Which means you'd never see it again."

"I want my baby! Nobody's going to take it away from me."

There was a silence. Finally Margo said, "What's the third?"

"You know."

"You mean, not to have it."

"Yes."

"I want my baby," Margo repeated in a dull voice.

It came to Alice that once before she had heard this kind of incantation, in which words lost their meaning because of the fixed idea behind them. Long ago. When Gene was eleven she bought him an elaborate electric train. That week he came down with the flu and in his fever kept repeating, in the same expressionless voice as Margo had just used, "I want my train, I want my train." She crossed over to the day bed and, sitting down beside Margo, took her hand. "You want the baby because you think it'll bring him back to you. It won't. You miscalculated once already. Now you're miscalculating again."

"What makes you so sure?"

"I'm not sure. But from the way he spoke to me, from the kind of person he is, I think the baby won't bring him back to you. Doing what you've done won't make him grow up; it only fills him with panic. And hate. I'm being frank with you, my child, because I don't want you to make the wrong move."

Margo seemed to be making an effort to be reasonable. "I've got to talk to him," she finally said.

"Have you tried?"

"Yes. I phoned him three times yesterday. He hung up."

"Margo, there's something more I have to say. It's terribly unfair of me to barge into your life like this giving advice you never asked for. But there is someone who has the right to advise you, and that's your mother. I'd feel so much better if you were home with your parents. That's where you belong at a time like this."

A look of horror came into Margo's eyes. "Oh, no! They must never know!"

"They love you. They'd understand."

"I could never do that to them. Never!" Her lips pressed together in a firm line. "Let's not even talk about it."

"Then you must decide for yourself." Alice held out her hands helplessly. "But how can you decide when you're so wrought-up? How can you realize that someday you're going to feel differently about him?"

"You don't know how I feel about him!" Margo's intensity startled the older woman. "I shall always love him. Always!"

"There is no *always*. We grow older, we change, and our love changes too. It may die, or turn elsewhere. There will come a time when he won't mean a thing to you."

"I don't believe it."

"Believe me, the fever passes."

Margo remembered that she, too, in her mind had compared love to an illness. "What if it destroys the patient?"

"That's why I'm pleading with you . . . not to let it destroy you. You're about to make a decision that'll affect your whole future. You've got to make it not in terms of what you are now, but of what you'll be five, ten years from now. Please try!"

Without warning the little oval face went to pieces. "I can't go on without him," she sobbed. "I can't." She bent forward, elbows on her knees, and buried her face in her hands.

"Sh, my child . . ." Alice took Margo in her arms and drew the girl's head down until it rested on her shoulder. She remembered the night of the party when she wanted to tell her to forget New York and go home. To free herself from the rat race while there was still time. Now it was too late. She stroked Margo's hair. "There, there," she murmured, repeating the words over and over like a lullaby.

The street was deserted. Margo walked up and down, stopping now and again to look behind her so that she would see him whether he came from Lexington Avenue or Park. The street lamp threw its glow on the black door of Judith's house, imparting to it a delicate sheen. By the curb a young tree lifted its puny trunk within the iron bars of its cage.

It was a little after eleven; she had been there since ten. She paused to rest before the adjoining brownstone, which had retained its old-fashioned staircase in front. Her heart jumped as she caught sight of him turning the corner. He was not alone.

She drew back into the shadow of the stoop. The two men came closer. Presently Bob moved into the glow of the lamp, and she recognized his companion—Paul Horvath. Bob was hatless; he was listening to what Paul was saying and broke into a laugh. How could he be so carefree, Margo wondered, when she was so miserable?

They said good night; Paul walked off toward Park Avenue as Bob entered the house. Margo hurried in behind him. When she came into the vestibule he was standing in front of the letterbox, keys in hand.

"Bobby!"

He turned, startled. "What are you doing here?"

"I had to see you."

There was a silence. Then, "Margo, you still don't understand," he said. "We've nothing more to talk about. If you and I had a quarrel I'd say, 'Let's talk it over.' But this is no quarrel. This is——" He paused, searching for the right word, "—the end."

"Don't say that, Bobby!" It was the look in his eyes that frightened her—a look from which all pity, all affection for her had fled. "It's not fair, what you're doing," she faltered. "We meant so much to each other. Suddenly it's over—just like that!"

"Just like that? Is that what you said?" He turned from her, addressing the letterbox. "She lives with me, she talks to me, she says she loves me, and all the time she hasn't the foggiest notion where I'm at. Christ, how can anyone be so stupid?" He looked at her coldly. "You don't know me at all. You were in love with someone who existed inside your own head and didn't resemble me in the least. Is that my fault or yours?" He inserted his key in the hall door.

She rushed forward and put her hand on his arm. "Bobby, please don't leave me like this. You're being so cruel I can't believe it's you. I know you're angry with me. Maybe you have a right to be—I can't judge. But try to remember, whatever I did, I did out of love. I swear to you!"

He turned back from the door and faced her. "You're forcing me to be cruel. Maybe that's what's bugging me." Suddenly his voice was quiet. "What Alice told you is true. I don't want the baby, I'm not ready to be tied down, and I don't want to go on as we were. If I told you anything else I'd be lying to you, and that would be the cruelest of all."

He was so cool, so outside it all. She gazed at him with torment in her eyes and began to cry.

"Tears won't change anything," he said. "You, being the person you are, had to play it the way you did. But the same goes for me. I can't be someone I'm not, so I'm giving it to you straight. Absolutely straight!"

Margo did not know which was more terrifying, his earlier anger or his present calm. In the face of this cold hostility what could she say? She withdrew her hand from his arm and looked at him in blank despair.

He was about to say something but changed his mind, stepped into the hallway, and let go the knob. The door swung closed, the latch slid into place with a click.

Margo turned and went out. She stopped in front of the next house, leaned against the balustrade of the brownstone stairs, then sank down on the lowest step. Her throat was dry, the strength drained from her body. Remembering the look in his eyes she knew, with a certainty that left no room for self-deception, what decision she must make. She had no right to bear his child.

A taxi passed. A gust of wind tossed the leaves that remained on the thin little tree by the curb. Three fell off and scraped their way fitfully across the sidewalk. She sat slumped over, staring vacantly before her. Lost.

7

The doorbell rang. Paul looked up in surprise; his friends knew that his mornings were devoted to work and never intruded. He crossed the room and opened the door. "Bob!" He was about to say, "What brought you here?" but changed it to, "What brought you out so early?"

"I—I was passing by."

"Come in."

Bob took off his short tan raincoat and dropped it on the armchair by the window. Then he gazed at the rug as though it were a matter of life and death for him to study its pattern.

Paul waited for the young man to speak, but Bob kept his eyes glued to the floor. "What is on your mind?" he finally asked.

Bob looked up, hesitant. His face betrayed his embarrassment. "I don't quite know how to say it. I hate to ask for favors, especially from you, but there's no one else I can turn to."

"What is it? Money?"

Bob nodded. "It's not for me—it's for a girl. I got her pregnant and she needs an operation."

"Oh." Paul gave the young man a quizzical look. "How much do you need?"

Bob thought that the abortion would cost around five hundred, but he was not sure. "Could you let me have six hundred?"

"Of course. But what if you made a girl pregnant every month? That would be something of a strain."

"Don't worry," Bob scowled. "It won't happen again."

"I'll give you a check." Paul went over to his desk, pleased that Bob had turned to him for help.

"Where can I cash it?"

"Anywhere. Have you a bank account?"

"No."

"Stop at my bank, around the corner." He handed Bob the check.

The young man took his coat. "I appreciate this, I really do." He brought his fist against his chin. "And it's a loan, Paul. I'll pay it back when I can."

"Don't worry about it. When will I see you?"

"When would you like to?"

"Tonight, after the concert."

Ordinarily Bob would have pleaded a previous engagement and postponed their meeting for a day or two. Instead he said, "Great. I'll be here at eleven thirty."

Paul was delighted at this response. Money, he felt, invariably complicated human relationships. For once it appeared to have had the opposite effect.

By noon Bob, with six crisp hundred-dollar bills in his pocket, was waiting for Alice to come from her class. She appeared with another woman whom she left when she caught sight of him. "Anything new?" she asked.

"I brought you some money for the——" He stopped, shying away from the word. "For Margo." He dug into his pocket and brought out the bills.

She glanced at them. Without knowing why, she wanted him to keep the money. Yet she was afraid that if she offered him the entire sum he would refuse it. She compromised. "I'll tell you what, we'll share it. Give me two hundred and hold on to the rest. You may need it."

"Why should you?"

"Well, Walter would have taken care of it if he knew. So——"

"It don't seem right."

"Take my advice." She took two of the bills and pushed his hand away.

He looked at the money. "I shouldn't have got you involved in this."

"Why? I'm glad you came to me."

"All the trouble I'm giving you."

She smiled. "Maybe I enjoy helping you."

He looked at her as if he saw her for the first time. "Really?"

"Really. Put the money away."

He obeyed. "Frankly, it never occurred to me." He thought a moment. "You're very kind."

Her face lit up. "I'm like most people. I can be kind in one situation, indifferent in another, perhaps cruel in a third. So it's very nice when someone comes along who gives me a chance to be kind. Maybe I'm the one who should be thanking you."

"I'm very lucky," he murmured. Abruptly the expression on his face changed; he looked tense and unhappy.

"Is there something else?" Alice asked.

"Yes. When you . . . when you go with Margo, I'm not coming."

"Why?"

"I can't."

"I think you should."

"I know, but I'm not going to."

She found it extraordinarily difficult to chide him. "Are you being fair?" she asked.

"No. But that's how it has to be."

"Then there's no point discussing it."

"You think I'm awfully selfish, don't you?"

"I've already told you, Bob, you mustn't ask me to judge you. Someday you'll see this thing differently and you may be sorry for the way you handled it, but you'll have to come to that yourself. It would help her very much if you went with us, and I think it's your duty. But no one can force you if you don't want to."

His face was sullen. "This is my problem and I have to handle it my way. Please try to understand."

"I'll try."

When he left Alice, Bob was confronted by a moral issue. Now that she was helping him pay for the abortion he ought to return the rest of the money to Paul. Yet the more he considered the matter, the more reasons he found for keeping the gift. He was forever going beyond his allowance; it would be good to have something to fall back on. Besides, Paul would never miss the money, nor need he ever know that it had not been used as he thought it would be. By the time he reached home Bob had overcome his scruples. The four bills found their way into the top drawer of the chest in his room.

Margo was ready when Alice came into the living room on Twenty-second Street. She sat upright on the sofa, in a navy-blue dress with a pink scarf tied around her neck. She was pale and quiet, her face set, her eyes red. Alice thought of a lamb being led to slaughter, and wanted to cry.

They were due at the doctor's at three o'clock. Alice sat down beside Margo and took her hand. "My child, you mustn't be afraid. You have a fine doctor; there's nothing for you to worry about."

"I'm not worried," Margo said listlessly. "I don't care what happens to me."

"Margo, you'll get over this terrible thing, and you'll begin to care all over again."

"No. Nothing'll ever be the same."

"Try not to think like that. No one can help you if you don't try to help yourself." These were the sterile phrases that had been repeated to her after Gene's death. They had not done her the slightest good yet here she was, passing them on to Margo.

The girl stared into space. "Do you know what it means to lose someone you love?"

"I do."

"Do you know what it means to lose a child?"

"I do."

"Then how can you tell me everything'll be the same again?"

Taking Margo by the shoulders, Alice turned her around so that they faced each other. "Many years ago I went through a terrible time. I felt I couldn't go on, the same as you. But I came through it and I'm glad I did. You'll come through too, and you'll be a better person for it."

"Why? Suffering makes you hate the world," Margo said bitterly. "Why should it make you a better person?"

"I don't know, but it does. And it'll make you a better artist too. When you'll sing of love and sorrow you'll know what you're singing about."

"I'll never sing again."

"Don't say that! The only thing that'll pull you through is your work. You must get back to it as soon as possible. You must say this to yourself every day, over and over until it sinks in." Alice put her hand under Margo's chin, lifting her head until their eyes met. "But before you start working again you ought to spend some time with your family. You can tell them you're run down and need a rest." In urging this was she thinking of Margo, Alice wondered, or herself? Was this responsibility greater than she could bear? "At a time like this you should be near your mother. She'll help you through the next weeks."

"Is he coming with us?"

"No."

Margo dropped her hands in her lap and kept looking at them. "How can he be like this? Doesn't he feel anything?"

"He's afraid; he feels guilty. He can't face it."

"Why d'you defend him?"

"I'm not defending him," Alice replied quickly. "I'm only trying to understand him." As she said this she became aware of the weakness of her position. By rights, her sympathy should have gone to Margo, yet it was the young man she was involved with rather than the girl. Was this why she was unable to judge him as severely as she should? She was trying her best for Margo, but with Bob she didn't have to try. She had only to lay eyes on him—no, only to think of him—and her heart melted. He was certainly not the kind of young man she would have wanted a son of hers to be; indeed, he was everything against which her middle-class outlook should have fortified her. Yet from the moment he had appealed to her for help she had found herself thinking about him and waiting for their next encounter. What she did for Margo was really done for his sake, but what she gave Bob was given spontaneously, for the joy of giving. She was grateful for the chance that had brought him into her life. He had reawakened something in her that she had thought was dead, something that she must never lose again. Of all who had crossed her path over the years, he was the one who had wrought this miracle. How, then, could she judge him by the standards she ordinarily applied to people? Even when he refused to accompany Margo to the doctor, even then she tried to understand—and forgave him.

It was time to go. "Dress warmly," she said, "it's raw outside." In helping Margo, she was thinking also of Walter. "You mean very much to my husband," she said as they went down the stairs.

Margo stopped, looking up over her shoulder. "He must never know about this."

"Of course not! But he wants terribly to be proud of you. Please try to remember this."

They came to the foot of the stairs. "I may be dead in two hours," Margo said quietly.

Alice put her arm around the girl's waist. "I told you, you've nothing to worry about."

The taxi went southward through the muted light of a gray November afternoon. "It's like in opera," Margo said. "When the heroine is unhappy, it rains." They came to the arch at Washington Square and turned west. "The night I met him, at your house, we came down here. To a place in the Village. He was happy listening to that awful music. All I got was a headache, but I couldn't tell him that. Funny, I've never liked jazz. The trees were bare then, like now, but everything looked so beautiful." She leaned her head against Alice's shoulder. "He should have come with us," she said, half to herself. "He would have, if he had a heart."

They alighted at the corner of MacDougal and Fourth Street. Taking Margo by the arm, Alice guided her toward one of the neat wooden houses, relics of another age, that abound in the Village. She rang the bell; they passed through a dark vestibule into a narrow hallway that led into the waiting room. The woman who greeted them had a large bosom. "Make yourself comfortable, honey," she said in the cordial tone of a hat saleslady. "Doctor'll see you in a minute." Alice assumed that she was the nurse even though she was not in white.

An old-fashioned tin sink stood in one corner of the room. It had a tarnished yellow faucet above which a huge fly, lone survivor of the summer, crawled gingerly across the wall. The doctor came in, a short man with a businesslike air. "How d'you feel?" he asked Margo, and without waiting for an answer turned on his heel. "Won't you come in?"

Margo glanced at Alice, who patted her on the shoulder. She bit her lip, rose, and followed the doctor into the inner room.

Bob sat in his room reading Camus's *The Stranger*. He glanced at his watch. Twenty to five. It would be happening now. He drummed his fist against the arm of his chair. There was that girl he had read about in the paper who died during an abortion; the doctor cut her body into pieces and stuffed them down the drain. If anything happened to Margo he would be the guilty one. Not legally, but that didn't change the fact. He would have caused the death of someone who loved him and would have to live with the knowledge for the rest of his life, the knowledge that he was a murderer. He felt like a murderer in any case. Had he not killed their love? Yet what else could he have done? Allowed her to hang on to him? Encouraged her to go on hoping? There were times when to be cruel was the only kindness.

All the same, he might have gone with them; he had behaved like a creep and felt ashamed. He tried to go back to his reading but found it impossible to concentrate. What if something went wrong? There was no point in telephoning her, she would not be home yet. He saw her lying on her back, naked; her arms and legs were severed, only the torso remained. *Girl found dead in doctor's office. Concert pianist's son implicated.* The breath went out of his body; he could bear the tension no longer. He threw on his coat, rushed out, and took a cab to Twenty-second Street. Traffic was heavy, he sat clasping and unclasping his hands as the green and red lights pierced the gathering dusk. Finally the taxi stopped at the familiar corner. He hurried down the block until he came to her house. Her window was dark; he crossed the street and began to pace up and down.

It was almost half past five; they should have been back. His anxiety grew, lending credence to his wildest fears. People were returning from work. A garbage truck made its way down the street; there was a clatter of ash cans. Boys were playing in front of the house next to Margo's; one of them hurled a ball against the stoop, which the others caught on the rebound with much shouting. The neon sign on the corner began its nightly gyrations. A taxi turned in from First Avenue. His heart beat violently; he walked quickly in the other direction so as not to be seen. When he glanced back Alice was helping Margo out of the cab. They went into the house.

Bob drew a sigh of relief and retraced his steps. He decided to wait for Alice and, finding himself near a grocery, sat down on a wooden crate in front of the store. The light went on in Margo's apartment. It had grown dark; the street lamps were lit. Presently Alice appeared in the doorway and crossed the street on a diagonal toward the grocery. She stopped short when she saw him.

He jumped up. "How is she?"

"So-so. She'll be all right."

"I got worried, so I thought I'd . . ." He stopped and began again. "I was wrong, I should've come with you. My imagination ran away with me, I was sure something terrible had happened."

"Would you like to see her?"

He shook his head. "What for? When you're finished with something you should make a clean break. Isn't that the best way?"

Alice sighed. "Who can say what's best?"

The boys had ceased their game, the hush of early evening settled on the street. "I want to thank you," he said, "for all you've done. I'd have gone to pieces if you hadn't come to my rescue. And I want to thank you especially because you did it for me, not for her."

She looked at him in surprise. "How d'you know?"

"I know."

Alice took his hand. She felt a twinge of guilt. Although she did not approve of him, she loved him almost as much as if he were her own.

four

1

Like all romantics, Paul ascribed magical powers to love. During the years when he was searching for it he told himself that if he ever found it again he would make it the focal point of his life. It seemed to him that when a man fell in love he ceased to be simply one of the millions of creatures on earth; he became unique, because there was someone among all those millions to whom he could relate every facet of his existence. This was the miracle of love, that it set apart the lover and his beloved, enclosing them in a oneness from which all others were excluded.

That autumn was illumined for him by the hours he spent with his idol; his life took on a new dimension. As he came out to conduct a concert he felt a special excitement because he knew that Bob was in the audience. He was even less attracted than formerly to the after-concert receptions and parties that studded the musical season, and accepted as few invitations as possible. It was infinitely more pleasant to return to his hotel, where Bob presently joined him.

When things went well between them they spent idyllic evenings together. Bob would be eager and giving; the older man, unwinding from the tension of his public career, would bask in the younger one's admiration and succumb anew to his charm. Unfortunately, things did not always go well. If finding someone to love solved certain problems for Paul, it created others. He had always known that love would bring out the best in him; it also brought out the worst. The very qualities that made him a great conductor—his need to dominate, to lead—made him a trying lover; he had to possess Bob, to govern his every act and thought. This required a submissiveness of which the young man was not capable. When they met at night Paul had to know everything his friend had done during the day. His curiosity extended beyond the boundaries of their friendship, taking in all that had happened to Bob since his childhood. Partly this interest was flattering, and stimulated Bob to remember details of his early years that he seemingly had long since forgotten; but it was also trying, since it forced him to reveal more of himself than he cared to. In either case he found himself in the grip of a powerful personality whose insatiable need to conquer brooked no opposition.

Paul was especially curious about all that concerned the young man's sexuality; his avidity for details was as great as Bob's reticence. He insisted upon knowing, to Bob's embarrassment, about each of his experiences, especially the early ones; when, where, with whom, how often. There was not much to tell. Bob's discovery of sex had been painfully tentative. The admiration his good looks aroused, instead of feeding his confidence, had somehow undermined it, so that he was incapable of taking the initiative; the best he could do was to leave himself open to seduction by anyone sufficiently interested to attempt it. Each of his adventures had then fed the erotic fantasies of his solitude, which both during his adolescence and later had constituted the greater part of his experience. His affair with Margo had marked a new phase in his development —for the first time in his life he had had the courage to assert himself. But of this experience he was determined to reveal nothing to his admirer. After a time, to conceal his shyness, he began to invent lecherous episodes designed to titillate Paul's appetite, and noticed that the more wildly improbable these were, the more eagerly Paul swallowed them. Bob was amazed to discover that the art of fiction was so much simpler than he had supposed.

The attention to detail characteristic of Paul's conducting manifested itself in every aspect of the man. With a persistence that maddened his young friend he tried to impose his own meticulousness upon a temperament which was alien to it. Instead of accustoming himself to Bob's chronic lateness, he never failed to be infuriated by it; or if Bob promised to perform an errand for him—to pick up a score or a book—and forgot, the result was an explosion of the first magnitude. It puzzled Bob that such trifles should be blown up into important issues and transformed into irrefutable evidence of his lack of character. Paul, it came to him, was assuming the overly critical role that his mother had played in his life; he resented it in the one as much as in the other. "You're becoming more and more like her," he would tell him. "What a drag!"

Behind Paul's tantrums was a desperate desire that the young man share his own involvement. The knowledge that Bob was incapable of this filled him with an anguish that all too easily transformed itself into rage. Thus, in his fear of losing Bob, he was driven by some perverse impulse to bring about the very thing he feared. After each of his outbursts Bob would disappear for a time; then would begin a frantic effort to lure the young man back. At the end of a sleepless night he would humble himself and pour out his heart in an abject letter. "My darling boy, please forgive me. Please come back to me. If you knew how deeply I love you, you would understand why I behave as I do. I should have pride and not tell you these things, but true love has no pride since its only pride is in loving. Have you ever read Beethoven's letters to his nephew? Where he writes, 'Only come to my arms, you will hear no harsh word. If you do not come you will surely kill me.' What more can I say? Only come to the loving heart of your faithful . . . Paul."

The nature of his work rendered him singularly vulnerable to emotional upheaval. As he explained to Bob again and again, if he were a doctor or lawyer he would have an office to go to and would spend his time with people, which would distract him and enable him to function no matter what his frame of mind. But, except for rehearsals, he was cloistered in his apartment for most of the day, studying the scores he was to conduct—he needed solitude for his work. But of what value was solitude if he lacked peace of mind? How could he concentrate on music if his thoughts kept reverting to an upsetting episode of the night before? His avoidance of emotional entanglements had been, indeed, a protective device; it had left him free to pursue his career with the utmost singleness of purpose. Now that he had surrendered to love he was acutely conscious of the threat this posed to his art, and kept imploring Bob not to do anything that would disturb him. Unfortunately, he had only one defense against his morbid vulnerability: he forestalled the hurt by inflicting it first. "If only I had as much talent for love," he ruefully told Bob, "as I have for music." To which Bob, with sudden insight, replied, "Know why you don't? Because your need for music is simple and straightforward, but when it comes to love you reach for it with one hand and push it away with the other."

Given these conditions, quarrels between them were as inevitable as lightning on a sultry day. If Bob allowed himself to be lured back after each flare-up it was because of his genuine admiration for the artist and the man. He recognized in Paul's character a dynamic force that was the antidote for his own irresolution. When they were together he felt himself surrounded not only by love but by strength. The reassurance that he derived from the older man was enhanced by the fact that he saw him as a symbol of power; Paul had achieved the fame and success he was quite certain he would never attain. He did not know enough about music to be able to judge the fine points of Paul's conducting, but he knew that he was in the presence of an artist and could not but hold on to a friendship that brought him into intimate contact with so distinguished a mind. True, he was terrified by Paul's outbursts and after each one vowed never to subject himself to another. But when peace was restored between them he forgot his vow as a child might. More accurately, he let the memory slip beneath the surface of his mind, to lie dormant until it would be reawakened—with accumulating bitterness—by the next crisis.

At the concerts he watched with fascination as the thin, ascetic-looking man in tails walked to the podium and curtly acknowledged the burst of applause that greeted him. The famous hands floated through the air. Bob followed the intense but subtly controlled gestures with which Paul put the orchestra through its paces. As when he had seen Margo on stage, he found it difficult to reconcile the public aspect of the artist with the private image of his friend; the authoritative figure on the podium bore no relation to the man who loved him. In the greenroom he stood in line with all the others who waited to shake the maestro's hand. Presently he made his way to the hotel. Another Paul was there to greet him, wearing the battered dressing gown with the maroon satin collar. The applause and the glitter were left behind as they withdrew into their private world. Bob was always surprised at the transformation.

Supper arrived. Since Paul did not eat before a performance, this was a full meal. Paul served his guest, heaping generous portions onto the young man's plate. "I like to watch you eat," he would tell Bob. Unlike Judith and the other artists of Walter Stern's circle, he had no need to discuss either himself or his concerts. If he mentioned them at all it was only to illustrate a point. Much more he wanted to know what Bob had done, thought, felt that day. His attitude shifted with his moods. Sometimes he spoke to Bob as to a learned colleague, sometimes as to a beloved son or trusted friend.

Whichever it was, within those four walls Bob felt protected. With unconscious coquetry he showed off before his admirer as a little boy might exhibit himself before a doting parent; he spoke with a confidence that he never achieved with others. One night, to Paul's delight, he held forth on his latest discovery —Proust. "I tried to read him again and again but those long sentences hung me up. I guess I must have dipped into *Swann's Way* a dozen times but never got anywhere. Then, about a month ago, I opened the book. I can't explain it——" He tapped his chin with his fist, looking mystified. "It was like a door opening. All of a sudden I was with it. The scene where the kid waits for his mother at the top of the stairs. Beautiful!" The catlike eyes lit up. "I discovered the trick of reading him. You have to keep going to the end of the sentence without letting yourself be turned off by all those asides. Straight through —bzzzzzzzzzzz." He thrust his hand through the air while he imitated the sound of a buzz saw. "Then you start the next sentence and do the same."

"You're forgetting to eat. It'll get cold."

The words tumbled from Bob's lips as, along with Paul, he succumbed to the sound of his voice. "The book is on two levels.

On one he's doing a satire of French high society, with a keen eye for all its pretensions. On the other he's describing his notion of love. He sees love as a delusion, because the one you love never loves you in the same way. That's why he's able to put his finger on the greatest fallacy of all. People fall in love to escape their loneliness; then they discover they're just as lonely."

"Eat, little one," Paul commanded. Bob smiled and obeyed.

Yet no matter how close they came to one another, the issue of sex remained unresolved between them—the older man's insistence rose in direct proportion to the younger one's reluctance. Paul's desire was nourished by the innermost forces of a volcanic temperament. He desperately needed the reassurance, the glow of possession which only physical intimacy could give him. Bob on the other hand approached the physical aspect of their relationship with increasing misgiving; it was the price he had to pay for the friendship, and he preferred to pay less rather than more. Inevitably the moment came when Paul tried to get him to bed while he tried to steer Paul to the door. He had an assortment of excuses to placate the older man: he was tired, he had to get up early the next morning, he had spent the night before with a girl. At this point, however, the most fervent protestations of friendship could not hide the fact that, whichever of them won, the other lost.

Thus they continued from week to week, their relationship surviving in the same way as a chemical solution in which the forces driving the molecules apart are precisely balanced by those holding them together. After each crisis Paul was persuaded that they had finally reached an understanding and would never quarrel again; he continued to believe this even though the next crisis would prove him woefully wrong. He conceived of friendship as a continuity—issues once settled ought never to raise their heads again!—and he clung to this illusion even though Bob and he seemed again and again to be starting from the beginning. Why, he asked himself, did they waste so much of their energy going around in circles when they could be moving forward to better things? Why, indeed?

2

Margo walked along the deserted paths overlooking the Hudson. The earth was bare and brown, preparing for winter; the low hills lay supine beneath a glowering sky. She faced a landscape from which all color and joy had fled. Abruptly her life had fallen apart, and she had neither the strength nor the will to put it together again.

It should have helped her to be with her parents and sister. Yet despite the love with which they surrounded her, their presence only intensified her grief. She was enough of an actress to fool them; she chatted, she smiled, she seemed to be her old self. But she realized with something akin to terror that she could never again return to the life she had shared with them. She had come back to her roots to find herself a stranger. Where, then, did she belong?

Her father was foreman in one of the local factories and kept his family in a reasonable degree of comfort. The kitchen was spotless and filled with things she remembered from her childhood. The flower boxes in the windows. The cream pitcher shaped like a strawberry. The ornamental plate that showed a windmill and a rosy-cheeked boy who wore wooden shoes and ate an apple. As she listened to her mother's small talk it seemed to Margo that if she could only confess her sins they would weigh less heavily upon her. But she would sooner have died. What would her parents do, she wondered, if they knew the truth? Would they throw her out, telling her never to return? Even if they did not, they would look upon her with different eyes; they would never love her again.

For them she was the gifted one who had been chosen to set the world on fire. How could she confess to them that the Margo from whom they expected so much was no more? It seemed to her that she could never again recapture the hope with which she had set out. Had so shattering a blow fallen later, after she had made a name for herself, she would have been able to withstand it. But it had caught her just as she was spreading her wings, when she was most vulnerable. She was scarred forever,

as some people were by smallpox, only there was no cure for
her illness.

How could this terrible thing have happened to her? Why?
Endlessly she asked the question, and found no answer. Her
mistake had been not to see him as he was, to attribute to
him qualities he did not begin to possess. But didn't people
usually idealize the one they loved? Was not this an essential
part of loving? Life, she realized, was no less cruel than
Bob. What room, then, could there be in it for someone as open
to hurt as herself? She sat by the pond where she had gone
swimming as a child and brooded on her wrongs, feeling utterly
alone.

On Sunday the sound of church bells floated through the air;
she accompanied her parents to the Lutheran church where
she had sung in public for the first time. Everyone remembered
her and treated her with the deference due a celebrity. "Gee,
Marge, it's been a long time," they said. "Guess we'll be hearing
you on TV one o' these days." Most of the girls with whom she
had gone to school were married; they would never know how
she envied them. Their way of life was untouched by the me-
tropolis that was only a few hours away; they rarely went to
New York, and when they did they could not wait to get back.
They tried to be friendly and she wanted desperately to respond,
but she had left them too far behind. What had taken their
place?

One afternoon she happened upon the book of Mary Garden's memoirs that Alice had given her. She tried to reread the
chapter that described Garden's debut as Mélisande in Paris.
Margo had found much to inspire her in the story of the great
diva. Now the book served only to remind her of a time when
she was still capable of dreams—the happy time that had disappeared forever from her life. She put it aside and wept.

She slept in her old room. The bed had a railing of four thin
iron columns at the head, painted white, matched by a shorter
railing at the foot. The faded yellow wallpaper showed a pattern
in which two roses alternated with green leaves. Long ago, as
she lay falling asleep, the roses would come alive in the dark
and move. Margo lay still under the quilt, staring at the wall.
What right had he to kill her love? What right had he to murder their child? He would go from one affair to the next, using
people, discarding them when he no longer needed them, breaking their hearts and their lives. She saw him as someone utterly

spoiled and selfish; she must strike back at him, to avenge not only the wrong he had done her but the pain he would inflict on all who had the misfortune to love him. Her grief gave way to anger. He hadn't heard the last of her. She would make him pay!

Just as, when she was pregnant, she had conjured up scenes of domestic bliss, so she now surrendered to visions of revenge. Her vivid imagination forced her to act out innumerable scenes in which she punished him for what he had done. These fantasies left her shaken, exhausted. She would awake in the middle of the night, her mind scurrying around and around like a mouse in a trap, refusing to leave her in peace until she wondered whether she was going mad. She waited for him, revolver in hand, and with a single shot repaid him for the agony he had caused her. No, death was too easy—it took only a moment. He must live, to expiate his crime in unending pain, day after day, month after month, year after year. A bullet in his spine would cripple him for the rest of his life. She saw him paralyzed in a wheelchair and gloated over the prospect. To achieve it, however, she would have to be a marksman. She abandoned the idea.

Finally her fevered mind turned to a simpler revenge: she would hurl a bottle of acid in his eyes. She pictured him groping his way through a never-ending night, his face disfigured beyond recognition, his beauty destroyed. She remembered his morbid fear of blindness. *To know that the world is full of color and not to be able to see it—that's the worst!* He had said this early in their friendship, when they were still happy. Without knowing it, he had pronounced his doom.

There was something compelling about this fantasy; it kept returning with the force of an obsession. She had read in the paper about a jilted suitor who poured Lysol in his sweetheart's face, and had wondered how a man could do this to the woman he loved. Now she knew. When she finished with him he would never forget her! Her face tightened, the tiny mouth expressing a determination that belied her fragile appearance. He must suffer for the love he had destroyed, for the life he had stolen from their child. He must be maimed even as she had been. Then —only then—could she bear to go on living.

The first snow of the year spread magic over the city. White flakes traced dancing patterns against the night. Within its iron bars the little tree in front of Judith's house looked more anemic than ever. Margo walked up and down, a slight figure in her belted leather coat. She stopped to tie her scarf over her hair and pushed up the collar of her coat. The damp seeped through her shoes; her feet were wet. She had always dreaded catching cold because of her voice. Now it didn't matter.

On Park Avenue the Christmas trees were lit in memory of those who had died in the war. Festivity was in the air, and the atmosphere of passionate merchandising that accompanied the holiday season. Margo reached the middle of the block and turned back, her eyes scanning the empty street. What if he were not alone? Then she would steal away and come another night. No matter how many nights she had to wait for him, he was not going to escape her.

She thrust her right hand over her coat pocket to make sure the bottle was there, and slid her thumb over the cork. There was something inevitable about the approaching encounter. What lay beyond she could not see; nor did it concern her. A car approached silently; the snowflakes glistened as they floated into the glow of its headlamps. *If I were a soldier I don't think I'd fear dying so much as losing my sight.* Her eyes glittered, and a smile crossed her lips.

She had lost track of time; it seemed to her she had been patrolling the street for as long as she could remember. She retraced her steps, and the breath went out of her body: he had just turned the corner of Lexington. He moved forward with that springy stride of his; he was bareheaded. Margo hid behind the staircase of the adjoining house. Her throat was dry, her heart skipped a beat; the blood pounded in her eardrums. She drew out the bottle of acid and, with a flick of her thumb, dislodged the cork. He was coming closer; he was only ten feet away. She stepped out from the shadows, holding the bottle behind her.

He stopped short. "Margo!"

She crouched forward and stared up at him, deafened by the pounding in her ears. "Now!" it roared. "Before he escapes!" His blond hair shone in the lamplight. How beautiful he was. As beautiful as on the night she met him, the night she first lay in his arms. "NOW!" She bent forward and stared into his eyes. Her mouth opened, but no sound came forth; she was shaking. The darkness whirled around her and became an abyss. Then a moan was torn from her throat, the agonized cry of her weakening resolve. "No! I can't." The bottle slipped from her grasp and was shattered on the pavement. She covered her face with her hands, sobbing convulsively.

He stared at her in puzzlement, then looked down at the fluid that sputtered and hissed in the snow, spreading a yellow stain at his feet. "What the devil—? What were you up to?"

She stood before him, shoulders hunched. "I couldn't!" she moaned. "I couldn't do it!"

"What's all this?" A wild suspicion flashed through his mind. He seized her by the shoulders. "You were going to—? My God!"

She lowered her face, her lips shaking. The accumulated despair of the past weeks was replaced by shame. She had the sensation of sinking to the lowest point of humiliation a human being could endure. "I couldn't!" she repeated, shaking her head as she bent abjectly before him.

The yellow stain had almost reached the curb. He let go her shoulders and looked at her as if he had never seen her before. "I'd have been blind." He said it quietly; he might have been talking of someone else.

"Yes. For the rest of your life."

A silence fell between them. At length, "You must have loved me very much," he said softly, "to be able to hate me so."

She shook her head, wiping her tears with the back of her hand. He brought out his handkerchief and wiped her cheeks. "I'd have deserved it, I guess. No." He shook his head. "Nobody could deserve anything like that. No matter what."

"I thought I could do it," she said in a toneless voice. "But when I looked up at you, I couldn't destroy you."

"You idiot! You'd have also destroyed yourself. Didn't you think of that? The newspapers, the scandal. Your parents. Walter and Alice. Everything would've gone down the drain. I'd have been blind and you'd have been ruined. Didn't that occur to you?"

"No."

"Just so you could act out a silly dream of revenge."

"I only——" She held out her hands, palms up, in a helpless gesture. "What's the use? How could I ever tell you what I thought."

"You must forget me. Forget everything that happened between us."

"I love you so," she said. "I wish I were dead."

"Margo, don't talk like that, it makes no sense. I'm the way I am and that's it. We could never make it together. Why kid ourselves?"

She gazed up at him. He stood against the curb enveloped in light, like a golden-haired creature from another world. The fever in her veins had ebbed, leaving behind an infinite weariness. She had the feeling of awaking from a nightmare, to discover with a gasp of relief that it had not really happened, that she had only dreamed it.

The snow wove a fanciful lattice against the darkness. She accompanied him to his door. Anger, grief, hate seemed strangely remote now. She had passed beyond feeling into an endless void, like the pink-gray void she used to see when as a little girl she pressed her eyes, tightly shut, against the pillow. It seemed to her that nothing could ever touch her again.

They stopped before the black door with its discreet red border. She drew a deep breath. "Forgive me. It wasn't your fault that you couldn't love me as I wanted you to." Already time was rushing between them; already her love for him, like her agony, was receding into the past. "You were so beautiful to me," she whispered. "I guess you always will be." She shut her eyes as if she would engrave on her memory what he looked like at that moment. "Thank God I didn't do it. I must've been mad."

"That future you were always talking about—— His face was grave and gentle. "Don't let anyone spoil it for you."

She looked up at him sadly. Suddenly she touched him lightly on the cheek, letting her hand linger a moment. Then she turned, a slight figure in a short leather coat, and walked off.

3

The year's end found Bob in a deep depression. Although relieved at his narrow escape, he was overwhelmed with remorse. What kind of scoundrel was he to have behaved as he had? Behind this accusation lay the humiliating knowledge that, confronted with the same situation, he would probably behave in the same way. When he shaved in the morning he studied his

face in the mirror, finding behind its chiseled features total un-
worthiness—and a capacity for cruelty that terrified him. He
took long walks during which he meditated on the nature of
good and evil. What was his life about? Where was he headed?
The questions remained unanswered.

His distress was compounded by his not having anyone he
could talk to. He had no close friends of his own age, and
Judith—even if he were willing to confess to her what had
happened, which he was not—was too occupied with her own
affairs to listen to his. Paul would be sympathetic, but he would
read his own meanings into the break-up with Margo; it was
better not to encourage him. This left Alice. Bob hated to sink
even lower in her estimation than he already had, yet at the
back of his mind he knew he would turn to her sooner or later.
On a Wednesday morning in January he waited for her after
her class.

Her face lit up when she saw him. "Bobby, where've you
been?"

"Hiding."

"I've missed you."

It cheered him to hear this. "How's your painting going?"

"I'm learning a lot. It's fun."

They walked toward Sixth Avenue. The air was sharp and
bracing, the wind tousled her white hair, and her face was
aglow. Her coat was open, revealing a light-green scarf around
her neck.

"You look wonderful," he said.

She glanced at him with solicitude. "I wish I could say the
same for you." They passed a telephone booth. "Let me make a
call," she said, "then I'll be free."

"If you're busy I can come another time."

She gave him a smile. "I'd much rather be with you."

Reassured, he watched her through the glass walls of the
booth. He could not be all bad if she greeted him so warmly.
As Bob told himself this, his guilt eased a little. She hung up
the phone and came out of the booth. "Now we can talk."

They went into the coffee shop on the corner; she made for
the table near the window. "This is where we sat last time."
When the waiter had gone she said quietly, "What's on your
mind, Bobby?"

"I want to know——" He stopped, growing red with embarrassment, but forced himself to continue. "I want to know if you think less of me because of what happened."

"Does it matter to you what I think?"

"Very much."

"I've already told you that it's not for me to judge you." She wanted to add, "I like you too much for that," but was shy. Instead she said, "How do you feel about it?"

He stared at the table top. "I feel like a heel."

Her face was grave. "I'd be lying to you if I said I approved of what you did. You failed Margo in the most terrible way. But, to be honest, she also failed you. She tried to get you into something you weren't ready for, and didn't realize what this would do to you."

"Then it wasn't altogether my fault?"

"When two people fail each other, who's to say which one is at fault?" Alice thought of Walter and herself. How would one apportion the blame between them? "She loved you and couldn't help herself. You did not love her and couldn't help yourself. What else can one say?"

"Are there no standards?"

"Of course there are, or you wouldn't feel the way you do. You are responsible, because if you hadn't made the first move nothing would have happened. But she asked you up that night and encouraged you, so she's responsible too."

In his confessional mood he wanted to tell Alice of his final encounter with Margo, but was afraid that this might tip the scales against him. The waitress brought a fruit salad for Alice and a hamburger for him. "It began so well," he said. "I never suspected how it would end. When I was a youngster my mother gave me a shiny, red apple, and when I bit into it I found a worm. What I had in my mouth turned bitter. That feeling has never left me."

"I'm sure you've eaten apples that had no worm."

"Yes. But I'm always expecting to find one."

"Perhaps that's why you do."

He thought a moment. "Those war films—I used to watch them and wonder how men could be that cruel. But I was just as cruel. More, in fact. The soldier doesn't know the man he's trying to kill. Besides, he has an excuse—it's kill or be killed. But I was brutal to someone who loved me. I keep asking myself, How could I?" He thought a moment. "People will do anything if they think they can get away with it. What they're afraid of is being found out."

"That's not true. You got away with it, technically speaking. No one knows except Margo and me, and no one ever will. Why, then, are you so upset? Because something inside you is passing judgment."

"Conscience? Maybe I only flatter myself by pretending I have one."

The waitress brought the check. Bob reached for it but Alice stopped him. "Let me take it," she said.

"Why? You did the last time."

"Because it gives me pleasure."

"You make me feel like a kid."

"I don't mean to." They came out on the street. She gave him her hand. "Don't neglect me. As you probably suspect, I love to see you."

"How can you? All I do is talk about myself."

She patted him on the arm. "I don't mind."

"You've a lot of patience."

"For you, yes," she said as she hailed a cab.

Bob buttoned his coat against the wind and set out for home. He had forgotten his gloves; the cold air nipped his fingers. He thrust his hands into his pockets, filled his lungs, and felt better than he had in a long time.

Crowds filled the shops on Fourteenth Street. Near the corner of University Place a little man stood selling handkerchiefs, a dozen for a dollar; his overcoat was too big for him, his lips were blue, and he held out his wares with a supplicating air. People passed him by as if he did not exist. Bob took a dozen, to encourage him. A little further on, a man was selling pretzels. Bob bought one and, munching the salty dough, cut across Union Square. Despite the cold, groups of men stood arguing vehemently around the statue of Washington. A tall man with bad teeth and an intense look maintained that Chinese communism was the real thing—what they had in Russia was a fake. Bob continued on his way. He would be much better off, he reflected, if he took greater interest in the fate of the world. He was too concerned with his own affairs to care—really—what happened to mankind.

The walk uptown did him good. What he needed was exercise. At college he used to work out in the gym; now he had drifted away from his former interest in his body. Two or three workouts a week would put him into shape. Turning the corner of Sixty-second Street, he wondered whether his mother was home. She had gone to Philadelphia to play a concert. He hoped she had not yet returned—the house was so peaceful without her.

Judith was in the dining room having a cup of tea. "Darling!" she called brightly.

Involuntarily Bob straightened. "Hi, mom. When did you get back?" He kissed her.

"A little while ago. How's my baby?"

"Not bad." He pointed to the plate of chocolate cookies in front of her. "First you starve yourself dieting, then you go on a binge."

"I know." She chuckled. "But I'm so exhausted, I need something to pick me up." She offered him a cookie.

"No, thanks."

His indifference to sweets was a perennial source of wonder to her. "How I envy you," she said, and stuffed the cookie into her mouth.

"How did it go?" he asked.

"Wonderful. Four encores, which is something for Philadelphia. And in Trenton they went out of their minds." Judith did not entirely fabricate her out-of-town triumphs; her memory merely retouched the truth to give it luster. "The reviews were sensational." Her bag lay on the table. She opened it and drew out two clippings.

Bob read them through. "Great!" he said, and put the clippings on the table.

She returned them to her bag, in order to exhibit them to Birdie. "Once you get out of New York there's a different attitude toward the artist. People want to hear you. They appreciate what you do, so you play better. There's too much music in New York—the public is fed up with it. They give you a fishy look when you come out, as if to say, 'Oh, it's you again!' You're licked before you start. And the critics! They should drop dead . . ." Judith reached for her fourth cookie. "There should be a law against playing in New York."

Bob enjoyed listening to her as long as she held forth on matters unrelated to him. He poured himself a cup of tea and sat down opposite her. Unfortunately the preliminaries were over. "I thought a lot about you while I was away," she said sweetly.

Not taken in by her tone, he waited for the onslaught.

"I realized," Judith continued, "that I have to take a stand. It would be more pleasant to let things slide, but that'll get us nowhere."

"Where d'you want us to get?"

She ignored the interruption. "I could let you keep drifting as you are. You'd love that and so would I, because then there'd be no hard feelings between us. But," she raised her hands slightly and let them drop, "it's not always possible to choose the easy way."

"I know. You have an obligation, etcetera."

"How did you guess?" She smiled, but her eyes took on a determined look. "So, young man, if you want to remain in this house you'll have to toe the mark. Comes September you'll go back to school and work for your degree. Once you've got that, we'll see."

His face hardened in the same way as hers. "What if I don't agree?"

"I said, 'if you want to remain in this house.' You're free to leave whenever you choose, but if you expect me to support you you'll have to do as I say. Doesn't that strike you as fair?"

"Is this an ultimatum?" It infuriated him that she put on this air of sweet reasonableness when she knew he had no alternative but to yield.

"You can take it as such if you like."

"I don't like."

"That's your problem, not mine." Again she raised her hands and dropped them, this time in a gesture of finality.

"I'll have to think it over," he said.

"By all means." She rose and cleared away the tea things. "You see," she added amiably, "you have no trouble in understanding me when you try." She mounted the stairs. "I have to get some sleep, darling, so try not to make any noise."

Bob went to his room. He picked up the first thing that came to his hand—a battered paperback—and flung it against the wall. Then he threw himself on the bed. He thought of all the biting replies he might have made to Judith's remarks, but realized that these would not have affected the outcome in the slightest. In the struggle between them he was helpless—she paid the bills; therefore she was in a position to call the tune. Was not this what the philosophers on Union Square understood by economic determinism? Money was power. Neither love, intellect, nor art—only money! That was the basic fact of life, everything else was window-dressing.

He ground his fists into the mattress. If only he could get out of this damned house and never see her again. His impotent rage transformed itself into a leaden weight that thrust against his temples, a throbbing that faintly echoed a forgotten pain of long ago, the self-inflicted pain of his childhood when he would bang his head against the pavement in order to spite her. His ear was pressed against the pillow; he shifted his position so as not to hear the beat of his pulse. The tension in his body grew until it was a hunger that demanded assuagement, a need that would not be denied. Each of his pores became a gaping little mouth crying out for the magic capsule that wiped away doubt and discouragement. He lay rigid. His heart was pounding, his muscles twitched, beads of sweat came out on his forehead. He put off the moment of surrender as if he were testing his power, yet even as he resisted he found relief in the knowledge that in the end he would yield. In the same way, when he was a boy, he would lie in bed determined not to play with himself yet know all the time that he would. Finally the tension became greater than he could bear. He opened the middle drawer of the chest and took out the pills that would lift the burden and set his spirit free.

He put on a record and lay down. Ravi Shankar. The tinkling of the sitar made fanciful patterns in the air. As he followed them a great peace descended upon him. Those delicate curlicues of sound, evanescent and remote, had been shaped by thoughts and feelings totally alien to those he had grown up with. Thoughts and feelings to which he seemed to be instinctively attuned. How gladly he would leave behind him the power-mad, money-mad world he knew, to find refuge on a mountaintop in Tibet where the mind could throw off the bondage of ego-striving and contemplate in silent rapture the mystery of Being. There, perhaps, was where he belonged. Here he certainly did not . . .

4

The window of Birdie's bedroom faced a blank wall. No shades had to be drawn when she was in bed with Walter. He had always associated love-making with the dark, but their afternoon sessions convinced him that it was more fun to see what you were doing.

The wall shut out the noise of the street; random sounds filtered in as from afar. In this room, Walter felt, the atmosphere was right. Sex enabled two people to create a world of their own, so private that no third person could even remotely conceive of it. This was one of the wonders of the act of love. Another was that it rejuvenated his body as no massage could have done. The orgasm seemed to release all the vital energy within him. His exhilaration more than compensated for the feeling of fatigue that sometimes overtook him afterward. Birdie was all woman in her response—submissive, tender, alive. "You're marvelous," he whispered, still breathing hard.

"Flattery will get you everywhere," she cooed.

"And you have a brain besides!" he added in a tone of incredulity. She beamed.

"Funny thing," he continued. "When I was young I couldn't imagine how anyone over fifty was able to feel passion."

"Now you know."

"Now I know. It's more precious too, because every time is one nearer the last."

"This we're not going to think about," she said, stroking his chest.

A muted light enveloped the room. Walter sighed contentedly, his hand cupping her breast, and emptied his mind of thought. Whoever invented woman knew what he was about.

Now that they had finished making love, Birdie's thoughts turned to business. Paul's contract with the orchestra was coming up for renewal. She worried about her artists; that was part of her job. "How did Paul make out?" she asked.

"The board had quite a discussion about him."

"Really?"

"No one denies he's a fine conductor. The public likes him too. Of course, he does play too much modern music."

"What d'you expect him to do—stick to Brahms?"

"Don't worry, he'll be re-engaged. To tell the truth, I'm a little worried about his personal life, but I didn't bring it up."

"I don't know what you're talking about."

"Yes, you do."

She was defensive now. "A person's private life, it seems to me, is his own affair."

"As long as he's a private person. When he becomes a public figure it's everyone's affair. Look, dear, I'm not being moral about this, only practical. If he likes young men that's his problem, but if he should ever get into trouble it would be very embarrassing for us."

"I'll never understand," she said vaguely, "how such rumors get started."

"Doesn't matter. They get around."

"You believe everything you hear?"

He grinned. "Your loyalty is touching."

With feminine perversity, as she was on the verge of winning her point she gave it away. "Look, honey, he doesn't conduct with his cock, so it's no business of ours what he does with it."

"Where did you learn such words?" Walter shook his head in mock reproof and sat up.

Birdie got out of bed and slipped into her yellow housecoat. Walter dressed. Now that the moment of parting was at hand, she became very quiet.

"What's wrong?" he asked.

"I hate to see you go."

"But we had a lovely time."

"That's why. I don't want it to end."

"Everything has to end. Life itself."

"A philosopher, on top of everything else." She gazed at him tenderly. "If you stayed it would be different. I'd cook dinner, we'd go to a movie or concert, or visit friends."

"If my grandmother had wheels she'd be a covered wagon."

"Don't you see what bothers me, Walter? It's all wonderful but so—temporary."

"Maybe that's why it's wonderful. Did you ever think of that?" He put on his coat.

She forced a smile. "All right. Let's be thankful for little blessings."

He knew that when she was in this mood nothing he could do would cheer her up. "Maybe they're not so little." He kissed her good-bye.

When he came out, a young moon was floating in the amethyst sky. He turned briskly up Second Avenue; the wind whipped through his hair and made his ears tingle. He went without a hat in winter; it made him feel younger. The evening rush had begun; traffic moved so slowly he practically kept up with it. New Yorkers were strange—rather than walk ten blocks they sat fuming in taxis that didn't move. He crossed the avenue and bought a *Post*.

When he came home Alice was out, which annoyed him. He asked the maid to fix him a sandwich, changed into slippers and the velvet jacket Alice had bought him and settled down in the living room with the paper. The Rouault was enveloped in shadows that gave its rich patina a deeper tone. He lit the lamp beside the sofa. Walter liked the *Post,* even though it was a shade Jewish for his taste. He began with page 5: the news from abroad, which disturbed him. We were overextending our commitments; sooner or later we'd get ourselves involved in a war that would do us no good. He turned to Leonard Lyons' column. Occasionally he found an item in it about someone he knew, which made him feel important. Years ago he used to wonder who read the obituaries; now he never missed them. Sylvia Porter reassured him about the future of capitalism. He dutifully read Max Lerner, whom he considered something of a bore, and enjoyed James Wechsler's liberalism because it corresponded to his own. Next he turned to Dr. Franzblau. As an amateur psychologist he never missed her column; she gave the same advice as he would have given. He liked to read about people's emotional problems; it made him feel more normal.

The stock-market report he left for last. The tiny figures filled him with excitement. He had the gambler's belief in the infallibility of his instinct—what he thought of as his luck. When he made a killing he felt like a darling of the gods; his sense of triumph bore no relation to the amount of money involved. Since he was essentially a rationalist, he tried to inject logic into the rise and fall of the market and felt that he should be able to predict its vagaries, but he was continually being taken by surprise. "When it goes up," he would say, "I don't sell, and when it goes down I don't sleep."

The paper finished, he put on Isaac Stern's recording of the

Mendelssohn Violin Concerto, dimmed the light, and made him-self comfortable on the sofa; he liked to listen to records lying down. It astonished him that people tried to attach precise meaning to music. For him its charm lay precisely in its in-definiteness. On one level he found its meaning to be purely physical: a visceral response to the sweetness of musical sound, to be enjoyed in much the same way as a sunset or a drink. Yet beyond that was a host of undefined emotions and images that this sound released in him, a sense of heightened awareness, of being afloat in a dreamlike world whose beauty could never be described in words. He preferred a limited number of works (most of them from the nineteenth century) to which he listened again and again, savoring his recognition of the melodies and the way the composer developed them. Although he had studied the violin in his youth, the memory of that attempt was so re-mote that for all practical purposes he considered himself a lay-man. A little better informed than most, but still in another class than the professional. Even though he was able to read notes, it would never have occurred to him to follow a composi-tion with the score; watching the printed page somehow took away from the magic of the sounds. Music for him was *the* poetic experience, especially since he never read poetry. As much as he liked to hear musicians discussing its fine points—their chief pleasure, it seemed to him, was to discover shortcom-ings that had completely escaped his notice—what he enjoyed most about it was to be able to immerse himself in it, to let it flow over him and feel its miraculous power to touch the heart.

The first movement ended in a burst of technical display. As the Andante began he heard the hall door open. Alice said some-thing to the maid and came into the living room. He sat up and turned off the machine. "Where've you been?" He sounded as if he had been counting the minutes.

"What's wrong?"

"You know I like you to be here when I get home."

"If you would tell me when you were coming," she said in a conciliating tone, "I'd make it my business to be here."

"I was hungry," he announced, still petulant.

"Couldn't Louise fix you something? The icebox is full."

"What kept you?"

"I was shopping. Before that I had lunch with a young man."

"A young man?"

"My dear, you sound jealous. How flattering!"

"I'm only curious."

"Oh. It was Bobby Conrad."

"Him? How come?"

"Very simple. He waited for me after my class and I took him to lunch."

"How long has this been going on?"

"We've had lunch a few times before."

"And you never told me?"

"Do I have to tell you everything? I didn't think you'd be interested."

"You know I am."

"So I've told you."

He looked puzzled. "When did this—uh—friendship develop?"

"It developed. I hope you don't mind."

"But why him?"

"You're funny, Walter. For years you've been telling me I ought to take an interest in young people, it would be good for me, and so forth. When I finally do, you complain."

"Sweetie, I'm not complaining. I'm only surprised you picked him."

She smiled. "Maybe he picked me."

"But he's such a schlemiel. Judith spoiled him. He can't stand on his own two feet, and he'll never amount to anything."

"Would that be a reason for sending him away?"

"No. I'm only saying that you might have picked someone more . . . promising."

"Walter, friendships aren't planned that way. They just happen. He's young and troubled, he needs someone to talk to, and I need someone to need me. It's as simple as that."

"I need a drink."

"No liquor."

He made a face. "Fix me a Compari. And don't forget the lemon."

She made the drink and brought it to him.

"I called Margo today. She's still in Poughkeepsie with her folks," he said peevishly.

"How is she?"

"Fine. I told her she must come back right away. Max has all sorts of things lined up for her."

"What did she say?"

"That she needs a few more days. I don't understand that girl."

"You mustn't push her. She's worked hard this year and needs a rest."

"Sure. But enough is enough. I want her here."

"You sound as if she was put on earth just to please you. Doesn't it occur to you, dear, that she has a life of her own?"

"Her life is her career, and at this point her career is in New York. Why d'you argue with me when it's so obvious?"

"Maybe it isn't." Alice murmured.

He glanced at her. Her eyes shone. With her pink skin framed by her white hair she looked, Walter thought, uncommonly pretty. "Your lunch date did you good," he conceded. "But you would pick a loser."

5

For a number of years Judith had thought of organizing a series of concerts devoted to the chamber repertoire, with the emphasis on works that were not heard as often as they should be. That winter she finally decided to launch the project. She saw herself creating something unique: a concert series directed by an artist, in which artistic considerations took precedence over all others. By a simple act of will she would end her long bondage to the commercial manager, and she was determined to beat him at his own game.

She discovered that she was capable not only of drawing up plans but also of carrying them out. A host of details engaged her attention—the planning of programs, the hiring of a hall, the selection of artists, and negotiations with their managers. Hitherto she had faced a man behind a desk who made the decisions; now it was she who decided. She swept through obstacles with irresistible gusto, her new activity absorbing her completely. The harder she worked, the better she felt.

Nor could she remain indifferent to the sudden change in her status. As an artist she was one of many competing for the favor of the public; as an impresario capable of engaging or rejecting other artists, she was someone to be reckoned with, courted, feared. In the complex web of rivalries and conflicting interests that made up the musical world of New York, she had gained considerable leverage for her own ambitions. Judith enjoyed her new-found power and, for the most part, used it well. On occasion she allowed personal feelings to sway her judgment, as when she decided against hiring an otherwise impeccable musician because he had once affronted her. There was nothing wrong, she maintained, in nursing a grudge; hating people was much too pleasant an activity to be taken lightly. Inevitably she made enemies, but this had to be accepted as part of the game.

In getting the series under way Birdie was of inestimable help to her. Birdie thoroughly understood the business end of the operation. She sent out the press releases and gathered the necessary mailing lists; more important, she was there to talk things over with at any hour of the day or night. "I don't know what I'd do without you," Judith said again and again throughout these months of close collaboration. They worked well together, chiefly because when there was a disagreement between them Birdie gave in. It was fortunate that her talent for publicity was equaled by her ignorance of music, so that Judith's decisions went unchallenged in the one area where she would have brooked no interference.

Although she was too much the soloist to have played much chamber music, the new series gave her a welcome opportunity to present herself to the public. She limited herself to two performances, so as not to appear to be taking advantage of the situation: the *Trout Quintet* at the opening concert, and a modern work on a subsequent program. Her affinity as a pianist lay with the German repertory of the eighteenth and nineteenth centuries—the music from Bach to Brahms—but she knew that in order to attract a sophisticated audience she had to include a sampling of twentieth-century works. She was devoting three programs to the masters of our time—Stravinsky, Schoenberg, Bartók—and decided that Paul would be the man to conduct those. Besides, his name would lend prestige to the undertaking. She had not heard from him since the summer; they had run into each other several times at concerts and he had been—in his remote way—fairly cordial. She felt awkward about telephoning him, but once she decided that her project needed him she let no other consideration stand in the way.

He sounded surprised when he heard her name. Judith indicated what she had in mind and suggested that they meet to discuss the matter.

"By all means," he said. "Where and when?"

She ruled out Birdie's office as too noisy; besides, since she had to persuade him to come down on his fee, she needed a cozier atmosphere. "I'd ask you up here," she said, "but my place is a madhouse—it's being painted."

"How about lunch tomorrow?"

That meant a restaurant, which would be too impersonal a setting. As though on an impulse. "Why don't I drop in on you this afternoon?" she suggested. "That is, if you don't mind."

"I would love it," Paul said, to hide the fact that he minded very much. The older he grew, the harder it was for him to say no. When he hung up he was possessed by the notion that she would guess, as soon as she entered the apartment, that her son had been there. But how?

Judith dressed with care and felt that she looked her best; yet, having relinquished him after his second visit to the seashore, her interest in him was purely professional. She threw a quick glance around her when he ushered her into the sitting room. "It's exactly as I imagined your place would be—roomy and old-fashioned." Her eyes rested on the Spanish chest. "That's a splendid piece, Paul." She admired the candlesticks, the crucifix, and St. Sebastian. He fixed drinks.

As on the night when they were side by side on the breakwater, she sensed his withdrawal. Once again she had the feeling of being in front of a door that refused to open. Seated in the armchair, she crossed her legs and described what she had in mind. She found him a sympathetic listener. Since he, too, had suffered from the interference of nonmusicians, the concept of an artistic venture run by artists appealed to him enormously. Besides, her enthusiasm was infectious. By the time she asked him to conduct for her he was as eager to do so as if he had originated the idea himself.

"There's only one problem," she concluded sweetly.

"What?"

"I'm afraid we can't afford you," She leaned forward, her dress cut low enough for him to see the valley between her full breasts. He raised his eyes to her face and kept them there. "Paul, I've told you about the project so you'd know what I'm trying to accomplish. If you feel it's worthwhile perhaps you'll take less than you ordinarily would."

Like many Europeans, he was embarrassed at having to discuss money with a woman. "Why don't you speak to Birdie Harris," he said hastily. "I am quite sure we can work something out."

"There, I knew you'd understand." Her mission accomplished, she sat back and made small talk. Paul, too, relaxed; now that they met as musicians, she no longer was a threat. They chatted well into the afternoon.

Despite her contempt for Max Rubin's preoccupation with money, it was apparent to Judith that her project could not get off the ground without it. She needed approximately forty thousand dollars for the series; half the amount was promised by a foundation on condition that she raise the other half. She obtained ten thousand from friends and decided that, instead of wasting time on fund raising, she would squeeze the remaining ten thousand out of Walter. The way to do that was to ask him for fifteen.

Walter's office was thirty-two stories above Madison Avenue. Judith had chosen the office for their meeting rather than his home, on the theory that he would be more generous if Alice were not there. The furnishings were fashionably modern; everything was upholstered in dark blue leather. Through an enormous window she could see Westchester and Long Island Sound. It made a great impression upon her that when Walter was called on the telephone he did not pick up the receiver but spoke into the air.

"I've come to hold you up," she announced, all smiles.

"I know that. The question is, How much?"

"Twice that," she answered, confident of her ability to handle him.

Pen in hand, Walter doodled idly as she explained what she hoped to accomplish. Despite his fondness for her, he was unable to work up enthusiasm for the project. It seemed to him that she was simply trying to further her career, which she would not have had to do if she hadn't quarreled with Max. "I'm with you all the way, my dear," he said at length, "you know that. The trouble is, I'm bombarded with worthy causes every day. It becomes a problem to take care of them all."

"Let's stick to mine for the moment."

"How much do you need?"

"Forty thousand for my first season. I got a grant of fifteen," she said, subtracting five thousand from the sum promised her by the foundation, "and raised ten. I need fifteen from you."

"Judith!" He went through the motion of wincing. His practice was to give small sums to causes he considered worthy, like multiple sclerosis or birth control for underdeveloped countries; larger sums to the more glamorous charities that brought the donor a measure of social prestige; and a few substantial gifts to the institutions closest his heart. Judith's attempt to enrich the city's musical life with performances of neglected chamber works was certainly a worthwhile project, but a little too special to engage his interest. "You're asking me to put up a good hunk of the money. Why?"

"In the first place, you understand what I'm trying to accomplish. In the second, there aren't many people I can turn to. Besides, I just don't have any ability as a fund raiser."

"On the contrary, I think you have a great talent for it."

A little flattery was indicated; Judith obliged. "Not everyone would be interested in the kind of thing I have in mind. Only someone with taste, and a sense of what ought to be done in a city like this. Besides, you can take it off your taxes."

Walter found himself at a disadvantage. Judith, for years, had been one of the chief attractions in his stable, and this was the first favor she had ever asked of him. His sense of style demanded compliance even if his heart was not in it. "I'll tell you what," he said. "I'll give you ten grand."

Judith was delighted that she had so accurately forecast his reaction. "You're a darling!" she cried with feeling, and gave him a hug. The check was in her bag when she left.

At dinner that night he told Alice of the visit. She showed her annoyance. "Why d'you let that woman take advantage of you?"

He knew she had a point. "I have to give away a certain amount this year. What's so terrible if I let her have some?"

"I'm not saying you should have turned her down, but you might have given her less. There are more important things you could support."

"What's wrong with supporting a project that a friend's involved in?"

"Would she still be a friend if you had said no?"

"She'd have had every reason to feel let down. Besides, she got together a good board of directors and she's making me chairman. I'll help her run the thing."

"You will, will you?" There was sarcasm in her voice.

"Why not?"

"Because anything Judith gets her hands on she'll run exactly as she pleases. How can you be so naïve?"

"Why must you always suspect people of the worst? Trouble with you is, you don't understand the artistic temperament."

Alice smiled. "The trouble with me is, I understand it too well."

Walter closed the discussion by disappearing behind his paper. Alice would never be convinced. Didn't she realize that music needed support; it always had and always would. On Broadway either a play made money or it closed, but concerts never paid and someone had to foot the bill. There was a cultural explosion in this country. If people like him didn't support it, who would?

He read the editorial and went on to the obituaries. No one he knew was in them.

6

It was almost midnight when Judith came home. As she opened the front door the telephone rang. She picked up the receiver.

"Philip! What a surprise!" He asked if he could see her. "I'd love it," she replied. "How about dinner Wednesday?"

"I mean now."

"Now? Where are you?"

"Midtown."

"What's it about?"

Ignoring the question, "I'll be right over," he said and hung up.

She had not heard from him since his marriage. Why would he be coming at this hour? Judith was mystified. Could he have quarreled with that French wife of his? The thought gave her a curious satisfaction. She put on fresh make-up, wondered whether she should change into a housecoat, and decided to remain as she was.

Philip looked worn when he came in. He took off his coat, threw it on the couch, sat down, and frowned.

"Well?" she said.

"It's . . . it's about Bob."

"Bobby?" Her heart gave a leap. "What's wrong?"

"Don't get upset. It's not serious. He got into a bit of trouble."

"What d'you mean?"

"It seems he forged some prescriptions for pills——"

"What?" She sprang up.

"——and got caught."

"You mean, he was arrested?"

"Calm yourself, Judith. I'll get him out."

"Oh, my God!" The breath went out of her body. "It can't be!" she cried.

"It's small potatoes, believe me. But I had to tell you."

"You mean, he'll have to go to jail?"

"No, he'll get off. His first offense. It was a foolish thing to do, that's all."

"How did you find out?"

"He was allowed to make one phone call."

She stared at him without comprehension. Then she said slowly, "You're telling me that my Bobby's been taking drugs, and got arrested, and now he'll have to stand trial. There'll be a scandal. My name'll be dragged into the papers." She rose and began to pace up and down, striking the palms of her hands together as she moaned, "Oh, my God!"

He seized her by the elbows and forced her to stand still. "Judith, hysterics will only make it harder for him. It's the kind of a jam a young fellow can get into, and there's no point carrying on as if he'd killed someone."

"He is killing someone," she screamed. "Me!"

"Stop being dramatic! You should be thinking of him."

"Fine family, the best schools. I did all I could for him. And now to have my name dragged in the mud." Her eyes were upon him, filled with despair. "Will it be hushed up?"

"I'll get it before a friendly judge. He'll get a suspended sentence, no more."

"But will the papers get hold of it? I'll die if they do!"

"There are dozens of cases like this every day. If he were the governor's son they would take notice. But court reporters wouldn't know your name—music is not their world. Don't worry, no one'll know."

"I'll know!" Her face stiffened. "And I'll never forgive him for this."

"That won't help him any."

"If all I've done for him hasn't helped him any," she said harshly, "what chance is there now?"

Philip glanced at his watch. "I knew you'd be upset, that's why I came. I've got to go."

"Do you need money?"

"I'll post a bond."

She slumped in her chair, crushed. "You have ten minutes of pleasure, then you're stuck with them for the rest of your life!" She clutched her head and began to sway back and forth, as if only now had she received the full impact of the blow. "That this should happen to me. What did I do to deserve it?"

"Judith, pull yourself together. Please." He left.

The clock punctuated the silence with its metallic click. She saw Bob's boyish face, and was sick at heart. After a time she arose and made her way downstairs to his room. She had thought they shared a life together, yet she didn't begin to know him— they were a million miles apart! She opened the door, flicked on the light, and stared at the familiar objects: his bed, his desk, typewriter, bookshelves, television set, record player. On the night table lay a copy of Henry Miller's *Nexus* and the paper knife encrusted with green and red beads that she had brought back for him from Venice. He used it as a book mark. No matter how curious she had been about him, she had never rummaged through his things. Now, alas, she had to. She went to the chest in the corner and opened the top drawer. The three hundred-dollar bills that remained of Paul's gift lay neatly folded in one corner. Judith wondered where he had obtained the money. In the middle drawer she found the envelope that contained her green-and-black pills, and realized why she had had to refill the prescription so often. Cigarettes lay strewn about; a little cloth bag held four white capsules and a tiny cube of what looked like sugar. She drew out a notebook, sat down on his bed and began to read what seemed to be notes for a novel interspersed with a diary. Her attention was suddenly riveted to what she was reading. "My mother is a bundle of contradictions. Is her ruthlessness born of strength or weakness? She can't make up her mind about anything. To hide her vacillation she leaps at the first choice that enters her head, and does so with such impetus that she gives the impression of being a woman of decision. As a result her friends say of her, 'There's a woman who knows her own mind.' People are naïve when it comes to judging character."

Judith wanted to stop, but curiosity impelled her to continue. "Her good qualities, such as they are, are spoiled by a lack of nobility. She's single-minded in pursuit of her goals, and can't relate to anything that will not serve her ambition. She's a taker, not a giver, and can be a bitch when it suits her purpose. These traits, nourished by a vast arrogance, have enabled her to parlay a modest talent into a sizable career. Although she believes she's looking for love, she don't have the faintest notion of what love is. Wouldn't recognize it if it hit her in the face. She's driven to destroy friendships, loyalties, ideals, and when she has nothing else left to destroy she'll end up by destroying herself."

Judith put down the notebook. So this was what he thought of her! He lived in her house and accepted her money, yet dared to write such filth about her. The gall! The deceit! The child she had cradled in her arms, diapered, fed, caressed, had grown up to sit in judgment upon her—an irresponsible weakling who would end by dragging her name in the mud. It was monstrous! At one stroke she could thrust him from her heart, and the great love she had felt for him would turn into hate. Was it possible for a mother to hate her own son? Why not, if he deserved it?

She looked within. Where had she failed? Was there any truth in what he said about her? Was she being punished because she was selfish, unfeeling, calculating? Because she used people? Because she could not give? She had failed as a mother, that was evident, just as she had failed as a wife. At least she had not failed as an artist. Bobby's slur on her talent she dismissed as malice. He didn't know enough about music to be able to judge. All he could do was to repeat the opinion of those who did not like her playing, probably because it made him feel like less of a failure himself. Well, she had news for him—she no longer cared what he thought of her. She sat staring helplessly before her, wishing she could fall asleep and never wake up.

The street door opened. She heard footsteps and hurried into the dining room. Philip came in first. "I got a postponement," he said. "Three weeks. A lot can happen in that time."

Bob was behind him. He kept his eyes lowered.

"Go easy on him," Philip said.

Judith stared at her son. "I don't want to see him," she muttered.

"Judith, that won't get us anywhere."

"What are we supposed to do—pin a medal on him?"

"He's had a rough time."

"*He's* had a rough time? I like that! And what've I had? A picnic?"

"Judith, it's late and I've had a long day. I just wanted to see that he got home." He turned to Bob. "Don't worry, everything'll be all right. I'll phone tomorrow and let you know how things look."

Bob came out of his silence. "Thanks," he said softly, "thanks for everything."

"Good night, Judith. And remember, he's upset enough, so don't you add to it." He patted Bob on the shoulder and left.

There was a long silence. Then Judith said in a low voice, "Nice doings. Very nice."

He remained silent, his eyes still on the floor.

"You should be ashamed of yourself."

For the first time he looked up. "I am."

"Delighted to hear it," she sneered.

He had spent the hours of his arrest in horror at the folly of his behavior and was prepared to be thoroughly repentant. Judith's tone, however, forced him to assume an air of bravado. "Yes, I am ashamed," he repeated defiantly, "not so much for what I did, although that was pretty stupid, but because I got caught."

"Then why did you?"

He was not sure whether her question referred to his misdeed or to his being caught. "There's no use my trying to explain. I got into it through someone else and things went wrong. You wouldn't understand."

"I'll tell you why you did it!" she hissed, glaring at him. "To upset me! Because you know it would kill me to have my name dragged into the papers. You have nothing to lose. You're a nobody and always will be. But I have a name, a reputation. I could be destroyed by a scandal like this. I suppose it would give you the greatest pleasure to see that happen!"

He felt himself on firm ground again. The disaster he had brought on himself had become something they could quarrel about, and the fiercer the quarrel, the better he could thrust the disaster out of his mind. "You're running true to type," he cried. "Even now you think only of yourself."

"And who were you thinking of when you got yourself into this jam? Me?"

"To tell the truth, I wasn't thinking."

"Why didn't you, damn it!"

"What interests me," he remarked in his most sardonic tone, "is that you're worried only because people might find out."

She sprang up. "Look, you! You get yourself arrested, you could be ruined for life, and you have the nerve to put me on the defensive. You insolent little—!" She choked with anger, unable to find a sufficiently annihilating epithet.

"It's true, though," he persisted.

She made an effort to regain control of herself. "I read the things you wrote about me in your diary," she said bitterly. "If I felt that way about someone, I wouldn't sponge off them as you've sponged off me. I wouldn't take advantage of their good nature."

He bit his lip. "So you went snooping."

"No. After Phil told me what had happened, I went to your room to find out a thing or two. I sure did."

Did she expect him to retract what he had written? "I'm sorry I offended you," he said calmly, "but I wrote what I felt."

"You should be ashamed to say such things about your mother."

"I'm not."

"I see." Her voice remained low despite the rage that was mounting inside her. "I also noticed three hundred-dollar bills in your drawer. To my surprise, since you're always telling me how broke you are. Who gave them to you?"

"I owe you no explanation," he said. What would she say if he told her that Paul had given him the money?

"I demand to know."

"It's no concern of yours."

"Oh, yes it is!" On an impulse she turned to the drawer and pulled out the money. "I'm taking it. As a down payment on what you owe me."

"You have no right to. Put it back."

"I have no right to?" Her fury exploded. "Who says so?"

"I say so." He, too, ordinarily indifferent to money, had found an issue on which he could make a stand. "It's my money. Give it to me!"

"I will not!" She closed her fist over the bills.

He sprang at her, grabbed her wrist with one hand while with the other he tried to wrench the bills from her grasp. She tightened her fist. Suddenly his arm was around her, and they stood locked in an embrace of anger and hate, pushing, tussling, each struggling desperately to gain possession of three bills that neither cared about. Finally she struck out at him with her free hand, her long, red nails clawing his cheek. He sprang back startled. There was the sound of paper tearing, and he held three half-bills in his hand while she clutched the other halves.

"You rat!" she screamed, finding the word at last. "You dirty little rat!"

His lips were trembling. He raised his hand to the scratch on his cheek; it was bleeding. In his rage he seized the first thing that came to hand—the Venetian paper knife—and hurled it against the table. It bounced up at a sharp angle, toward Judith, and struck her in the throat. For an instant its sharp point touched her skin, then it fell to the floor.

They stared at one another across an abyss, the knife between them. "I didn't mean to——" he stammered.

She found her voice. "That's right, murder your mother! What else?" She went up to him, raised her hand, and slapped him with all her might. "Get out! D'you hear me?" she screamed. "I never want to see your face again! As far as I'm concerned you're dead. And may you live to regret this night, God damn you!"

He covered his cheek with his hand. His face was white. "It's you who'll regret it!"

"Get out of here!"

Bob realized that he still held the three torn bills; he slammed them on the table and grabbed his coat. Judith dropped down on the green velvet couch, sobbing. The tears streamed down her cheeks.

7

Bob walked along the empty avenue. He had no idea where he was going, but the steady beat of his footsteps on the pavement had a quieting effect upon him. His face felt hot in spite of the wind. He took out his handkerchief and dabbed it against the scratch on his cheek; the bleeding had stopped. The coffee shop on Fifty-seventh Street was still open. He would have liked a cup of coffee but realized that he had come away without any money. Turning left, he continued until he reached the square that overlooked the river.

It was laid out as a diminutive park, with concrete walks instead of lawns. Two pale lamps cast a melancholy glow over the empty benches. As he walked down the ramp that led into the square, he glanced up at the tall building on the right where Walter and Alice lived, and remembered the night he met Margo. He crossed the square to the river side, where a squat stone wall was surmounted by a railing of semicircular iron prongs whose tips curved inward. To prevent people from jumping? Queensborough Bridge floated on its massive piers in an aura of gray light, the latticework of its towers outlined hazily against the night. Below him the river gleamed darkly, taking on a dirty-green tinge as it flowed into a pool of light under the bridge. On the opposite bank the Pepsi-Cola sign still wrote its message against the sky. He stared at the buildings on the island in the middle of the river. They had an unreal look.

His bravado had faded. With a sickening sense of shame he reviewed the events of the past twenty-four hours. Each detail of his arrest had etched itself in his mind, never to be erased. The fingerprinting. The taking of his picture, with a number underneath for identification. The police officer with a red face and bulbous nose who kept calling him by his first name. The meal of two hard-boiled eggs, toast, and coffee that was shoved under the iron door of the detention pen. The barred windows. The tiers of bunks on which lay, in attitudes of apathy or defiance, his companions in degradation. This was the day he had touched bottom. It would remain, he knew, the bitterest memory of his life.

To be arrested was in itself no disgrace. Throughout history men had defied the Establishment because of something they believed in and had been imprisoned for their pains: Socrates, Cervantes, Raleigh, Dostoievsky, Thoreau, Debs. But he did not have their excuse. He had undergone the ultimate in humiliation for no lofty ideal but because of a stupid blunder; he had failed to evaluate the consequences of his actions and ended in a dreary cage together with a pimp, an automobile thief, a heroin pusher, and a quiet little man who had made improper advances to a detective in a subway toilet. The hours he spent with them had forced him to re-examine his life, to trace each link in the chain of events that had brought him to jail. Of the actual forging of the prescriptions he preferred not to think; it had been suggested by a crony while he was high and had not the faintest notion of the risk he was taking. His aim, rather, was to discover what had led him to this idiotic act; yet whenever he fastened upon a cause he realized that this actually had been a result, the real cause lay farther back, so that his investigation ultimately led him to events that lay at the outer rim of memory. He had started out so auspiciously, his childhood had been so full of promise . . . What had gone wrong? The familiar sense of betrayal tugged at his heart. Once again he had bitten into the apple and found a worm.

Was there a malevolent fate at work in the world, as men had believed since the beginning of time? Or did each man carry his destiny within him, unconsciously contriving his own defeats, shaping his own experiences until they all resembled one another like a series of portraits by the same painter? As he looked about the cell it was clear to him that his fellow prisoners could, with justice, claim to be victims of fate, but not he. He had had all the advantages they dreamed about. How, then, did it happen that he ended up in their company? He had tried to heighten his awareness of life, to free his soul from the bonds that imprisoned it. Like Icarus, he had flown toward the sun only to drop from the heights into this filthy hole. Suddenly the warnings of the moralists, the platitudes he had shrugged off, turned out to be true. Somewhere along the line his judgment had been impaired until he could no longer recognize an act of folly as such. Or could it be that deep inside him he wanted to be caught, wanted to be punished? For what?

Bob grasped the semicircular prongs and bent forward until

they pressed against his chest. He watched the river as it swirled toward the black piers of the bridge. To his surprise the current moved northward—the river seemed to be flowing upstream. He recognized that he stood at a crossroads in his life; he could drift no longer—that part of the trip was over. His goal had been to find something more real than reality, but in his attempt to do so he seemed to have lost touch with reality altogether. Was this why he had come to grief? Was reality what he had tried to escape from or what he had hoped to escape into? Which was really real—the private dream-world that swam out of his pills or the cell in which he had spent the darkest night of his life? Which, then, was the illusion? This was clearly a philosophical problem, and a philosopher he was not.

Could it be that his mother was right after all? She refused to acknowledge the validity of his dream world, she accepted only the standards of the Establishment. Would it be a sign of his growing up that he, too, accepted them, or would this be the ultimate capitulation? Might it be that rebellion demanded sterner stuff than he was made of? To be a true rebel one had to be able to throw off the prejudices of one's society—neither to trample upon them nor defy them, but to rise so far above them that they ceased to exist. One who felt only contempt for the law had no qualms about coming into conflict with it, an inner conviction sustained him in his hour of need; the lower such a man sank in the estimation of the "squares," the higher he held his head. Bob let out a sigh. He had never even remotely achieved this conviction. His trouble was that fundamentally he had never freed himself from his mother's values; he had rejected her notion of success only because he was secretly afraid he might not achieve it. His rebellion was a fake. What better proof than the fact that, at his first brush with the law, instead of holding his head high he had been overwhelmed with shame and remorse? He had always looked down on his mother and her friends as bourgeois. How strange to discover that, deep underneath, so was he.

The wind blew his hair over his forehead; he jabbed it back. It astonished him that, after having fought his mother so bitterly, he evaluated himself pretty much as she had. He was a dropout. And in order to cease being one he would have to surrender what he prized above all else—his freedom. *Oh, freedom, what crimes are committed in thy name!* Who said that? In all

that he had done, good and bad, there had been only one purpose—to find a shortcut to freedom. He had not found the one
he was looking for. Was there another? As he gazed at the water
swirling below him, the answer floated up from the back of his
mind. Yes! The shortcut many men had taken, some in despair,
others out of weariness or resignation. Whatever their motive,
this was the path to ultimate freedom. It required only that a
man conquer within himself—for a moment—the animal wish
to live. He had but to leap over the rail to throw off the tyranny
of the world, to free himself forever from the burden of false-
hood, vanity, desire, ambition that deluded most people into
thinking themselves alive. He contemplated the idea without
surprise, as if—without his knowing—it had been part of his
thinking for a long time. Yes, it was true that he stood at a
crossroads. But the choice before him was not whether he should
go right or left. The real choice was whether or not to go on
at all!

He tapped his fist tentatively against his chin and stared at
the river. We didn't miss not having been alive during the thousands of years before we were born. Why, then, should we miss
it after we were dead? Could it be that the sense of pure being
he had sought to achieve was to be found only in nonbeing?
That the only significant experience, ultimately, was nonexper-
ience? Wisps of foam swirled across the river's gleaming surface.
He followed their turbulent course as if only they could give
him the answer to his question. Presently he glanced around
him; the plaza was deserted. He slipped off his coat and dropped
it on the ground. Then he stepped on a bench and, firmly grip-
ping one of the prongs, swung himself up and into a crouching
position on top of the railing. The iron felt cold and hard
against his palm. Stretching his arm, he leaned out over the
river. Directly below him the water splashed against its stone
bank and receded in little eddies that disappeared in midstream.
He had only to loosen his grip and he would plunge into eternal
darkness; a single movement of his hand and he would be free
forever. He saw his body hit the water, his face sucked under
by the current that swept him toward the piers of the bridge;
his head split open as it hit the stone, the golden hair he combed
so carefully straggled in the water like seaweed, and the body
he had been so proud of, that had brought him such a diversity
of sensations, pleasures, feelings, became a bloated corpse, rot-

ting and dirty green like the river itself. Suspended between life
and death, he gazed at the abyss below him. The wind whistled
in his ears, and something inside him said no. Over and over
again, louder and stronger—no, No, NO! He felt a cramp in
his arm, his wrist was throbbing with strain from the weight of
his body, but his fingers retained their grasp on the icy prong.
They were stronger than his will. They refused to let go.

At last, tugging at the prong with all his might, he pulled himself back from the abyss; he jumped from the rail and dropped
in exhaustion on the bench. He rested his head against the
back of the seat and became aware that there were tears in his
eyes. They rolled down his face to his lips and had a hot, bitter
taste. Was he weeping at the end he had narrowly escaped? Or
because he had been unable to let go? A chill damp floated up
from the river; he sucked in the air until his lungs were full and
slowly exhaled, then picked up his coat and spread it over him
like a quilt. He lay very still, reflecting that he could have been
dead by now. The thought was both grotesque and terrifying.
Yet he felt a great joy that he was able to think it, and was
thankful for whatever it was that had kept him from jumping.
Did that take greater courage than he possessed, or would it
have been the ultimate cowardice? He tried to debate the pros
and cons of the matter, but he was too tired. This, too, was a
problem for a philosopher. He knew only that he was glad he
had not let go. The "No" that had held him back was really a
"Yes!"

His legs were numb; he stood up and put on his coat. A bus
glided across the bridge, looking like a toy. There was a hum
in the air; somewhere a bell rang. The noises of the night had
a fresh sound, as if he were hearing them for the first time. A
vast calm hung over the city. He felt infinitely relieved, for he
knew that he would never again try to die.

He had no desire to return home. Where was home? The
house he had shared with his mother? He tried to think of her
dispassionately but was too tired to sustain the effort. Their love
was overlaid with so much bitterness that he wondered if they
would ever find each other again. Meanwhile, where could he
go? He thought of Margo's apartment on Twenty-second Street,
with the neon sign on the corner pumping intermittent waves
of light into the living room. If he could go to her and beg her
forgiveness for the hurt he had inflicted upon her. But there

was no returning; he had failed her too miserably. How strange, that his mother should have brought sorrow into his life because she did not love him enough, and Margo because she loved him too much. Would anyone ever give him the right amount? He thought of Alice, asleep in her room high above the river, and turned around to face the apartment building that overlooked the square. Would she be angry with him if he rang her doorbell at this hour? Her husband certainly would. She was able to do for him the one thing his mother never could—she accepted him as he was, so that he didn't have to lie or apologize or defend himself. How pleasant it would be if we could pick our parents as we picked our friends, because we liked them and felt at ease in their company.

A dark-gray mist enveloped the river. He dug his hands into his coat pockets and crossed the square; he never wanted to see it again. There was only one place he could go to at this hour—Paul's. He would have to walk. He turned into Fifty-seventh Street as a taxi drew up at the house where Alice lived. Ahead, the traffic lights changed from red to green; except for an occasional stroller, the streets were deserted. He glanced at the clock in the coffee shop; it was ten after two. The air was cold. Bob turned up his collar, hunching his shoulders so that his ears were protected. The antiques in the shop windows looked more interesting than in the daytime, probably because the lights were dimmed. People were strange: they lived in twentieth-century houses and wore twentieth-century clothes, but wanted eighteenth-century clocks and chests so that their friends would think they had a grandmother. He passed what he considered the most interesting window on the street—IBM—where a lively text explained the newest computer. He read a few words mechanically, and continued his way.

A sharp wind rushed down Fifth Avenue, as if someone had left a window open in the park. He felt hollow inside, his head was light. He had the impression that if he spread his coat to either side like a sail, the wind would carry him off the ground. Instead he plodded on toward the West Side. The coffee shop on Sixth Avenue was full of people; Bob crossed the street and made his way to the hotel.

Paul looked at him sharply when he came in. "Who scratched you?"

"A woman."

"Naturally. Where've you been?"

"By the river."

"What were you doing there?"

"I tried to jump in."

"Very funny. You look frozen."

"I am." He took off his coat and dropped it on the chair.

Paul took the coat and hung it in the closet. "Hungry?"

"Starved."

"Why didn't you eat?"

For answer Bob turned both his trouser pockets inside out.

"Oh. I'll send the boy for a sandwich." He telephoned down to the lobby, and fixed Bob a Scotch and soda. "What happened?"

"I had a fight with my mother. I left for good."

"I see." He handed Bob the glass. "What about?"

"About nothing and everything. We just don't mesh, I guess. No use talking about it." He sipped his drink. A feeling of utter exhaustion poured over him. He lay down on the bed. "I'm sorry to barge in on you like this."

"I was up anyway."

"You don't mind?"

"Of course not." Paul came beside the bed and took his hand. He was delighted that the young man had no one else in the world to turn to. And Bob knew it.

8

Max sat on the sofa in his oval-shaped living room. He leaned toward the armchair occupied by Margo. "If you were my own daughter I couldn't be happier. So help me!"

"I'm happy too, Mr. Rubin," she said quietly. Her black dress accentuated her pallor.

"A year in Germany!" Walter beamed. "It's wonderful."

Max assumed his most oracular manner. "A year in Germany will give you what you need. If Max Rubin tells you, you can believe. It's a shame our young singers have to go to Europe to get experience, but what can you do—we have no opera houses. Over there every city has one. You'll sing three Butterflys in

Frankfurt, three in Stuttgart, two Mimis in Dortmund. Where else you would get such a chance? Myself, I don't go to Germany. After what they did, I don't have to look in their faces. But for you it's different. You're not Jewish. Besides you were a baby when it all happened. They're good to Americans. I have a few who made fine careers there." He never said *singers* or *artists;* the noun was understood. Max opened his notebook and turned the pages until he came to hers. "See." Her name was written on top in his large scrawl, and underneath it the list of her engagements. "Not bad for a beginning, what you think?"

Walter scanned the list and turned to Margo. "Aren't you thrilled?"

She smiled faintly. "Of course I am."

"But you're so quiet."

"Why she should make a noise?" Max interposed. Now that she was one of his, he put the best possible interpretation on whatever she did. "If you told her five years ago she's going to Germany to sing opera, she would jump with excitement. Today she's ready for it, so she takes it——" He stopped, looking for the right word.

"In her stride," Walter prompted.

"—like it's natural," Max brought out deliberately, to put Walter in his place. "I'll be honest with you, I like this better. There's a kind of a girl that jumps all over the room, whenever you look at her she's making with the eyes and hands and everything else, already she's a prima-donna. But when you get her on the stage, from all this business comes nothing. Then there's the kind who sits without saying 'boo,' you don't even notice her. But when she get's on the stage she's like a house on fire." He patted Margo's hand. "By me it's all right. Why you should put on a show for us? Better you should save it for the customers."

He went into the kitchen and came back with a tray on which stood three glasses of champagne. He served domestic rather than imported, on the theory that when people were busy talking they never noticed the difference. Walter handed Margo her glass and took his own. "To your success in Germany."

Margo smiled. "I remember you told me I mustn't drink while someone is toasting me."

"Nonsense," Max snorted. "Drink up."

She sipped the wine. Max pointed to the photographs on the

wall. "When you make your debut in New York you'll give me your picture. Autographed, of course. I'll hang it there." He gave her a majestic kiss on the forehead. The visit was over.

Walter's car rolled down Broadway. The city throbbed with the expectancy of early evening; Margo, pensive, watched the lights flash by. Columbus Circle swarmed with automobiles. The park was veiled in a purple dusk. She turned to him. "What if Max hadn't taken me on? I mean, suppose I hadn't gotten this far. Would you feel that all the time and effort you put into me were wasted?"

He thought awhile before answering. "I wish I could say that the pleasure was in doing it and the result didn't matter, but it's not true. If you didn't make it I guess I'd feel you had let me down. Yet even as I say this I know it could never happen."

She looked away. Would he ever know how close she had come to letting him down? "But it mightn't depend on me," she said. "I could try my best and still nothing would come of it."

"That could be only if you didn't have the stuff. But you do."

The car pushed its way through the bedlam of Times Square and reached the quieter streets beyond. She was silent. Finally she said, "Sometimes life gets complicated. A person might have talent but fate is against him and he never becomes what he should have been."

"Then he wasn't meant to get there in the first place. The real artist never allows anything to stand in his way."

She dropped her hands in her lap and stared at them. She had dreaded the visit to Max. Yet now that it was over she was glad to have gone through with it.

He glanced at her in the half darkness. "You're very quiet tonight. You're different somehow."

"In what way?"

"I don't know. If Alice were here she'd know. A man can't tell about these things. You're more . . . withdrawn than you used to be."

She sighed. "Maybe it's because I overdid things a little this year."

"And you're not as excited about singing in Germany as I hoped you'd be. I suppose Max is right. Once you're ready for it, you take it for granted."

They rode in silence until the car stopped in front of her

house. The chauffeur alighted and opened the door; Walter helped her out. She looked up at him. "I want you to know," she said earnestly, "that if anything ever becomes of me, it'll be thanks to you."

He grinned. "It's been a long road, and I've enjoyed every bit of it."

"And don't think I'm not thrilled about going to Germany. I am."

He held her hand between his. "My dear girl, I'm so excited I could shout."

The nymph on Max's mantelpiece showed half-past six. The old man stirred the strawberries at the bottom of his yogurt and studied his notebook with a satisfied air. Frankfurt, Stuttgart, Dortmund—all this took doing, and only someone with Max Rubin's connections could have done it.

Now she was on her way. He heaved a sigh and closed the book. In this world of lies and hatred and cruelty only one thing mattered—to create! A song, a picture, a poem. Or a star . . .

He finished his yogurt, pushed the green leather armchair into its horizontal position, and dozed off.

five

 The new year brought Paul one of the
happiest periods of his life. For the first time since his youth he
experienced the joy of a complete relationship. Bob was de-
pendent upon him for money, affection, encouragement. In giving these Paul not only had the satisfaction of fulfilling his
friend's needs but also enjoyed a sense of power over him.

Although his apartment was large enough for two, it was soon
apparent that Bob could not remain there. Paul had to be alone
when he worked. His home was his citadel; whoever invaded it,
no matter how dear, threatened his inner life in the most direct
way. Besides, his neatness was compulsive; the young man's
casual way with clothes, books, and records never failed to irritate him. The problem was solved by a little studio he rented
for Bob on Seventh Avenue, around the corner from his hotel.
They dined together every evening, except when Paul conducted; on those nights they met after the concert. For the rest
of the day each had the freedom he needed.

Paul attached little importance to money. From his mystical
youth he had carried away a notion that there was something

immoral about it; he gave away considerable sums to charity and to help young musicians. He was thus prepared to assume his new responsibility, recognizing that Bob could not very well accept a nine-to-five job if he was to make a serious effort to write. All the same, it surprised him that an able-bodied young man should have no qualms about allowing someone to support him. He had had to work hard to make his way in the world, whereas Bob had everything handed him on a silver platter. Paul realized that Bob's generation had different values from the Spartan ones he had grown up with; indeed, it was this difference that fascinated him. Yet, in his ambivalence, he went from one extreme to the other. At times he indulged Bob's every whim; then—as if to make up for it—he became close-fisted and complained about some petty expenditure. When they were together Paul wanted, above all, to speak of love; instead they were continually discussing money. Which infuriated him and strengthened his secret conviction that he would never be loved for himself.

Bob was trying his hand at a play. Neither the conflicts of the drama nor the artifices of the stage came easily to his type of imagination, since his nature leaned toward improvisation and diffuseness. He might have succeeded with lyrical mood-pieces. Instead, he was tackling one of the most tightly organized of literary forms. His models were on the one hand the plays of Chekhov, on the other those of Pinter and Beckett; he did not suspect how carefully made, despite their seeming looseness, these were. The play was about himself and Margo. Although there had been no dearth of drama between them, this was not easy to capture within the confines of a three-act form; nor was he sufficiently removed from the experience to view it with the necessary detachment. If the venture was sound from a psychological standpoint in that it afforded him an outlet for his guilt, it nevertheless demanded the one kind of writing in which he was bound to fail.

He was not able to work well during the first days after his quarrel with Judith; he was not only shaken by that but fearful of what might happen to him in consequence of his arrest. He was especially worried that Paul might find out about his predicament, even though there was not the remotest possibility that the only two people who knew about it—his mother and his lawyer—would betray him. He called Philip daily for reassurance; but no matter how earnestly the lawyer tried to dispel his fears, he fell prey to terrifying visions of being sentenced to jail and disgraced forever. His anxiety grew apace when the trial was postponed twice; Philip was determined to bring him before a sympathetic judge.

Finally, on a rainy morning in February, he took the subway to Centre Street and made his way into a huge gray building. Justice was dispensed on the third floor. Philip was waiting for him; they sat on a bench awaiting their turn. The room was filled with defendants and witnesses, lawyers and policemen, who milled about while a gravel-voiced attendant imposed order upon the assemblage. Bob was silent while Philip haggled with the policeman who had arrested him; the room and its people seemed part of a nightmare. He gave a start when his name was called. Sick with shame he stood before the bar while the judge, a little, bald man with a sallow complexion who looked thoroughly ordinary despite his black robe, gave him a brief lecture and a suspended sentence. It was over. The case had not been important enough to attract anyone's attention. "You were lucky," Philip told him sternly.

Bob's brush with the law had one important result: it freed him from further desire for psychedelic experience. The connection he had established between pills and dazzlingly beautiful visions was permanently broken, its place taken by vastly different associations—the iron bars of the detention pen, the curved prongs of the railing by the river, the depressing courtroom on Centre Street, the harsh voice of the judge. He had been catapulted out of his dream world; the awakening was too painful to go through again.

Painful, too, was the thought of his mother, and all the more so because her disapproval had turned out to be so well justified. He knew he had to go home to fetch some clothes and his typewriter, but could not bring himself to face her. In the end he tried to pick a time when she would be away. He telephoned first; his heart jumped at the sound of her "Hello." He hung up and called back an hour later; there was no answer. Bob took along his keys, let himself in, and was strangely moved to see his room again. He slipped his typewriter into its case and stuffed an assortment of shirts, socks, and shorts into a valise. He had intended to go through his papers and destroy what he could not take with him. Instead he sat on the bed, glancing idly

around him. The Venetian paper knife lay on his desk. He
transferred it to the top of the chest, where he would not have
to see it. The three vertical bars outside his window seemed
uglier than ever despite their coat of shiny white paint. Was it
their function to lock out the world or to lock him in? Now
that he was taking leave of it, he loved his room more than ever.
But the time had come to say good-bye. Life was a process of
outgrowing . . . people, places, things . . . until one outgrew
life itself. The thought brought a gentle melancholy. He roused
himself and opened the top drawer of the chest, half expecting
to find the three hundred-dollar bills. Then he heard the front
door being opened. Seizing valise and typewriter, he slipped out
through the rear.

Most of all he was troubled by his dependence on Paul. The
situation had been different with his mother—he had lived in
her house and had been part of her household. Now, on the
other hand, he was a burden to someone who was under no obligation to look after him. He felt that he had to give something
in return, which made the giving more difficult; besides, there
was an irreconcilable conflict between his gratitude and his need
to feel free. He told himself that this was a temporary arrange-
ment, and that things would change as soon as he had finished
his play. All the same, instead of enjoying the quiet of his little
studio he felt restive in it. Finally he tried to find a part-time job
that would not interfere with his writing. He scanned the help-
wanted advertisements and faced the realization that, as far as
the labor market was concerned, he was hardly a saleable com-
modity. What was he equipped to do—sell shoes at Macy's?

The opening concert of Judith's series took place at the beginning of February. Paul felt that he had to go and asked Bob
to be early for dinner. Bob arrived forty minutes late.

Paul was seething. "You know I have to be out of here by a
quarter past eight."

"So you'll miss the first number." This was the first concert
of his mother's that he would not hear; the thought disturbed
him.

"I'm sitting in a box. Everyone can see me walk in late." He
picked up the phone and ordered dinner. "What kept you?"

"I was at the library reading. Suddenly it was six-thirty. I ran
out, but the bus took forever."

"Why didn't you take a cab?"

Bob's answer was to turn his trousers pockets inside out.

"But I gave you fifteen," Paul remonstrated, "only the other day."

"That was half a week ago." It galled him to have come to Paul for pocket money like a little boy. "What d'you want, an accounting?"

"Not at all! You know I do not begrudge you the money, but you should know what you do with it."

"Suppose I buy a little notebook and enter every item. Rubber bands, eight cents. Chocolate bar, ten cents. Typewriter ribbon, fifty-two cents.

"Nice way for you to talk. After what I am doing for you." Paul immediately regretted the words.

"Ah, now I'm not being grateful. Is that it? We'll have two minutes of silence while I try to appreciate all you've given me." He dropped to his knees in front of Paul and salaamed.

"Stop it, you idiot! Get off that floor!"

Bob raised his voice. "You want gratitude? Here it is!" He salaamed again.

There was a knock on the door; the young man leaped to his feet. The waiter wheeled in their dinner. While Paul and Bob watched in silence, he raised the side leaves of the portable table and placed their chairs.

"Do you have to embarrass me?" Paul brought out darkly after the waiter had left. "He could hear you."

His anger was contagious. "I know I wished myself on you," Bob cried, "but you don't have to do me any favors. I'll leave any time you like."

"God damn it! You come late, you behave in a completely unreasonable way, then you talk as if I am to blame."

Aware that he was in the wrong, the young man had to strike back. "I'm sick of it!" he shouted. "Sure, you're doing a lot for me. But it just won't work. I feel hemmed in, my life is not my own!"

"Then make it your own! There is only one way—to stand on your own feet. To take a job and work for a living as everyone else does. As I did when I was your age."

"Now you sound like my mother. For all the fancy talk about art, deep down you're a money grubber like the rest of them."

"At least I make my own instead of waiting for someone to give it to me."

The little muscles in Bob's jaw twitched. "All those sweet words about sharing our lives and giving me the chance I need —what was all that? Garbage?"

"No. I meant what I said."

"But now that you have to shell out it's beginning to hurt. Is that it?"

"No, that is not it!" Now Paul raised his voice. "What hurts is that you give so little in return for what you receive. Let's face it, my friend, you are a taker, not a giver. And always will be."

"Maybe we should start clocking it. So much for a kiss, so much for an embrace, twice that for a night in bed. Like those hustlers you used to go with. Is that what you want?"

"You need not look down on them!" Paul shot back. "In a way they were more honest than you. At least they gave good value for what they received." Long-accumulated resentments surged through him in a torrent of bitterness. "In your own way you are a hustler too," he snapped, "except that you hold out for more." The deep-set blue eyes were ablaze. "Must be the Jew in you!" he added, as the torrent swept him beyond his intention. "The eternal kike!"

Bob's face went white. For an instant he had the hurt look of a child who has been slapped and doesn't understand why. His features tightened, the lips shriveling to a thin line, and that wild look came into his eyes. "You—!" He choked. Then his hand shot out over the table. He seized the cover of the chafing dish nearest him and hurled it across the room. The disc narrowly missed Paul; there was a crash as the missile hit the mirror on the wall. The second cover smashed into St. Sebastian, shattering the glass that covered the print; the third caught one of the candleticks on the Spanish chest. Bob stood still an instant, staring before him in bewilderment; suddenly he heaved the tureen of split-pea soup on the sofa. The thick fluid splattered over the flowered cover in a viscous green stain, followed by the dish with the veal Parmigiana. Veal and melted cheese spread over the floor as knives and forks hurtled through the air. Half a grapefruit caught Paul in the chest; he ducked the other half. Plates and coffee cups fell at random over the room and were joined by the fruit salad that was to have been their dessert. Now the table was bare. Bob surveyed his handiwork, seized his coat, and ran out.

Paul sank into the chair behind his desk and gazed at the shambles. With a terrible sinking of the heart he knew that he had lost his friend. What madness had caused him to bring about the very end he feared? He buried his face in his hands.

There was a knock on the door. The bellhop stuck his head in, and a look of amazement spread over his face. "Mr. Horvath, what happened?"

"Nothing. Nothing at all." Curtly he added, "Clean it up!"

2

Paul tried to keep his mind on the music. The *Trout Quintet* was one of his favorite works. He followed the unfolding of the variations. How fascinating it was to watch Schubert's imagination at play with the theme. This was the noble chamber-music style of which only the Viennese masters knew the secret. Judith did not. Chamber music demanded that each performer subordinate his personality to the group, but she asserted herself where she should have been self-effacing. In addition, instead of leaving the piano closed she had had the lid raised, which aggravated the imbalance. Her tone was lovely but she constantly called attention to the piano part, now hurrying forward, now holding back, overlaying the noble simplicity of Schubert's line with unnecessary decoration. The fault, Paul decided, stemmed from her temperament rather than from lack of understanding. She was too much the soloist to be part of a team.

She was wearing the same dress as on the night he conducted the Mozart concerto for her. He did not ordinarily notice what women wore, but for some reason he remembered that flame-colored gown. It seemed a little tighter; she had put on weight. With her jet-black hair and high color she was a commanding presence on stage. He recalled the two evenings with her at the seashore, especially the uncomfortable hour on the breakwater and his precipitous escape. The memory of that night, when he held Bob in his arms for the first time, filled Paul with an anguish so intense that he felt he must cry out. All his life he had dreamed of finding someone like her son, and now he had driven him away. Yet even as he lacerated himself with futile regrets, he could not shake off the suspicion that in some mysterious way the break was inevitable. One lost what one loved, if only because one was too eager to hold on to it.

He saw again the blotches of pea soup on the couch and the broken crockery. There was the hurt expression on Bob's face and that wild look in his eyes. Paul sighed. How could he have brought himself to say such cruel things to someone he worshiped? He must have been mad. We knew ourselves only on the surface. Deep underneath were unsuspected forces that seethed like lava at the bottom of a volcano, waiting to erupt. He tried to find comfort in plans for a reconciliation. He would humble himself before the young man and beg his forgiveness. But he knew Bob too well to fool himself; the damage could not be repaired. Too late, his heart cried out. He had lost his beloved forever . . .

The finale began; strings and piano bandied about a little tune in Hungarian style, filled with the grace and longing that were Schubert's alone. Paul listened, carried away. Out of his fears, his sorrows, and his loneliness man created the ideal domain of art, an enchanted garden where his spirit was purged of its dross. Was not art the only true refuge, enabling us to rise above our limitations and attain the highest of which we were capable? Paul rested his head on his hand. The melody returned, warming him with its tenderness. His eyes filled. He knew only that the heavenly sounds had exorcised the demon within him, dispelling his grief by lifting him into a purer realm.

There was much applause at the end of the quintet. He was glad, for Judith's sake. It occurred to him that if the audience had known more about chamber music they might have been less enthusiastic. People did not know what they were listening to; they didn't trust their ears. They believed what their friends told them during intermission, or what the critics told them the next morning. This was as true in Paris, London, Vienna, and Rome as it was in New York. Which explained why the musical public was more unstable, more susceptible to the winds of fashion than the theater or art public. People knew what they were looking at in a gallery or in a theater; in the concert hall you could sell them anything. Paul scowled at the thought, since it made his own success seem spurious, yet he knew he had won it through steadfast dedication to his ideals. Maybe a few did know and influenced the rest . . . The players took their bows; Judith looked radiant. He noticed that she consistently stood in front of the others—in her mind she was the leader of the group. Paul smiled. One had to admire ladies who played chamber music in public. As somebody said about dancing bears and lady preachers, the wonder was not that they did it well but that they did it at all.

Later, at Walter and Alice's, he told Judith how much he had enjoyed the concert. She sat on the sofa, legs drawn up under her—she had taken off her shoes and her wide skirt fell in shimmering folds over the side of the couch. Paul covered his misery by being unusually pleasant. The more he smiled, the more miserable he felt.

Walter, glass in hand—he was drinking soda, but at least it looked like a highball—glanced contentedly around the crowded room. All the ingredients of a successful party were present: plenty of food and drink, and a group of pleasant, well-dressed people who acted as if they liked being with each other. Timing, too, was important—a party should be intense but brief. For this reason he preferred after-concert receptions—people arrived at eleven, buzzed around for an hour, and ran.

It was essential to his enjoyment that the permanent members of his circle be present. He looked around to see where each of them was. Alice, standing at the table, was serving lobster salad. Birdie was bouncing around in the vestibule, her shrill laughter floating above the din. Judith held forth on the couch. Max Rubin perched on the edge of his armchair with the irritated look he assumed whenever he had to listen to her. Paul, as usual, lent distinction to the room. Margo was missing because she was in Munich. So, to his surprise, was Bob. "Where's your boy?" he asked Judith.

"He had a terrible cold," she answered smoothly. "It's the first concert of mine he's missed, and he was so disappointed. But I made him stay home."

She returned to her discussion with Max. Now that she had launched her own series, she addressed him as one impresario to another. She was determined to show him that she had forgotten the unpleasantness between them. "What you don't realize, Max, is that there's a new public for music, and it's much more knowledgeable than the old. Sooner or later you'll have to take their taste into account. Look at tonight. A program of top caliber, and the hall was filled."

"The hall was papered," the old man said testily.

"That's not true." She turned toward the vestibule. "Birdie," she called, "Max thinks the hall was papered. Was it?"

"I should say not," Birdie lied. In any case, it was only half papered.

"Tsk!" The old man looked skeptical. "Birdie knows her business. She'd fill a hall if she had to drag them off the sidewalk."

"The important thing," Judith said in her loftiest manner, "is not whether they paid for their tickets. What matters is that they came and listened to the music."

"You can afford to say that because your expenses were covered," Max retorted sourly. "I hear you got a grant." He was tactful enough not to mention Walter's contribution. "So you're not depending on box office. That's a horse of a different color."

"True," Judith conceded. "But within five years, I'll bet you, the series will break even."

"I should live so long."

Guests were leaving; Walter saw them to the door. Finally only an intimate group remained. Now he could relax. He took a plateful of food and settled in an armchair, prepared to enjoy what he regarded as the best part of the evening. Precisely at this point someone mentioned the trial of Nazi war criminals in Frankfurt.

"Those trials are a farce!" Judith exclaimed. "A dozen Germans are picked for punishment so that all the others can say, 'They did it. They're the guilty ones.' It's as obscene as their crimes were."

"It's their way of admitting their guilt," Walter said uneasily. Conversation in a drawing room, he felt, should be mild and pleasant.

"On the contrary," Judith persisted, "it's their way of escaping their guilt. Look at the verdicts. A man found guilty of killing two hundred thousand people gets two years in prison. I suppose that's fifteen minutes for each one he killed. It's madness."

"I don't see what purpose is served," Paul interjected, "by

harping on these matters over and over. Twenty years have passed. It's time we began to forget."

"Forget?" Judith's eyes opened in amazement. "Six million Jews were gassed and you want us to forget?"

"You sound," he retorted, "as if they were the only victims. After all, it was a world war. Other nations suffered too, including the Germans." He disliked intensely the tone of this discussion. "We keep hearing about the six million. More likely it was two."

"What's that you said?" She stared at him.

There was an awkward silence; Paul faced the others across a widening gulf. He was aware that he had said the wrong thing and wanted to explain, but in his embarrassment made matters worse. "I'm only saying that when the Jews keep shouting about their fate they show the same aggressive qualities that made the Germans hate them in the first place." He stopped, as if he were trying to formulate his ideas in as fair a spirit as possible. "The Jew is a curious mixture. He has a spiritual heritage, yet he is not really—how shall I put it?—spiritual. He has a religion, yet in the deepest sense he is not religious. He was able to survive down the centuries through aggressiveness and double-dealing, and these are the qualities he most often shows to the world. Is it any wonder that these are the qualities the world dislikes in him?"

"You know what?" Judith paused a moment before striking home. "You sound like a Nazi yourself."

"Judith!" Walter jumped up, his role as host outweighing all other considerations. "You shouldn't make statements like that. Would Paul be in this house if he were a Nazi?"

The temperature in the room had dropped perceptibly. "I only meant," Paul said, "that if the Jew would——"

"We know perfectly well what you meant!" Judith shouted. "According to you it's the Jews' fault that the Nazis decided to exterminate them." She jumped up and swept the room with a dramatic glance. "I don't know how the rest of you feel, but I'm not staying here to listen to this antisemitic bilge."

Birdie put out a restraining arm. "Judith, you're putting words into the maestro's mouth. How can you call him anti-Semitic when——"

Judith pushed the arm aside. "I know, you're going to tell me some of his best friends are Jews."

Birdie gestured round the room. "Well, aren't we?"

Paul looked genuinely puzzled at the storm he had stirred up. "All I meant was that every nation has its good and bad traits. Scotchmen are considered tight, Italians are called irresponsible, Spaniards cruel. Why should Jews be so sensitive if their unpleasant traits——"

"Because," Judith interrupted, "neither Scotchmen nor Italians nor Spaniards went through Buchenwald and Auschwitz. That's why. I don't want to hear any more of this!" She rushed into the bedroom where the women had left their coats.

Birdie followed her. "Darling, you're all worked up for no good reason."

"What's that?" Judith exploded. "No good reason?"

"Sh . . .'

"Don't you shush me! If more people called a spade a spade there'd be less of this kind of talk. You people make me sick. No principles. No guts. You're all afraid to stand up to him!" She grabbed her coat, strode to the vestibule, and without bidding the others good night slammed the hall door behind her.

Alice turned to Walter. "Won't you see her to the elevator?"

"Certainly not!" he said angrily. "Not when she behaves like this."

"Then I will." Alice rose and went out into the hall.

"I am terribly sorry," Paul said to Walter. "I assure you I did not mean to give offense."

"Of course not. How about another drink?"

"It is late. I really must be going."

Birdie came in with her coat on; Max followed suit. By the time they reached the elevator Judith was gone. On the way down Max turned to Birdie. "She has a violent temper, that girl. You ought to tell her."

"She was upset."

"So? Do we make peepee in the middle of the room just because we feel like it? We learn to control it. That's what she has to learn."

Birdie smiled. "She never will."

The old man rolled his head from side to side. "Oy, will she pay for it."

When they came out Judith stood at the curb looking for a taxi. Paul turned quickly to Birdie. "Say good night for me. And do tell her how sorry I am that she misunderstood——"

"Don't worry, maestro, I will."

He walked off with Max. Birdie approached Judith. "You shouldn't have taken on like that, my dear. Paul was sorry you twisted his words."

Judith pretended not to hear. "I always thought there was something peculiar about him," she said quietly.

"Look, Judith, he's not Jewish and you can't expect him to feel the same as we do. You're not being realistic."

"Are you? We're sitting together, friends and colleagues. All of a sudden there's a line down the middle of the room, he's on one side and we're on the other. That's how it happened in Berlin and Vienna. That's how it could happen here."

"You're being morbid," Birdie cried. "Absolutely!"

Upstairs, Walter paced the living room in a rage. "Who the hell does she think she is, breaking up a party like that?"

Alice came to Judith's defense. "What the maestro said touched off something deep inside her. It meant more to her than any party."

"This wasn't *any* party, it was my—I mean, our party. I don't like an evening to end on a sour note."

"Don't worry about it, dear. They had a perfectly good time. Ask them again and they'll all be here."

"It's just that," he persisted, "she never considers anyone but herself."

"You finally discovered that?" She smiled, but in order to be fair to Judith added, "How many of your friends do?"

He went down to buy the *Times,* and was still disturbed when he stopped in at Birdie's. She was in a thoughtful mood. "Something came to an end tonight. I have a strange feeling that our little group—Alice, you, me, Judith, Paul, Max—will never be together again."

"Ridiculous! Why should we break up?"

"I don't know. But I can't help thinking it was our last time."

"Sweetie." As he took her in his arms, he wondered if she was right.

3

The street lamp threw its glimmering light over the little square by the river. Bob leaned against the railing, his back to the curved prongs. He looked up at the eighteenth floor. The light went out in the large oblong window beside the terrace; he knew that the party was over, and crossed the square.

The doorman looked at him dubiously. "Are you expected?"

"No. Just say Bob Conrad is downstairs."

"Their company left."

"I know."

The doorman plugged in the wire. "She says for you to come up."

Alice was waiting for him at the door. "Bobby! How nice to see you." She held out her hand.

"I hope I'm not disturbing you." He smiled feebly. "This is no time for visiting."

"Come in." She saw the distraught look on his face. "I'm sorry you weren't at the party."

"I couldn't make it," he brought out vaguely.

"Take your coat off. They're cleaning up. Let's go where we won't be disturbed." She led the way to the study, which was lined with books and had two leather chairs. She sat down in one and pointed to the other. "Now . . . tell me."

He stared at the rug. It seemed to him that if he were to tell her everything, the poison festering inside him would vanish. But how could he? It would be like stripping naked in front of her. Yet how could he ask her to help him if he began by being dishonest with her? In the end he made a clean breast of it— from his arrest and the night in jail to the break with his mother, his attempt at suicide, and his going berserk that evening at Paul's. He went on and on, keeping his eyes on the rug most of the time but raising them every now and then to hers. And as he spoke the terrible burden that had weighed him down seemed to ease a little. The one detail he withheld was the nature of his relationship with Paul, representing him as a friend of his mother's who had been kind to him. Even when a person stripped, the figleaf had to remain. At last he was done. He sat back in his chair and took a deep breath. "Well, I feel better now."

"I'm glad you came, Bobby. And I'm glad you told me what you did." A gentle smile crossed her lips. "It means you trust me."

"I do."

"What now?"

His fist went up against his chin. "I really don't know."

"It doesn't have to be settled tonight. Think about it during the next few days—I'm sure you'll see your way."

Walter had returned. He heard them and came into the study.

"We have a visitor," Alice said, as if it were the most natural thing in the world for her to be entertaining a young man at two in the morning.

Walter took his cue from her. "Hiya, Bob." He extended his hand.

Alice rose. "I've asked Bobby to stay over."

"How nice." Walter managed to sound unsurprised. "I hope he'll be comfortable."

"I know I will," Bob interjected, trying not to show how grateful he felt.

Walter gave Alice a questioning look. "He'll sleep in—?"

"The guest room," Alice said smoothly, although she had not thought about where to put him until that moment. Turning to Bob, "Come, I'll show you where it is," she said and preceded him down the corridor. She hesitated a moment before she opened the door. "This was my son's room." She switched on the light, raised the Venetian blinds, and opened the windows. "It needs a bit of airing. Otherwise it's ready." She pointed to the closet. "You'll find some night things in there." Bending over the bed, she turned the coverlet.

"It's very kind of you——" Without giving him any warning, his lips began to tremble; he turned his face away. Then, steadying his voice, "I wish I could tell you how much this means to me," he said.

She put her hand on his shoulder. "You don't have to." She kissed him good night and shut the door behind her.

Walter was waiting for her in the bedroom. "When did all this happen?"

She shrugged her shoulders. "How should I know? It happened." She paused before Gene's picture on the sideboard and the vase of fresh wildflowers near it. An hour ago she had not dreamed that someone would be sleeping in his room. Now that Bob was there, she was glad of it.

4

Paul sat at the back of the bar, staring into his vodka and tonic. He had not visited Patty's Corner in months. It depressed him to be back. The bar was as dark and crowded as ever, and Patty's baritone hadn't changed—if anything, it was more raucous. Her rendition of "I Rise When You Enter," against the familiar background of arpeggios, enchanted her admirers.

For the hundredth time his thoughts reverted to Bob. He went over their friendship from beginning to end, probing for the point where he could tell himself, "I should have done this instead of that"; but each incident led inevitably to the next. As the plant was contained in the seed, so the entire relationship—with all its frustrations and torment, its excitement and ecstasy—was prefigured in their first night together. No matter what course he would have pursued, the final result would have been the same. There was a malevolent force at work in the universe that took pleasure in defeating man—or pushed him to defeat himself. Paul remembered how, in one of his frantic notes to Bob, he had quoted Beethoven's letter to his nephew. The mightiest genius of his time humbled himself before a thoroughly ordinary young man who could not bear the sight of him, and the more the great man implored, the more eager Karl was to escape him. A mysterious chemistry determined the interaction of two personalities. Try though they might, it could not be changed . . .

He found it curious that he should have quarreled with both mother and son on the same evening. She was an imperious woman. If he had not been so upset he would never have been so maladroit. Most people did not take offense if you suggested that their nation or race had some unpleasant traits; they accepted the opinion in the friendly spirit in which it was given. Not Jews! At the slightest hint of criticism they became infuriated and considered you an enemy, no matter how kindly tney had felt toward you a moment before. A stiff-necked, tiresome people. Even their own God—as the Old Testament made clear —could not bear them.

"Nureyev was *wonderful*," the young man at his right exclaimed, and looked around to make sure that he had been heard. "I adore *Giselle*," his companion replied. Paul turned away so that he would not have to see them. On his other side stood a blond youth, slender and attractive like all the anonymous young men he had found at Patty's. He thrust a cigarette between his lips, went through the motions of looking for his lighter; then, with the familiar tightening of his throat, turned and said, "Would you have a match?"

Their conversation followed the well-worn path. It turned out that the young man's name was Tim, he came from Boston, and was looking for a job. By the time they left the bar they were friends. They took a cab to the West Side. Paul entered his hotel alone; the young man was to follow.

The debris left by Bob had been cleared away; the room looked itself again, giving Paul the impression of a stage set that had been shifted for the next scene. Not even when Tim came in could he shake off the sadness that had haunted him all evening. He fondled the young man, and a terrible longing for Bob swept over him. The stranger asked him to turn out the light; from the hallway, a faint glow filtered in through the old-fashioned transom. Paul took off his clothes and lay down on the bed, watching Tim undress. Presently the young man stood naked before him, his shoulders outlined against the half-light. He approached the bed; Paul sat up expectantly, raising one arm in a gesture of welcome. The young man bent over him.

Suddenly a fist shot out of the dark and crashed into Paul's forehead. He looked up in bewilderment as expectancy gave way to fear. "Please—!" he stammered, "Please—!" The fist descended again, knocking the breath out of his body. Before he could cry out, another blow fell on his face and another; the darkness exploded into floating points of light, a constellation of stars. Then, as the blows continued to rain down upon him, it grew dark. His body sagged; his head hit the floor.

Tim turned on the light and cast a practiced glance around the room. He threw on his clothes, went through Paul's trousers, and pulled out the wallet which he emptied of its contents— three ten-dollar bills and two singles. He thrust these into his pockets and tossed the wallet on the floor. Stepping over the prostrate body he made his way to the Spanish chest, opened the top drawer, and emptied the white box that contained Paul's cuff links and studs. Next he went through the middle drawer and found the envelope that held the conductor's ready cash—three fifty-dollar bills and five twenties. Then he made his way back to the bed.

Paul's head lay tilted to one side, out of line with the rest of his body as if it had been snapped off. A thin stream of blood descended from his nostril to the corner of his mouth; his lips hung open, he was breathing with difficulty. Tim spied the ring on the fourth finger of Paul's right hand. He knelt down, yanked off the ring and held it up against the light to appraise the garnet in the setting. He was about to leave when he noticed the crucifix on Paul's chest. With a swift pull he broke the thin gold chain from which it hung. Paul's head fell back to the floor with a thud.

The telephone began to ring. Tim gave a start and stuffed the loot into his pockets. He glanced round him, seized his coat and fled.

The telephone stopped after six rings. After an interval it began again. This time it rang nine times before it stopped. Birdie hung up and looked at her watch. It was twenty to three and she was worried; Paul never stayed out as late as this on the night before a concert. She had been calling him at intervals since midnight, knowing that he must be upset over the unpleasantness at the party. She decided to try again at three.

When she received no answer she became worried. She telephoned the night clerk and inquired if he had seen the maestro. The clerk recalled that Mr. Horvath had come home about an hour before. Birdie hesitated no longer. She threw a coat over her shoulders, hurried downstairs, and took a taxi to the hotel. She rang Paul's bell. Silence. She tried the door and found him lying in a pool of blood, his face swollen, his right eye blackened. Birdie let out a scream, collected herself, and ran to the phone to summon the clerk. She lifted the receiver only to thrust it down again, called her doctor instead, and asked him to come right away. Then she went to the bathroom, held a towel under the cold faucet, and tried to stanch Paul's wound.

The following morning Birdie informed the manager of the orchestra that the maestro was confined to his bed with a severe case of pneumonia; the doctor had forbidden all visitors until the fever passed. The afternoon papers carried her story, and by the time Birdie saw Walter she almost believed it.

Walter pursed his lips. "Sounds fishy to me."

"What's fishy about catching pneumonia? He's been run-down all winter, and the weather's been terrible. I'm surprised he held up as long as he did."

Walter shook his hand in the air in a gesture of skepticism. "Something doesn't jell."

Birdie shrugged wearily. "I knew a psychoanalyst from Vienna. He used to tell me what a funny lot the Viennese were. They sat at their cafés, watching. If a man crossed the street with a woman, it meant they were having an affair. If he crossed with another man, he was a queer. And if he crossed alone, he masturbated." She laughed shrilly. "New York's getting to be the same way."

At the concert that afternoon the orchestra was led by the assistant conductor, a comparatively unknown young man who, without a rehearsal, turned in a beautiful performance. The next morning his picture was on the front page of the *Times*. Thus, inadvertently, young Tim from Boston helped launch a brilliant career.

5

Paul lay resting. His head was still bandaged, but the swelling on his face had subsided. He shuddered to think of what might have been the outcome of his escapade. He could have bled to death, and the affair could have been plastered over the papers —*Famous Conductor Found Unconscious in Hotel*. He thanked the merciful Father who had brought him through this trial with nothing more than a scare.

But why had he been so sorely tried? Why had God seen fit to inflict this humiliation upon him? Paul buried his head in the pillow as though to escape the question. He had followed his lust wherever it had led, and it had led him into the valley of the shadow of death. Time and again he had heard of the dangers to which his pursuit of beauty exposed him, yet he had persisted in his folly. His narrow escape was a warning: if he did not mend his ways he ran the risk of a violent—and shameful—end.

His gaze turned inward. How could he, for the satisfaction of a momentary impulse, have jeopardized his career, his reputation, his life? He thought of himself as a rational human being who was widely admired for his intellect. How could he be guilty of such recklessness? Could it be that what we called an artist's intelligence—his ability to think and feel clearly within the confines of his art—had nothing to do with his ability to solve the practical problems of life? Or was it that, to punish himself for his deviation from natural law, he secretly desired to destroy himself?

The explosion of Tim's fist against his head seemed to have pushed aside his involvement with Bob. It was obvious that he was not destined to find love. At this stage in his life he probably was not even capable of it. A great weariness pressed upon his heart. If only he could crawl out of himself, become someone else! He heaved a sigh. In losing Bob a phase of his life had come to an end, a precious gift of warmth and light had been snatched from him forever. He stared somberly at the lithograph of St. Sebastian, from whose frame the splintered glass had been removed. We all had our cross to bear. Was this his?

Painful, too, was the recollection of his battle with Judith. He had had no desire to attack the Jews; as she herself recognized, some of his best friends were. Besides, would it not be foolish to attack them in a city like New York where there were millions of them? All the same, one grew tired of their complaints. They seemed to regard themselves as the only victims of history, forgetting that millions of non-Jews had died in the war too. Had they been killed as soldiers they would have had no special claim to sympathy. Well, was not the extermination camp simply an extension of the battlefield? Life was cruel, nature pitiless; certain organisms were chosen to survive while others perished. Everyone knew these truths. All that Hitler did was to act upon them. The convulsions of nature created new forms; so, too, the convulsions of history, by wiping out the weak, left more room for those who survived. The strong were meant to inherit the earth; inevitably they aroused the envy of their inferiors. Nature herself was aristocratic: one sperm out of millions was chosen to create life; the rest were doomed to die. Similarly millions of nonentities peopled the earth only because out of them might arise the chosen one—the leader. To him alone was it granted to fulfill his destiny.

In Paul's hierarchy the artist ranked even higher than the

statesman or warrior. The ideal world created by the artist balanced the ruthless one of nature. It was a hermetic universe based on the perfect synthesis of intellect and emotion, in which cause led to effect by the noble logic of the creative mind. Yet even in the frictionless world of art the cruel laws of natural selection prevailed: only the most talented survived; all others were doomed to fail. The great artist was to be envied because through him other men were able to transcend their limitations. He incarnated the finest to which mankind might aspire.

Paul lay still, following the play of his thoughts. How ironic that he, who had encompassed the highest level to which a man might rise, should also have sunk to the lowest. If the truth about him were known, the public that regarded him with reverence would heap upon him their utmost contempt; they who now welcomed him with applause would dismiss him with jeers and hisses. How could vile corruption exist side by side with the most ardent longing for perfection? Or was each the necessary counterpart of the other? What if God and the Devil were not two opposites, as he had always believed, but two parts of an all-embracing whole, each needing and nourishing the other? How else account for the fact that an omnipotent God had never wiped out the Devil, and for all His championing of good had always permitted evil to flourish? The thought was appalling, yet it brought Paul a modicum of relief from his self-loathing and even offered him an explanation for his otherwise incomprehensible behavior. In his perplexity he found refuge in his favorite author, who understood so well the duality in man's soul. "Let them say no more," St. Augustine wrote, "when they perceive two conflicting wills in one man, that the conflict is between two contrary souls, of two contrary substances, from two contrary principles, one good and the other bad." For this profoundest of saints, good was not so much the absence of evil as the conquest thereof. "I will now call to mind my past foulness and the carnal corruptions of my soul; not because I love them, but that I may love Thee, O my God. For love of Thy love I do it, reviewing my most wicked ways in the very bitterness of my remembrance, that Thou mayest grow sweet unto me."

He heard the hall door being unlocked; it would be Birdie. He had given her the key when the nurse was dismissed. She clomped over to the bed with an air of synthetic cheerfulness. "Well, how's our patient today?"

"Much better."

She took off her coat and pulled a chair beside the bed. "Maestro, that's what I like to hear."

He still found it hard to believe that he owed his life to this plump little Jewess. She had been the soul of discretion in shielding him from the snooping of reporters and the solicitude of friends. The thought that she had seen him lying helpless on the floor, his secret revealed to her gaze, overwhelmed him with shame. One thing alone mitigated his embarrassment: she managed to make him feel that he did not have to explain anything, that whatever had happened did not in the slightest alter her regard for him, and all she wanted was for him to get well. To such devotion he could not help responding.

"I have been thinking," he said.

"What about?"

"A man's life falls into periods. He may not be aware of it at the time, but on looking back he can see the divisions, like chapters in a story. I feel that a chapter has just come to an end."

"How d'you mean?"

"I should like to return to Europe. I have been here now for twelve years. I feel it is time to go back."

"But the public adores you, maestro. You've had a terrific success here."

"True. But one must know when one's time is up. One must not overstay. My roots are there, and that is where I belong."

"But they're offering you a three-year contract."

He shook his head. "No. I will finish out the season and go. I can always come back and guest-conduct if I like. What I need now is a change."

"Aren't you allowing a single——" She stopped, looking for the right word. "—a single accident to influence you more than it should?"

It was the first time his unfortunate encounter had been mentioned between them. Paul stared before him as if he had not heard her. How could he tell her that what had happened was no accident, it was implicit in his whole manner of life? "I have thought it over carefully," he said smoothly, "and I am quite certain this is what I want."

Birdie seemed to be on the point of remonstrating but thought better of it. "I'll be sorry to see you go," she said with feeling. "Absolutely."

"You did a good job for me."

She gave him a worshipful smile. "With such material it was easy."

Her acceptance of his decision brought home to him that she knew why he had reached it. "I want to thank you for——" The bony face tightened, the steel-blue eyes seemed to sink deeper into their sockets. He forced himself to continue. "—for everything you did."

"My pleasure," Birdie said in her best cocktail manner.

"I mean, you took very good care of me and——" he grew red, "—I am most grateful."

"Think nothing of it. You are a great artist, and I would do anything in the world for you." It was time to change the subject. "You're looking much better, maestro. The swelling is down. All sorts of people have been dying to see you, but I told them you weren't strong enough yet." She looked appraisingly at his black eye. "I think in a day or two you might have visitors. I'll bring you a pair of dark glasses."

He lowered his eyes. "Good."

Birdie picked up the telephone. "I'll order lunch," she said, "then I've got to fly."

He rested his head on the pillow. As he watched her he realized that there was no one in the world who knew as much about him as she. How strange!

6

The passing weeks brought no abatement of Judith's anger at her son. The break between them, she felt, was not simply another in a long series of quarrels. It was different in kind, and seemed in some fundamental way to have changed her feelings toward him. For years she had made herself believe that there was no problem between them—no matter how severe—that could not be solved. Now, in a mood of disenchantment, she swung to the other extreme and became convinced that the distance between the generations was too great to be bridged. Would the two of them ever find their way back to each other? She doubted it.

Although she kept few secrets from Birdie, she had refrained from telling her about Bob's brush with the law and the rift between them; but her reluctance to reveal this was outweighed ultimately by her need to confide in someone. Having made Birdie swear never to repeat it, she told her the whole story and harangued her with increasing vehemence to prove that she was in the right.

For once Birdie disagreed with her. "I think you were too hard on him."

"On the contrary, I wasn't severe enough."

"Many young fellows get into trouble of one kind or another. What's so unusual about that?" Birdie felt that, compared to what had happened to Paul, Bob's escapade was small potatoes.

"It was a terrible shock. Try to imagine what it means to raise a child, to give him every advantage, and suddenly you find out things about him you never dreamed of. I felt I no longer knew my own son."

"He was in a tight spot and needed your sympathy. Instead you gave him hell."

"The trouble with this generation is they get too much sympathy." Judith's dark eyes unloosed their thunder. "When we were young, if something went wrong we blamed ourselves. Nowadays they read Freud and prove to you that it's all your fault."

"Well, isn't it?" Birdie inquired brightly.

"If you were a parent you'd sing a different tune. No matter what you do for them it's not enough. The world owes them everything, and it's always the world that's wrong." Judith's lower lip pushed forward in her obdurate way. "Believe me, they're monsters. Consider yourself lucky you don't have any."

"Still, when the chips were down you were not behind him."

Birdie's unexpected opposition impelled Judith to reveal more than she had intended. "I was so upset I did something I'd never done before. I searched his room. I guess I was trying to find some explanation for what had happened, and found his diary. You should have read some of the things he said about me."

"Ah, your vanity was hurt!"

"Why not my sense of loyalty? When I was his age I respected my parents, I felt I owed them everything. But these monsters don't know what gratitude means. For them it's a dirty word."

"You had no right to read what he wrote about you.

"My dear, you're missing the point. He shouldn't have written it. What's more, he shouldn't have allowed himself to think it. This, I guess, is what I can't forgive."

That week Birdie reported to Judith that Bob was staying with Walter and Alice. Judith was relieved. Convinced that Bob and she needed a separation to regain their balance, she was especially pleased about Walter's involvement. She had always regretted the absence in Bob's life of an older man whom he could emulate. Walter had both feet on the ground and would be a good influence. In regard to Alice, whom she described as "that cold fish," her feelings were less charitable. She had never thought a time would come when she would be jealous of Alice. Now, to her amazement, it had.

"He'll turn on the charm," she told Birdie, "and when he does you'd think butter wouldn't melt in his mouth. It's the same as when he was little and visited his father over the weekend. I was the ogress because I had to discipline him all week, but his father let him do whatever he liked, so it was all fun and holiday. He'll get on with Alice all right. She'll tell him that everything he does is fine."

"That's what he needs right now. You'd be the worst thing in the world for him, and he for you."

Judith was silent. Finally, "I'm afraid you're right," she said reluctantly.

Philip refused to accept a fee for his services; she went to his office to thank him. "Tell me," she asked him, "where did I fail? What did I do that was wrong?" How strange it was that hardly a memory remained to her of the time she lay naked in his arms. Where did passion go when it ceased to exist?

"Don't blame yourself, Judith. Bob's generation grew up after the war. How can you expect them not to be affected by it."

"You're not answering my question. What did I myself do that threw him off?"

"I'm trying to tell you it's not a question of what you did or didn't do. We're living in a crazy time."

Judith, unconvinced, pursued her own line of thought. "I failed as a wife. I failed you as a friend. Now, worst of all, I failed as a mother."

"You're making too much of this squabble. Both of you will get over it and go on as you did in the past."

"No, Phil, something happened between us that I don't think can be patched up. It's a terrible thing to lose a child, but I've lost him. There's no use kidding myself." Her lips curved a wry smile. "It's a funny thing. The world thinks of me as a success, and I feel like a complete failure."

"How about your success as an artist? Maybe your real talent lies there."

She sighed. "I'm not even sure of that. Besides, if you think one makes up for the other, you're mistaken."

He remembered the time when he was still attracted to her. "It's not all black and white, Judith. We fail in some things and succeed in others. The two are all mixed up."

She leaned forward and tapped him lightly on the wrist. "Well, then, it's the mixture I don't like."

She threw herself into the work connected with her concert series. Neither the thought of Bobby nor the absence of a man in her life could dampen the exhilaration she found in directing the project. The first concert had drawn excellent reviews, the second had a full house. Max Rubin might regard her as a tyro, but she was more closely attuned than he to the temper of the time. The curiosity of the public was whetted by the novelties on her programs. True, she had no real understanding of modern music, but she had a shrewd sense of what was currently fashionable and a natural flair for putting together an exciting evening. By the end of the third concert it was apparent that her series would be successful; in other words, her deficit would be no greater than she had anticipated.

Her one failing as an administrator was that she could not delegate authority; she insisted on making every decision herself. Partly this was due to her conviction—Birdie regarded it as arrogance—that in certain matters she knew better than everyone else, and partly to her need to feel indispensable. In any case, the succession of lunches, meetings, and dinners that filled her days served to distract her from her inner turmoil. She had a talent for creating storms; every week brought at least one crisis. She bullied or cajoled her way from one to the next, weeping, threatening, imploring as circumstances dictated, and reached the day of the concert in a state of hysteria. Then the event came off—to everyone's astonishment, including her own —with brilliant success, and she was ready to repeat the pattern in preparation for the next.

Judith belonged to a rather large class of persons who assume that their private concerns are of overwhelming interest to their friends. That winter, no matter where she was, her conversation revolved around her series. She had always enjoyed talking about herself, and now had a perfect excuse for doing so. She had solved, rather well she thought, the delicate problem of her own appearance on the series. Having played in the first concert, she did not schedule herself again until the last; for the following season, too, she arranged to take part in only two concerts. She called a meeting of her board of directors to discuss her plans for the future. Judith did not expect her directors to direct, and would have been resentful if they had tried. Having picked them herself, she knew that they would approve whatever she did.

The meeting took place on a sunny morning in March in Walter's office. She sat at the head of a long oak table, facing the window that overlooked Westchester and the Sound. She wore her black and green tweed suit and felt that she looked her best; she wanted to be both businesslike and feminine. Speaking with assurance, she presented to her board a sober appraisal of her achievements for the first season and her hopes for the second. As she had anticipated, they were unanimous in their approval.

Walter, watching her, thought she did well. He asked her to stay after the others had gone. "There's something I've been meaning to ask you," he said when they were alone. "It's about Margo Scholtz."

"Margo? How is she doing?"

"She was a sensation in Germany."

"How nice." Like many artists, Judith disliked hearing about anyone else's success.

"Max thinks she'll be making her debut at the Met next year. It's practically in the bag. Anyway——" He assumed a casual air so as not to appear to be asking a favor. "—I thought she might sing at one of the concerts next year."

"You mean, in my series?"

He noticed that she said *my* instead of *our*. "Yes. I would be very pleased."

Judith smiled sweetly. "I'm having only chamber music in the series. No opera."

Walter smiled too. "I'm sure there's plenty of chamber music with voice."

"There is, but I wasn't planning that sort of thing."

"Can't your plans be changed a little? After all, the programs for next year haven't been printed."

She sighed, with a show of patience. "Walter, darling, I've already decided what I want to do. Where would I be if I changed the series every time someone asked me to?"

"Someone isn't asking you to. I am."

If he had not mentioned Max she might have been more tractable. As it was, her lower lip thrust forward obstinately. "Look, Walter, the whole point of my going into this was to create a series where only musical values would be considered."

"You sound as if Margo were a second rater. She's tops!"

"I'm sure she is," Judith said dryly. "But I've already told you —she doesn't fit my plans."

"You mean, you're going to turn me down?" He looked at her, incredulous.

"Of course I'll turn you down if you try to interfere in artistic matters." The smile was still there but the sweetness was gone. "I never would if you asked me a personal favor. But you're asking a musical favor, which is something else again."

"When you asked me for the money," he said, resentful that he had to remind her of this, "I had other plans too. I changed them because you wanted me to."

"True. But just because you gave me a couple of thousand dollars doesn't mean you can dictate policy."

"I don't want to dictate policy. I gave you the money out of friendship and I expect you to act the same way. I'm not asking anything for myself, but for a young artist in whose talent I believe." He remembered Alice's remark the night he told her about the ten thousand: *Anything Judith gets her hands on she'll run exactly as she pleases.* It infuriated him that his wife was right.

"Friendship is one thing, music is another. I'd love to oblige you, but I've created a certain approach for next year's series, and Margo doesn't fit in with it. I'm sorry."

"Why d'you need a board of directors if you decide everything your own way?"

"Look, Walter, I swore to throw off the interference of the Max Rubins. Would there be any point in doing that if I substituted another kind of interference? Now be an angel and drop the subject. Please!"

Walter drew a breath. "Very well. I guess I can't convince you." It had never occurred to him that she might refuse his request. Obviously he had been taken by this power-mad, unpredictable woman. He had planned to ask her to lunch; now that was out of the question. Chatting amiably, he escorted her to the elevator.

He returned to his office in a fury and summoned his secretary. "Take a letter, please." His fingers drummed on the desk as he dictated. "Dear Judith, I do not feel that I can remain on the board of directors of an organization in which my suggestions receive so little consideration. I therefore submit my resignation, effective immediately. I regret this step because I have enjoyed our friendship through the years, but my idea of friendship is apparently different from yours. Sincerely, Walter." He had this sent off special delivery. Now he was ready for lunch.

Birdie was appalled when Judith told her what had happened. "You must be out of your mind!" she shrieked into the telephone.

"Why? Because I stood up for a principle?"

"Principle, my ass! What harm would it do if Margo sang, if that's what he wants."

"You don't understand," Judith retorted hotly. "I'm the one who fixes policy for the series. Once I begin to take orders from anyone, I might as well give up. The project would lose its direction and become a rich man's plaything. Is that what you want?"

"It's you who don't understand. You've made a colossal mistake, my dear. You've just lost your main supporter."

"Stop being dramatic. We parted on very good terms."

"I know Walter. You don't."

Judith stuck to her guns. "I believe in what I'm doing, and I can't let Walter or anyone else order me around. That's why we're surrounded by mediocrity. People do what's expedient— no one stands up for what he believes."

"Aw, nuts! You need Walter, he doesn't need you. It's as simple as that! I worked so hard to get his support for us, now you've thrown it down the drain."

"Maybe I don't want his support on those terms. I've got to live with myself."

A feeling of helplessness descended upon Birdie. "Sometimes I think you have one goal in life—to make things as hard as possible for yourself. And me."

"If you try to build something worthwhile," Judith orated, "you've got to expect hardships. How else can it be?"

"I'll only say this, my dear. If you continue this way you won't build anything at all—you'll only destroy. Take my word."

"Whose side are you on anyway?" Judith asked testily. "Naturally you see it his way. But I don't have to. After all, I'm not in love with him."

Birdie sighed. What was the use? "I should hang up after that remark, but I won't. I wish to hell I could drum some sense into you. Take my advice, make up with him if it's still possible. That's all I have to say."

Only after she received Walter's note did Judith realize that she might have gone too far. She telephoned him the next morning. "Walter, darling," she cooed, "I'm terribly sorry about the misunderstanding. You know how confused I can get. Of course Margo can sing on one of the programs, if that'll please you. I'd like nothing better."

It was too late. Walter had decided that Margo could do without her, and so could he. "My dear," he said crisply, "I must admit I was hurt by your attitude, but let's not talk about it now. I'll phone you in a week or two. I'm sure it'll work out."

"Good," she said brightly. "Don't wait too long." She hung up, disturbed. Could it be that Birdie was right?

Walter decided to say nothing to Alice; he could not bear to hand her such a victory. After three days, however, he weakened.

She listened till the end. "What am I supposed to say? 'I told you so'?"

"Naturally."

"Well, I won't. Are you going to call her?"

"Of course not. When I'm through with a person, it's for good. She doesn't know it yet, but she will."

Alice made him a sandwich. He ate it and felt better.

7

Judith looked forward to the final concert of the series; she was playing Hindemith's *Kammermusik II*. She had never performed a modern work in public, and was doubly eager to do well since Paul was conducting the chamber orchestra.

She realized as the weeks wore on that she should have left herself more time to learn the music. Hindemith's idiom eluded her; one had to come to it, she suspected, either early in life or not at all. She let Birdie take over the chores of the project, and spent three hours at the piano every morning. But she was not concentrating well: the telephone kept ringing, she had too many things on her mind. She thought of withdrawing, which would be tantamount to confessing that she was not equal to the task; besides, at this late date it would not be easy to find a replacement. And so she continued the struggle, even though her apprehension increased as the date of the concert grew near.

The rehearsal took place on a rainy morning in the last week of April. Birdie called for her at ten. Judith had not slept well.

"Your suit's divine!" Birdie crowed. "Positively." She thought Judith had on too much make-up but said nothing.

Judith settled back in the taxi. "I hope Paul will be friendly. I haven't seen him since we had that argument at Walter's."

"He's not the kind to bear a grudge."

"That's what you think. I hear he had an accident."

"Who said? He had pneumonia. A bad case of it."

"Oh. I must have mixed it up. Is he all right?"

"He's fine." Birdie was relieved that Judith had heard nothing more specific. She had done everything to scotch rumors, and had even remembered to slip the night clerk a ten-dollar bill. Somehow things got around. What a town this was!

Judith opened her music. "I'm terribly nervous," she said, turning a page.

"Darling, you always are when you have to play. Remember?"

"But this time I have a feeling it won't go."

"Where did we hear that one before?" Birdie inquired of the top of the cab.

They arrived at the hall. Birdie took a seat at the back of the orchestra; Judith deposited her coat in the artists' room and made her way onstage, automatically assuming the assured manner with which she faced the world. The men were at their places; Paul, on the conductor's podium, was marking the concertmaster's score. He wore a black turtle-neck sweater, against which his face stood out with unwonted pallor. He glanced up from the stand. "Good morning, Miss Conrad." His tone was polite but distant.

Judith was taken aback by his formal manner. "Good morning," she answered brightly and sat down at the piano. Although she had memorized the piece, she decided to play from the music. She opened the score and put her handkerchief in the left corner of the keyboard. Her hands felt cold; she rubbed one against the other. Paul stepped on the podium, lifted his baton and rapped on the stand.

The men began the Allegro. Written during the twenties, this was an impetuous movement in Hindemith's early style, based on frequent changes of meter and tricky crossrhythms that required the utmost precision. Judith, in her nervousness, took the opening passage a little too fast. Paul stopped the music; they began again. Her right knee was shaking; she tried to watch his baton but had difficulty with the beat; she seemed to be following the orchestra instead of the other way around. At one point, where the piano had a bravura passage based on thirty-second notes, she came in a beat too soon. Paul rapped on the stand; the men stopped. He stepped off the podium and went to the piano.

"You know what the trouble is?" He rubbed his hand against his jaw, as though trying to decide how to explain it to her. "You are playing this as if it were Chopin or Schumann. But you cannot take liberties with Hindemith's rhythm. The retards are written into the music, all you have to do is to play the notes in time." To illustrate the point he brought his palm down on the piano top in an even succession of beats. "Otherwise I cannot follow you. In other words, no interpretation." He made the word sound reprehensible. "Shall we try again?"

"Of course." Judith smiled to hide her embarrassment. She realized at once that he had put his finger on what was wrong with her approach. She looked into his eyes, the cold blue eyes of a fanatic; their remoteness unnerved her. "It would help, maestro, if you made the beat a little clearer."

"Clearer?" He looked puzzled, as if to say, *At this point in my life I have to learn how to beat time?* He shrugged. "I'll try. It will also help if you watch me." He stepped on the podium and rapped on the stand. The men began again.

Judith tried to play the notes strictly in rhythm, but her hands were shaking. This lean, athletic music needed a steady pulse; hers was uncertain, even erratic. And at the back of her mind was the suspicion, ever more insistent, that she should not have wandered into unfamiliar territory, she should have stuck to what she knew—Beethoven, Schubert, Schumann. Suddenly Paul's voice slashed the air. "Why don't you count, Miss Conrad!" he commanded, his voice brusque, unsparing. "Count!"

Judith swallowed hard. Abruptly the façade she presented to the world—the smooth façade that had taken a lifetime to build—began to crumble. She stared at the printed page; the notes trembled and blurred over. She had the feeling that this could not possibly be happening to her, it was happening to someone else, she was dreaming it. She plunged ahead even faster, unable to hold back. Suddenly, in the middle of a phrase, she broke off; her hands fell helplessly to her sides. "I—I'm terribly sorry, maestro." She tried to steady her voice. "I haven't been well. I thought I'd be able to play this morning, but——" Her voice dropped to a whisper, "—I'm afraid I can't."

Paul laid his baton on the stand and looked up from the score, glowering. His face was stony. "What do you propose to do, Miss Conrad?"

She felt the eyes of the players upon her. Her lips trembled. "I don't think I can play the concert," she brought out in a barely audible voice. "We'll have to find someone else."

"The concert is two days away!"

She lifted the handkerchief from the side of the piano and twisted it in her hands. "We'll have to do the best we can." Her face was going to pieces; another moment and she would burst into tears. She sprang up, ran off stage into the artists' room, threw herself into the chair in front of the dressing table and, dropping her head on her arms, began to sob.

Birdie hurried in and came behind her. "Sh . . . there, there . . ." She put her hands on Judith's shoulders and moved them up and down in a circular motion.

Judith looked up with bleary eyes. "I've never been so humiliated. He's a monster! A sadist!" She dropped her head; her shoulders shook. Birdie resumed her massaging.

When Judith had quieted down somewhat, Birdie went out on the stage. The men had gone; Paul was still on the podium, leafing through the score. Birdie went up to him. "You upset her dreadfully."

"Why does she attempt this kind of music when she has no understanding of it? Vanity, nothing else! Woman's vanity. Am I supposed to have patience with that?"

"You could have been a little kinder."

"I cannot be kind to what is not good," he said coldly. "That sort of kindness only encourages mediocrity."

"She's not mediocre."

"I agree. That is why she should have known better than to undertake this." He made a mark on the score. "What will we do now?"

"Try to find another pianist, I guess."

"Impossible. The concert is Wednesday."

For once Birdie was caught without a plan. "Shall we cancel it?" she asked, her heart sinking at the thought. There could be no worse way to end the series.

He thought a moment. The thin lips curved a smile. "Why do I not play it myself? And conduct from the piano."

Birdie looked as if she had been saved by a miracle. "Maestro, that would be wonderful!"

"Why not? I have not played in public in years, but I used to." The more he considered the idea, the better he liked it. "Besides, this is my farewell appearance in this country . . . probably for a long time to come. It will be a pleasant way to say good-bye."

The publicity woman awoke in Birdie. "What a story! Judith fell ill at the rehearsal and you stepped in at the last minute. Great. Absolutely!"

Judith spent the rest of the day in bed. Paul's "Count, Miss Conrad!" continued to ring in her ears. Her head ached; she tried to wipe from her mind the memory of her disgrace; she wanted to be left alone. No, what she really wanted was to go to sleep and never wake up. Finally she took two pills and went to bed. She was alone in Penn Station, her train was leaving; a fat conductor in a gleaming helmet bawled into a megaphone at the top of his lungs, "ONE! two, three, four; ONE! two, three, four," over and over again with ferocious emphasis on the *ONE!* She ran forward, valise in hand, but the faster she ran the farther the train receded, and the chug-chug of the engine became, as she awoke, the furious pounding of her heart.

The next day she stayed home. Since the newspapers duly carried Birdie's story she could not very well show herself. She was relieved at not having to perform; at the same time she had an irrational desire to hear Paul play the *Kammermusik* and with difficulty restrained herself from attending the concert. At eight thirty her restlessness reached its peak. She pictured the audience entering the hall, the hum of expectancy, the lights dimming; she missed the excitement and the familiar faces, her imagination endowing the scene with an allure that intensified her disappointment. Birdie had promised to telephone her the instant the concert was over. Judith went to the closet and drew out the pale-green dress she had intended to wear. Next to it hung the flame-colored Balenciaga in which she had played the Mozart concerto with Paul almost two and a half years before. She remembered the moment in the greenroom, after the concert, when she had felt herself surrounded by everything in the world that had meaning for her: her son, her lover, her friends, her public. Now Phil was gone, Bob was gone, Walter was gone, Paul was gone. If only that moment could have lasted. But time—in life as in music—could not stop. The minutes died even as the notes did, to be followed by others that either were forgotten or echoed feebly across the vast space of memory.

Judith returned the dress to the closet and tried to remember what Bob had written about her playing. She had not looked at the diary since the day she read it; she could not recall his words. She found herself going downstairs to his room, driven by some irrational force to tear open the wound he had inflicted, to add more pain to what Paul had dealt her. She opened the door and switched on the light. The room was as the cleaning woman had left it. She went to the chest and opened the middle drawer. Her fingers brushed a sheet of paper. She pulled it out. "My darling boy, please forgive me, please come back to me. If you knew how deeply I love you . . ." She glanced at the signature and gasped; her face changed color as she sat down on the bed and reread Paul's letter. Slowly the pieces fell into place. That night on the breakwater when he pretended to have a headache. Later, when she stood on the landing and heard their voices through the door. At last the puzzle was solved. It couldn't be true, she told herself, and knew that it was.

She looked up helplessly. Wherever she turned, vileness! A fierce resentment flamed in her. Was there no end to the sorrow she must bear because she had a son? No end to the shame he visited upon her? Yet it was Paul rather than Bob on whom, finally, she vented her anger. The pure artist dedicated to his ideals. Pure, indeed! The hypocrite! Her underlip pushed forward and a determined look settled on her face. What he had done to her was child's play compared to what she was going to do to him. She would unmask him, blow his career to smithereens! She glanced at the clock; it was almost nine-thirty. Intermission time. She had a vivid picture of herself rushing out on the stage waving the letter, shouting, "Stop the music! I can tell you what your great Paul Horvath is really like!" She sat very still, her mind whirling around and around, playing a hundred variations on the theme of her triumph and Paul's disgrace.

She had lost all desire to reread the diary. Instead, taking the letter with her, she returned to her room and waited for Birdie's call. At last the telephone rang.

"Darling, the maestro was fabulous. Absolutely!"

Judith's voice quashed her ecstasy. "Birdie, I've got to see you."

"What happened?"

"I can't tell you over the phone."

"Don't you want to hear how the concert went?"

"No. Come right over."

Birdie arrived half an hour later and plumped down on the green velvet couch. "What's up?"

Judith waved the letter before her face. "Read this. I found it in Bob's room."

"For God's sake, are you still snooping?"

"I came upon it by chance." While Birdie read the letter she paced up and down, arms folded imperiously across her chest. At length she stopped and faced the sofa. "What d'you think of that?"

"What d'you expect me to think?"

She glared at Birdie. "He's not going to get away with this!"

"How d'you mean?"

"I'm going to raise such a stink he'll never show his face in New York again. I'll send him right back to his Nazi friends where he belongs."

"On what basis? All it says here is that he loves Bob. Is that a crime?"

"You know very well what it says. He can go to jail for a thing like this. If I had my way," she added with venom, "he would."

"But you don't have a leg to stand on. Even if this means what you think it means, Bob is over twenty-one. Whatever he and Paul did—if they did anything—is their affair."

"You mean to say he can come into my home and lead my son astray and I've no way of striking back? Is this what you're trying to tell me?"

"I'm not so sure about your son being led astray. Nowadays young people know everything. And try everything."

"Bob never did this kind of thing!" Judith shouted.

"That's what I'm trying to tell you."

"I mean, until Paul put such ideas into his head. 'My darling boy . . .' It's sickening!"

Birdie looked at Judith as if she were earnestly trying to follow the workings of her mind. "Judith, how can you speak of creating a scandal? Your own son is involved. D'you want to ruin him? Don't you realize there's only one thing you can do about this."

"What?"

"Forget it!"

Judith saw her fanciful structure of revenge crumble to the ground. "And to bring Beethoven into this," she cried, as if she had not heard what Birdie said, "of all people! It's disgusting!"

"Beethoven couldn't care less. Judith, listen to me. I can understand your being angry at Paul because of what happened the other morning, but the argument was about music, not about anything personal. If you want to strike back at him as a musician I'll buy that. But to strike back at him in a personal way is childish. Besides, it won't get you anywhere." She was about to add that the entire discussion was irrelevant since Paul was returning to Europe; but his departure from the orchestra had not yet been announced, and she was too annoyed with Judith to give her the pleasure of hearing about it before everyone else.

Judith stared at Birdie. "Whose side are you on anyway?" she brought out fiercely. "The other day you took Walter's part against me. Now you take Paul's. Is this what I'm paying you for? To be loyal to my enemies?"

Birdie's body stiffened as if she had been jerked upright on a wire. "Are you saying I'm not loyal to you?" she cried, a look of righteous anger pouring through the contact lenses. Turning sideways, she appealed to an impartial judge. "I work myself to the bone for her, I take everything she hands me without a word of complaint, and she has the gall to tell me I'm not loyal to her!" The dirty-blond bun at the back of her head bobbled precariously as her voice rose in a crescendo: "You don't think you're getting your money's worth? Is that what's eating you?"

"Don't twist my words," Judith shouted. "What's eating me is that when I have a fight with Walter you stick up for him, and when I have a fight with Paul you stick up for him. Is that being loyal to me!"

Birdie sprang up. "I'll tell you what I'm loyal to. Common sense! When I see you going haywire, whether it's with Walter or Paul, it's my duty to tell you so. And if you think that's being disloyal, then I'm disloyal!"

"Common sense?" Judith had never before heard this tone from Birdie. She did not like it. "If you had a shred of common sense in your head would you be in love with Walter? Would you go around thinking Paul is God?" Her voice went up half an octave. "And don't sound off about how you work yourself to the bone for me. That's what you're hired for! That's your job!"

"Oh, no, it isn't!" Trembling, Birdie put her hands on her hips and faced her adversary. From the depths of her there welled up the grievances accumulated over the space of a decade, no longer to be repressed. "It's not my job to be at your beck and call twenty-four hours a day. To 'yes' you all the time. To suffer your whims and tantrums! You think I was hired for that?"

Judith looked at her in astonishment. "How dare you speak to me like this!"

Birdie made a gesture of impatience. "Come off it! Who d'you think you are—a queen? You're living in an unreal world, my dear! I'll tell you who you are—I've been wanting to for a long time. You're a bully! A tyrant! Like those people who take jobs in prisons so they can lord it over everybody else. You're a self-centered, power-mad bitch, that's what you are!" Having quoted Walter without being aware of it, Birdie stopped short, appalled at what she had said. It was too late.

A look of disbelief froze Judith's face. "Get out," she screamed, her eyes blazing, "before I——" She choked.

"Don't worry, I'm getting out. I've had enough of this shit!" Birdie grabbed her coat and retreated toward the door. "Find someone else to do your dirty work. To bow and scrape and take your bullying. And be as loyal as I've been." One hand on the doorknob, she fired her parting shot, "Believe me, it won't be easy!" She slammed the door behind her.

For an instant Judith stood still, regal in her rage. Then consternation descended upon her. She heard the staccato of Birdie's heels on the stairs. "Come back!" she called. "D'you hear me!" She flung open the door and rushed out on the landing. "Birdie!" She leaned over the bannister. "Come back!"

The heels continued their descent. The door of the vestibule swung open. Then shut.

Judith pulled herself erect and returned to the parlor. The letter lay on the sofa. She picked up the sheet, crumpled it between the palms of her hands, and hurled it on the floor in impotent fury. Then she flung herself on the sofa, face down, her fists pounding the faded green velvet cover until tufts of dust issued from it. All of a sudden she left off and lay quite still. With an immense ache in her heart.

8

"What are your plans, maestro?" Birdie spooned up the last of the Peach Melba; the ice-cream spread so sweet a coolness in her mouth that she forgot the calories. Her stormy encounter with Judith had faded from her mind, supplanted by the quiet charm of this good-bye supper in Paul's apartment.

"Plans?" Paul, facing her across the narrow table on wheels, sipped his coffee. "I really do not know." He put down the cup. "I have been conducting steadily since I was twenty, and I think I need a vacation."

"You wouldn't know what to do with one."

"Perhaps vacation is not the right word. Call it a period of transition."

"Transition?"

"In a symphony people listen for the main themes, but the transition passages are just as important. I seem to be in one of those at the moment."

Birdie did not see what he was driving at, but she was sure it was profound and nodded appreciatively.

"During the Middle Ages," Paul continued, "men took time to meditate. Our lives are too crowded; we're afraid to hear ourselves think. I should like to spend a few months thinking things out for myself."

Birdie turned to her coffee; Paul poured himself a second cup. "I'm sorry to have been so brusque with Judith," he said. "Was she very much upset?"

"Yes."

"Is that what she wanted to see you about?"

This was a strange question, Birdie thought, from one who as a rule was so reserved. He was obviously more disturbed about his behavior toward Judith than she had suspected. "She had several things on her mind. Anyway, we quarreled. And broke up, after nine years."

"I'm sorry to hear it."

"Strange, that I should lose my two most important artists on the same night. That's how the cookie crumbled."

"You sound as if you regret it."

"I regret that you're leaving, maestro. I enjoyed my work with you and I'll miss it. As for Judith, not really. It was in the cards. Remember what you said—that a person should know when their time is up? The years I shared with Judith were the years when she was on her way up, which made it fun. Now— I don't know—I won't say she's on her way down, but she certainly isn't going up any more."

He offered her a cigarette, took one himself, and sat back, inhaling slowly. "Max Rubin says it is difficult in this country for a woman pianist, especially if she is American. That is part of her problem."

"There's more to it than that, maestro."

"I know, you will tell me her personality is at fault. But that is such an American view. In Europe an artist is judged by his talent. In this country you have to have a talent for public relations as well."

Birdie smiled. "Or if you don't, you've got to hire someone who has." She pointed a forefinger at her chest. "That's where I come in."

"You do it extremely well."

She felt a glow of pleasure at the compliment. "Are you packed?"

"There is not much." He pointed to two valises that lay open in the bedroom. "People clutter up their lives with things. I have tried not to. Everything I need has to fit into those two bags. A few special things," he pointed to the Spanish chest, "I will have sent."

"Where to?"

"Berlin. I go there first." He snuffed out his cigarette. "Perhaps you will come?"

She decided to be honest with him. "Not Berlin. Shall I confess?—I wouldn't like to hear German spoken all around me. I guess I saw too many movies about Nazis."

"You forget, it is the language of Goethe and Heine."

"Still . . . Maybe we'll meet in London. I'm sure you'll be going there."

He nodded. Then he cleared his throat nervously. "I wanted you to have a keepsake, but I could not imagine what you would like. I am not very good at this sort of thing." His face showed his embarrassment. He went into the bedroom and returned. "This baton was given to me by Bruno Walter when I was beginning my career. I should like you to have it. And this book." He handed her a copy of Beethoven's sketchbooks. "And those ——" He pointed to the two silver candlesticks under the picture of St. Sebastian.

"Maestro, you shouldn't!" she cried, deeply moved.

"I think you will enjoy them."

"They're beautiful!" She opened the book to the title page on which was written: *"For Birdie Harris, Colleague and Friend. With profound gratitude. Paul Horvath."* "Maestro, it's most kind of you. I shall treasure these as long as I live."

"I am so pleased that you like them."

She glanced at her watch; it was close to one. "You're sure you wouldn't like me to see you off tomorrow."

He smiled. "Quite sure."

"Well, then . . ." She rose. "Whenever we went on a journey, my mother would sit down for a minute and look around the room, so she wouldn't miss it. Don't forget to do this."

He glanced around. "I will not miss it," he said softly.

She gave him a searching look, as if to imprint his features on her memory: the high, intellectual forehead, deep-set blue eyes, thin lips, and sculptured outlines of the ascetic face. She held out her hand; he bent over and kissed it. As he did, Birdie had the feeling that this was one relationship in her life where everything had gone right. Between them there was no unfinished business. She had done her best for him and he had brought out the best in her. It was a good feeling to have.

six

Bob opened his eyes and glanced about him; it still surprised him not to awake in his old room. He remembered the passages in Proust where the "I" of the novel described his tortuous reactions to the rooms he slept in. Bob smiled; his, fortunately, were simpler. Sunlight lay in golden streaks on the carpet. He folded his hands behind his head and stared absently at the ceiling. Since he had been staying with Walter and Alice he had been getting up much earlier. The morning air had a freshness that delighted him; he took a deep breath. This springtime held a special quality, as if he were convalescing from an illness; he did not let his mind dwell on the events that had preceded. Suddenly, miraculously, life had become possible again.

The closet door was open, revealing a neat row of plastic bags. It surprised him that Alice should have held on to her son's suits and coats all these years. He wondered what Gene had been like. Would they have been friends if they had met? He doubted it; the sixties were too far away from the forties for them to have spoken the same language. Bob pushed back the sheet and lowered his feet to the floor; he had retained his habit of sleeping in only the lower half of his pajamas. He stretched his arms, cracking the shoulder bones, and pushed back his hair. The golden patch on the carpet had moved closer to the window. He watched the traffic on the river; on the opposite shore the roofs and smokestacks of Astoria huddled together. If he leaned to the right he would be able to see, far below, the little square with its railing of semicircular prongs. He preferred not to. Instead he went to the bathroom and turned on the shower.

When he came out, Alice was in the alcove off the kitchen; they had breakfast. She pointed to a small white box on the table. "For you."

He opened it and saw a wrist watch. "Oh, you shouldn't have."

"I noticed you didn't have one."

"I left mine home. Maybe I lost it."

"How can one lose a wrist watch?"

"Very easy if you have a talent for it. You take it off and don't remember where you put it."

She smiled. "It's remarkable how indifferent you are to things."

"They only clutter up a person's life." He was quoting, without being aware of it, one of Paul's maxims.

"Most people love things."

"Maybe I will some day. Anyway, thank you very much. I'll take good care of it." He fastened the watch around his wrist, wound it, and held out his arm to admire it.

He finished his eggs; Alice poured him another cup of coffee. He looked up, thoughtful. "May I ask you a question?"

"Yes?"

"What d'you think I ought to do now?"

"How do you mean?"

"I feel I've come to the end of a thing. I'm fed up with writing for the time being. I'm not even sure I've got what it takes. What next?"

"I was hoping you'd ask me," Alice said quietly. "I think you should go back to school and get your degree. It may surprise you to find that I see eye to eye with your mother on this, but I do."

"It don't surprise me at all. As a matter of fact I was thinking about it."

"Why were you so against it when she suggested it?"

"Hard to say. The way she pushed for it turned me off. Now

I've come to it on my own. The only trouble is, I have no way of financing it."

"Walter and I will be glad to——"

"I couldn't accept that. You've already done too much."

"You could take a student loan. There are such, you know. Or borrow from your mother——"

"No, I couldn't take it from her," he interrupted. "Anything she gives comes with strings attached."

"Then take a loan from us. You'll pay it back when you can. By the way, your mother phoned this morning."

His heart skipped a beat. "What did she say?"

"She asked to see me."

"What about?"

"She didn't tell me. You, I suppose."

"I'm not ready to go back yet."

Alice was silent awhile. Then, "Bob, I'd like very much for you to stay here," she said. "I think you know that. But only if your mother approves. Otherwise I'd feel I was coming between you and her, and that's not a good feeling to have."

His face thrust forward, intense. "Don't send me away. Please."

She smiled. "You sound like a little boy when you say that."

He drew out a sheet of paper. "The money you gave me—I wrote down what I spent it on. Here it is."

"That's all right. I don't have to see it."

"I'd like you to." This was his only way of telling her, since he could not bring himself to say it, that he was no longer on drugs. To return to his former ways would mean that he was unworthy of her friendship, and the loss of that, he knew, would be a far greater deprivation than any he imposed on himself.

"I see," she said, glancing down the list of items, "that you still have some cash."

"Yes. If you don't mind, I'll keep writing down what I spend it on."

"I don't mind."

"How strange, that a chance meeting with you should have changed my life."

"You were ready for the change."

"Still, that's what did it."

Alice looked at him intently. "Don't you want to see her?"

"Did she say she wanted to see me?"

"No."

"Then I'd rather not. I'll go out before she comes. I planned to go up to Columbia and find out about their summer session."

"I'll tell her."

"Will she be surprised!" He pictured Judith's face when she learned where he had gone. "I'm glad we had this talk," he added. His mother, he remembered, had always described Alice as cold, yet this was the last adjective he would associate with her. Actually his mother was the cold one, for all her histrionics. It was she who could not give.

Judith arrived after lunch. She glanced with interest around the living room. "I've never seen it in the daytime," she said, assuming her most ingratiating tone. "The Rouault has more color to it." She sat down on the couch that faced the painting. "How's Bob doing?"

"Fine." Alice noticed that she had put on weight.

"Did he know I was coming?"

"Yes."

"Didn't he want to see me?"

"That's what he asked about you."

"Oh." She sounded disappointed.

"He went up to Columbia to find out about this summer. He's going back to school, as you wanted him to."

"So he finally came around to it. Good. How did all this happen?"

"What?"

"You and him."

"I ran into him one day and asked him to lunch with me. Then he got into difficulty with a girl, you were away, and he needed someone to talk to. That's how it went."

"A girl?" Judith sounded relieved. "Who?"

"He didn't tell me and I didn't ask."

"How did it turn out?"

Alice shrugged. "Could have been worse."

Judith leaned forward, her casualness dropping from her. "Alice, shall I be frank? I'm jealous as hell of you."

"You have no reason to be."

"Yes, I have. He's finding something in you that he never did in me."

"Only for the time being. Sooner or later the two of you will make up."

"No, I'm not right for him. I never was. Maybe you're what he needs."

"You're making me feel guilty, Judith. That's not fair. I'm terribly fond of your boy and he's welcome to stay here as long as he likes. But only if you approve."

"As a matter of fact, I do. I've a lot on my mind at the moment, and I just couldn't handle him too. We'd only irritate each other." She concentrated on the Rouault for a moment. "But I didn't come here to discuss Bob." She hesitated, as if trying to decide how to begin. "I have to make plans for next year. My series was a success but I don't know whether I can go on with it, and before I reach a decision I'd like to know how Walter feels about it. He probably told you that we quarreled."

"Yes."

"It was my fault, I admit. I didn't realize it meant so much to him to have Margo sing, and I shouldn't have said no. But that's water under the bridge. What upsets me is that he's still angry with me. After all, we've been friends for fifteen years. If he'd be willing to make up with me and come back on the board, I might continue with the concerts. Do you think you could talk to him about it?"

Alice looked at her in surprise. "That would be interfering, and I never do that. Walter would resent it, and he'd be right. He was quite upset by what you did. I don't think you can count on him, certainly not for next year."

"I see." Judith's lips curved a mechanical smile. She saw her plans crumble; a blind rage took possession of her, all the more intense because she had no legitimate object on which to vent it. Walter, Alice, Bob, Birdie, Paul . . . they were all against her! She saw herself as the victim of a gigantic conspiracy whose sole aim was to put obstacles in her path, and a wild, irresistible impulse gripped her to strike back as hard as she could. "There's something you ought to know about Walter," she said quietly, her voice taking on a honeyed tone. "About Walter and Birdie. People won't say anything to you, but I'm speaking as a friend because I think you have a right to know." Having delivered the blow she sat back to observe its effect.

Alice felt the color drain from her face. For an instant she was going to show Judith the door. Instead she folded her hands in her lap and looked at her calmly. "Why do you think I ought to know?"

"Don't you?"

"No. Anything that concerns Walter is his problem, not mine. And don't tell me you're acting as a friend. You're angry at Walter and you're angry at me. This is your way of striking back at us."

"I acted with the best intentions!" Judith cried hotly.

"What you really wanted, I guess, was to spoil my day."

"You mean to tell me you prefer to live in a fool's paradise?"

Alice rose. "I don't think I have to discuss my private life with you. If you don't mind my saying so, we're not that close. And now, if you'll excuse me . . ."

Judith rose too, smiling to hide her discomfiture. "What a strange attitude for you to take."

"Judith, this is kid stuff. We're too old for it—we don't have time enough left." She led the way to the vestibule. "Sooner or later you have to make peace with the world, otherwise it'll destroy you. But to do that you must first make peace with yourself. And you haven't." They reached the door. Alice held out her hand. "You're an unhappy woman, Judith, and I feel sorry for you. Good-bye."

"Good-bye." Judith's lips were still curved in a mechanical, slightly foolish smile.

Alice returned to the living room, sat down and stared at the rug. So it was Birdie, with her fat behind and shrill laugh. What in the world did he see in her? Mainly that she was not his wife. If she had been, he'd be running to someone else. Yet, come to think of it, if he had to play around it was better for him to pick somebody close to home than to become involved with some floozie who might give him trouble. Why, Alice wondered, had her suspicions never fallen on Birdie? Probably because she had always considered her a little ridiculous. It showed, however, that they were being discreet, which was something to be thankful for.

Her discovery changed nothing; it merely gave a name to a situation that had existed long before. She remembered her overwhelming sense of betrayal when she first learned that Walter was unfaithful. Time had robbed the ancient hurt of its power. She did not understand men, so she would never know what drove Walter. What was he trying to prove? But now that she was able to view their life together objectively, she was glad she had stayed with him. In some strange way he was loyal to her even when he was jumping into bed with the Birdies of this world. It was this that bound her to him, and—who could say? —perhaps even some residue of her former love. In her own way she, too, had been unfaithful, seeking through her attachment to Bobby a fulfillment that Walter was unable to give her. Would he have been so willing to let Bobby live with them if he had not understood this. The only thing that puzzled her was his taste. Birdie, of all people. She pictured the long nails that were a shade too red, the spiked heels that were a little too high, the tight skirt a little too short. It was Birdie, curiously, she felt sorry for.

She walked down the corridor past Bob's room. The door was open. He had made his bed and put everything away. Someday he would have to go back to his mother. For the time being, though, he was hers to love and take care of. She had him on loan, as it were, and she was going to make the most of it. Alice sighed. Life itself was on loan; it wouldn't do to be greedy. Let Walter take his pleasure with that ball of dough. As long as she had Bobby she would not complain.

2

Judith regretted her visit to Alice: the memory of it filled her with shame. What had she hoped to gain by telling Alice about Walter's infidelity? Her behavior was reprehensible from every point of view, and doubly so because the victim was someone as decent as Alice.

Taken separately, the events that had upset her that winter were not too shattering. Anyone could quarrel with a friend or two, any mother could have a run-in with her son, any artist could make a poor showing. Such mishaps were to be expected in everyday living and had to be taken in stride. All the same, the defeats she had sustained in the past months seemed to be indicative of something deeply wrong with her life. She had always thought of herself as a favorite of fortune; she now began to feel that fate was turning against her. Ever since her childhood she had had the impression that she was moving steadily forward. All of a sudden the path had broken off; she did not know where to take the next step.

Despite the success of her concert series, Judith realized that she could not undertake another season. She dreaded this decision so much that she put it off from day to day. She told herself that she would find other backers to take the place of Walter, as well as someone to replace Birdie; she even drew up a list of programs and chose the artists she intended to engage. Yet she knew all the time that she had lost her momentum: she no longer had either the desire or the energy to continue the project. She thought of turning it over to Max Rubin, or trying to run it jointly with him; but this—assuming that she could persuade him to join her, which was by no means certain— would wipe out everything she had hoped to accomplish. Indeed, it would only prove that Max had been right from the beginning. Bewilderment settled upon her. The year had begun so full of promise, the concerts under her direction had brilliantly fulfilled that promise. Yet she saw herself forced, by an unfortunate combination of events, to abandon what had given her such joy to build. The prospect sent her into an acute depression.

In her overwrought state she became aware of impulses in her nature that were the opposite of those she associated with herself. She had always considered herself a woman who made decisions easily. She now discovered that what Bob had written about her in his diary was true: her decisiveness was a cover-up for her inability to make up her mind. Inexplicably the most trivial detail—whether to go shopping or not, whether to wear one dress rather than another—became an excuse for painful vacillation. The pros and cons were so evenly balanced that, whichever path she chose, she at once regretted not having picked the other. The result was an almost total paralysis of will.

She had always been acutely conscious of the passage of time. There was so much to accomplish that she had not a moment to waste. Now, contrariwise, she would let hours slip by while she sat immobile, staring morosely before her as she brooded for the thousandth time on the chain of events that had brought her to her present pass. Her only salvation, she knew, was work: she decided to give a recital in the fall and began to learn two compositions she had never played before—the Fantasy of Schumann and Beethoven's Sonata Op. 110. Her practicing had been the focal point of her existence; once she was at the piano she had shut out everything else. But she no longer commanded this power; her thoughts kept wandering. Worst of all, she did not feel the delight in playing that had sustained her since child-hood. What had served as the mainspring of her life seemed to have lost its impetus; indeed, she no longer cared whether she played badly or well. Judith could not understand this change in herself. Her last line of defense had broken down, leaving her helpless, terrified.

She was astonished at the strength of irrational impulses which, like the one that had dictated her disclosure to Alice, seemed to lead her away from her goals rather than toward them. Increas-ingly concerned about her weight, she would embark enthu-siastically upon one diet or another; but after concentrating for three days on steak or Metrecal, she would throw principle to the wind and surrender to an orgy of French pastries or a marsh-mallow sundae with pecans. Or, in an attack of hunger that was like a fever, she would devour whatever was in the refrigerator. The result was that, just when she had worked out a perfect formula for losing ten pounds, she gained five, which in turn brought on such a fit of discouragement that her raids on the icebox increased in ferocity. She bulged, she overflowed her suits and dresses; at the same time she could not bear to have them let out, since this would constitute too open an admission of defeat. So she continued to squeeze herself into clothes that were too tight for her, consoling herself with the thought that any-one who liked her would not like her less because there was a little more of her.

Sleep, which she had always regarded as a friend, now became an undependable visitor. She would go to bed exhausted, yet the instant her head touched the pillow she was gripped by an unrelenting wakefulness. Her thoughts ran rampant, her nerves became taut like the strings of a violin scraped by an implacable bow. She heard the beat of her pulse against the pillow and would shift her position to escape its disquieting rhythm. Silence enveloped the city, broken by stray noises—the moan of an alley cat, the honking of an auto horn. She lay very still, pretending that she was about to doze off, but the ruse did not work. What if she had forgotten how to fall asleep? What if she would never sleep again? She arose, turned on the light, opened a book or magazine; but after an hour she was more wide-awake than ever. By this time half the night had passed. She took two sleeping pills and returned to bed. Finally consciousness slipped away from her, but her anxieties followed her into her dreams, clothing themselves in horrendous nightmares from which she awoke with a cry. In the morning her head was heavy, she needed a different pill to raise her spirits and give her the energy she lacked. Thus she gradually accumulated an armament of little bottles—powders, pills, capsules, syrups—from which, in the manner of the hypochondriac, she hoped to assimilate the vitality that her nervous system was less and less capable of supplying.

In a curious way Judith had relinquished for herself the possibility of love. She came to regard it on the one hand as a youthful indiscretion that she had outgrown, on the other as a kind of dangerous infection against which she must guard herself at all costs. Having lost the courage either to give or receive it, she freed herself from its summons by continuing to separate love and sex, as she had done on that rainy night in Cleveland. When her loneliness got the better of her she would stop in at one of the cosy little bars on Lexington Avenue where transient conversations ripened into casual intimacies—what she called taking pot luck. It fed her vanity that she could still attract a man, especially since she attracted him not on the basis of her mind or personality but because of her body, overripe though it was. These conquests were sufficiently pleasant to salve her ego yet not absorbing enough to threaten her freedom. They were stimulated by erotic fantasies in which she would transform herself in her imagination into someone else, according to her whim of the moment: a young girl having sex for the first time, or an aging prostitute earning her living the hard way. Imperceptibly degradation had become part of the thrill she found in sex; her assumption of a self-demeaning attitude toward her partner of the evening heightened her enjoyment. Like an actress who lives her part until the fall of the curtain, Judith would play whatever role her fancy suggested to her, until the climax of physical satisfaction freed her from any further need for pretense. There was only one requirement in this fantasy—that she never play herself. Her adventures, therefore, revived for her the excitement of the masquerade, conjuring up a world of voluptuous pleasure bathed in a golden haze, into which she was helped by an obliging stranger who, once he had performed his part, could be conveniently forgotten. Sometimes there was a return engagement, although Judith ordinarily preferred a new conquest. What she recognized as passion was perhaps only curiosity. Even if she saw the stranger a second time, the contact, as impersonal as possible, had the advantage of leaving her real self untouched, thereby guarding her against all possible hurt.

She had always loved May in New York, when the cold and dampness finally disappeared and the puny tree in front of her house took a new lease on life. This May, however, was a melancholy one. A wall seemed to have gone up around her, shutting out the light and warmth of the sun. Imprisoned within it, she could not see that the prison was of her own making; she only knew that her life had become bleak and barren. And so she sat in her music room, now devoid of sound, embittered, brooding, feeling sorry for herself, finding relief from time to time in uncontrollable fits of weeping.

Toward the end of the month a cousin whom she had not seen in years invited her for a weekend in Philadelphia. Judith thought the change would do her good and accepted; on the appointed day she took an early train at Penn Station. By the time the train approached Newark she regretted having gone. Why should she spend three days in the company of a woman with whom she had nothing in common except their grandmother? She saw herself immersed in hours of small talk, making a futile attempt to revive associations that had lapsed long ago. She decided to return home and telephone an excuse. Bag in hand, she alighted at Newark and took the first train back to New York. On the way she was assailed by remorse: her cousin had probably gone to considerable trouble. By the time the train pulled into the station Judith had decided she could not possibly disappoint her. The solution was simple: she took the next train out. On her way to Newark her previous doubts returned, and with them her desire to return home. She saw herself spending the next ten hours in the tunnel between New York and Newark, unable to make up her mind. All of a sudden a sentence flashed across her mind as clearly as if someone had written it on a blackboard: "I'm having a nervous breakdown." Why hadn't this occurred to her before? She returned home, telephoned her cousin to say that she was not feeling well, and went to bed.

An immense stillness pressed down upon her, hemming her in. She lay staring into the dark. How could she go on? Where was she to turn?

3

For three weeks every June Max Rubin played the loving father: his son Jerry would arrive from San Francisco with Frances and the two boys. Suddenly the quiet, oval-shaped living room would change its character: the couch became a double bed, cots were set up for the boys, quiet gave way to perpetual din. From the moment he heard his daughter-in-law's "Hello, poppa," delivered in a whining voice that combined reverence with a plea for affection, he would freeze within. The remainder of the visit Max passed in an irreconcilable conflict between his kindlier impulses and his basic desire that they go back to San Francisco and leave him in peace.

Jerry was the offspring of Max's second and least successful marriage. Jerry's mother had inspired Max with a cordial dislike, a good deal of which had rubbed off, Jerry felt, on him. He was a violinist in the San Francisco Orchestra. His appointment to the second-violin section was greeted by a cruel remark on the part of his father that he never forgot: "Some people were born to play second fiddle." At least he played a good second fiddle. Jerry was the great disappointment of Max Rubin's life. His father had named him Jascha and had entertained the highest hopes for him; the boy was taught the violin from the time he was eight. Both the violin and the teacher were, as Max put it, the best that money could buy. Jerry was one of the last pupils of Leopold Auer, teacher of geniuses. Auer was in his eighties by then, and deaf. He would rouse himself from time to time to emit a solemn "Dunt scretch!" But Jerry hated being Jascha and became Jerry as soon as he could. He was a quiet, affable lad who grew into a quiet, affable man, and he was delighted at being able to put three thousand miles between himself and Max. Was he supposed to kill himself because his father wanted a great violinist for a son? Big deal.

In Jerry's view Max epitomized what he called the Fifty-seventh-Street way of life. This was a manner of thinking and living that required all the qualities he lacked: talent, ambition, insatiable hunger for fame, and the ability to step over as many dead bodies as necessary in order to achieve it. Fifty-seventh Street was "Big Time." The center of the world. At the opposite end was the placid life he had built for himself in San Francisco, that exactly suited his modest needs and attainments. He enjoyed his work in the orchestra; every Tuesday night he played string quartets; he loved Frances and his two boys. And San Francisco had, for him, one supreme advantage: it was not New York.

Jerry had inherited his father's round head. He was a little taller. His body had become soft and plump through lack of exercise. He put too much butter on his bread and smoked more than was good for him. His gray eyes—his mother's eyes—were his most attractive feature; they were bright, timid, and kindly. Even now his father was the dominating force in Jerry Rubin's life. As a result he found himself in the curious position of measuring all things, whether he liked it or not, by the Fifty-seventh-Street values he had rejected. He saw Max as a little Napoleon, a tyrant whom he feared as much as he hated, and loved as much as he feared. To his San Francisco friends he would say, "You want to see what kind of father I got? Look!" and would hold out a large framed photograph that was signed, "For my son Jerry. Sincerely yours, Max Rubin."

Why, then, did he interrupt the even tenor of his summer vacation by a visit to the Great Man. Partly because the love was still there, corroded though it was by hurt and bitterness; partly to see old friends and show Frances—a San Francisco girl —the sights; partly because he wanted his boys to get to know their grandfather. Perhaps, too, something in Jerry needed to become again, if only for a while, the awed stripling who had trembled before the fulminations of the Great Man. But most of all Jerry wanted to show his father how wrong it had been to try to force on him a career for which he was not suited, to prove to his father that he had made it in his own way. So he wasn't Isaac Stern. So what!

Despite the good intentions on both sides, the instant he came into Max's presence the old patterns came to life. Between them obtruded the knowledge that Jerry was an obscure musician from the West Coast while his father lived among the great ones of the earth. At once Jerry lost what little assurance he had. A sickly grin fastened itself on his pasty white face; he kept clearing his throat and looked as if he were about to apologize for being alive. Max's innate sadism came to the fore. "I heard a good one today," he brought out innocently. "You know the definition of *wunderkind?* The *wunder* goes and the *kind* remains." A peal of laughter followed this sally, to which Jerry responded with a mirthless chuckle. Why didn't the old man drop dead?

Nor did Max take to his grandsons. True, they were going to perpetuate his name, but that was no great shakes—there were plenty of Rubins in the world. He disliked their raucous "gran'pa" as acutely as he did their mother's whining "poppa"; it made him feel old and Jewish. Once he finished questioning them about their age and how they were doing at school, conversation lagged. Lenny was a senior in high school, Ralphie was in the eighth grade. Max nodded his delight at this information, gave them each a dollar and told them to go buy themselves an ice-cream soda.

Frances was no help. She was an efficient wife in her own bailiwick, but in front of the Great Man she went to pieces— either she giggled nervously or she whined. Trouble began the very first day. Max proposed taking them to a restaurant. "Poppa," Frances remonstrated in her high-pitched voice, "in a restaurant they feed you poison. I'll make you a home-cooked meal like Jerry's momma used to make." Max's gorge rose. The last thing he wanted was to be reminded of Jerry's momma. Besides, it bored him to eat at home. He enjoyed the excitement of restaurants, the special attention of the maître d', the running into acquaintances at Sardi's or the Russian Tea Room, the whispering and craning of necks at his arrival. Instead of that, what would he have? Chicken in the pot, a schlemiel of a son for company, and heartburn. "All right, we'll eat home," he said, making every effort to look pleased. After all, how long was three weeks?

Very. His guests had a genius for getting in his way. They upset his schedule, intruded when he was on the telephone, and were noisy when he took his afternoon nap. Max relinquished his green leather chair and barricaded himself in the bedroom, spent as much time as possible at the office, and showered them with tickets to concerts, ballets, and plays. They were still in his way. He failed to realize that what disturbed him was not the amount of time they spent in his apartment but the threat they posed to his style of life. In addition, they were driving him out of his mind.

The climax came at the beginning of the second week, when Max was awakened from his nap by a thud and a scream. He came out of his bedroom in a rage and found Frances haranguing Ralphie. "Wait'll gran'pa finds out!" she whined. "You'll get it." Max's glance automatically swept the mantelpiece. One of the urns that flanked the bronze nymph was missing. Jerry held the urn in one hand and a fragment of its black marble base in the other. Frances turned to her father-in-law. "He knocked it down," she confessed in an agony of embarrassment.

"How could he?" Max snapped. "It was on the mantelpiece."

"Leave it to him. He was chinning, so he knocked it down."

"Chinning?" Max cried. "What is chinning?"

"He hung from the mantelpiece and tried to pull himself up. Wherever he goes he finds something to hang from."

Max glared at the boy. "What are you, a monkey? You know how long I have this set?" He waved an arm at the mantelpiece, where the clock in the nymph's belly showed twenty past three and the surviving urn stood in its usual place to the left. "Forty years! Your father was still a baby when I bought it. So Ralphie Rubin has to come from San Francisco to chin on my mantelpiece and break my antiques!"

At this insult Ralphie let out a howl. Frances turned white. Her lips began to tremble. "If that's how you feel, poppa, we can go home. This minute."

Max, ignoring her, poured his wrath on the boy. "Why don't you go to a gym if you want to chin? Why don't you go to Central Park and play ball like other boys? D'you have to hang around the house and drive me crazy?"

"Poppa, that's no way to talk to your grandson," Frances cried, on the verge of tears.

At this point Jerry took a deep breath and entered the fray. "Look, it's not as if he killed someone." He held up the urn and fragment. "It's only a *thing*, so what's all the fuss?" It astonished him to be talking back to the Great Man, yet there was no retreating now. "You can replace things. It's human beings you can't replace."

Max turned upon his son. "Hoo-hah. Such deep thoughts all of a sudden!" He was so astonished by the firmness in Jerry's voice that his rejoinder missed the sarcasm he intended it to have.

Jerry stood his ground. Glancing down at the urn, "A little

piece chipped off, that's all," he said. "So let's not make as if the world ended. It can be fixed with glue."

"Glue?" Max sneered.

"Yes, I'll glue it together."

"How you can glue marble?"

"Nowadays you can glue anything. Then you'll keep that corner turned to the wall, and no one'll know."

"I'll know," Max declared tragically.

Jerry swallowed hard and fired his final shot. "So you won't tell anyone." They stared at each other, separated by four decades of incomprehension, and it seemed to Jerry that he would love the glued-together urn for the rest of his life.

Max was about to reply but caught the look of astonishment that this interchange had brought to Ralphie's face, and realized that he had lost the battle. "Here," he said to the boy, drawing a dollar bill from his wallet, "go buy yourself an ice-cream soda."

Ralphie took the dollar and bolted. Jerry went for the glue. Frances wiped her eyes. Max returned to the bedroom but was too agitated to resume his nap. He needed this excitement like a hole in the head.

On the following day he found a solution. "I'm taking you all to Miami Beach," he informed them lovingly. "It'll be a vacation for me too. I made reservations at the Fontainebleau Hotel." He pronounced it *fountain blue*. "We're leaving Thursday." However, on Wednesday night he announced a change of plan. "Something came up I didn't expect. I'll have to stay here over the weekend. But it don't pay to change the reservations. You go ahead tomorrow and I'll join you Monday."

Jerry was not taken in by the ruse. "He's getting rid of us," he told Frances.

"You and your suspicions."

"You don't know him like I do." Jerry smiled. "Even if he won't come, we'll be in Miami. Nothing wrong with that."

"Miami in June? I'd rather be in the Congo."

"Stop exaggerating. It's become a year-round resort."

"If it's a year-round resort, smarty, why do they charge you half price in summer with meals thrown in?"

"Anyway," Jerry persisted, "the rooms are air-conditioned."

"So we travel three thousand miles to see poppa and end up in an air-conditioned room?" Frances thought hard. "He wouldn't pull a trick like that."

"There's no trick he wouldn't pull if it suits him. Monday we'll get a telegram saying he can't come but we should enjoy Florida anyway. Y'know what?" Jerry's gray eyes filled with glee. "That's exactly what we'll do."

They left on Thursday, and Max's life resumed its normal rhythm. The couch ceased to be a bed, the cots were removed, the oval living room regained its charm. The bronze urn, with its glued-on corner turned to the wall, looked as good as new. On Monday morning he had his secretary send a telegram to Miami. He was careful about the wording, as he wanted the message to ring true. It read: "Sorry, detained by emergency. Will try to join you soon as I can. Enjoy yourselves. Sincerely yours, Max Rubin."

That afternoon he came home in a relaxed mood. He installed himself in the green leather chair, tipped it back to its horizontal position, and celebrated his liberation with a delicious cigar.

4

The room had mahogany wainscotting along the walls and wooden shutters through which filtered slanting rays of light. From the top of the bookcase a bronze bust of Sigmund Freud looked down benignly on the armchair in which sat Dr. Franz Wittenfels. He spent hours in this chair listening to the stream of memories, confessions, associations that flowed from the couch before him. At the moment he was listening to Judith.

Dr. Wittenfels was a tall, heavy-set man in his late sixties. He was Viennese; that is, he was born in Prague, came to Vienna to study medicine, and remained there until the entrance of Hitler reminded him that he was a Jew. He had abandoned his medical studies shortly after he fell under the spell of Freud, and was one of the last survivors of the band of disciples that surrounded the master in the 1920s; he spoke with the authority of one who had inherited the mantle. Wittenfels had Olympian contempt for the shoemakers—as he called them—of the New York Psychoanalytic Society, and carried on endless polemics with them over points of doctrine so subtle that they could be

understood only by the initiate. In these he proved to his satisfaction that they had not the remotest comprehension of what
analysis was. Wittenfels was a forceful personality whose impatience with the ineptitudes of his fellow men made it a little
difficult for him to get on with them. He wrote a great deal; his
wife, much younger than he, called him in her divorce suit "an
Ego with a typewriter." His eyes were sharp and looked at you
as if they were trying to see through you. He cleared his throat
portentously before he spoke. Psychoanalysis, he often said, was
the disease for which it presumed to be the cure. He had an
abiding interest in the creative process and wrote several papers
on the psychopathology of the artist, an area in which he followed the lead of Freud's studies of da Vinci, Shakespeare, and
Dostoievsky. Judith met him during the early forties, when she
moved widely in refugee circles, and was attracted to him because of his interest in music. Wittenfels, when he arrived in
this country, was astonished at the popularity of Sibelius, who
was never played in Vienna. "Why you listen to Sibelius when
there is Mahler?" he asked contemptuously. In the next two
decades he had the satisfaction of seeing his faith vindicated, as
the public shifted its loyalty from the Finnish composer to the
Austrian.

Seated behind the couch, Wittenfels could see his patients
without their seeing him, so that he might more effectively surprise their unconscious. Judith's unconscious resisted him. "You
mean to tell me," she said, glancing up at the bronze bust, "that
in order to understand what I'm going through we have to go
back to when I was three years old?"

"Why not?" His guttural accent made him sound like one of
those Nazi officers in Hollywood movies. "You react to the
present, but the seeds of the present are where? Far in the past!"

Judith mused on this. "And if we dig up the past things will
change for me now? Am I supposed to believe that?"

"Why it is not possible? When you respond to a situation is it
because of the woman you now are? Of course not! It is because
of the little girl you are long ago, because of what she feels about
her parents and her parents feel about her. Is that not true?
Why all your experiences resemble one the other? Because on
all of them you impose—yes, you impose—the personality of
that little girl."

"And if we dig far enough and long enough into the past that
personality will change? You really believe this?"

Wittenfels nodded. "Very much I believe this." He divided mankind into two groups—those who had been analyzed and those who had not. The first group he further divided into those who had been analyzed by him and those who had not. It was his firm belief that anyone who correctly followed the tenets of Freud could be cured of whatever ailed him. The psyche was able to change, if led adroitly from one level of understanding to the next; the neurotic, overwhelmed by life, could learn to cope with it, if guided by a skillful physician of the soul such as himself and not by one of the shoemakers. Unlike them, he did not regard a medical degree as an essential part of the analyst's equipment; he held a doctorate in psychology. (This point constituted another bone of contention with his American colleagues.) Indeed, he considered analysis to be not so much a science as an art. In any case, he regarded Judith as lucky in having come to him instead of to them, and repeatedly told her so.

"And you, doctor," she persisted, "could you change? Could you acquire another personality, another way of looking at life?"

"Who is the patient here, I or you?" Wittenfels laughed. "A person can change if he wants it enough. To do this he must overcome everything in him that does not want it."

"If you wanted it hard enough, could you change the color of your eyes?"

"No, but I could change what they see and how I interpret what they see."

"Doctor, we're playing with words. According to you I could change if I really wanted to. If I don't, you say it's because I don't really want to be cured. Very well then, my illness is not that I'm ill but that I don't want to get well. So cure me of that!" She lay back, delighted with her unassailable logic.

Wittenfels leaned toward the couch, suddenly confidential. "All of you here come looking for a miracle. You want I should wave a wand and—one, two, three—you become someone else. Can I a miracle make? Can I change in one month or two or three the habits of the mind that have been for thirty, forty years? The whole psyche must want to change, not only with the lips. This is not easy."

Judith, for no apparent reason, remembered an evening when she was eleven. "My parents had to go somewhere and told me I was old enough to stay home by myself. When they left I tried to do my lessons but I felt they didn't really love me or they wouldn't have left me alone. I began to cry, and I wouldn't go to bed until they returned. I remember this as vividly as if it happened last night." It seemed to her she could still hear those childish sobs.

"Maybe you are jealous of your mother, you want your father to go with you instead of with her. Maybe you feel very guilty because you want this. It is not possible?"

"Everyone goes through this sort of thing. I was an only child and wasn't used to being left alone. Naturally, the first time they did it I felt neglected. What's so significant about that?"

"Nothing, except that it leaves an impression on you which it does not leave on another child. Perhaps you become convinced that night that you are not worthy of being loved. Perhaps that impression stays with you when you grow up."

Judith shrugged. She resented having to pay him forty dollars an hour twice a week, which was more than she could afford. Much of her time she spent in sparring with him—what he called her resistance; the rest went into dredging up stray memories of the childhood patterns which, according to him, had warped her until she had become the woman she was. The greater part of this seemed futile to her; still, she looked forward to the hour with him. It was comforting to know there was someone she could talk to about herself without shame or inhibition; to articulate her fears, anxieties, disappointments; finally, to make contact on whatever level at a time when the ability to make contact seemed to be slipping from her grasp. She continued the sessions, on the theory that if they would not help, neither could they harm. Besides, what else had she to cling to?

5

The air was acrid with fumes and smoke, the nights were humid; then the sun rose and the city seemed to float on waves of light. From his room high above the river Bob could see the boatloads of tourists gawking at the skyline of Manhattan. Despite the heat and the dirt he loved New York in the summer. People looked friendlier.

He had resumed his studies at Columbia and was taking three

graduate courses. The return to a disciplined manner of existence was more pleasant than he had anticipated, providing him
with a specific goal and the kind of framework his life had
lacked. It occurred to him, as he looked over the past, that he
had misunderstood the nature of freedom. He had thought of
it as an absolute good, and in his search for total freedom had
ended by becoming its slave. By relinquishing part of his freedom, on the other hand, he felt more free than he ever had before. Hegel had expressed it well: freedom was the recognition
of necessity.

He looked forward to the mornings on campus. The red and
gray buildings were the embodiment of everything he regarded
as academic—solid, respectable, square. His professors were
scholarly pedants who read their lectures badly and seemed afraid
of their shadows. Bob watched their mental gymnastics with a
kind of fascination even though what they offered had little in
common with the great masters of poetry and prose whose names
they mouthed. As he walked along 116th Street, with the im-
posing library on one side and the seated marble figure of
Columbia on the other, the university appeared to him like an
enclave cut off from the turbulent life that surrounded it. What
would happen, he wondered, if the world outside ever invaded
this cloistered retreat?

The most pleasant part of his work was the reading. Before
him stretched the vast panorama of English literature. He was
attending a seminar on the Victorian novel. Thackeray, Dickens,
Sir Walter Scott, George Eliot, the Brontës—how swiftly the
hours passed in their company. He was enthralled by the music
of their prose, the vividness of their characters, the scope of
their imagination. From a welter of wonderful coincidences and
mistaken identities, misplaced wills and mysterious aunts travers-
ing eerie corridors in deserted manor houses, there emerged a
world in which the quest for love and sex, wealth and power
was as intense as in his own, a world whose men and women
seemed astonishingly real to him no matter how greatly their
speech and clothes differed from his. Was it not a miracle that
words could preserve intact the personal vision that had inspired
them, and could communicate that vision to men of another time
and place? This was true immortality, perhaps the only one that
mattered: the triumph of language over the corrosive power of
time.

When his classes were over he repaired to the gymnasium where he worked out with weights, ran around the track, and swam. He remembered the summer before at the seashore: the swimming had been better there, but he felt more at peace with himself now. He thought of Paul. On several occasions he had been on the point of telephoning him to tell him how much he regretted his behavior. When he finally did, Paul had already left for Europe. Perhaps it was just as well. The friendship was doomed to fail; nevertheless the manner of its failing troubled him. There ought to be, he felt, a degree of style in human relationships. By any standard his conduct had been less than stylish.

He had failed to respect Paul's love, just as he had failed to respect Margo's. We owed something to those who loved us even if we did not share their feelings. This was one of those moral principles (like the injunction not to kill) that could not be proved by logic but had to be accepted on faith. Suppose Margo had carried out her decision to blind him; he would have been punished and her life would have been ruined. Although she was unable—luckily—to go through with it, the moral problem remained: what right had he to push another human being to such despair? Beyond that loomed a larger question—To what extent could anybody be held responsible for someone else? This, it seemed to him, was the basic issue of all morality.

He was having his first taste of family life. After the haphazard way in which Judith ran her household, it was pleasant to be in a home where meals were served on time. He submitted cheerfully to the discipline that this imposed upon him and was careful never to keep Walter and Alice waiting. He was expected to join them for a drink a little after seven; dinner was at seven thirty or, if they had guests, at eight. After dinner he was free to spend the evening with them or return to his room to read. At first his friendship was mainly with Alice; he felt shy with Walter and sensed that Walter was equally constrained with him. Gradually, however, a relationship developed. Walter interested him, representing as he did the man of practical affairs who was at home in the world—a type with whom Bob had never had contact. They would discuss the events of the day, on which they generally disagreed, or books. Walter did not read much fiction; he would skim through a novel if people in his circle were talking about it, or a detective story before he went to sleep. But he liked to discuss literature for the same reason he enjoyed discussing music: it made him feel cultured. They would walk along the river on Sunday mornings, Bob surprised at how well they hit it off. "Tell me," Walter asked, "what are you reading?"

"*Wuthering Heights*. I'm doing a paper on Emily Brontë."

"I saw the movie years ago. With Merle Oberon. God, she was beautiful."

"Before my time."

"I was supposed to read the book when I was at college. Never got around to it."

"It's an extraordinary work. Imagine a young girl hidden away on the moors of England creating Heathcliffe. The lonely rebel who defies society and all its conventions. What a bold conception. Probably the first appearance in literature of Nietzsche's Superman, fifty years before Nietzsche. She was a genius."

Walter was infected by his enthusiasm. "This is how they should have taught us," he said. He was beginning to enjoy the young man's mind.

Best of all Bob liked his conversations with Alice. With her he was at his best—confident, considerate, relaxed—the kind of person he had always wanted to be. He was giving her, he realized, the affection that should have gone to his mother, and felt guilty about this. Judith was frequently in his thoughts. The complex fabric of their relationship, woven in equal measure out of love and hate, had grown unaccountably vague in his memory, except for certain scenes that lit up the dark landscape of the past. One such scene returned again and again to torment him: the moment when he threw the knife on the table and it glanced her throat. He remembered how they looked at each other. "She brought out the worst in me," he told Alice. "I'll never know why."

"Maybe both of you were too wrapped up in each other."

"The vibrations were wrong between us, no matter how we tried."

"Sooner or later," Alice said quietly, "you'll have to go home."

"Why?"

"You'll never forgive yourself if you don't make up with her."

"For years the room I slept in was home to me. Now home is here. You know, I scarcely remember the other."

"What's real to us is here and now. Once you're back you'll forget this one."

"Oh, no," he exclaimed with fervor, "I never will!"

She took care not to impinge upon his freedom. As though sensing his dread of involvement, she made him feel that she expected very little of him, and he was grateful. "People talk about how wonderful it is," he told her, "to be in love. What they don't say is how wonderful it is not to be. Look at me. I feel free at the moment. Free to keep my mind on my work."

"That's only because you're still recovering from what happened. Once you're well, you'll want to get involved again."

"Why couldn't we be like the amoeba, which divides in two whenever it feels like and don't need anybody else?"

She smiled. "I don't think you'd find that very interesting."

"Maybe not. But it sure would solve a lot of problems."

"We heard from Margo," Alice said. "She's had a great success in Germany."

"I'm glad for her." His face fell. "I hate to think of how I behaved."

"It's over, so there's nothing to think about. She's coming back this winter. She may be singing at the Met."

He was thoughtful. "She almost didn't make it."

"But she did. That's what counts."

It was time for him to go. He gathered his books. Before leaving he kissed Alice. "Thanks. For everything."

The summer unfolded in serene, sun-drenched days. He took each as it came, determined to enjoy it to the full. The future would take care of itself.

6

A gray light filtered through the wooden shutters under the benevolent gaze of Freud. "It'll be fun," Judith said, "to get away for awhile."

"What you want, even if you do not know it," Dr. Wittenfels replied, "is to run away."

"Who am I running away from?"

"Me."

"Why?"

"Because you are afraid if you come to me you get better."

"You know, doctor, you're so eager to find hidden meanings, I think you don't even hear what I say."

"Why you spend so much time fighting me? It is your time, you are paying for it."

"Don't remind me."

"Then why you waste it? And why you hate so much to pay me? All of you the same way are. A fur coat, yes; a motor car, yes; but to pay the doctor who tries to put your life in order, no. Why so?"

"You tell me."

"Because you are ambivalent to me. You do not think I can help you."

"To be honest with you, I don't."

"Then why you come if you think I can do nothing? To win an argument with me? Do you not see that if you win, you lose? Only if you lose the argument do you get well."

"I haven't been to Europe in five years. I think the change'll do me good."

"How there can be a change if you take yourself with you? Your problems go where you go."

"But if a person hasn't been anywhere in five years, are you trying to tell me it won't do him good to get away for awhile?"

"You are not well now, you should not make such a trip. And alone."

"Don't worry, I can take care of myself. Once I'm there I'll feel better."

"Impossible!"

Judith's underlip came forward obstinately. "I'm going," she brought out petulantly.

"Go, go," he said, annoyed at her stubbornness. "You will come back to me. If you know what is good for you."

It rained the day she left for London. Judith took this as a bad omen. She slept most of the way; when she awoke the plane was flying into a gray dawn. The same kind of panic attacked her as on the train to Trenton. Why London when what she wanted was warm weather and cloudless skies? She had played there on her last trip abroad—two concerts in Wigmore Hall—but that was hardly a reason for returning now. She suddenly saw herself trapped in a cold, rainy city, screaming with boredom. By the time the plane landed she had reached a decision; she canceled her stopover and proceeded to her final destination —Rome.

She had been in Italy briefly on her last visit; this time she was eager to explore Rome. She went back to the hotel she had stayed in, a rambling structure near the Pantheon with a huge courtyard, enormous rooms, old-fashioned balconies, and faded carpets along its silent corridors. The sun was shining, the sky was blue. She loved everything about the city—its architectural splendor, its majesty, even the hordes of tourists who worked their way with guide books and cameras from one landmark to the next. She discovered a confectionary shop whose ice-cream was heavenly, and contrived to be in its vicinity several times a day. She found the Italian temperament operatic but enchanting, and never tired of walking through the teeming streets. Everything about the city spoke of the past: the remains of ancient Rome that showed like an undergarment in the most unexpected places, the Baroque fountains, the narrow streets without sidewalks in the medieval part of town. It was a masculine city, she decided, just as Paris and Venice were feminine, and its theme was the passing of time. Time as the eternal element of both change and continuity, that destroyed stone and marble yet also preserved them. At midday, before setting out on her rounds, she would step into the Pantheon for a brief visit with Raphael, Corelli, and Queen Margaret of Savoy. Here time had stopped; it was dark, cool, and infinitely quiet.

The Pantheon put an end to the solitary phase of her stay in Rome. As she came out on its broad steps one afternoon, her eyes dazzled by the sunlight, a familiar face swam out of the crowd. Philip. They had made no effort to see each other in New York, but their meeting in a strange city was an occasion for rejoicing.

"Imagine running into you here!" he exclaimed. "One chance in a million."

"Not really. All the Americans go to the same places, so we'd have met sooner or later. Where's Andrée?"

"On the Via Veneto. Shopping."

She saw his eyes linger on her figure. "I know, I'm bursting at the seams. It's that marvelous ice-cream they have here, I just can't resist it."

He grinned. "You were never strong on resisting."

Having been alone for almost a week, Judith enjoyed having someone to talk to; they spent a pleasant hour together. Now that she did not have to win or retain his love, she felt at ease with him. It was his first visit to Rome, and he, too, had fallen under its spell.

Judith sensed that he was eager for her to meet Andrée and invited them to dine with her. When they arrived at her hotel that evening Philip was a little tense; he obviously was apprehensive as to how his wife and former mistress would hit it off. Judith felt at a disadvantage because of her bulk; her successor had the figure and elegance of a Parisienne. She wore a navy-blue silk dress trimmed with white; her light-brown hair, parted in the middle, met in a low bun at the back of her neck. Judith covered her awkwardness by assuming an exaggeratedly cordial manner. Andrée's opening remark "I 'ave 'eard so much about you" did not augur well; it always stopped Judith cold to be told this. Before long, however, she decided that she liked Andrée. The woman was sensible and forthright, without being in any way interesting. If this was what Phil had preferred to her, that was his problem.

They dined on the terrace under a sky spangled with stars. Warmed by wine and a flavorsome meal, their conversation grew more and more animated. By the time dessert arrived Andrée, who prided herself on her ability to read palms, was studying Judith's. "Oh," she cried, "I see a veree eenteresting—'ow you say?—adventure. Weez a tall, dark man, veree 'andsome. And young!" She threw back her head and laughed. Judith did too.

Andrée's prophecy came true sooner than might have been expected. The following day, when Judith left her hotel, she passed a sidewalk café on the north side of the piazza. The young man seated at the end table was dark and handsome, as she had been promised. It was as if he had been waiting for her. He rose as she walked by, caught up with her, and walked by her side. She observed the proprieties by pretending not to notice; finally she glanced at him and smiled. He smiled back. It was as simple as that.

His name was Aldo and he came from Amalfi. He was extremely proud of his English, which he spoke haltingly; he had learned it from a book. He had been a clerk but at present was unemployed. His black hair was thick and curly; he looked at the world through a pair of large brown eyes that resembled a cocker spaniel's and would have been expressive if they had had something to express. When he smiled he showed two rows of even white teeth, and he smiled often. He spent the afternoon with Judith and ended up in her room. It was obvious that Aldo did some of his best work in bed; his love-making had the professional touch. His adroitness with American ladies of a certain age was aided by a trick of the imagination that enabled him, when he shut his eyes, to substitute Sophia Loren in their stead. Aldo's body was lean and bony, the ribs showed, his chest was covered with hair. His favorite expression was, "The signora, she like?" To which Judith replied, "The signora, she like very much."

Philip and Andrée had invited her to dinner. She wondered if she should bring Aldo. She asked him if he would like to come, whereupon an eager look lit up his big brown eyes; he was perpetually hungry. Judith decided that he was much too attractive not to show off, and telephoned Phil to inform him that she was bringing a friend. "It's really your doing," she said to Andrée when they arrived. As she was about to introduce him she realized that she had forgotten his last name, if she had ever known it. "This is Aldo Cavalli," she said, giving him the first name that popped into her head.

"No, Pazzarelli," Aldo gravely corrected her.

"Of course," Judith said smoothly. "Cavalli is his middle name."

In the following days the four of them were inseparable. Judith was astonished that they got on so well together. Her surprise was shared by Philip and Andrée, who were planning to go to Greece and suggested that Judith and Aldo come with them; they would spend a few days in Athens and take a trip through the islands. Judith thought this a capital idea. Having always believed in traveling alone, she now discovered that a congenial foursome could be more fun.

Aldo did not have much to say, but what he said was basic. He readily accommodated himself to Judith's wishes, especially if these involved the two occupations he liked best—eating and making love. Judith found him enchanting. She surrendered to him with an abandon that delighted her, and emerged from his ministrations immeasurably refreshed. Aldo made her feel like a woman again, and a desirable one at that. Coming at a time when she had begun to lose faith in her power to attract men, this was an achievement for which she was properly grateful.

The subject of money did not come up between them, at least not immediately. Aldo was obviously penniless, and it seemed only right to Judith that he be her guest. She would have liked to help him with his rent and living expenses but was afraid he would be offended; she contented herself with buying him useful gifts—a wrist watch one week, several sport shirts the next. Aldo came to the point in a most delicate manner. His mother, he informed her, needed an operation; could the signora lend him twenty thousand lire? When Judith realized that he was asking for not much more than thirty dollars (she never could remember whether to divide or multiply by six hundred), it seemed like a trifling sum compared to what he had given her. The signora, she assured him, would be delighted to give him the money. A few days later it turned out that his sister needed five thousand for a pair of shoes. And so it went. He seemed to have a large family but their needs, by American standards, were modest.

Aldo loved opera; he had the soul of a tenor. His usual stolidity disappeared when the radio in Judith's room emitted a familiar aria by Verdi or Puccini. He would sing along ecstatically; on a sustained high note his right hand would describe an all-inclusive arc from the region of his heart to the universe. Judith's stay in Italy had not caused her to change her low opinion of Italian opera. However, when Aldo suggested that they attend a performance at the Baths of Caracalla—Philip and Andrée seconded him with enthusiasm—she agreed.

They dined early and reached the Baths as the orchestra was tuning up. Philip thought it a stroke of genius to present open-air opera among Roman ruins; Judith, on the other hand, was contemptuous from the start. She complained about the hard seats; the little cushions they rented reminded her of third-rate summer concerts in the Lewisohn Stadium. The crowd, the soda vendors, the carnival atmosphere that pervaded the Baths struck her as thoroughly appropriate to what she regarded as the lowest form of music.

Aïda, in this setting, took on heroic proportions; the figures on stage were larger than life. Their Egyptian costumes fooled no one; they were, as Verdi had conceived them, true Italians. No one in the cast was great but all were excellent, and they were singing music that was in their blood. Nothing could upset their beat or their phrasing, not even when the wind blew down a palm tree. A cold mist began to rise from the Baths. Judith had not been warned to bring a sweater and felt chilly; Aldo draped his jacket around her shoulders. The second act was spectacular. Camels and elephants joined in a triumphal march worthy of a conqueror; Radamès arrived in a chariot drawn by four white horses who galloped to the edge of the stage. The granitic melody of the March rang out from sixteen trumpets with shattering effect; the audience cheered; Judith was a minority of one.

They went for refreshments during intermission. "Waz eet not wonderful?" Andrée exclaimed.

"It was so vulgar," Judith deflated her, "I was appalled."

Andrée looked at her in surprise. "I thought eet was beautiful."

"The Italians have no musical taste," Judith pontificated. "Serious music is completely beyond them. All they know is this kind of circus. Disgusting!"

"But Verdi, Puccini," Andrée persisted, "zeez are great composers, no?"

"No. The great composers," Judith answered categorically, "are Bach and Beethoven, Mozart and Haydn, Schubert, Schumann, Brahms."

"Maybee for you. But for people oo do not understand music zey are very deefeecult. Schumann, par exemple. He bores me."

At this remark Judith forgot that she had become quite fond of Andrée; she knew only that one of her idols was being attacked. "And what makes you think you're qualified to give an opinion on Schumann?" she brought out, fixing Andrée with an icy stare.

Andrée's face showed her astonishment at this change. "Eet eez only my opinion," she said amiably, "but I 'ave a right to eet."

"No, you don't!" Judith announced, her voice rising. "Only people who know what they're talking about have a right to their opinions."

At this point Philip intervened. "Sh . . . people are listening."

Judith turned upon him. "Don't you shush me!" she cried in the tone she had used when they were lovers.

Philip was not cowed. "This is no way to talk to my wife."

"What am I supposed to do? Listen to idiotic statements and let them pass, just to be agreeable? Thank you! That's not my style."

"The old Judith," he cried. "I was wondering when the sweetness and light would end."

"Don't give me that!" she shouted, her anger rising to the surface. "I'm sick of people who compromise. Compromise on what they believe, what they feel, what they think, just to be pleasant!" She turned to Aldo. "I've had enough of this. Let's go home."

Aldo had followed the conversation as best he could, bewildered by the turn it had taken. The realization that Judith was ordering him to leave agitated him so deeply that he forgot his English. "Voglio intendere il atto terzo," he exclaimed. "Il atto terzo è molto bello. Bellissimo!" He flung out his arm in its customary flourish.

"You can stay and hear the third act if you like," Judith said coldly. "I'm going!" She removed the jacket from her shoulders, handed it to him, and walked off in the direction of the gate.

"You'd better take her back," Philip said.

Aldo glanced tragically from Judith's retreating form to the stage, torn between the two. Then he remembered which side his bread was buttered on and ran after her. Philip, his face grim, took Andrée's arm; they returned to their seats.

In the cab Judith sat staring before her, throwing an aggrieved look now and again at the back of the driver's head. Once they were back in the hotel she exploded. "Ignoramus! Probably heard three notes of Schumann in her life and thinks she's an expert!" She realized that the idyllic foursome had been irretrievably damaged. Her regret made her more determined than ever to prove herself in the right. "And the way he backed her up. 'This is no way to talk to my wife.' Who the hell does he think she is?" Judith did not have to be told that the trip to Greece was off, but she had to establish the fact that the decision was hers. "I have to listen to this kind of drivel? I've nothing better to do? That's my trouble—I get too friendly with people, then they take advantage of my good nature!" She suddenly remembered that Aldo had been reluctant to leave the theater. This disloyalty could not possibly spring from his love of opera; she found a baser motive. Turning upon him the full blaze of her eyes, "And don't think," she struck out, "that I didn't see you flirting with her all through dinner. It was disgusting!"

"Signora!" Aldo cried in tender reproach. He planned before the evening was out to ask her for fifteen thousand lira for his aunt Carmela, who had a goiter.

"Knees touching under the table. And hands. I'm not blind!" It made Aldo more desirable in her eyes to believe that another woman was after him. Besides, she enjoyed the thought that

Andrée, whom Philip had preferred to her, was now unfaithful to him.

"I swear, signora!" Aldo brought out operatically. "Lo giuro!"

"You two were having your little secrets all along."

"Signora!" Aldo held out his hands in a gesture that protested his innocence.

His helplessness added fuel to her rage, which carried her farther than she had intended. "You're all alike, all of you. Trash! Gigolos!" Startled at her use of so unsavory a word, she repeated it.

It was, unfortunately, a word he understood. His face went white. "La signora è pazza!" he shouted. "Pazza!" He wanted to strike her but, remembering his Aunt Carmela's goiter, he threw himself on the twin bed nearest the wall, buried his face in the pillow, and groaned.

Judith's nerves were at breaking point. Although she felt remorseful, she was not going to ask his forgiveness. She took off her clothes and made ready for bed. Because of Aldo's presence she omitted the ritual of cold cream; she lay down on the other bed, her back to him, and pulled the sheet over her.

She knew she would not be able to sleep. Presently she rose, proceeded to the bathroom, and took two sleeping pills. She went back to bed, still without a word, and turned out the light. She wanted to tell Aldo that she regretted what she had said but a drowsiness enveloped her, sparing her the confession.

Aldo listened to the quiet rhythm of her breathing. He cautiously lifted his head from the pillow and turned around. She lay in semidarkness, head thrown back, mouth open. In sleep her face looked bloated, imperious. "Messalina!" he whispered between clenched teeth, the epithet summing up all he knew of Roman history. A deep revulsion filled him for all the rich bitches from America to whose desires and insanities he was a slave. He felt sorry for himself; he knew he was made for better things. Because of this crazy woman he had missed the beautiful third act by the Nile and the beautiful fourth act in the tomb. "Maledizione!" The signora was a horror and he never wanted to see her again. He eased himself over the side of the bed and, stepping noiselessly on the worn carpet, made for the door. On the way he passed the dresser on which lay the signora's handbag. It was a large black-leather bag that contained the signora's cash, traveler's checks, airplane ticket, passport, and wrist watch.

Aldo thought of his Aunt Carmela's goiter and sighed. He lifted the bag from the dresser, reached the door and, with a final look of hatred at the plump figure on the bed, tiptoed out of the signora's life.

7

Judith opened her eyes. The sun was shining; she felt refreshed. "Aldo!" Upon receiving no answer she turned around to the empty bed. He must have gone home in a huff, she decided, and smiled at the recollection of their quarrel. He would turn up for breakfast; Aldo was not one to miss a meal.

She snuggled against the pillow, luxuriating in the feeling of relaxation that pervaded her body; she had slept well. Having upset her companions the night before, she now felt warm toward them: quarrels never failed to rid Judith of the venom stored up in her, leaving her sweet and clean. She would phone Phil and Andrée after breakfast and tell them how sorry she was. Toward Aldo she felt particularly affectionate. It was ridiculous of her to accuse him of flirting with Andrée, who adored Phil. As for her calling him a gigolo, she felt deeply contrite; the best apology would be three silk ties from Gucci. A devil got into her when she lost her temper; she must learn to control it, she really must.

It came to her that she genuinely liked Aldo. She enjoyed his simplicity of mind and heart; he had an animal quality that she found most attractive. She wondered whether it would be possible to bring him to New York. He could make himself useful in an export-import house that did business with Italy, or in one of those chic Italian clothing shops that were springing up all over town. The smell of coffee drifted in from the hallway; she was hungry. She decided to telephone Aldo; he had left a number where he could be reached. It was not where he lived; his family, he explained, could not afford a phone. She had written down the number, and looked for her bag. When she did not find it on top of the dresser she looked through the drawers, then in the bathroom. Suddenly she knew.

She sat down on the bed, crushed. That she should have taken up with a common thief! It would not have been so bad had he walked out on her while she was angry with him. But that she should have discovered his treachery when she was feeling so affectionate toward him . . . The shame of it overwhelmed her; she felt doubly humiliated because, knowing what he had done, she still liked him. If she had not called him a gigolo he would not have behaved like one. It was her fault, if you came right down to it.

She surveyed the extent of her loss. He had left her without cash. The passport and airplane ticket could be replaced, but that would involve a lot of red tape. She had written down the number of her traveler's checks, she could not remember where. If he tried to cash them he would be caught, and it would serve him right. The watch was no great loss; it was a gift from her second husband and she had never liked it. Still, the thought that it was now in Aldo's possession filled her with rage. She would notify the police and put him in jail, where he belonged. A cruel satisfaction possessed her, until she remembered what a juicy morsel this would make for the newspapers. *American pianist victimized by young Italian.* You spent the first half of your life trying to get your name in the papers, and the second half trying to keep it out. How was he able to leave the hotel with her bag? Through the service entrance, of course. He was probably in cahoots with the night clerk; this kind of thing happened all the time. It humiliated her that her life should resemble a third-rate movie. She would have to get in touch with the embassy over her passport, and notify the airline that her ticket was missing. If she admitted that her bag had been stolen, the hotel would investigate; the less she said, the better. Probably the best way would be to tell them she had left it in a taxi.

She would have liked to crawl back into bed and forget her predicament, but she had to do something. The only thing she could think of was to call Phil; he would know what to do. Yet how could she bring herself to tell him? How could she say—? Her face went hot. It was bad enough that he had learned about Bob's misconduct; this was even worse! She sat without moving, staring before her. Her head ached. Finally she telephoned Philip's hotel. He was out, as was Andrée. She left a message for him to call her as soon as he returned. There was nothing for it but to wait until he did; she was not up to settling this dreary business by herself. What had she done to deserve it? The more she pondered the question the more agitated she became. She felt a burning in her eyelids and began to sniffle; suddenly tears rolled down her cheeks. She leaned over to reach for the box of tissues on top of the dresser and caught sight of herself in the mirror. She looked a mess without her girdle, her breasts hanging down, stomach bulging, her dyed hair straggling over her shoulders, chin sagging, skin rough and flabby. A silly woman in a ridiculous pink nightie weeping because she had to inform her friends that the handsome young man who had been squiring her had made off with her purse. She slumped forward, her shoulders shaking. "It's too awful," she sobbed, "I try my best and it's no use. Why?" she demanded of the mirror. Its silence released a fresh stream of tears. "It's no use!" she moaned over and over, racked by sobs yet aware throughout that she was making a spectacle of herself.

Presently the spasm passed. She roused herself, pulled two tissues from the box on the dresser and blew her nose. There was a knock on the door. She gave a start. Had he returned, remorseful? A surge of hope made her realize that she would take him back in spite of all. For an instant she was certain everything would turn out well. Yet she waited before replying, as if to stave off the disappointment she would feel if it turned out not to be he. The knock was repeated. "Who is it?" she called, and was answered by the bellhop.

Crestfallen, she went to the door and opened it. He handed her an envelope: a gentleman had left it for the signora. "Grazie." She shut the door and tore open the envelope. Her passport, ticket, and traveler's checks lay inside. He had kept the cash and the wrist watch. The bastard! Her anger gave way to a feeling of relief that she no longer had to reveal her mishap to Phil. What a stroke of luck that he was not in his room when she called. It maddened her that, despite what Aldo had done, she regretted his departure. With him gone, there was no point in her remaining in Rome. She would go to Greece with Phil and Andrée, if they still wanted her. If not, she would fly home.

She felt hollow inside: she had not had any breakfast. Yet she was too upset for anything as substantial as scrambled eggs; she craved something sweet. She telephoned the desk and ordered an espresso with four of the little chocolate cream puffs that were a specialty of the house; they were filled with a light yellow

custard that slithered down your throat with marvelous ease.
When the tray arrived she gazed at the four cakes in dreamy
anticipation, lifted one after the other from its corrugated paper
wrapper and washed it down with a mouthful of coffee. If anything could take the place of Aldo, this was it.

The telephone rang; it was Andrée. "You called?"

"Yes. I'm sorry about last night." The custard had lifted her
spirits. "I get so easily upset these days. You must forgive me."

"Of course. Do not worry about eet."

"I'm glad you feel this way. Where's Phil?"

"Een zee lobbee."

"Could I see him for a few minutes."

"I will send 'eem at once."

Judith noticed that Andrée made no mention of their meeting
later in the day. "Thank you so much," she said in the honeyed
tone she reserved for the amenities. "See you soon, my dear."

When Philip arrived she was dressed. She greeted him effu-
sively. "Did Andrée tell you I apologized to her?"

"Yes."

"I'm sorry I lost my temper last night."

"You're always sorry later. Why d'you do it in the first place?"

"Let's not go into that. I asked you to come up so I could ask
you one question. Do you and Andrée still want me to go with
you to Greece?"

He hesitated. "Judith, we've had a wonderful time with you in
Rome, Andrée as well as I. Matter of fact, she got to be real
fond of you. But after last night I'm afraid it wouldn't work.
You see, it's our first vacation in years. We want to relax, and if
you came along we'd be weighing our words for fear of provok-
ing you. I'm being honest with you because I think that's what
you want me to be. I'm sorry, believe me."

"Very well. Then I'll go home."

"What about Aldo? Why don't you take the trip with him?"
She smiled. "Enough is enough."

"That's up to you. You do understand about Andrée and me."

"Of course."

He cleared his throat. "Judith, I hate to bring this up, but
I think I ought to say it. You're letting yourself go in every way,
and it's not good. I have a feeling you're a bit on edge. Why
don't you do something about it?"

"Like what?" A note of irritation crept into her voice.

"That's for you to decide. I just thought I should give you my impression. As a friend."

Her withdrawal was automatic. "Thanks. As a friend."

They parted warmly, promising to see each other in New York although both knew they would not. Judith felt sad after he left. For the first time it appeared to her that Dr. Wittenfels might have been right—she should not have undertaken the trip in her unsettled state of mind. She went out on the balcony. The city lay before her, its skyline dominated by the glittering dome of St. Peter's. The glow induced by the cream puffs had passed; it saddened her to think that her holiday was over. Already Aldo was a memory, soon Rome would be one too. Everything passed, joy, sorrow, life. Why did people make such a fuss?

The following morning she took the plane to New York. Below her the coastline receded, the Mediterranean was a dazzling blue that reached as far as the eye could see. The thought of going home did not dispel her sadness. Where was home? Where did she belong? Judith watched the fleecy little clouds that floated beneath her window. She was as rootless as they.

She dozed off and dreamed that she had been packed into a wooden crate. She tried to force her way out but the sides would not give. Suddenly they fell away and she was free to go. Where? The signposts had been removed, and she did not know what street she was on.

She awoke, gripped by a feeling of apprehension that she was unable to shake off. What was she afraid of? She could not say.

seven

Walter welcomed Margo with a hug, then held her at arm's length. "You've changed."

"How?"

"You're different. More——" He hesitated. "What's the word I'm looking for?"

"Poised?"

"Could be." He glanced at her clothes. "And more stylish."

The dark little face was illumined by a smile. "You mean more expensive."

"But the real change is inside. You seem more sure of yourself."

"That's a nice way of saying I'm older."

They reached his car. The porter piled her luggage into the compartment; they took the road from the airport. "Glad to be back?" Walter asked.

"Yes. I loved Europe, but sooner or later you have to face New York. That's the final test, I guess." Under their thick lashes her eyes shone.

He watched her closely, seeking a sign of the old Margo. She moved differently, with a quiet authority that she had never had before. He was happy to observe that she had adopted none of the artifices he disliked in prima donnas; she did her acting on stage.

He had always thought her pretty; now she was beautiful. "I passed the opera house yesterday and there was your name, right under Nilssen's. What a thrill to see it." He leaned toward her. "Scared?"

She knit her brows, searching for the answer. "I don't think so. By the time it happens you're ready for it. Otherwise it wouldn't happen in the first place. Of course, there's always the possibility that it won't come off as you had hoped. But——" She shrugged.

He patted her hand. "It'll go fine."

"I'll do what I can." She said it matter-of-factly, and he knew that she was not afraid.

"How's Alice?"

"Fine. Can't wait to see you."

"Max?" It was a measure of her new status that she referred to him by his first name.

"Excited about your return. He's got all kinds of things lined up for you."

"And Paul?"

"Left us. He decided to return to Europe."

"Why?"

"I never figured it out. He was doing very well but his roots are over there, I guess. Strange man. Hard to get close to."

"Who took over?"

"No one as yet. We'll have a year or two of guest conductors before we decide."

"How's Judith?"

Walter's face darkened. "I haven't been seeing her. We had a run-in. Didn't I write you?"

"No."

He was about to tell her that she was the cause of it but changed his mind. "Judith's a difficult woman," he said, "and not a very good friend. She tried to make up afterward but I was firm. Life is too short for that sort of thing."

Margo watched the shop fronts speed by. "And Bob?" she asked casually. She felt a tightening at her throat, but the emotion passed. This, she reflected mournfully, was our only revenge against those we had loved too well: ultimately they lost their power to make us suffer.

"He's living with us."

"How come?"

"Judith was giving him a hard time. Then Alice and he became buddies—I never discovered how—and she asked him to stay." He was about to add, "It gets Alice off my back" but changed to, "It gives her someone to think about, which is good for her. Seems to be working out for him too."

The car approached the bridge. It was the hour when a lavender tint warms the afternoon air. Seen from the Queens side of the river, the city seemed to be floating in a haze, its towers imponderable, miragelike. "It looks like something out of a fairy tale," Margo whispered, moved. "This incredible city. I realize now how much I missed it."

The heartless Princess of China turned brusquely toward the little slave girl who refused to betray the name of her beloved. What gave her this strength, Turandot demanded, even under torture? Liù stepped forward humbly. *Principessa, l'amore . . .* Margo's voice soared into the hushed auditorium, limpid and warm. Far behind her were the years of preparation, the grinding hours when breath and muscles had been honed into a perfectly controlled instrument. Now she could rise above technique, so that the sounds issued not so much from her throat as from her mind and heart—she was the music, her body the instrument through which the composer's vision came to life. A dark tremolo in the cellos and basses ushered in the melody in E-flat minor that Puccini marked *con dolorosa espressione;* slowly the crowd fell back, leaving Liù alone in the center of the stage, a slight figure bent forward in an attitude of humility. She sang of her secret love that sought only to give and demanded nothing in return, and the music lifted her sorrow to the ideal plane of art, transfiguring it, so that she was not only little Liù singing of her prince but everyone who had ever loved in vain, who had suffered and had been defeated.

Walter listened, enthralled. He thought of the girl she was when he first met her and of the long road they had traveled together. He had been given the rare joy of helping to create an artist. Yet even in this moment of triumph he knew that she would have attained her goal without him; he had only smoothed the way. Nothing he had done in his life seemed to him as worthwhile as this, or had given him such pleasure. A sustained note soared aloft, of such beauty that tears filled his eyes and he took himself to task for being sentimental.

Alice remembered the night of her party when she wanted to urge Margo to forget her ambitions and go back to Poughkeepsie, marry a pleasant young man, and raise three children. Was advice of any kind ever right? And the gray November day when she brought her to the doctor. She glanced around at the bemused throng. Would they ever know what torment had gone into the making of this golden voice? Of what importance was that? It was the result that mattered.

Bob followed the ascending curve of the aria. As on the evening when he heard her sing *Butterfly* at Juilliard, he tried to reconcile his image of the girl he had held in his arms with the artist on stage. Art, he reflected, supplied the necessary distance between the emotion and those who were to feel it, lifting it above the personal so that it could be shared in public—without embarrassment—by complete strangers, each of whom experienced the emotion in his own way. He winced when he remembered how unworthy he had been of her love. Yet what had passed between them belonged to another period of their lives and was inevitable in terms of what they then were. Gradually he yielded to the pathos of the opera—it was Liù he was listening to rather than Margo—and his guilt dissolved in the grand gesture of the Italian style.

Birdie, sitting behind Alice, felt depressed. Paul's departure, on top of her quarrel with Judith, had left a blank in her list of artists that would not be easy to fill. She thought of the years of promotion that went into the making of a career, the thousand and one details for which, as she grew older, she had less and less patience. When she was young it had all seemed so glamorous —the people, the concerts, the press releases, the parties. Now she found it a bore. She had set her heart on a career: why would any dame want one when she could stay home and let her husband do the worrying? An idyllic vision rose before her of the married woman who in the morning slept as late as she liked, spent a relaxing hour at the hairdresser, had lunch with friends, passed an hour or two with the latest novel or working in the garden, and at five put her mind on preparing dinner. This was the existence she should have striven for. Her gaze rested on the back of Walter's neck. How well she knew its well-groomed look—the neck of a man who thoroughly enjoyed life. She should have freed herself from him long ago and found a husband. He didn't have to be rich, just comfortable—a solid, kindly individual who would give her the simple things of life and spare her the heartaches. Oh, she had been foolish, foolish, and Margo's voice was so heavenly that she wanted to cry. Absolutely.

The melody came to its agonizing end. Liù seized a dagger from the nearest soldier and stabbed herself in order not to betray her prince, but Calaf was too wrapped up in his love for Turandot to fathom the depth of hers. Staggering forward, she touched the hem of his robe and fell adoringly at his feet. A burst of applause exploded in the theater, punctuated by bravos and the special excitement that grips an audience when a new star rises on its horizon. Margo, outstretched on the stage, knew she had conquered. The long upward climb was over; the promise had been fulfilled.

Walter turned around and smiled at Max, who sat next to Birdie. The old man shook his head. "You knew she had it, I knew she had it, now they all know." He grinned with delight, for he had her under a five-year contract.

When the curtain calls were over they went backstage. She had taken off her costume and had removed the grease paint; she wore a blue dressing gown and looked radiant. Her parents and sister hovered about her, proud and a little astonished that this wondrous creature belonged to them. Walter had sent roses, for which she thanked him with a kiss. Max, Birdie, and Alice embraced her in turn; then Bob stood before her. Betraying no surprise, she greeted him as she had the others. He kissed her lightly on the cheek.

It was arranged that, since she was not yet dressed, Walter would bring her family to the party at his house and send the car back for her. They all left, except Bob. The official smile vanished from her face. "Why did you stay?"

"Because I wanted to tell you——" That night in front of his door, the sound of glass against the pavement and a yellow stain spreading over the snow. "—you were terrific."

She said nothing.

"No, that's not what I wanted to tell you. You've heard it from everyone. I only wanted to say——"

She looked up at him gravely. He pressed his fist to his chin in the gesture she knew so well. "I'm sorry for what I did to you. Forgive me."

There was a puzzled look in her eyes. "What does it mean, to forgive? These are words. What do they mean?"

"Tonight . . . your triumph . . . I almost spoiled it for you."

"I almost spoiled it for myself. That terrible thing between us . . ." She knit her brows. "It's as if it happened to someone else. Someone who was me."

"We're both different now. Say you forgive me."

"I guess I do, because I feel nothing." She put her hand over her left breast. "Nothing at all, except when I'm on stage making believe I'm somebody else."

"You will be a great artist."

She sighed. "That first night. When you left you said, 'Don't worry, I don't stick pins in butterflies.' "

"I didn't mean to."

"But you did."

"That's why I'm asking you to forgive me."

Her eyes rose slowly to his. "Strange. First I loved you so much I could have died for you. Then I hated you so much I wanted to destroy you. And now, I feel nothing. I didn't think there'd come a time when you'd mean nothing to me."

"That's not true," he said vehemently. "I'm part of your past. Part of what you had to go through in order to become what you are."

"What I mean is, I'm free of you at last."

"Then let me bring you to the party."

Margo thought a moment. "No, it would be false. I dreamed of it so much, that I'd sing the way I did tonight and then we'd go out together. But it didn't happen like that. It's too late to pretend."

"I'm staying at Walter's. How will it look if I come in without you? How will I explain it?"

"Say anything. Nobody listens, haven't you discovered that? Say I asked you to do an errand and I'll be along any minute."

"You really don't want me to bring you?"

"No. That free of you I'm not." She smiled sadly, pulling her dressing gown around her.

He moved toward the door. Just before he opened it he turned around to look at her once more. "Oh, Bobby!" she cried, and her voice was like her voice long ago, "I loved you so!" Her hand returned to her breast. "And now it doesn't hurt any more There's only an emptiness."

She put her fingers over her lips as if to stifle a cry. He left.

2

Alice had gone before the others so as to be at home when her guests arrived. She fluffed up the cushions on the couch, rearranged the white chrysanthemums in the vase on the piano, and glanced around the room. Everything was ready.

She stepped out on the terrace. It was a mild November night. The river gleamed in the darkness. The bridge hummed, its gray latticelike structure floating above the black bastions at either end. On the opposite shore the neon sign still proclaimed the virtues of Pepsi-Cola. Alice filled her lungs and frowned. Another party. Tonight, though, was special. Walter had invited several of Margo's teachers and a contingent of young musicians who had been her classmates. She made a mental note to pay special attention to Margo's parents.

Paul would not be at the party; she regretted this. Of all Walter's friends, he was the one to whom she had felt closest. She was sorry, too, that Judith was not coming. It was ridiculous of Walter to hold on to his anger, especially now that Bob was a link between them. Judith was often in her thoughts. What right, she asked herself, had she to enjoy Bob as much as she did when his own mother never saw him?

The bell rang; she went to the door and welcomed Margo's parents and sister. Max arrived with Birdie. Then Bob, alone. The room filled with people, most of whom she did not know. They kissed one another, chattered, and spilled ashes on the rug; the barman poured drinks. Walter, his face pink with excitement, made the necessary introductions. Finally Margo arrived. The company broke into applause when she entered. She wore a white satin sheath that left one shoulder bare; silver earrings gleamed against her skin. Her friends crowded around her, champagne was brought in for a toast.

Alice went into the dining room, lit the tall white candles in the silver candelabra, and took her place at the table. The cream-colored lace cloth was covered with huge platters of cold meats, cheeses, and salmon; musicians loved to eat. Walter came up with his plate. She scooped up a helping of sliced cucumbers and tomatoes. He tasted the salad appraisingly. "Honey, the dressing is just right. It's a good party, don't you think?"

"Yes, dear." She glanced at his plate. "All that salmon? You know it's full of salt."

He assumed his Do-we-have-to-go-through-that-again look. "This once won't harm. After all, it's a special occasion."

"When isn't it?"

Max approached the table with Birdie in tow. "The lox is delicious," he said.

"How many times must I tell you," Birdie shrieked, "that's not lox, it's Nova Scotia salmon."

"Lox shmox, as long as it tastes good."

Walter turned to Birdie. "You were right."

"What about?"

"The night Judith lost her temper with Paul. You had a feeling it was the last time we'd all be together."

Alice regarded Birdie with new interest. It remained a mystery to her what Walter saw in this plump creature with the huge dirty-blond bun in back of her head. A study ought to be made, she decided, of the kind of women men chose when they were unfaithful to their wives. If the mistress was like the wife, the husband obviously was looking for a substitute; but what if she was as different as could be? Did this mean that he was trying to make up for his disappointment? Alice sighed and put another helping of salmon on Birdie's plate. All this dabbling in psychology would get her nowhere. Whatever the reason for his choice, one thing was certain: he lacked taste.

Her heart expanded as Bob approached the table. Of all the people in the room he was the only one who gave her pleasure. What would she do when he went back to Judith? She put the question out of her mind. "Are you enjoying yourself, Bobby?"

"The party's jumping." He grinned.

She heaped his plate with food; he moved off to make room for others. Soon Margo came up. "You must be famished," Alice said.

"I am. I never eat before a performance."

Alice filled her plate. As she did she remembered that they were standing at about the same spot the night she said to her,

"Why don't you go sit with Bob Conrad. He's all alone." How different Margo's life would have been if she had not said it. And Bob's. And her own. He was still sitting alone. "Why don't you have some beer with your supper?" she said to Margo.

Alice fixed a plate for Margo's father. He was a raw-boned man with large hands and a weather-beaten complexion. At first he sat stiffly, intimidated by his daughter's friends, but after a few drinks he relaxed. He had a theory that all New Yorkers were crazy. It added to the strangeness of the evening that he was in a room with so many Jews. As Alice came up he repeated, with all the joy of discovery, "New York's all right t'visit, but I sure wouldn't want to live there."

Margo's mother shook her head in agreement. A short woman with a round face, she had been agreeing with her husband for thirty years; this certainly was no time to strike out on her own. Although the room was the most luxurious she had ever been in, she made it a point not to be unduly impressed; nor did she take to the curious company her daughter kept. Confining herself for most of the evening to "Thank you very much," she let Margo's father bear the brunt of the conversation.

He squinted at the Rouault. In the rosy glow induced by three scotches, the fanciful shapes of the French painter took on a bizarre quality. "Now take this modern stuff," he said with a lordly gesture. "Where does it get you? Tell me, did you ever see man or beast look like that?"

Alice handed him his supper. "It may seem strange at first, Mr. Schultzberger," she said, "but if you look at it again and again it begins to make sense, and you might even get to like it."

"That'll be the day," he retorted with gusto, and concentrated on his plate.

Supper was over, people left; by half-past one the last guest had departed. Walter sat down and made his usual declaration: "This was one time I enjoyed my own party," He beamed at Alice and Bob. "What a night!"

"Now you can relax," Alice said.

"Yes." In his most casual manner, "I think I'll go down a bit, the air'll do me good. Besides, the reviews'll be out soon."

"It's a bit raw, dear," Alice said evenly. "Put on your coat." If he had to have a good-night kiss from Birdie, that was his affair.

The barman emptied the ash trays. From the kitchen came the

hum of the dishwasher. "Let's unwind a bit," Alice said to Bob after Walter left. She fixed two drinks and led the way into Walter's study. "Did you get to talk to her?'

"Yes." He stared into his drink. "I asked her to forgive me."

"What did she say?"

"What could she say? Will I go through life asking people to forgive me?"

"We don't go on making the same mistakes."

"You mean, we make others?"

She smiled. "When you'll feel strong enough inside, you won't hurt those who love you. So there won't be anything to forgive."

Bob was silent. Alice said, "I've been thinking of your mother."

He looked at her inquiringly.

"I can't help putting myself in her place," Alice continued. "It's a terrible thing to lose a son."

He ran his hand through his hair. "What are you getting at?"

"You've got to make up with her. Phone her."

"What if she says for me to come home? How can I tell her that home is here?"

Alice steeled herself. "Sooner or later you'll have to go back."

"You mean, you want me to?"

"No, Bobby, I don't. But that doesn't change anything. As long as you remain here it means I'm keeping you from her. Much as I love you, and I love you very much, I'd feel guilty for the rest of my life if I did that."

He stared moodily before him. "Some people bring me down, others lift me to my top level. That's what you've done for me, and I'll always be grateful."

"She means well."

"What good does that do?"

"Besides, she's alone now. She needs you."

"Then why don't she call me?" His eyes were bright with reproach. "She knows where I am. All she has to do is lift the phone."

"Maybe her pride won't let her. Or she feels that she failed you."

A wan smile crossed his lips. "We failed each other."

"Bobby, you'll never forgive yourself if you don't ask her forgiveness."

"Were you forgiving in your life?"

"Not as much as I should have been. But I keep trying."

He moved his glass from side to side so that the ice clinked. "All right, I'll call her one of these days. Just let me work up to it."

"It doesn't mean we'll stop being friends. This'll always be your second home. It does mean you'll be doing what you should."

He sipped his drink in silence. Then, "I liked hearing you say you love me very much. Thanks." He kissed her good night and went down the corridor to his room. Just before going in he turned. "Matter of fact, I love you too."

She sat with a quiet smile on her lips, nursing her happiness. Walter had Birdie and she had Bob. A fair exchange.

3

Birdie studied her long nails and brought out with conviction, "She knows."

Walter sprawled on the couch, a glass of ginger ale in his hand. "What makes you say that?"

"It's . . ." She twiddled her fingers in the air to suggest an intuition too subtle for words. "I feel it."

"Who'd have told her? You don't suppose anyone would go up to her and say, 'Alice, your husband etcetera etcetera.' You don't know Alice—she's very proud. She'd stop them before they got started."

Birdie was not impressed. "All the same, she knows."

"So she knows." He raised his glass and took a sip.

Birdie had let her hair down, which gave her a softer look. "You don't understand. The point is not whether she knows or not. It's that I don't feel right . . . about us."

"Are we on that again?"

"We are. You think I like to go around like something out of *Back Street?*"

"But what am I to do? I have deep feelings about you, as you know. And I have deep feelings about Alice, as you also know. Am I supposed to kill myself?" He assumed the air of helplessness that was his best defense. "It'll all work out if you'll only give it a chance. Patience . . . the one thing nobody has."

"Listen to him." She put all the satire she could muster into her voice. "A philosopher!"

"There's only one way to win an argument with a woman." Walter sat up, put down his glass, and pulled her to him. "You look very pretty tonight. Why don't you stop fussing and give me a kiss?" He nuzzled his cheek against hers.

"It's late, Walter. I've a rough day tomorrow."

He ran his hand over her hair. "Put your mind on now."

Birdie was not in the mood for pleasure, but she firmly believed that a woman should never refuse her man. She let him pull down the zipper of her housecoat and undo her brassiere. When they were in bed together she wondered how many women in the world spread their legs for a man solely out of desire to please him. Probably millions. Fortunately they did not have to feel passion, they only had to lie back and receive it.

Walter's hands slid over her body, fondling her breasts and thighs; he knew how to arouse her. From simulating desire she passed over to feeling it. As she responded to the rhythm of his body she forgot the hard day that awaited her and yielded to the delight of holding him in her arms.

In the midst of that delight she was startled by a sound between a groan and a gasp. It took her an instant to realize that the sound came from him. His body stiffened with a convulsive jerk, then went limp and slumped on hers.

"Walter!" she cried, clutching him to her. He did not answer. She repeated his name and heard the rasp of his breathing; he was gasping for air. "My God!" She stifled a scream and turned sideways so that he rested on the bed. She held him in one arm; the other shot out toward the light. His face was ashen. She shook him without realizing what she was doing. "Walter! Are you all right?"

He looked as if he were trying to remember where he was. "I have a pain. Here." His hand slid with difficulty over his body and stopped below the left shoulder. "Must be——" His face tightened, lips compressed, then the spasm passed. "—something I ate." His head dropped onto the pillow.

She jumped out of bed. Bending over him, she helped him turn on his back. "Lie still," she commanded. "I'll get a doctor."

She threw on her housecoat and picked up the telephone beside the bed, but thought better of it and went to the one in the kitchen. She called the same doctor who had helped her the night she found Paul unconscious, and heard herself explain that Walter and his wife were visiting her when he was suddenly taken ill. "We made him lie down but he's feeling worse. I hate

to drag you out like this, but I think you ought to see him."
She returned to the bedroom. His breathing was quieter now,
although his hand was still pressed against the left side of his
chest.

Suddenly she saw the situation with merciless clarity. Walter
found in her apartment. The newspapers. The scandal. A cold
fear poured over her. Then she collected her thoughts.

What to do? The answer came clear and urgent. Call Alice!
She did not know the number, since she rang him only in his
office. She pulled out the telephone directory and began to leaf
through the pages. Her hands were trembling; she remembered
that the number would be in her little book. When she found it,
her courage broke. How could she face Alice? She stared at the
telephone, unable to make a move. Finally she roused herself,
pressed her lips together, and dialed.

"Alice?" Her voice was firm, almost chatty. "It's Birdie. I'm
sorry to disturb you so late. Walter dropped in for a nightcap and while we were talking he began to feel bad. He thinks
it's something he ate." The pretense collapsed; her voice
dropped to a whisper. "I think you'd better come."

There was a silence. Alice said, "Where are you?"

"Fifty-second. Two forty-nine."

"I'll be right over."

She returned to the bedroom. He lay on his back. A greenish
pallor had spread over his cheeks; beads of sweat daubed his
forehead. His belly rose and fell with his rapid breathing. She
covered him with a sheet and went into the bathroom. Taking a
towel, she held it under the cold water, wrung it out, returned
to the bedroom and spread it across his forehead. Then she
sat down on the edge of the bed and buried her face in her
hands. Convinced that he was going to die, "Oh, my God!" she
muttered and began to cry. It came to her that he would be
found naked; she sprang up and went to the chair on which he
had left his trousers and underwear. She brought his shorts to
the bed, inserted his feet in the leg holes and, taking care to
move him as little as possible, drew the garment slowly along
his legs and thighs. It would be necessary, she saw, to lift him
slightly in order to pull the shorts into position. She decided not
to—let them think what they pleased.

The sound of the bell made her start. She ran to the vestibule,
pressed the buzzer and opened the door. Footsteps came up the
stairs. Alice's face was tense. "Where is he?"

Birdie led the way into the bedroom.

"Did you call a doctor?"

"Yes. He'll be here any minute."

Alice came beside the bed. She bent over Walter, rearranged the compress and smoothed his hair back from his forehead. She raised his arm, which had slipped over the side of the bed, and placed it gently at his side. Then she went into the living room and sat down on the red hassock. Birdie followed her.

The bell rang again. It was the doctor, a little man with reddish hair and watery eyes. Birdie showed him the way. He nodded curtly to Alice, disappeared into the bedroom and shut the door behind him.

The two women sat facing each other. Alice folded her arms in her lap. She saw her surroundings with abnormal clarity: how ugly the room was, with its lamps and knickknacks and over-stuffed furniture. She noticed that Birdie looked more human without that atrocious bun on her head. At the same time she was occupied with an altogether different train of thought. The first night she went dancing with Walter. Prohibition was still in effect, so they went to a speakeasy and he had to say his name through a little hole in the door. When they returned from their honeymoon he took her in his arms and carried her across the threshold. Now he lay helpless in this hideous apartment where he found the happiness she had failed to give him. The thought filled her with resentment. It was not right that she should be sitting in the middle of the night on a ridiculous red hassock in this dumpy little woman's living room. It was not right that he should die. But what had right or wrong to do with it? Foolish, foolish man. Not wicked—only willful and vain . . .

Out of the wild seething within her, her voice came calm and even. "You should always wear your hair like this, Birdie. It's very becoming."

Birdie, seated on the sofa where Walter had sat an hour before, turned her head. She stared at Alice as though she had not heard the remark. Then she said, "You didn't sound surprised when I phoned. You knew."

"I knew."

"Who told you?"

"Does it matter?"

"I'd like to know."

Alice's eyes came to rest on the Picasso print. Underneath, on an end table, stood the two ornate candlesticks that had belonged to Paul Horvath, looking magnificently incongruous in their new setting. Alice thought of the summer Gene was born; they took a cottage at the seashore. Walter was working in her father's firm and was beginning to make a name for himself. He came home at six and took a swim before dinner. She would sit on the veranda with the baby while he swam back and forth in front of the house, splashing, doing somersaults, showing off. The sand was soft and white on the south shore. When they walked on the beach it made a crunching sound under their feet. The world was young then and full of sunshine . . .

"I didn't mean to break up your marriage," Birdie said.

"You didn't."

"I mean—how can I explain it to you?"

"You don't have to."

"I didn't mean to take him away from you."

"Nobody ever takes anyone away unless he's ready to go."

"It just happened. You understand."

"I understand."

"I never felt right about it. Honestly."

"I believe you."

The door opened. Both women jumped up as the doctor came in. He turned to Alice. "I called the hospital, Mrs. Stern. The ambulance is on its way."

"How is he?"

"Too early to say. He's had a coronary, but it could be worse. Let's get him to the hospital, then I'll know more."

"I'll come with you."

"Of course. You can ride in the ambulance or in my car."

"I'd rather stay with him."

"Good. I'd like to call in a heart specialist, if it's all right with you."

"Do whatever's necessary."

They heard the ambulance arrive. Two orderlies came up the stairs with a stretcher. Walter did not stir; his eyes were shut. Barely touching him, they removed his shorts, slipped a white garment over him, laid him on the stretcher, and carried him down. The doctor, with a good night to Birdie, followed them.

Alice went to the door. She reached for the knob and stopped. The women looked at each other. "I'm sorry it had to be like this," Birdie said.

Alice nodded but said nothing. She went down the stairs. Birdie hastened to the window and leaned out. The tops of two automobiles gleamed under the street lamp, the doctor's coupe a black rectangle, the ambulance a long, narrow oblong shaped like a hearse. She watched the orderlies slip the stretcher into the back of the ambulance. One of them remained with Walter, the other went to the front and took his place beside the driver. Alice sat next to him. The doctor entered his car and drove off toward Second Avenue, followed by the ambulance. Birdie watched until they turned the corner; then the street was quiet. A light shone on the top floor of the house across the street. The night air had a rawness that made her face smart. She raised her hand to her cheek and realized that it was wet.

Alice sat on the bench outside the emergency room. She had dozed fitfully through the night and seen a gray November dawn float up over Central Park. She shut her eyes. When she opened them again both doctors stood before her. She jumped up and turned to the specialist. "How is he?"

"He's pretty sick, Mrs. Stern, but he has a chance."

"Thank God!" Her lips shook. She began to sob.

The younger doctor put his hand on her shoulder. "Why don't you go home and get some rest. You can come back later in the day. By that time we'll have him in his room."

"Thank you. Thank you for all you've done."

She made her way out. Fifth Avenue looked strangely empty in the early-morning stillness. A garbage truck clattered past, a mailman unlocked the mailbox on the corner and emptied its contents. Alice wiped her eyes and called a cab.

4

Time stopped. He lay inside the oxygen tent as in a womb, suspended in a gray void without beginning or end. In that primordial stage he absorbed the nutrients piped into his veins, excreted them, and—most important of all—continued to breathe.

Days passed. Slowly, thought and feeling returned to him; he became aware of his body as a newborn infant might. The will to live asserted itself. He was not so much afraid of dying as reluctant to leave life when there was still so much to do, hear, see, feel. He had no right to complain; younger men died. What he was slightly ashamed of was that he was not yet ready to go; he wanted one more year, like a greedy child begging for one more chocolate. Sooner or later there had to be an end—the last day, the final hour. Didn't his heart realize this. Apparently not.

He had enjoyed his life. Now, because a few blood vessels had worn out, he might have to leave it. What an absurd reason for dying. Someday there would be a supply of spare parts that could be installed in the body whenever heart, kidneys, or liver wore out. What a pity he was born too soon. Meanwhile he had only his doctors to depend on; they came several times a day to map their campaign against the dread enemy from whose embrace he shrank. They tapped him, felt him, X-rayed him, and made idiotic little jokes to cheer him up. "How's the young man today? We'll soon have you playing tennis, no less." Out of politeness he would crack a smile. In the battle that was being waged over him he was not only participant but spectator, looking on and wondering what the outcome would be. Then the sedatives took effect, he lost interest, and fell asleep.

Even in his desperate hours he did not turn to God and was proud of it. He rejected the notion of a merciful Father in heaven who received His children into eternal life; this was the grand illusion, a myth invented by man to make dying easier. It was monstrous to think that if his heart sustained a little more damage, the whole complex of dreams, ambitions, and desires named Walter Stern would cease to be. Monstrous or not, this was the fact and he had to face it. To take refuge in a vision of life after death would be as childish as to believe in Santa Claus. When you stepped on a cockroach it ceased to be. Man was like the cockroach, except that he had a brain capable of concocting the fantasies he needed in order to continue living. The most daring of his fantasies was God, the most consoling of his myths the immortality of the soul. Granted, it was less painful to die if you believed, but in order to believe you had to relinquish reason. This was a price Walter refused to pay. A rationalist he had lived, and a rationalist he was going to die.

His fear of death took, instead, the form of a vague regret for the things he had not done. If he could have another chance he

would be a better father, also a better husband. More faithful?
No, but more considerate. He loved women too much to give
them up for a single one; it was an illusion to think that man
was made for monogamy. This was another of the myths propa-
gated by Judeo-Christian morality, and not even convincingly—
the patriarchs of the Old Testament never limited themselves to
one wife. If he had it to do over again he would have more
women, not less!

He especially regretted his inability to relate to anything larger
than himself. Once he had passed through his youthful period
of radicalism, he had lived solely for himself. His needs and
desires had made up the sum total of his existence. But couldn't
this be said of most men? In our world it was dog eat dog. Our
kind of society accentuated man's competitive instincts—in a
word, his selfishness. In such a setup would not the perfect
socialist be as great an anomaly as Christ himself, were He to
come down to preach His philosophy of the poor and the meek?
Walter looked back on his philanthropies with genuine pleasure.
Still, it was easy to give money if you had it; what he had not
been able to give was himself. This incapacity for total commitment came to plague him now, adding to his reflections a
delicate aroma of guilt that proved to him how sensitive he was.

Where, he wondered, did the poor go when they fell ill?
Certainly not to private rooms overlooking the park, attended
by nurses around the clock. They lay in wretched wards listening
to each other groan, belch, fart, snore—this was where he would
now be if he did not have a fair amount of the green stuff. Was
it any wonder that men sold their souls for it? Someday, perhaps,
mankind would attain an ideal society in which a person would
have all his needs satisfied simply because he was a human being.
Until that time, however, you had to grab all you could, because
if you didn't take care of yourself, who would?

If only he had done something important with his life. (He
could not regard making money as important, much as he enjoyed having it.) If only he could have risen above his bourgeois
self. He wished he had been someone else; above all, he wished
he had fought in the war. Perhaps if he had taken part in the
most important happening of his time he might have achieved
the total commitment he was incapable of attaining by himself. In the sharing of hardship and danger for a common
cause did not a man transcend his ego, rise above his selfishness?

Wasn't this what we admired in the citations for heroism and the awarding of medals—especially posthumous ones: that a man had risked, even sacrificed his life for others? Or were the heroes singled out for these honors precisely because they were the exceptions, whereas most men thought only of saving their own skins? He would never know. What disturbed him was the inequality that ruled the lives of men. In war some were killed or maimed while others returned safe and sound; in peace some were rich while others were poor, some were well while others suffered from all kinds of diseases, some died young while others lived to a ripe old age. How absurd, then, to conceive of a loving Father who allocated these diverse destinies, how childish for men to imagine that there was someone up there who cared for them. On the other hand, since no one had ever discovered by what system the Deity allocated good and bad, how clever it was—in a vulgar sort of way—to try to bribe Him with an occasional prayer, donation, or good deed!

The hospital was a self-contained world whose rules were specifically designed to exclude everything outside it. To begin with, the hours for meals bore no relation to the practice of sensible people: breakfast was at seven, lunch at eleven, dinner at five. Between these three landmarks his day was punctuated by a succession of minor events that unfolded in unvarying pattern: the examining of his pulse, blood pressure, heart, urine, and so on. The nurses who attended him tried to be friendly; one with buck teeth and a horsey face invariably began the day with a cheery "And how are we this morning?" For all their attention to his wants, their interest in him was impersonal. For them he was something to be bathed and sponged, changed from one robe to another, put on the pot or taken off it. The main event in his day was the arrival of Alice. He expected her at ten. If she was five minutes late he sulked or made a scene. She was his one link with the life he had known; he needed her to remind him who he was.

During the first weeks of his recovery he was not able to say much to her, but he had to know she was there when he drank his orange juice, took his nap, or had his dinner; in short, all day. His improvement was measured by the energy with which he bullied her into gratifying his whims. She fed him, read to him, and listened patiently to his complaints, most of which concerned the things he was not allowed to eat. Walter gradually moved from an infantile to an adolescent stage, in which he took an impish delight in disobeying his doctors' orders. It was as if, along with his desire to get well, he was driven by a need to do whatever would impede his recovery: he went to the bathroom before the doctor pronounced him ready for it, sat up for longer periods of time than he was supposed to, and secretly telephoned his office. When these infractions came to light he confessed with a satisfied grin on his face, with the result that Alice, in order to watch him, was forced to come earlier and stay later. What he really wanted was a plateful of strawberry ice cream; when he was fourteen he had had his tonsils taken out and was given all the ice cream he could eat. Alice finally discovered a dietetic ice cream that she used as a bribe, promising to bring him more if he behaved himself.

He had always enjoyed the view from his apartment on the East River; he now discovered the delights of facing west. How gentle were the winter sunsets. The light faded imperceptibly, moving from yellow to gray to lavender to purple; color drained from the sky, leaving the outlines of buildings etched in black. From his window on the seventh floor he rediscovered the charm of nature. Central Park stretched before him in an endless expanse of bare trees. This was nature as Walter, a true city dweller, preferred her: not wild and free but tamed within formal gardens and alleys—nature in a corset, as it were. There was a snowstorm. The next morning, as if a magician had waved his wand, the park was transformed into a scene of dazzling white. In the distance figures skimmed across the skating rink, boys threw snowballs and fashioned snowmen. Walter watched, enchanted. His whole life would have been different, he informed Alice, if they had lived on Fifth Avenue instead of Sutton Place.

He vaguely remembered the night he was taken ill; he had a recollection of Alice at his bedside in Birdie's apartment, but could not decide whether he had imagined this or she had indeed been there. The simplest way was to ask her; he did not quite know how. He felt that he owed her an explanation, but the longer he put it off, the more difficult it became to bring up the subject. Finally, one afternoon when he awoke from his nap, he found the courage. "We ought to have a talk, you and I."

"What about?"

"All sorts of things."

A quizzical smile flitted across her lips. "Meaning—?"

"About you and me and . . . other people. There's a lot you must be wondering about."

She took his hand. "Look, dear, there's only one thing on my mind, and that's for you to get well. There'll be plenty of time later to talk about you and me—and other people."

Relieved, he let the matter drop. Yet Birdie was in his thoughts too. Much as he had enjoyed her, he had no desire to see her; he somehow held it against her that he had been stricken in her arms. Although he thought of himself as a rationalist, Walter had his superstitions. He knew that she was not to blame for his heart attack; the fact remained that she had brought him bad luck. She had also brought a wonderful thing into his life; but already, without noticing it, he thought of her in the past tense. He was not unmindful of his obligation to her; he was simply not yet certain what form it ought to take. Should he put her in his will? Settle an annuity upon her? Perhaps an outright gift? How could one translate into dollars and cents six years of affection and care, especially when the six years had ended so disastrously? In other words, how much? The question remained unanswered. There was only one sensible course: to postpone the matter until he was well enough to discuss it with his lawyer.

Quiet winter days, each bringing him a step closer to recovery. One morning Alice leaned over him, her face pink and girlish beneath her white hair. "The doctor says you're going to be as good as new."

He felt so happy he could have shouted.

5

It seemed to Judith that a wall was going up around her, cutting her off from the life she had known. The world, she found to her surprise, was quite ready to go on without her. Walter and Alice would continue to give their parties, Birdie would go on oohing and ahing, Max would promote his artists, Paul would conduct, Bobby would weave his daydreams, and Philip would try his cases whether she was part of their lives or not. It was possible to drop out of life, just as it was possible for a person to go under at sea, without leaving a trace. Social life—the pleasure people presumably found in eating, drinking, working, playing, and sleeping together—was a monstrous hoax designed to hide from each of us how alone he was. Now that she had discovered this, she could never be fooled again.

She forced herself to go out occasionally. She would squeeze into her clothes—she had put on eight pounds since her return from Europe—rouge her face, pile her blue-black hair high on her head, and sally forth to visit friends. But it required an ever greater effort for her to be with others. She would pretend to be amused by the gossip of the music world, so as to hide the boredom that weighed her down and the anger that seethed within her. What would happen, she wondered, if she were suddenly to stand up and cry, "Why don't you all drop dead!" She found it more and more difficult to keep up the pretense; increasingly she preferred solitude. Alone in her house she could relax; there was no one she had to please, no rules of the game she had to follow. She had been engaged, she now saw, in a desperate effort to make a place for herself, and had cluttered her life with people if only to give herself the illusion that she was at the center of things; but she had always been an outsider, and an outsider she had remained.

Where was the sense of expectancy that had urged her on since the beginning of her career? Was she beginning to face the fact that the promise could never be fulfilled? More and more she felt like the victim of a conspiracy. Why had the world turned against her? Or was it she who had turned against the world? She had a recurrent dream that she controlled a magic ray capable of wiping out all life on earth. On the appointed day she unleashed its power and only one being remained, a mannikin with long eyelashes arranged in V-shaped clusters, as on a doll she had had when she was ten. Judith awoke filled with bitter hate.

The succession of moods through which she passed was determined less by external events than by some inner compulsion; she was their prisoner and could not escape. She would sit idle for hours on end, gripped by a vast regret as she reviewed the course of her life. At every point of decision, it seemed to her, she had taken the wrong turn. Regret, she told herself, was futile; what was done was done. Yet, against her will, her mind con-

tinued its interminable cycle of self-torment. For years she had
seemed to be moving steadily forward; now the journey had
ended in the middle of nowhere, like one of those surrealistic
staircases in a painting by Chirico. How had she stumbled
into this blind alley? More important, how was she to get out?

She spent hours in Central Park watching the swans in their
stately progress across the lake, or walking along deserted alleys
to the Mall. The stillness accorded with her mood; she felt protected against the relentless city outside. Squirrels leaped across
the paths bent on mysterious errands, their eyes darting nervously from side to side. They, too, were determined to get
there. But where was "There"? On her way home a gaping
emptiness spread inside her; she felt drained of energy, almost
faint. She stopped at the nearest Schrafft's and devoured a
double portion of ice cream garnished with syrup, whipped
cream, and nuts. Assuaged, she continued on her way, but after
she had traversed a few blocks the emptiness returned, demand-
ing another infusion of energy. One afternoon she ate three
banana splits in a row. Mysteriously her abnormal craving for
sweets kept pace with her weariness of the world, the one seeming to nourish the other.

Her mind began to play strange tricks on her. One afternoon
a black truck rode past her. She was persuaded that if it turned
the corner, something terrible would happen to her. On another
occasion, her eyes glued anxiously to the sidewalk, she felt com-
pelled to step on every crack in order to ward off an unknown
evil. Convinced that she had missed one, she retraced her steps
and repeated the procedure. The following day the ritual involved touching each lamp post she passed. One morning she
awoke convinced that a woman she knew was saying terrible
things against her. She spent several hours defending herself
against imaginary accusations until, unable to bear her anxiety
any longer, she telephoned her traducer and was greeted with
such friendliness that she wondered if she had been mistaken.
There followed a suspicion she could not shake that she had
cancer; it took a hectic week of X-rays and examinations before
this specter was laid. Each bout of anxiety dominated her attention for hours or days on end, and was followed by a short period
of calm before the next began. At the end of each she was willing
to concede that she had been the victim of a delusion, but this
did not prevent her from letting herself be victimized a day or
two later by its successor.

Worst of all were the bouts of depression that returned with increasing frequency. A black despair would descend upon her for no apparent reason; she would stare listlessly before her while her mind whirled around and around in its dark prison. Her anguish was like a physical weight that pressed down upon her, enveloping her in a gloom that colored all her thoughts and feelings. This malaise was not attached to any particular idea or image: it was sorrow in the abstract, as it were, which she must suffer as long as the attack lasted, and which she was convinced—each time she fell under its shadow—she would never again be able to shake off.

Nonetheless it was in a defiant mood that she paid her last visit to Dr. Wittenfels. She seemed to enjoy showing him how little he had helped her. He was not discomfited. "You put on much weight," he remarked acidly.

"So what?"

"You are eating compulsively."

"And enjoying it."

"Aha. The pleasure goes into your mouth instead of where it should go."

She flashed her sensual smile at him. "Maybe I like it better that way."

"Why you want to be a little girl when you can be a woman. You think it is easier?"

"Now that you mention it, I think it is."

"Oh, no. You are very mistaken."

"Could be I've had enough of the other."

"So you take revenge on men for the pleasure you have given them. You let yourself grow fat. Then they do not want you and you are safe."

She thought. "You have a point there. What if I'm through with men?"

"You think they betray you?"

"No. Life betrayed me."

"Aha. You feel sorry for yourself. It is not very original. Shall I tell you the truth? Life does not betray you. You betray yourself."

"Can't you understand, doctor, that your view of life is too simple? You have a few standard goals—love, sex, work, success —and if your patient goes after those he's doing fine, or so you think. All my life I went after them, I thought that if I got them I'd find happiness. I know better now. Shall I tell you the truth? I don't want them any more. According to your way of thinking I was well then and sick now. According to my way of thinking I was sick then and well now. Because for the first time in my life I'm free." It came to her that the norms Dr. Wittenfels held out to her were the same ones she had held out to Bob. The circle had been completed: for Bob she had represented the Establishment against which he rebelled; for her Wittenfels was the Establishment and she was the rebel.

"There is no freedom," he said. "This is a dangerous illusion. The insane are free, because they throw off the laws of the real world. And the dead are free. To be alive and sane means to accept reality."

"The dangerous illusion is wanting happiness. I'm cured of that."

"No. You are cured of wanting life, which is not the same thing. From this people die."

She smiled. "Doctor, you don't understand. There comes a time when the struggle drops away from you. You're cured. I've lost my drive and I'm not in the least sorry. It pushed me on and on all these years, but I no longer want to get anywhere or fight for anything, I just want to be." Wasn't this what Bob had said he wanted?

"Man was not made to be. He must do. Look what he creates out of his discontents. You want a return to the Garden of Eden? It is not possible."

She stood up, facing him. "Doctor, for some people life may end long before the heart stops. They've done what they had to. If they hang around it's only because they're waiting. My life is over. It has reached its natural end. Now there's only the coda. You know, when a piece is finished it has said what it had to say, the coda rounds it off a little."

Wittenfels gave her a piercing glance. "It is lucky you are not the suicidal type, otherwise I worry about you. But you love yourself too much to do yourself harm."

"Good. Then you've nothing to worry about."

"Why you still fight me? Do you not remember what I tell you? If you win over me, you lose. If I win over you, you have a chance."

"That's how you see it."

He held out his hands in a gesture of defeat. "There is nothing more I can say. If you do not listen to me, how I can help you?"

She glanced around her. The bust of Freud gazed down on them benignly. Dust motes danced in the slanting rays of light that filtered through the shutters. She was glad she would not see this room again.

At parting he made one more attempt. "You will come back?"

"No, doctor."

His face was grave. "I warn you, Mrs. Conrad, you need help. Your hatred of yourself has become hatred of the world. In the end it will destroy you. I am not joking."

She held out her hand. "Thanks for trying."

He shook his head. "You are a very difficult—how you say? —customer."

"I'm afraid I'll have to find my own way." She smiled and left.

Later, in the stillness of her house, she pondered his words. Her difficulty, she realized, was that she had no faith in his power to help her. She had put behind her forever his concept of life as ego assertion. How, then, could she listen to him preach an idea that she had outgrown?

That night Guiomar Novaes was giving a recital in Carnegie Hall. Judith toyed with the idea of going, but it required too much effort to get dressed again; besides, she would find it depressing to hear another woman pianist. Instead she poured herself one more vodka on the rocks, her third. The liquor made a little burn in her throat and spread a warmth through her veins, enveloping her in a pleasant haze. On the way to the bathroom she stopped before the tall mirror in the hall. She stared at herself under the harsh light of the hallway and did not like what she saw. She was fat, her stomach was bloated, her skin was coarse, her eyes lacked luster. Suddenly she hurled the contents of her glass at the mirror; the vodka splashed across the shining surface and dribbled down, blurring and distorting her reflection. She stood watching, empty glass in hand, and laughed contentedly at her resourcefulness in wiping out what she did not wish to see.

By the time she went to bed her contentment had worn off. Afraid that she might not be able to sleep, she took two pills; then she forgot she had taken them and swallowed two more. As she lay in the dark waiting for them to take effect, it occurred to her that Wittenfels probably was right. She was permanently cured of that nasty ailment known as life, and glad of it.

6

The day came when Walter was allowed to have visitors. Max Rubin was the first. The old man was more crotchety than ever. He complained about his artists, gossiped about other managers, and with portentous shaking of his head deplored the state of the world. Then he led the conversation to what he really wanted to know. "Tell me, Walter, were you afraid?"

Walter pretended not to understand. "Of what?"

"Of dying. What else?"

Walter pondered the question. "With all the stuff they gave me, I was too doped up to feel much of anything. No, I wasn't afraid as much as sorry. I was sorry to be leaving it all."

"You didn't——" Max shot a glance from under his bushy eyebrows. "—pray?"

"I should say not! Even if I'd wanted to, I wouldn't have given Him the satisfaction." Walter laughed. "But I had no desire to. It's not true what they say about needing God when you're dying. My head was muddled, but not that much."

Max nodded appreciatively. The two atheists spent a pleasant half hour bolstering each other's faith in the nonexistence of God, and came to the conclusion that men had invented Him mainly in order to feel a little less unimportant in the universe. After Max left, Walter turned to Alice with an amused expression. "Whaddya know! He came here to find out if he'll be able to face dying."

"Did you encourage him?"

"Of course. He went away feeling better. He won't admit he's afraid, but he is," Walter crowed, as if the old man's fear were a victory for him.

Bob came every day on his way back from school, bringing him books: *Alexandria Quartet, Ship of Fools, Fox in the Attic,* and paperback collections of short stories. Durrell's novel was too richly orchestrated for Walter's taste; he did not have the proper kind of imagination for it, and after several attempts gave up. *Ship of Fools,* on the other hand, he finished.

Bob discussed the book with him. "Some writers build a novel, others weave it together, Katherine Anne Porter crochets it. She arranges thousands of details into tiny patterns. Sometimes the details hide the story, but in the end they add up; you forget the details and remember the story. This is the method of the short-story writer applied to the novel. Strangely enough it works."

Walter listened, surprised as always that Bob derived so much more from literature than he did. He liked the short stories best of all. One or two, and he was fast asleep.

Toward the end of the week, just as Bob was getting ready to leave, Margo arrived at the hospital. She brought a huge fruit cake wrapped in tin foil, that her mother had baked especially for Walter. He insisted on tasting it at once.

Margo also brought good news. On the strength of her success as Liù she had been assigned the roles of Butterfly and Mimi. Walter beamed. "Lying here," he told her, "I went over my life pretty thoroughly. The thing I was proudest of was you." She took his hand and brought it to her lips.

Alice cut the visit short lest they tire Walter. Bob accompanied Margo down the long corridor to the elevator. Neither spoke. They came out on the street. "You want a cab?" he asked.

"Please."

He was about to hail one but thought better of it. Turning back to her, "Perhaps we could see each other," he said uncertainly.

She looked up at him, "What for?"

Her calm unnerved him. "Maybe we could——"

"No," she cut in, "we couldn't. It didn't work when I needed you, why would it work now?"

"Don't it mean anything to you that I want to see you?"

She thought a moment. "In a way it even offends me. Why should you want to see me? Is it that you feel sorry for me? You don't have to. Is it that I've become glamorous for you? That would be childish. In any case it doesn't matter, since I've no wish to see you."

"Honest?"

"Honest. You see, Bobby, I don't love you any more. This may sound strange to you, but it's true."

"I see." He scowled and added defensively, "I thought I'd ask."

She sighed. "There's no need for us to be polite. You meant too much to me for that."

"Do you hate me?"

"No. I'm indifferent. Not all the way, though. I haven't for-given you—or myself—for the baby." Her calm suddenly dropped from her. "Oh, Bobby," she cried, "we should have let it live. We had no right to——" For an instant the dark, little face was twisted with sorrow, then she regained her composure. "It's no use, Bob. If we ever meet again it'll be by chance. As strangers." She looked up at him resolutely. "That's how it has to be."

"Will you let me kiss you good-bye?"

"No." She smiled. "I couldn't bear it."

He put her in a cab and went his way.

Birdie telephoned. Walter signaled to Alice to say that he was asleep. She asked Birdie to call back in an hour.

"Tell her I'm not seeing anyone yet," Walter said.

"Max must have told her he saw you, so she'll know I'm lying." Alice fell silent. Then, "You'll have to see her sooner or later, dear."

"What'll you tell her?"

"To come this afternoon."

Birdie arrived at four. Alice greeted her, explained that she had some shopping to do, and left. Birdie took the chair beside the bed and studied Walter's face. "You must have had a ter-rible time." There was tenderness in her voice.

"It was pretty bad." A born actor, he had no difficulty in sug-gesting the ordeal he had been through. All the same, the sub-ject bored him. "You've changed your hairdo," he said.

Birdie had discarded the bun. "Do you like it?" she asked, im-mediately coquettish.

"Very becoming." She seemed different somehow. Then he realized that the difference was in him; he no longer had the slightest desire to feel her breasts or pat her behind. He became aware of the ticking of the clock. Unable to think of what to say next, he lowered his eyelids to indicate fatigue.

"When will you leave the hospital?"

"Depends. The doctors are vague about it. But the worst is over."

"My poor darling."

This was precisely the tone he wished to avoid. He shut his eyes and sighed. "I was lucky—it could have turned out worse." He did not mean to imply that she was responsible for his plight, but if she chose to take it so he had no objection. The silence flowed between them in an ever widening stream. At length, "What've you been doing with yourself?" he inquired.

"Waiting to see you."

His left hand slid up over his heart, as a warning to her that tender avowal was strictly forbidden. She took the hint. "I'm afraid I'm tiring you," she said.

"It's all right. What time is it?"

"Twenty past four. I'll go."

"No, stay a little longer," he said listlessly, "then I have to rest. Doctor's orders."

She made small talk. At half past four she rose. "I think you've had enough of me."

He did not contradict. "Thank you for coming." He sighed and, without opening his eyes, added, "It was good to see you."

She stood very still, obviously waiting for him to ask her to come again. Finally, "Good-bye, Walter."

"Good-bye." A deeper sigh. "Thanks again." He watched her go. A part of his life was leaving him and he had no wish to hold it back.

Birdie stomped down the corridor, her spiked heels going clackety-clack against the stone floor. She sat down on a bench and began to cry. The elevator door opened. She blew her nose and hobbled inside.

She walked slowly down Fifth Avenue, dabbing at her eyes. *Thank you for coming. It was good to see you.* The sonofabitch. Who the hell did he think he was? Not a kiss, not even a handshake. Was this how a great love affair was supposed to end? She turned into the park and walked toward the ice-skating rink. The refreshment counter offered a wide selection of candies. She bought an Oh Henry! sat down on a bench, and watched the skaters. That night, when she saw the ambulance ride off, she knew right away it was all over between them. Six years of her life gone, and a girl wasn't getting any younger. She would have to begin all over again, only this time there must be no mistake. Absolutely.

Birdie bit into the candy bar. The sweetness of the chocolate mingled with the bitter taste of her tears. For years she had wished she were free of him. Now that she was, why was she crying?

eight

 Walter was dressed by the time Alice and Bob arrived. Leaning on Bob's arm, he made his way down the corridor to the elevator. Alice followed, carrying his valise. They came out on Fifth Avenue; Walter took a deep breath. "Everything looks as if I were seeing it for the first time." He buttoned his coat. The park, he decided, looked prettier when viewed from above. Seeing it from across the street was like sitting too close in a theater.

The living room was full of sunlight when they came home. Walter sat down. "Whaddya know, I made it." He glanced around him and grinned. The room was as he remembered it—cool and immaculate.

"Now I can stop being your mother," Alice said. As if this had reminded her, she turned to Bob. "Did you phone her?"

"Not yet."

"You said you would."

"I didn't get around to it."

"You should."

"Why?" Walter interposed.

Alice gave him a must-you-interfere look. "Darling," she said evenly, "if you quarreled with a son, would you want it to go on forever?"

"But he's doing very well here. Why change?"

"Because Judith is alone."

"You mean, you want him to leave?"

"I'd like him to stay forever, but it wouldn't be right."

"I must say, I don't agree with you," Walter said emphatically.

Bob was amused that they spoke about him as if he were not there. "Matter of fact, I'd like very much to call my mother. But it's not easy for me. Maybe," he looked at Alice, "you could prepare the way, sort of."

"We'll phone her while Walter takes his nap."

"It's that urgent?" Walter asked, petulant that his opinion had been disregarded. To Bob, "Now that I've gotten used to you, you have to leave. It's not fair."

The young man smiled.

Walter, trailed by Alice, walked slowly down the hallway and into the bedroom. He glanced at the twin bed he had not occupied in years. She opened a window. "Shall I make up the couch in the study?" she asked.

Casually, "I think I'll lie down here." True, he had sworn never again to sleep in their bedroom, but that was in a previous existence. Now that he needed her, ancient grievances went by the board.

Alice, without a word, turned down the bed. Walter took his clothes off; she tucked him in. As he dozed off he reviewed the doctor's parting instructions. Avoid worry, tension, excitement. No drinking, smoking, or rich foods. A nap in the afternoon and, as soon as he felt up to it, a long walk daily. Sex, he noticed, was not included in the list of forbidden activities. Small comfort. Nothing could be farther from his mind.

Alice returned to the living room. "What's the number?"

"Butterfield eight, two four five one. Are you going to call her now?" The breath went out of Bob's body.

"Why not? Would you rather I didn't?"

"Let's get it over with."

Alice dialed. "Judith?"

Judith was emerging from a drugged sleep. "Yes?"

"It's Alice Stern."

Judith came awake. "Alice! What a surprise!" Her voice took on a honeyed quality. "How *are* you?"

"Walter's been ill."

"So I heard. Is he better?"

"He came home this morning."

"Wonderful! And how's my boy?"

"He's right here. I'll put him on." Alice handed the receiver to Bob.

Judith wanted to say, "Not yet." She needed a little time. Then she heard his voice, "Hi, mom."

"Bobby!" She bit her lips to keep them from trembling.

"How are you, mom?"

"All right, I guess." She pushed her hair back from her forehead. "And you?"

"I've gone back to school. As you wanted me to."

"I'm glad." Her anger was gone! She felt only love for him, and forgiveness. The realization brought tears to her eyes.

"I'd like to see you, mom."

"I'd like to see you."

"When?"

"Any time, Bobby."

"I could stop by this morning, on my way to school."

She did not wish to tell him that this was too soon. Then she heard him say, "Or tonight, on my way home."

She relaxed. "Tonight would be fine. Where d'you eat?"

"At school. Gives me an hour more in the library."

"Then you don't want me to make dinner?"

"No, I have to study for an exam. I'll come by around nine."

"Good. Bless you." She hung up, relieved that she did not have to prepare a meal for him. She was not in the mood.

That afternoon she took a long walk. She was exhilarated at the prospect of seeing him, but also apprehensive. She must not do anything, she told herself, to upset him; she would keep the evening light and gay. It struck her that she was like a woman awaiting a lover of whom she was not certain; she laughed. Somewhere in the course of the afternoon she bought the cakes he liked best—macaroons and chocolate eclairs—and a TV dinner for herself. The dinner was mediocre but had the virtue of needing no preparation. She enlivened it with a glass of red wine and a cigarette. There was an accumulation of dishes in the sink; she washed them and put them away. Then she went to her room to dress.

She was glad he was coming at night, when she looked her best; she piled her blue-black hair high on her head, put on heavy make-up, and dimmed the lights in the music room. It was a little after eight; she still had an hour. She looked through the piles of music on the floor, pulled out Schumann's *Scenes from Childhood,* and went to the piano. She loved the quality of naïve wonder that vibrated through these little pieces, even their fanciful titles: *About Strange Lands and People, A Curious Story, Blindman's Bluff,* and the rest. She began the first one, softly. *Innig* was the direction Schumann used more than any other—Judith translated it as intimate, heartfelt—and it applied particularly to these lyrical pieces. She had not touched the keys in over a week. How beautiful the piano sounded.

Suddenly she felt that she was not alone. She turned. "Bobby! When did you come in? I didn't hear the bell."

"I let myself in."

"My precious boy!" She rose and put her arms around him. "You look surprised. Have I changed so?"

"Not at all. You look fine, mom," he lied. He was shocked at ᴊer appearance. He had always seen her through the adoring eyes of the child; now he saw her as he would any woman. She was fat, her face was puffy, the skin coarse and too heavily rouged, the eyes ringed with greenish shadow. Only her smile was the same, a little-girl smile with a curiously sensual, even lascivious quality. "It's wonderful to see you." He bent over and kissed her. As he did, he wondered whose lips had touched hers last and was embarrassed at the thought.

She released him and stepped back to study his face. "You're as handsome as ever, Bobby. Even more. You look . . . how shall I put it . . . more mature." She fixed him a drink and sat down on the sofa. "Well, tell me all."

"It's good to be back."

"After the fancy apartment you've been living in, this must look pretty shabby to you."

"Oh, no," he brought out decisively. "It's home!" But she was right. The room seemed smaller, as if it had shrunk during his absence. He had always thought it elegant, with its French doors, waxed floor, and long, black Steinway. He was suddenly aware of the piles of music against the wall, the magazines and newspapers strewn everywhere. They made the room look as disheveled as she.

"Let's face it," she said. "I was never much of a housekeeper."

"You had other talents, mother."

"How's school?"

"Would you believe it, I'm enjoying it."

"Then why were you so against it when I kept telling you to go back?"

"I had to be against, I guess. If you said white I had to say black. I'm sorry I behaved as I did."

"Maybe the time came, and you were ready for it." She thought a moment. "There's something I'd like to ask you. While you were away I found a letter addressed to you. From Paul Horvath."

He made a face. "Let's not go off on that, mom. I didn't come here to be cross-examined."

"Still, I'm curious."

He looked at her. Would she never learn? Yet what if he answered her question? What if, instead of permitting her to put him on the defensive, he tried to explain? "It's very simple, mom," he said evenly. "Since you read the letter you know. He had a thing for me. It didn't happen to be my kind of thing. He was a lonely man and, I don't have to tell you, a great artist. I tried to give him as much as I could. Unfortunately, it wasn't enough. What more can I say?"

"I see." She thought a moment. "Bob, I appreciate it when you're honest with me. I really do. One more thing. Alice mentioned that there was a girl. Who was it?"

"What's the difference? It's all water under the bridge."

"Was it Margo Scholtz?"

"Of course not. What put that into your head?"

"I just wondered."

He leaned forward pleadingly. "Mom, why can't you and I be friends? Not mamma and baby, but friends."

She straightened, as though to fling back the imputation that she was prying. "I'd like nothing better."

"Then why, instead of harping on the past, can't we make a fresh start? Being friends means that we respect each other's privacy. Is that so difficult?"

"I guess that's the kind of thing you and Alice have."

"As a matter of fact, yes. We don't pry into each other's lives. We have no right to."

"But she's only a friend. I'm your mother."

"If you'd forget that once in a while we would do much better."

"Darling, I don't want to quarrel with you. God knows, I feel friendly toward you." With an imperceptible tremor in her voice, "Are you coming back?" she asked.

"I'd like to. That is, if you want me to."

Her eyes were upon him, brilliant, intent. "You're saying this only to please me. You'd rather remain there, with her."

"Why would I want to remain there?"

"Because she makes you comfortable."

"But this is my home. I grew up in this house, I belong here." He scowled. She saw right through him; she was a witch. He came over to where she sat, kneeled before her and took her hands in his. "Mom, you're alone and you need me. Of course I want to come back." He wanted her to believe this. To bolster his case, "Alice thinks I should too," he added artlessly.

"Naturally. Her conscience hurts her. You think it's fair of her to take my son away from me?"

"Mom, lay off." It startled him that he found her nearness distasteful; she used too much perfume.

Judith put her hand on his wrist, and noticed his watch. "She gave it to you?"

"Yes."

"When I gave you one you always forgot to wear it."

"Don't tell me you're jealous."

"D'you take me for a fool? Of course I am." Throwing back her head, she let out that low melodious laugh of hers.

He grinned. "I'll tell you what, mom. Try to take me as I am and you'll see, we'll get along fine."

"I'll try." She smoothed back his hair and kissed him on the forehead. Coquettishly, "Would you like me to play for you?"

"You know I would."

She sat down at the piano and leafed through the music on the rack. "Remember the *Scenes from Childhood?* I used to play them for you when you were little. Instead of telling you a story. Which would you like to hear?"

He did not recall their titles. "Whichever you like."

"Your favorite was *Träumerei*. I guess it's the prettiest." She played the familiar melody very simply, letting it sing, but bringing out the subordinate lines as well. At the climactic high note she paused an instant, as if she were reluctant to take leave of it.

Bob recaptured the mood of wonder with which he listened to her playing when he was a child, and felt ashamed of the unkind thoughts he had harbored during their conversation. She was an artist, she was his mother, and she needed his help. How un-gracious of him, then, to sit in judgment upon her. She played three more of the Schumann pieces; they chatted after each. He told her about the courses he was taking, about his professors, for whom—with the exception of Lionel Trilling—he had scant respect, and about a paper he was writing on Emily Dickinson. He noticed the small clock on the piano. "It's after eleven! I still have some work to do."

"When are you coming . . . home?"

"Tomorrow, if you like."

"Wonderful."

"I'll stop by on my way to school. Around noon. I'll bring some of my things and my typewriter. The rest I can pick up later."

She accompanied him to the door. "D'you have a muffler? It's cold out."

"Yes, mother." He took his coat from the closet and drew out the muffler he had tucked inside the sleeve.

"What a pretty one. Did Alice buy it for you?"

"No," he lied, "it was my Christmas gift to myself."

She smiled and patted him on the shoulder. "You're saying this to make me feel good." She held up her face. He kissed her.

"It was good that you came, Bobby." She held him to her. "Things'll be different from now on. You'll see."

"I know they will."

"Till tomorrow, then."

"Yes, mom." He went into the street. At the curb, the tree in the iron cage raised its thin bare branches to the lamplight.

2

She lay hands folded under her head, enjoying the sense of ful-fillment that Bob's visit had left with her. Her fears had been groundless; the evening had turned out to be simpler than she had anticipated. No trace remained of her resentment; she loved him again as she did when he was little. They would wipe the slate clean, they would never quarrel again. The thought brought a feeling of peace.

She rose, went downstairs to the kitchen, and spied the fancy white box near the sink. Oh, dear, she had forgotten to serve the cakes she had bought for him. After a night in the frigidaire they would lose their freshness; she put them on a plate, which she took with her to the music room. Seated on the sofa, she stowed away four macaroons and two eclairs, eating slowly, purposefully, with an extra measure of delight because she knew she should not. It came to her that, eager though she had been for the reconciliation, she did not really want him back. Living together meant adapting to his needs, and this required a greater effort than she was capable of at the moment. All the same, she was pleased that he cared enough to want to return. She finished the last cake, licked her fingers, and sighed contentedly. Happiness was a fresh chocolate eclair.

The telephone rang. Who could it be? She did not answer, in order not to break her mood. After seven rings it stopped. She had begun by wanting so desperately to succeed. As an artist and as a woman. Now she desired only to be free of desire. To rest. The heart was rebellious and continued to want things. One had to conquer its greediness. That was the beginning and end of wisdom.

She sat down at the piano and played the last of the Schumann pieces, *The Poet Speaks*. She had always approached music as a performer, concerned about projecting it to others; for once she was playing for herself. The rich sonorities of the Steinway reverberated through the high-ceilinged room, caressing her ear. It seemed to her the little piece contained a secret she had fathomed at last. She played it as she had always wanted to play, from within the music, with no alien thought interposing between herself and the notes. She sustained the final chord with the pedal. The sound died away slowly, and there was silence.

She poured herself a vodka on the rocks, and another. She did not have the craving for liquor that she had for sweets; she drank only because it relaxed her. After the third vodka she could feel herself unwind. A pleasant drowsiness enveloped her; her mind surveyed the landscape of the past. She had had everything she wanted . . . the admiration of the crowd, the devotion of friends, the passion of lovers. There was a time when she had only to snap her fingers and men came running. She sighed. It was in the nature of life to slip away no matter what you did, leaving behind a few memories tinged with regret. She had enjoyed the passing show, but its day was over. Now it was night, and time to sleep.

She made her way to the bedroom, a trifle unsteadily, took off her clothes, removed her make-up, and washed her face. The cold water was refreshing. As she put on her nightgown she remembered Bob's expression when he saw her that evening. Had she changed so much? She returned to the mirror. As always, the roughness of her skin distressed her. She wondered whether to rub cold cream on her face and decided that it wasn't worth the effort. Yawning, she lay down and turned out the light.

The instant her head touched the pillow her drowsiness vanished; the tips of her nerves grew taut to breaking point. Judith knew she was going to have an attack of insomnia. She sat up, poured half a glass of water from the carafe she kept on the night table, reached for the little bottle beside it and swallowed three pills. She lay down again. While waiting for the pills to take effect she fastened her mind on the ticking of the clock, arranging the beats now in groups of four, now in waltz time. Unexpectedly she was walking through a subterranean garden that had a fountain in the center. The paths were laid out in symmetrical patterns, and on one side was a row of tall pine trees like those in the gardens of the Villa d'Este. She wore a white chiffon dress, her hair hung loose over her shoulders, she was young. An orchestra was playing beside the fountain; a large sign announced *Schumann Symphony*. This puzzled her: she did not recognize which symphony it was. She decided the sign must be a mistake, they probably had forgotten to change it after the preceding number. The music surged forward with powerful accents; now a clarinet sang the melody, accompanied by the strings. She felt the melody in her fingers, as if she were playing it on the piano.

The music stopped. Jets of water shot up from the fountain, glistening in the sunlight. She stood still, afraid that if she were recognized she'd be told to leave the garden and would never be allowed back. A terrible anguish gripped her throat, choking her. She awoke. Her mouth and nose had been buried in the pillow; more than half asleep, she turned on her side and sucked in a breath of air. She had only one desire—to return to the garden, never to leave it again. They were punishing her, they were sending her away because she had forgotten to take her pills.

Her hand reached for the little bottle, she wanted to swallow three more but lost count. To make sure she added a few, then a few more, stuffing the green-and-black capsules into her mouth as if they were candies, washing them down in mouthfuls of water. Her head fell back on the pillow. She looked for the garden but could not find it. Suddenly she caught sight of the tall pine trees and felt a rush of happiness. She was wearing a flowing gray gown with parasol to match; she was older now. The orchestra played a romantic melody that sounded like Tchaikovsky even though the sign still said Schumann. Again they were threatening to send her away. She did not want to miss the music, she begged them to let her stay. Her hand struggled free and found the bottle. One, two, three, four? She tried to remember how many she had taken but it was too difficult. The empty bottle fell on the floor, the garden began to float and dissolve in waves of music, soft gray waves lapping her ankles knees hips breasts shoulders, gently soothing, cool waves that rose to her mouth and nostrils, she might escape them if she lifted her head a little but she had no desire to move, she wanted only to lie still perfectly still floating without effort on the shadowy sea of gray. The music sounded from afar, barely audible now. A melody gentle and sweet like a lullaby bringing with it an endless peace that enveloped her as she floated without effort into the gray void the immense void of nonwilling nondoing nonhating nonstruggling nonbeing . . .

3

The valise lay open on the bed; Bob arranged his shorts, shirts, and socks in neat tiers. He left off packing when Alice called him to lunch. "I should have gone after breakfast. I wanted her to find me there when she got up."

Alice put a helping of tuna fish and sliced tomatoes on his plate. "How was your visit?"

"Not bad. We both tried. One thing upset me."

"What?"

"I realized I didn't really want to go back. She knew it too."

"How could she?"

"She knows me so well she can hear me think. It's a hassle, especially when I'm thinking one thing and saying another."

"That's easy to remedy. Say only what you think."

"Not so simple. When I'm with her I feel I've got to assure her all the time that I love her. The harder I try, the less I make it. Suddenly whatever I say sounds phony."

"That'll pass."

"What if it don't?"

Alice looked at him, and her face was firm. "It wouldn't matter. You're not going back because it's easy. Certain things in life we have to do whether we like it or not."

"You mean, I have to stay with her even if we bug each other?"

"I wouldn't say that. But you must make every effort to be patient and understanding. It's your duty."

"Why shouldn't pleasure guide us rather than duty?"

"I don't know. You're the philosopher, Bobby, not I. All I know is that people who do only what they find pleasant end by caring only for themselves. How can anyone like that be happy?"

"When I hear this I don't have the guts to answer 'The strong man follows his own will and considers only his own pleasure.' Maybe someday I will."

"I hope that day never comes. It'll mean that you never learned what life is about, or love. If that happens I'll feel sorry for you." She put a second helping on his plate.

They finished lunch. Bob fitted his typewriter into its case and pushed the rest of his things into the valise. "I won't try to thank you for what you've done," he said as she saw him to the door. "I never could."

"You don't have to. Matter of fact, I did very little."

"You came along as I was falling apart. You picked up the pieces and put them together again. That's all you did."

She put her hand on his arm. "Spend the week with your mother and come Sunday for dinner. Maybe she'll come too."

"But Walter's angry with her."

"After what he's been through, that kind of thing doesn't matter any more. I'll tell him I asked you to bring her."

"I'd like to say one thing." He hesitated, scowling to hide his embarrassment. "It sounds awful sticky, but I hope I'll be worthy of all you did. Everything lies ahead of me. I don't know my way yet and I'm not sure where it'll lead, but I want to be a good person. I honestly do."

"What do you mean by good?"

He pondered the question. "I want never again to have to say to someone, 'I'm sorry for what I did. Forgive me.' If I can get through life without that, I'll be satisfied."

She smiled. "My dear boy, you'll have every reason to be. As long as we're confessing, let me say this. You're so conscious of what I did for you that you forget one important thing. What you did for me."

"Like what?" He knew, but wanted to hear her say it.

"Like making it possible for me to worry about someone." She put her hands against his face. He kissed her.

Ten minutes later Bob stood in front of Judith's house. He let his eyes linger on the glossy black door with its thin red border, took out his keys, and let himself in. Leaving the typewriter and valise at the foot of the stairs, he opened the door of the dining room. "Mom!" There was no answer. He bounded up the stairs two at a time. In the light of day the music room seemed to be in greater disorder than ever. He noticed the plate on the sofa, covered with empty cake wrappers. The door of her bedroom was open. Puzzled, he looked in.

She lay on her back across the bed as if she had rolled off the pillow, head hanging over the side, hair spilling onto the floor. Her face had a bluish pallor; her eyes were open in a blank stare. "Mom!" he cried and ran to the bed, pulled her up by the shoulders and shook her. "Mom!" He put his cheek against her nostrils. A wild cry broke from his lips, the room reeled. He knew only that he must get her to breathe again. He lowered her head to the pillow, turned her over, leaped on the bed and, straddling her body as he had seen lifeguards do, began to press his hands against her ribs.

A feeling of unreality enveloped him: this was not actually happening, he was imagining it, he would wake up at any moment and discover it had been a dream. He continued his attempt to resuscitate her, his hands moving automatically in and out, until the thought he had been hiding from himself broke through: it was too late! He leaped from the bed. His glance fell on the empty bottle on the floor; near it lay two green-and-black pills. He picked them up, dropped pills and bottle into his pocket, and ran out of the room. He threw himself on the sofa, face down, and began to beat his fists senselessly against the green velvet top. Suddenly he stopped, dropped his head on the couch, and lay quite still. He must call her doctor.

Once the doctor came everything would be fine. He pushed himself off the sofa, took a step toward her room, and decided to use the telephone in the kitchen instead. He ran downstairs and dialed. "Doctor Glauber? This is Bob Conrad. I just found my mother——" An invisible hand clutched his throat; he was unable to bring out the word. After a moment he added, "—unconscious."

The doctor asked how she looked. Bob disregarded the question. "I'm trying to get her to breathe. You better come over."

Now he felt calmer. He had left her lying face down on the bed, he must go back, turn her over, and shut her eyes. The prospect of returning to her room filled him with fear. *Death be not proud though some have called thee mighty and dreadful* —— He could not remember the next line. What was he afraid of? Death was nothing more than the absence of life. He strode purposefully half way up the stairs, stopped, turned back, and dropped into a chair by the table in the dining room. He folded his arms on the table and rested his head on them, ashamed that he was unable to face her.

The bell roused him. He jumped up to let Dr. Glauber in. Bob led him up the stairs to her room. The wispy little man had guessed the truth. Blinking his watery eyes, he said, "Why don't you wait out here." Bob went into the parlor.

Soon Glauber joined him. "Looks to me like an overdose of sleeping pills."

Bob turned. "It wasn't suicide," he cried vehemently. "It couldn't be."

"I didn't say it was." The doctor stepped near the piano, noticed the empty glass on the rack, picked it up and smelled it. "Why d'you say it couldn't be?"

"Because I was with her last night. She was making all sorts of plans for the future."

"I see." Glauber put down the glass, thoughtful. "I know she couldn't sleep because I prescribed the pills for her. Sometimes they take too many without realizing it. Besides," he pointed to the glass, "she was drinking. It's a dangerous combination." He foraged in his bag, drew out a blank form, and began to write. "Death from natural causes. That's how I'll report it." He put away his pen and went over to Bob. "I'm sorry," he said softly. "Your mother was a remarkable woman."

The doctor left. Bob sat down on the bench in front of the

piano, his back against the keys. It was very still in the house. He roused himself and, almost as though drawn there against his will, returned to her room. Her head rested on the pillow, a little to one side; her eyes were closed. It seemed to him that she was frowning slightly, as if she were unpleasantly surprised. Her nightgown had slipped down, leaving her right shoulder bare. He sat down at the foot of the bed; the shock and the horror had passed, leaving only sorrow. He had feared death because he had never seen it; actually there was nothing fearful about it. He remembered that he had found her nearness distasteful the night before, and felt ashamed. Her face no longer repelled him; he liked it without make-up, the features strong, imperious, with the rough-textured skin she was so concerned about. *Have I changed so much?* It grieved him that he had caused her to ask this. The contradictory feelings she had inspired in him dropped away, revealing what they had so effectively hidden as long as she was alive—she was the one who mattered, the one he loved. She was the one he had had to fight and run away from, yet by that token she had been the center of his life. Long ago she had left him standing alone and disappeared into the crowd. He was convinced she was never coming back and let out a cry—the cry that now rose within him from the depths of his childhood, echoing across the chasm of the years so that he must press his lips into a rigid line to restrain it. This time she really was never coming back. He bent forward and laid his hand on her bare shoulder. How strange that he had never been able to tell her how much he loved her. Now that he could, she was no longer able to hear him. Was this the irony of death, that the knowledge it brought came too late to be of use?

He had not intended that the knife should hit her; how surprised they both were when it did. *I'm sorry, mom, for the things I did to you.* The words marched over the rim of his consciousness, stately and futile. As long as she was there he somehow was still a child; everything he said and did was important because she attached importance to it. By dying she had turned the tables on him, she had taken away his power to affect her. Why had she picked this moment to pull out on him? Was this her way of punishing him? From here on, nothing he did or failed to do could move her. They could never hurt each other again.

Forgive me, mom. What more can I say? He sat quietly, his hand still on her shoulder. Finally he rose, bent down, and kissed her on the forehead. There surged through him a sorrow more intense than any he had ever known. Too late, too late . . . The words tolled mournfully through his brain. Quietly, unashamedly, he wept.

Late-afternoon grayness enveloped the music room. Alice sat on the sofa where Judith had sat the night before.

"If I'd have gotten here sooner," Bob said, "I might have saved her."

"People always feel that way when someone dies. How could you have saved her if she didn't want to live?"

"It wasn't suicide. The doctor said it could have been an accident. If I had stayed over she might still be alive."

"Look, Bob, everyone feels guilty at a time like this. Why don't you think of how much pleasure you gave her last night. She knew you were back at school, which meant a lot to her, and that you were coming back to her, which meant even more."

But not enough to keep her from pulling out. He pushed the thought from his mind. "You learn a lot when someone dies—how you really feel about them and how much they mean to you. Trouble is, it don't do much good

The doorbell rang. Two men arrived from the funeral parlor with a long wicker basket. Alice showed them into the bedroom; they needed a dress to bury her in. Bob went to the closet. His glance fell on the flame-colored Balenciaga that had been her favorite concert gown. Out of the submerged world of his childhood rose the memory of ancient heroes whose swords were buried with them. He pulled out the dress.

They asked him to leave the room while they put the body in the basket. Bob returned to the music room and stood by the window, looking out. Presently Alice joined him. The men carried the basket out of the house and slid it into the waiting hearse.

"When I was a kid," he said, "if something unpleasant came along, I'd keep wishing that time would move back a day so I could pretend it hadn't happened. I never understood why time couldn't move backward as well as forward."

She turned away from the window. "We have to go."

They reached the lower floor. "I'll take a look at my room,"

Bob said. He opened the door and let his glance rest on the things he knew so well. On his desk lay the knife. He picked it up.

"What's that?" Alice asked.

"A souvenir she bought me from Venice." Resting the blade against his forefinger, he twirled it round and round, its green and red beads glinting gaudily in the gray light. "I'll take it with me."

He stopped at the foot of the stairs where he had left his valise and typewriter that morning. It seemed a lifetime ago.

4

Birdie's glance swept the chapel. A full house. Judith would have been pleased. They couldn't all be friends of hers; some people went to funerals because they had nothing better to do. The coffin stood in front, closed, its mahogany top adorned with a spray of white lilies. Soft harmonies on the organ made an appropriate background for the subdued hum of talk. Birdie was not sure what was being played; it sounded like Bach. She looked around to see whom she knew, and recognized a number of musicians.

Everyone rose as members of the family, led by Bob, entered and took their places in the front pew. The rabbi mounted the podium and opened his prayer book. He was a youngish man who relished the sound of his voice. "I waited patiently for the Lord," he intoned, "and He inclined unto me and heard my cry. He brought me up also out of a horrible pit, out of the mirey clay, and set my feet upon a rock, and established my goings." The rabbi officiated in the reformed temple Judith's parents had attended long before his time. Although he had never met her he had thrown together what he regarded as an eloquent eulogy, based on information given to him by a second cousin who had not seen her in twenty years.

Birdie tried to work herself into the proper mood, but without success; she felt nothing. She had been Judith's confidante and slave, yet once the association was broken none of the emotions attendant upon it had survived. She assumed the grave mien appropriate to the occasion, but the rabbi and his psalms were lost upon her; she turned instead to the secret joy that flooded her heart. His name was Ben—Dr. Ben Weiss, if you please—her dentist. She had known him for years and had never thought of him one way or another until a month ago, when she offered him two tickets for the debut of one of her artists. To her surprise he had asked if she would go with him. She said yes, and he had invited her out the next week and the next. He was neither as interesting as Walter nor as rich, but he was kind and thoughtful, a widower with two grown children—no problem. And he treated her like a queen. What a pleasure it was to walk out with him for all the world to see. He had not yet been in her apartment; she met him downstairs. This time there would be no slip-up: Ben was not coming up until the engagement ring was on her finger. This time she was out for the real thing, and something told her that she was going to get it. Definitely.

"As the hart panteth after the water of brooks, so panteth my soul after thee, O God. My soul thirsteth for the living God: when shall I come and appear before God?" Alice followed the rise and fall of the verse. Funerals and weddings stirred something deep and immemorial within her. She had been much upset that morning when Walter insisted on attending the service even though he was not yet permitted to go out. She had finally appealed to the doctor, who ruled that if he was going to stay home and fret, it would do him less harm to attend. As long as he avoided stairs. Walter would never change. The instant he knew something was bad for him he had to do it. She glanced at him. His eyes were shut; he looked bored. His lack of religious feeling never failed to astonish her.

How could a person not believe in God? Who had planned it all? Who ran it all? It wasn't necessary to follow a specific religion, but how could anyone doubt that there was a First Cause? Her eyes returned to the coffin. At last that tempestuous heart was at rest. She remembered the morning when Judith came to tell her about Walter and Birdie. How unhappy the woman must have been to stoop to such malice. The lilies were lovely. She made out Bob's face. He looked pale and drawn; he hadn't slept for two nights. He still could not accept his mother's suicide—if it was that. Who could say what had gone on in Judith's mind? In any case her suffering was over.

"We shall remember her as a devoted daughter, a loyal wife,

a loving mother . . ." The pious platitudes dripped off the rabbi's lips, wafted through the air on that institutional voice. Walter made a grimace. "That's our Judith all right," he whispered, nudging Max. Why didn't the clown get it over with so that they could go home? Or if he did have to go on and on, why didn't he paint her as she was? An arrogant bitch who made trouble for herself and gave trouble to others. The rabbi obviously didn't know Judith but his listeners did, so whom was he fooling? Walter decided that at his funeral he wanted a few psalms to be read, that was all. He would have to put it in his will. One word about him and the rabbi would forfeit his fee!

He glanced across the aisle at Birdie. Her new hairdo was a great improvement. He tried to catch her eye but couldn't. It would be nice to see her, not for any hanky-panky—he was in no mood for that—but for old-times' sake. Margo sat two rows in front. He had brought her Bob's request that she sing at the service and was delighted when she said yes. The morning would not be a total loss.

"We shall also remember her as a gifted artist who brought beauty and joy to thousands." The voice went on to explain that music had much in common with faith. Max suppressed a yawn. Did a rabbi have to explain to Max Rubin what music was about? The old man took out his handkerchief and mopped his forehead. In the presence of death he could think of only one thing—how good it was to be alive. When his turn came he hoped he'd go quickly. We came into this world with a cry and left it with a groan, yet in between it could be lots of fun. He viewed Judith's death as conclusive proof that the God he did not believe in was on his side. Look how much older he was, yet he was going strong while she pffffft! He always said she was too smart for her own good. It was not right for a woman to be too smart; this was still a man's world. He had never liked her when she was alive, so there was no reason for him to like her because she was dead. Still, he felt sorry. So many people without a shred of talent lived to be ninety, it was a pity when an artist died who still had something to give. With each such death there was a little less talent in the world, a little less excitement. With each such death, even if it was someone not under his management, Max Rubin felt a little bit diminished.

He shifted uneasily in his seat; he had to go to the men's room. His bladder had been giving him trouble lately; when he held back too long he couldn't go at all. If this windbag didn't shut up soon he'd pee in his pants. The old man smiled. Wouldn't that be something.

Bob kept his eyes lowered; the rabbi's eulogy embarrassed him. He seemed to be watching the ceremony from the outside. It bore no more relation to his sorrow than the rabbi's description of his mother bore to her. He wished he were alone in the chapel so that he could feel close to her and capture something of what her life and death meant to him. The only effect of this public ritual was to take her away from him. Was this the real purpose of the funeral service—to distract the mourners with a stream of words that prevented them from facing their grief? The rabbi finally stopped. There was a brief prelude on the organ; Margo rose and went to the front of the chapel. He had wondered if she'd be willing to sing at the funeral. He should have known she wouldn't turn him down.

Bist du bei mir, geh' ich mit Freuden zum Sterben und zu meiner Ruh' . . . Philip followed the curve of Bach's noble melody. He remembered Judith as she was when they first met and as she was in Rome when they parted for the last time. Between the two encounters her life ran its inevitable course in pride and willfulness. It startled him that at a solemn moment like this he remembered so vividly the physical side of their relationship. The woman who swamped him with her desires, whims, and tantrums; the woman who promenaded along the Via Veneto with her ludicrous young Italian; the woman in the coffin—they were one and the same. The thought disturbed him. He was glad he had helped her when Bob was in trouble. From where he sat he could see the young man. If he had had a son he would have liked him to be as good-looking as Bob; yet in a curious way physical beauty seemed to harm rather than help those who had it. Was it because their power to charm weakened their character? On second thought, Philip decided, he would prefer a son of his to be average-looking. This was no problem: Andrée was safely past the child-bearing age.

The rabbi was back on the podium, intoning the prayer for the dead: *Ayl molay rachameem shochayn hamromeem* . . . O God full of compassion who dwelleth on high, grant true rest beneath the shelter of Thy divine presence . . ." Andrée listened with surprise to the rabbi's translation of the Hebrew; it resembled so closely the prayers of her Catholic childhood. Her thoughts reverted to Judith. She knew they could never have been friends; a woman like Judith was too far removed from her own experience. The same was true, she reflected, of most of the people in the chapel. Her knowledge of life and death had been shaped by the war, and bore not the slightest resemblance to what the middle-class women around her knew. She had come as a stranger among them, and a stranger she would remain. It did not matter, because Philip was beside her. In her youth she had held out her arms to embrace the world; now she no longer needed to because she had him. Could the world exist for one solely in terms of another person? Why not, if one loved him enough? Andrée looked down at her hands folded primly on her black dress. She was a lucky woman.

"The Lord is my shepherd, I shall not want. He maketh me to lie down in green pastures, He leadeth me beside the still waters." The congregation rose as two young men in black wheeled the coffin down the aisle, followed by the intoning rabbi, Bob, and members of Judith's family. It was over. Walter sighed; he was hungry. Max stood bent slightly forward in acute discomfort. Birdie's eyes followed the casket as it rolled past. Ben was taking her to lunch.

The crowd spilled into the street. The coffin was lifted into the hearse, three limousines drew up for those who were accompanying it to the cemetery. Margo stood with Alice and Walter; presently Max joined them, feeling much better. Philip and Andrée chatted with Birdie. Soon Ben appeared. The groups overlapped, and Birdie unexpectedly found herself face to face with Walter. Her lips parted in a gracious smile. "Walter," The t came out very sharp, "I should like you to meet my friend Dr. Weiss." There was infinite pride in her voice. She turned to her fiancé. "Ben, this is Walter Stern. And Mrs. Stern. Old friends of mine." After a few perfunctory remarks she took Ben's arm, and they went off.

"I hear they're getting married," Alice said.

Walter's eyes followed Birdie. "I wish them luck." He was delighted: Ben, clearly, was no bargain.

"How was it?" Ben asked when they were across the street.

Birdie's spiked heels clattered over the pavement. "Very sad." She was in a philosophic mood. "You live, you struggle, suddenly it's all over. Makes no sense." She let out a deep sigh.

"Where would you like to eat?"

"You name it."

"How about Chinese?"

"I'd love it." She squeezed his arm.

5

Shafts of light slanted through the shutters. "How you know about me?" Wittenfels asked.

"I was going through her papers," Bob said, "and found some checks made out to you. Also one of your books."

"Which one?"

"The Need for Love."

"Aha. She was reading it? Unfortunately it does not do her any good. Why you want to see me?"

"I want you to tell me if you think it was suicide."

"May I ask why you need to know?"

"I need to know."

"Then I tell you. I do not think she says, 'I am going to kill myself.' It is not simple like that." Wittenfels knitted his brow. "You understand, we all have a will to live and a will to die. If the will to live grows weaker and the will to die grows stronger——" He moved his hands through the air, one up and the other down, to indicate the upsetting of the balance. "Suppose a man falls asleep when he is driving his car, he is killed. It is not suicide exactly, but his will to live is not strong enough to keep him awake. No? The same with your mother. I warn her that she must come back to me or she will be in trouble. But her will to live is not strong enough to make her listen."

"You mean to say you could have . . . saved her?"

"Who knows?" Despite this assumption of humility, Wittenfels' tone indicated he thought just that. "I can only save her if she wants it."

"Why wouldn't she?"

"Who can say? She has a theory that the physical span of life is not the same as the psychological. Which means, sometimes a man dies before his life is finished, sometimes a man's life is finished long before he dies. It is an interesting theory. I must think about it." Bob had a feeling this would appear in the analyst's next book.

"Certainly with Mozart or Schubert——" Wittenfels liked to choose examples from the ranks of the great German composers "—we know they die too soon. We also know many people who die too late. It is possible that your mother dies at the right time, when her life—psychologically—is finished."

"I have this irrational feeling that she did it to punish me."

"It is as you say, irrational. Children forget that their parents have a life apart from them. Your mother's life and death belonged to her alone. Any decision about them she makes for herself, not for you."

"Did she ever mention me?"

"Yes."

"What did she say?"

"Not much. We have not many hours together. When she speaks it is mostly of herself. But she tells me that you are very handsome and that she loves you very much."

"I wish she had made me feel that."

"Maybe she tries but you are not convinced. Children do not believe that they are loved. They are never convinced. Why you smile?"

"Just thinking. I felt my mother didn't love me enough. A girl I knew felt I didn't love her enough. Someone may feel that about her. Somebody else will feel it about him. So it goes, an endless chain of people who go through life wanting to be loved more, always more. Is anybody ever loved enough?"

Wittenfels smiled. "If you think not badly of yourself you will feel that you deserve love, then you will be loved enough." He saw Bob to the door. "She was a woman of great talent, your mother."

"You mean, as a pianist?"

The doctor held out his hand. "Also as a woman."

Bob left him feeling better, although he could not have explained why.

6

Birdie wore a ruby-red housecoat that Walter had never seen before. "Don't tell me," he said, "that you love him."

"Why should I love him? He's kind, he's considerate, he makes me feel I'm the most important woman in the world. So why should I love him? I should come crawling back to you so you can kick me in the teeth a little harder." She passed her hand languidly over her permanent wave. "Don't be a fool, Walter. I not only love him, I adore him."

"But he's a nothing."

"Is that what you came to tell me?"

"No. I wanted to see you."

"Then I'll tell you." She tugged at the housecoat between her breasts, where it was a little tight. "He's good enough for me. I've never been so happy."

"A Bronx dentist—is that what you wanted?"

"It's what I want now. And if you want to know the truth, I'm damn lucky to get him."

"When's the wedding?"

"Three weeks from now. Why? D'you want to come?"

"No. As a matter of fact, I won't be in New York. Alice talked me into a vacation. We're going to Barbados for a month. Bob's coming with us."

"Okay. Then you can send me a telegram."

He looked at her. Miraculously, she had regained some of the allure she had had for him before he went to the hospital. "How about a kiss? For old-times' sake."

She looked him in the eye. "Honey, you can kiss my ass."

"Nice way for a lady to talk."

"That was no lady," she said in the tone she reserved for the punch line of jokes. "That was the girl you slept with."

He sighed. "I can see," he said ruefully, "this is not my day."

"Definitely not."

He rose to go. His glance rested on the brooch of little diamonds and sapphires on her bosom. "At least you're wearing the pin I gave you. I'm glad."

She glanced down at it. "A little something to remember you by."

Walter paused before the end table on which she kept Paul's baton and silver candlesticks. He slid his forefinger appraisingly across the base of one of the candlesticks. "Very fine." Then he picked up the baton. "Paul's?"

"Yes."

"Well, I hope you'll remember us both with pleasure."

"Absolutely." She followed him to the door. "Okay, one kiss," she relented. "But a short one. I don't want to be tempted."

He took her face between his hands and kissed her decorously on each cheek. Then, "Don't mind what I said about Ben," he brought out quietly. "I was just being mean. As a matter of fact, I'm very happy for you."

7

Alice looked out of the window. The sky was blue—perfect flying weather. She finished packing their bags; Walter's was a problem because he insisted on including all sorts of things "just in case." She had fifteen minutes more, which would suffice for the final chore before their departure. She went to Bob's room and opened the closet door.

Walter came by. He watched in amazement as Alice removed from the closet their son's suits and coats. She piled the garments, in their neat mothproof wrappers, on the bed. "Sweetie, what are you doing!"

"Emptying the closet. So Bob'll have room for his things when we get back."

"Oh. And what are you going to do with those?"

She passed her hand in a caressing gesture over the top garment. "A man is coming to pick them up. They've hung here long enough, let others get some use out of them."

"Styles have changed."

"They can be cut down or sent overseas. Lots of poor people will be glad to have them."

"So the time came."

"Yes. I don't need these to remind me of Gene. Actually I didn't in the first place."

"That's what I tried to tell you."

She sighed. "I suppose I wasn't ready. Now I am."

"I'm glad." He sat down while Alice continued with her task. "I guess the island'll be a lot different from what it was like when we were there. Remember?"

"Of course I do. It took us almost a week to get there."

"That was before the tourists discovered it."

She smiled. "You forgot to pack your bathing suit, and some-one at the hotel offered to lend you his. He was twice your size, in those days men wore tops when they swam, and you looked a sight in his suit."

"All that empty land near the beach. We should have bought some." He shook his head ruefully. "Now it's worth a fortune."

The doorbell rang; the man had come for the clothes. Then Bob returned from a last-minute errand, and they were ready to leave.

The "No Smoking" sign went on. Alice opened a copy of the *New Yorker*. Walter kept looking out the window, afraid he might miss something. Bob, on the aisle, fastened his seat belt. The air was filled with gentle music, of the kind supposed to be soothing at take-off. A stewardess passed with a tray of chewing gum. Alice took some. The giant plane moved toward the runway.

"We should have gone first class," Walter said.

"Why? It's a short trip." Alice tossed her white hair back from her face. Her dark-blue coat emphasized the pink freshness of her skin. Her eyes shone.

"Food's better," Walter said.

"I'm not paying fifty dollars for a steak."

"All the drinks you want."

"You're not supposed to drink. Remember?"

"Fewer people."

"I'm not a snob. Besides, there's only two seats in a row. We couldn't be together."

"Okay, you win." He opened his newspaper.

Bob turned to Alice. "What's Barbados like?"

"White sand. The ocean is green by the shore and blue further out. You lie in the sun and forget the world."

The motors hummed; suddenly the sound grew loud and tense. Alice shut the magazine. The plane trembled and shot forward with such power that nothing in the world could stop it except another plane. Walter had taught her to concentrate her anxiety on the first and last minute of a flight. In between she relaxed. As they sailed into the air she put one hand on Walter's, the other on Bob's. "I didn't think we'd make it," she said softly.

The plane soared over the flatlands of Long Island, up toward the sun. Then it turned southward over the sea and left the city far behind.